OF FATHERS AND FIRE

FLYOVER FICTION
Series editor: Ron Hansen

"There is something timeless and mythic in Wingate's prose. The hardscrabble prairie life depicted here, with crisp, vibrant characters seeking their place in the world, has the same spiritual complexity of Flannery O'Connor, the same moral weight and imagination. Vital, timely, and unforgettable, Wingate's story brings us into the heart of America so that we might ask questions of our own hearts, our own minds, and our own souls."

—Patrick Hicks, author of *The Commandant of Lubizec* and *The Collector of Names*

"Hate and love, secrets and redemption, prayer and violence, all these swirl together in this beautiful, brutal whirlwind of a novel fueled by elemental flames of the human heart. Like some mystic prophet, Wingate delivers signs and wonders in generous abundance."

—Neil Connelly, author of *In the Wake of Our Vows*

"Few writers write as fearlessly about matters of faith as Steven Wingate. The characters are vivid and compelling as they search for answers and connections, ever on the perilous road to either destruction or redemption."

—Robert Garner McBrearty, Sherwood Anderson Foundation Fiction Award–winning author of *Episode* and *A Night at the Y*

"*Of Fathers and Fire* employs magical realism in a way that few American writers have been able to achieve. . . . Beautifully detailed, from the geography of Colorado and Nebraska to the trivia of daily living. Steven Wingate has an eye for the peripheral, the seemingly insignificant, the almost forgotten. Much of the novel's power comes from Wingate's juxtaposition of the mundane with the miraculous."

—Mary Clearman Blew, author of *Ruby Dreams of Janis Joplin*

"A wonderfully strange and compelling coming-of-age novel that delves into the deep pull and dangers of religion, the grace of music, and the importance of finding one's own path. . . . This is a beautiful book of a son seeking the truth, both personal and existential—which is, after all, the best quest any of us can go on."
—Laura Pritchett, author of *Stars Go Blue*

"Deeply felt, subtly innovative, utterly compelling, Steven Wingate's *Of Fathers and Fire* is an excellent novel by a talented novelist who deserves—and with this book I feel certain will find—a wide audience."
—Robert Olen Butler, author of the Pulitzer Prize–winning *A Good Scent from a Strange Mountain*

"Steven Wingate has a rare feel for American landscapes and for our recent past. I admire his willingness to tackle genuinely controversial topics—including religious vicissitudes and our complex visions of masculinity. Wingate's keen sense of language houses an equally keen compassion for human plights."
—Elizabeth Kostova, author of *The Historian* and *The Shadow Land*

"Steven Wingate writes so well about teenagers and parents, belief and doubt, saxophone playing and rain making, and the kind of small town where everyone knows everyone. *Of Fathers and Fire* is a magical and deeply satisfying novel."
—Margot Livesey, author of *Mercury* and *The Hidden Machinery*

Of
Fathers
and Fire

A NOVEL

Steven Wingate

UNIVERSITY OF NEBRASKA PRESS   LINCOLN

An earlier version of chapter 1 was previously published as "The Beake Street Circus" in *Vagabond: Bulgaria's English Monthly* 39–40 (December 2009–January 2010): 78.

Publication of this volume was assisted by a grant from the Friends of the University of Nebraska Press.

Library of Congress
Cataloging-in-Publication Data
Names: Wingate, Steven, author.
Title: Of fathers and fire: a novel / Steven Wingate.
Description: Lincoln: University of Nebraska
Press, [2019] | Series: Flyover fiction
Identifiers: LCCN 2018044510
ISBN 9781496211866 (pbk.: alk. paper)
ISBN 9781496215048 (epub)
ISBN 9781496215055 (mobi)
ISBN 9781496215062 (pdf)
Subjects: | GSAFD: Fantasy fiction. | Science fiction.
Classification: LCC PS3623.I6623 O3 2019
| DDC 813/.6—dc23 LC record available
at https://lccn.loc.gov/2018044510

Set in Stempel Garamond by Mikala R. Kolander.
Designed by N. Putens.

OF FATHERS AND FIRE

I

Saturday, July 5, 1980

Tommy Sandor was the kind of teenage man-child who liked to flex his neck in mirrors. A bull neck, a badass neck that made sure people thought twice about punching his face. Defiant, cable-like muscles between his shoulder blades held his spine straight up and his shoulders back. Nobody dared take a swing at Tommy Sandor unless they were ready to kill him, he believed, because that's what they'd have to do to keep him from fighting back. He pictured himself a few years older, with missing teeth and a Fu Manchu mustache like Jack Lambert, the Pittsburgh Steelers linebacker he used to want to be, back when he called himself a linebacker.

But that was months ago. Tommy smiled at his broad, bare chest in his bedroom mirror, ran his hand through his buzz-cut towhead hair to get the sweat out, and grabbed his saxophone case. Inside it sat a 1962 Selmer Mark VI tenor, made the same year he was conceived, which the music teacher at Widefield High School called the best sax ever made. He'd found it in the trunk of a totaled Buick at the junkyard, and most of its keys still worked. Tommy glanced at the subway map of New York City taped to his wall—J train, 7 train, 3 train—so he could quiz himself about the stations on his way to the abandoned church on Tumbleback Road, where every night he played his tenor like a man burning alive.

His father would be riding one of those trains right now, Tommy thought. Sax case in hand, knowing he'd never get famous but still playing because the music grabbed him by the throat and pulled him. He'd be on his way to the Village Vanguard or Arthur's Tavern or one of those loft clubs Tommy read about in the *New York Times* at the library. Did he ever wonder if he'd left a piece of himself behind on the dry, cracked plains? A child he never even knew existed?

"Hey, motherfucker," Tommy told his father as he flipped off the map. Drake, that's what his mom said the man's name was. "Bet you never played a sax this good in your whole life, huh?"

Tommy knew how stupid he sounded, talking like a New York street rat when he was just some hick from a nowhere town that people twenty miles away didn't even know existed. Drake was the real deal, though. A Lower East Side scumbag, living the junkie life like so many sax men before him. Charlie Parker and John Coltrane until they died. Sonny Rollins for a while. Tommy pictured his dad getting off the subway train, climbing past the piss-smelling drunks, and hauling himself up the stairs of the Second Avenue F train station. Then loping down the street, dodging people who thought he owed them favors, to his apartment building in Alphabet City. Or maybe to the bed of some other woman he'd tricked into loving him. A woman he'd ditch before she even knew she was knocked up, like he did to Connie Sandor at the Red Willow County Fair in McCook, Nebraska, in July of 1962.

Fuck him. Fuck that loser who couldn't even stick around to give his son a name. Tommy got sick of looking at his mirror and strode through the kitchen, where his mom's state patrolman boyfriend, Dan Stannard, had left his dirty dishes on the table yet again. Connie sat on the couch watching TV with the sound down while she paid the bills, waiting for the nine o'clock news to start. She still wore her white work blouse, which showed more skin than Tommy needed to see. Than any man needed to see, if you asked him.

"Hey, Tom-Tom," Connie said, stretching an auburn curl down

to her freckled cheek and flicking it up past her eyebrow. "I need to get this cut soon, don't I?"

"Don't get it cut too nice." Tommy leaned against the archway between the kitchen and living room. "You don't want a better man than Sheriff Bullshit noticing you."

"Stop saying that. It'll make life easier when you have to call him 'Dad.'"

"I'll call him 'Dad' once. When you give me my thousand bucks and I—"

"Go to New York, I know." Connie tucked her lanky calves beneath her rump and shot Tommy the *You'll learn someday* smile he hated most. "All you know about New York is what you picked up from watching *Barney Miller*. That and the library books you stole."

The news came on, and Tommy walked over to turn up the sound. Theme music swelled as the anchorwoman smiled at the anchorman, then she narrowed her eyes and set her jaw as a big American flag and the number 243 popped onto the screen beside her. The hostages in Iran were still in Iran, she said. The sick one was still sick, and Americans were fed up with being weak. Americans wanted someone with the courage to do what needed to be done before we lost our place in the world forever, and Jimmy Carter did absolutely nothing. Next came Ronald Reagan at a rally, with people climbing over each other to touch his fingertips like he was the saint of America.

"You fill out your draft card?" Connie asked. "Or are you back to wanting to join the marines?"

"It's not the draft, Mom, it's Selective Service."

"My dad joined when he was seventeen. He didn't wait for anybody to *select* him." She noticed her son's chest when he flexed his shoulders, just like he wanted her to. "Put a shirt on, Tommy. You'll catch cold walking home."

"Might not be walking home if your boyfriend's coming back over tonight."

"Can't I try to love somebody?" Connie shifted on the couch, pulling her skirt down to cover her knees.

"Maybe you should try loving somebody who isn't married to somebody *else*."

"They're hardly married. Haven't been for years."

"Married's *married*, Mom. There's no *almost* about it. Isn't that what his brother's always preaching on the radio?"

"Put a shirt on." She picked up a bill from the table and tried to hold onto her smile. Tommy was slipping away, but that's what boys did. "Don't want to drive all those girls out there too crazy."

"What girls?" he said. At least she got a smile out of him. As Tommy stepped outside, Connie tried to remember him before he got muscles and zits, before he started talking back and screwing girls. Before the sax obsession and the jazz books under his mattress like porn, before running toward Jesus and running away from Jesus and not talking about Jesus at all. The little boy who used to follow behind her singing for no good reason was now lost forever to hormonal rage and that stupid noise he called bebop. Tommy opened the door to retrieve his hat—green and Australian and ratty, a three-dollar Goodwill special with the brim buttoned up on one side—from its peg by the door.

"Can't leave without that," Connie said as he slapped it on his head.

"Nope." He blew her a kiss so she'd know he still loved her, and then he was out on the streets. Though you couldn't really call them streets because there wasn't an inch of asphalt in Suborney, Colorado, except for the parking lots at Pete Sowell's gas station and Jeff Heagren's junkyard. Suborney was a junkyard town, where all the crap nobody needed in Colorado Springs went to die, and if you took away Sowell's and Heagren's, you had nothing but twenty-eight houses—counting the empties—and forty-three people. Waiting-to-die ex-farmers mostly. Not the ones who sold their farms to buy giant houses in Colorado Springs, like some of them did, but the ones who got foreclosed on and barely had enough money to buy a shack in a junkyard town that could blow away without anybody noticing.

Tommy walked up Mangum Street past the Mukasics' house. Jim and Marcine, sitting on their blue plaid couch watching a rerun of *Alice*, had been waiting to die the longest. He had to remember to take their trash to the dump—that's the other thing Suborney was famous for, being on the way to the dump. Half the people who set foot in town came for Heagren's junk and the other half for Sowell's gas after they dumped their trash.

"G'night, Tom-Tom," called Julie Parness from the next house. She was a little young for Suborney, only fifty, but made up for it by being the kind of drunk who slept until afternoon. She swung silently on her front porch swing, its chains sprayed with WD40 every Sunday so they wouldn't creak against the eye bolts. Tommy only waved back at Julie, wanting to save his breath for the scale that rolled through his body.

$$D F G A\flat B\flat C D\flat D!$$

The low D was hard to hit, since that key wouldn't close all the way, and for some reason the high C gave him trouble too. But he didn't mind because the bad keys gave him notes that bent and songs that sounded like nobody else's—that didn't even sound like bebop, to be honest. He'd felt those notes bending themselves into a scale in his bedroom after supper while he clenched his teeth and listened to Sheriff Bullshit lecture his mom about the Ayatollah. Jimmy Carter wasn't doing shit to stop him because he was the biggest pussy America ever put in the White House, but Reagan—who for sure was no pussy—could make this country stand up for itself again. If we have to march into Iran and kill the bad people so the good ones can be free, he said, then so be it. Because freedom's the most important thing, and if Americans don't stand up for it all over the world, what good are we?

Uh huh, his mom said back, nodding along to the idea of a war that her own son might die in. Tommy had almost bitten his tongue in half listening to Stannard's bullshit, and now he was desperate to get his lips around that mouthpiece and say a few things back. He passed the big oak tree at the end of Mangum Street that must have had a hundred yellow ribbons on it for the hostages, then took a right onto Road X. How stupid it was, how much like torture, that his dad came from a part of New York that had Avenue A and B and C, and here he was stuck at the ass end of nowhere with Road X and Y and Z.

Shithole town. Shithole life. Tommy knelt to open his sax case, pulling out a reed and sticking it in his mouth to wet it, then walked double-time toward the church switching hands on the case every fifty paces. He'd walk all the way to New York like that someday, getting his arms strong and stopping to play wherever he felt like it. Gas stations, highway exits, the middles of fields, abandoned store-fronts. Making himself a genius, the way Sonny Rollins did by playing on the Williamsburg Bridge every day, until he was ready to show up at one of Daddy Drake's gigs. He'd blow on that busted Selmer like nobody else on the fucking planet, with more *attack* than anybody because he focused all the hate and lostness inside himself down to a single note that blasted out of his bell like shrapnel.

Drake would hear it and know *This is my son*. He'd take Tommy out to meet every big-time sax player he knew, saying, "You gotta hear my kid, man. Plays like a wild animal that just got a soul."

Someday, Tommy believed. But first he had to get out of Suborney. He skirted along Road X by the widest bend of Suborney Creek, which barely reached his shins this time of year. He waved at the storage shack across the water on Carl Mangetti's land, where he used to go when he felt like running away from home, then watched his feet to keep from stepping in the dog shit that Sam Kurtep never bothered picking up. Next came Tim Fiddler's house, with its big white cross in the front yard. It had the number 243 painted on a sign where Jesus's head would be and another saying NUKE IRAN where his feet would be.

Wouldn't Jesus hate that? Tommy couldn't tell anymore what Jesus would hate and not hate. Some people said he didn't hate anything at all, and other people had a huge list of things he hated that looked exactly like their own list. The Ayatollah, any kind of Arab, plus the Commies and the faggots and anybody who didn't love the American flag. And if you weren't white? Then tough shit. There were plenty of people like that in Colorado Springs, getting on the TV and radio and telling the whole country that taking American hostages was the first shot in a new holy war. One of them was on the radio that blared away on Fiddler's empty porch, saying he'd fly over and kill the Ayatollah with his bare hands if Carter let him.

"You think God wants the Ayatollah shaming our country?" the voice asked its listeners. "Or do you think God wants somebody to show the Ayatollah who's boss?"

For Fiddler, that *somebody* was Ronald Reagan. A REAGAN COUNTRY banner filled his whole front window, and a big American flag hung by the door, touching the ground the way Tommy's ex–Air Force history teacher in eighth grade said that no American flag should ever do. People like Fiddler loved their country and their God, all right—at least enough to send teenage kids halfway around the world to kill and be killed. Every second Tommy spent in Suborney ripped him up because everybody in town was for Reagan, Reagan, Reagan, like America was dying and nobody else had the balls to bring it back to life. Even Ed Dolman, his asshole boss at the junkyard who never gave a shit about politics until Reagan came along, had a sign in his window saying THE TIME IS NOW.

"Hey, dumbass," Tommy told the house. "You vote for him, you go fight for him."

But Dolman was probably up in Colorado Springs, out chasing tail and violating parole. He'd spent three years at the state pen in Cañon City for stealing a truckload of Puma sneakers and inherited his parents' house while he was locked up. Didn't even lift a finger for it. Tommy flipped the bird at Dolman's front door and turned left onto Tumbleback Road, getting ready to lean into the wind because he was on the stretch that gave the road its name. Where the wind blew back and forth across the plains, funneled almost into a whirlpool by the big lump of Lester Hill no matter what direction it came from. A quarter-mile of road where everything that wasn't nailed down tumbled into Suborney, then tumbled back out again, sooner or later.

Tumbleweed sometimes, but mostly junk that didn't quite make it to the dump or didn't want to stay there. A gallon bottle of Clorox bleach, cut in half to make a scoop. Sunday comics and restaurant placemats and Polaroid photos, stuck in the weedy ditches on either side of the road. A Styrofoam box from a Big Mac. Soda cans, beer cans, milk cartons, a worn-out folding sun visor for somebody's front windshield. As sad as the junk made Tommy, he found a beauty in it that made the songs he carried in his chest rise closer to his lips. It was *his* junk because Suborney was *his* town—the place he had to fight his way out of to call himself a man. He had to love that junk because he came from it. Its molecules were in his lungs and blood, and when he escaped his prison and looked back, he'd have to thank the junk for giving him the desperation to break out.

Tommy almost fell over from leaning into the wind because it was barely blowing that night. A few paper scraps lifted and floated and fell again, but the heavier stuff stayed still. It was the hushed, not-quite-baking part of July, before the ground got hard as cement and grew cracks and people started praying for rain. When he got to the abandoned church, the wind stilled completely. Not even the tall grass in the roadside ditches moved—like the sky itself had stopped, waiting to hear Tommy play his sax.

It was a white church with a stone foundation, older than anybody in town. Paint worn off by the weather, revealing bare wood beneath. A bell tower too rickety to climb. He stopped halfway up the rotting steps and stared at the big double doors as if someone were waiting for him inside. That couldn't be because it was abandoned before he was born, and only he and Dolman used it. Tommy knocked anyway.

"Anybody here?" he asked, pulling the left door open. Inside, things looked the same as ever. Boards up where the windows should be. Same junk as always, waiting until Dolman had the guts to quit Heagren's junkyard and open the store in Pueblo that he kept jabbering about. Same sewing machines, ten-speeds, crates of red roof tile. A tuxedo wrapped in plastic, a red bathrobe with yellow birds on it, six TVs, an encyclopedia set with *N* and *H* missing.

Tommy stepped to the little round stage he'd made in the center of the church floor, cleared of junk and lit by a single bulb he'd rigged up the day Dolman taught him to jack electricity from power lines. Then he stepped into the nook he'd made next to his stage so he could spy on the crowd while he put his tenor together. He could peek out from behind the imaginary curtains of some imaginary jazz club, gauging the vibe as he twisted the curved metal neck onto the Selmer's body and tightened it down, then twisted the mouthpiece onto the corked end of the neck.

Always put it together standing up, Drake reminded him. *Your breath has to come out of your lungs straight, so get your mouthpiece right for how you're standing that night.*

Tommy nodded and reset his strap, then set the wet reed on his mouthpiece and slid on the ligature. He peeked at the crowd again—mostly rich-looking white people tonight who didn't know shit about jazz—and reminded himself not to care about them. What happened in that circle was between him and his sax, and it would happen whether anybody else heard it or not. He stepped under the light with his lips around the mouthpiece, and the scale that had been rumbling through his blood all day rose up to his tongue.

He almost started with the low D but didn't because the messed-up key made it so hard to hit. Tommy wanted to play the notes like he *was* the notes, so he started off with an animal shriek at high F—the highest note his Selmer could get. *I am here and you cannot stop me and I will say what needs to be said*, that note told the world. Then he gave out a tremulous middle G, almost a whisper, before he leaped up to a high B♭, putting a growl into his breath that the sax sent back through his bones until his breath faltered and the note broke into a squeak.

Doesn't matter if you're any good, his father said. *Everybody teaches himself. Even the great ones.*

Tommy nodded and picked notes that he knew the Selmer could play and held them, whole and pure, like they could save his life. Like they *had* to. Then he picked up a bit of melody, gliding and looping between the iffy high C and B♭ and A♭ before slipping down to a soft middle D♭ with all the keys open. Then the whole scale changed, and he got lost in it like his dad always wanted him to. Drake told Tommy to move his head around to pull the music closer, like it was an antenna luring down signals from outer space. Once a signal found him, he'd hold still, and that's when the real music would hit.

Because scales don't belong to you, Drake whispered. *There's not a single one you can play that hasn't been played before. You move your head to catch one, then you let it flow through you till it starts breaking you down. Because the song wants you. It's out there, and it wants to be born in you.*

❊ ❊ ❊

Tommy didn't know how long he'd been playing on his back, pressing the side keys wildly until his sax sounded like a squealing radio stuck between stations, when he heard footsteps and a little rattling sound. He opened both church doors, and the footsteps came closer. A bigger animal than him, that's all he knew at first.

"Who's that?" Tommy growled, striding onto the landing with the sax against his bare chest. Then a man came around the corner and stood at the bottom of the stairs. In Tommy's flashlight he looked like a cross between a leftover hippie and a Mexican picker. Crusty black work boots, thick and muddy calves, cutoff army camo shorts, a red United Farm Workers T-shirt. A big barrel chest and a neck even thicker than Tommy's own. A mountain of a face, turned away and showing only its left profile, with a big muttonchop sideburn that came to a point in the middle of his cheek. On his head sat a yellowing straw hat with the brim curled up on both sides, like Tommy only saw on pickers. "Who are you?" Tommy asked him.

"Name's Richard Thorpe," the man said, his voice rumbling up from that barrel chest like he tried not to use it much. His hand reached out, halfway between a shake and a wave, and Tommy saw cigar-thick fingers that looked like they'd all been burned. "You?"

"I'm Tommy Sandor. Where you from? You coming up where I can see your face?"

"I'm from all over." Thorpe stepped toward Tommy's flashlight and looked him up and down, still not showing his face straight on. It was a hard face, tight as a cue ball and red from too much sun, with a scraggly patch of scruff running from his lower lip to his chin. Tommy thought he looked anywhere between thirty and forty, though it was hard to tell with all the weather on him. Thorpe turned and finally showed his right cheek—it looked caved in, like a blur on his face. Weak and broken, with a lazy eye that twitched in the flashlight's beam.

"What happened to your face?" Tommy asked.

"Guy hit me with a brick."

"What for?"

"Get me to turn the other cheek. Where'd you learn to play that sax, Mr. Sandor?"

"I taught myself. Plus my dad was a sax player. It's in my blood."

"Was?"

"My mom says he doesn't even know I exist, so yeah, he's kinda *was*. She won't even tell me his fucking last name."

"House of God there," Thorpe said, pointing inside and then up at the sky.

"Nope. They took the spell off it, way before I got here."

"That's called deconsecration," Thorpe said, and the big word made him sound smarter than Tommy thought. More Jesus-y than he looked too.

"You Baptist?" Tommy asked. "Pentecostal? Or are you in one of those roll your own churches?"

"We roll our own, pretty much." Thorpe looked behind him up Tumbleback Road as if the other part of *we* would be there.

"Are you the kind of Jesus freak who loves Ronnie Reagan?"

"Never met the man," Thorpe said, pausing to let Tommy stare at the bashed-in side of his face. "Just to let you know, we're going to start this church up again. That junk's got to go."

"Says who?"

"Says the man who owns the building." He tapped himself on the breastbone. "But you can keep playing for now. Jesus might even like it, don't you think?"

"I don't know what Jesus likes and doesn't anymore," Tommy said.

"Welcome to the club."

Thorpe backed down the steps and studied Tommy like he had to run off and draw a picture of him from memory. Then he held his right hand in front of him, cupped as if waiting for Tommy to drop in a few coins, and it trembled like an old man's until his fingertips slowly clamped against his palm. It creaked back open, the fingers spreading against their will, and flicked itself shut again like a snapping turtle's jaws. Then it loosened up and fell back to normal, as if the whole thing had been nothing but a cramp.

"Wind coming," Thorpe said, jutting his chin at Lester Hill. "Rain too. I've been out there, I've seen it. G'night, Mr. Sandor."

"Yeah. See you around."

"Yes sir. That you will."

Then Richard Thorpe went, with his big loping steps and his little rattle, back around the corner of the church where he came from. A new scale shot down through Tommy's head, and he ran inside to blow on his sax, feeling his fingers work that scale even before his lips clamped around the mouthpiece. But Tommy heard Thorpe's rattle again, and the scale passed through him without sticking. Drake had told him about that too. Sometimes a lost song came back, and sometimes it was gone forever, missing its one chance at living on earth. Afterward you have to believe they'll keep coming for you, even if it feels like you've lost the right to get any more of them.

Tommy looked up Tumbleback Road, like Thorpe had, but saw nothing. Not even the waving ghost of his best friend, Wesley, killed in the only house on the road seven years earlier. He went back to his stage and tried to blow on his sax, just any old scale, but nothing came because he kept feeling Thorpe spying on him through the cracks in the plywood that covered the windows. Which was bullshit because he figured Thorpe wasn't the kind of man who spied on people. He walked straight up to you, daring you to stare at that bashed-in cheek of his, and said exactly what he wanted to say.

That's what Tommy wanted to do with his sax, though he couldn't even get his lips on its mouthpiece long enough to try. *If you don't live it, it won't come out of your horn*, he heard Charlie Parker say. Maybe that's why he couldn't play right now, because he hadn't lived enough. Seeing a grown man like Thorpe, a bigger animal than him, showed him that he was just a boy even though he had the biggest muscles in town. A boy who could still become too many different things. Sax man. Marine. Jesus freak, just to piss his mother off. Linebacker, if he kissed enough ass after quitting the team. There were too many Tommies, all trying to live together inside of one body, and he either had to grow big enough to fit them all in or kill some off.

Tommy put the Selmer in its case and looked for Thorpe outside. He circled the church three times and climbed the steps to look at Wesley Perrin's house again. That's when he felt the wind, a little rustling in the bushes at first and then a gust coming straight at the church, hard enough to slam the doors shut behind him. Flecks of rain hit him, then big, full drops. No dust in this rain, like Suborney usually got in July. He stuck out his tongue to taste it—sweet and clear, not acidy at all. For a solid minute the wind and rain went on, blasting Tommy's face and cooling his chest. Then it slowly died down to a *tit-tat* here and there.

He laughed and ran his hand through his wet hair, then the wind reared up and knocked him back against the church doors like it was after him and him alone. Nothing else on Tumbleback Road moved at all. A paper plate and a Styrofoam cup that had blown in from somebody's Fourth of July barbecue sat there in the tall roadside grass, twenty feet from Tommy but not moving an inch. Another gust hit his face, with a mist of water that pinpricked his skin, but still nothing around him moved. He crouched down to feel the bottom step—bone dry. He felt the side of the church, ten feet from where he'd gotten wet, but there wasn't a drop on it. Water on the doors and on the landing and on him but nowhere else.

Richard Thorpe did that, Tommy told himself, looking down at his right hand as it slowly opened and closed in imitation of the man. He walked to the road and touched it—the same old dirt Suborney always had in July, ready to start begging for even a taste of rain. He climbed back up the stairs and flung open the church doors, then stood there, knowing the wind would come back. It pushed him inside, trying to shut both doors on him, but he kept the left one open with his shoulder, laughing like he and the wind were brothers playing a game only they knew.

He watched that paper plate and Styrofoam cup by the edge of the road, but they still didn't move a damn inch. One last blast of wetness hit his face, and Tommy went back inside, turning off the light so he could listen to the wind better as it kept coming for him, hurling itself against those doors. *Maybe it's another song*, he thought, *coming down to me in a shape I don't know yet.*

2

Sunday, July 6

Tommy spent the night in his hammock behind the church, then started the day with the only ritual he'd kept from his days of wanting to be a linebacker and a marine. Sprint to Suborney Creek, do fifty push-ups, fifty squats, and twenty-five pull-ups on a tree branch. Next, hang by his knees for ten slow sit-ups. Last, swing like an orangutan through three more branches before missing the fourth by an inch, as always, and dropping to the ground in midstride.

Shouldn't you be going to church? he heard a voice say, *instead of showing off how strong you are?* But it wasn't Jesus talking, like he'd hoped—the impossibly tall and broad-shouldered Jesus he dreamed of bumping into one day as he rounded a corner, who'd sit him down and tell him exactly what he had to do with his life. Instead, the voice belonged to Tami Willer, the biggest Jesus lover in Suborney if you asked her, though nobody ever saw her go to church. For Tami, Jesus was a set of rules that matched the ones she grew up with, and anybody who didn't have those rules couldn't have Jesus. Tommy passed the place he called home and saw Dan Stannard's Ford F150 there, tailgate to tailgate with his mom's blue Chevy LUV pickup, and he set the sax inside the kitchen door to avoid being under the same roof as Stannard even for a second. He flipped the Ford a bird and jogged over to Pete Sowell's gas station, where Pete had his wife's car parked in front even though he could walk from his house to the store in a minute. Tommy opened the door, and a dull cowbell clanged.

"You think you're fooling anybody with that car?" he shouted to Pete, though he couldn't see the man. "Everybody knows where you live."

"It's for out-of-towners," Pete called from the storeroom. "Don't want 'em thinking the place is closed just 'cause it's Sunday."

"I could get a couple junkers from the yard."

"Nope. People can sniff out junkers."

Pete came out and handed Tommy a day-old bagel with cream cheese and ham, then gave him his work for the morning. Clean up the counter from last night, when Brent Spoliak and Cam Yorney stayed late and drank all the beers. Take the trash to the dumpster, put out new cereal and fruit cocktail and tuna and beans, then break down the boxes they came in. Tommy liked Pete, who'd lived in Denver and Kansas City and at least had some stories to tell that weren't about the military or farm foreclosures or jail. Pete seemed all out of stories, though. He leaned over his cash register and yawned.

I saw somebody at the church last night, Tommy opened his lips to say, and Pete looked up at the sound. But Tommy had spent eleven years in Suborney being a kid without secrets, and he didn't want to spill his shiny new one just yet. He bit the bagel to keep himself from talking.

"You see any strangers around here last night?" Pete asked. "Phil Luder says he saw a guy walking around. Looked like a Mexican but didn't walk like one."

"How the hell do Mexicans walk?" Tommy stuffed the bagel between his teeth and pulled the trash bag out of its barrel. He'd hang onto the truth until he had to let it go, just like his mom did. She'd waited fourteen years to tell him his father's name, hadn't she? He could wait a few days to tell people Richard Thorpe's. Tommy took the trash out and wondered what Drake would say about holding back the truth like that. Sitting in his Alphabet City apartment by a window with the shade pulled down at dawn. Nothing but a silhouette strung out on heroin.

We all got our lies, he slurred, watching light leak through the cracked, yellowed edges of the window shade. *Some people just got bigger lies, that's all.*

Dad? Tommy asked, walking in front of the window and turning into a silhouette himself. Ready to kneel down and pray and beg Drake to get clean. *Tell me what you need to get off the junk, Dad,* Tommy said, but Drake just shook his head. Then the real Tommy Sandor, the one closing the dumpster behind Pete Sowell's gas station in Suborney, Colorado, knelt down and asked Jesus who he'd be if he stopped trying to save his father. If he couldn't save the guy in his own mind, why bother thinking he could ever do it in real life? Why bother with New York?

The next stop in his day was Jeff Heagren's junkyard, where he'd promised to work a few hours even though the place was closed on Sundays. He'd worked there since June of '77, when half of Suborney turned to junk after the creek overflowed its banks and relocated a dozen houses. Today he had to empty out a flatbed so Heagren could pick up more junk that night. Tommy always got there before Dolman, which never surprised anybody who knew them both. Since they wouldn't give him a key for the padlock on the main gate, he climbed the twelve-foot fence and swung his leg over the one spot where there wasn't any razor wire. He started in on the flatbed, which had a load of commercial washers and dryers that Heagren had pulled from a Laundromat about to get bulldozed. He had to drive the truck to the big sheet metal shed, get the washers and dryers onto the forklift, and stack them up along the far wall. The cab of the flatbed was too tall to drive all the way in, but Tommy backed the load between the shed's doors so at least he wouldn't have to work outside once the sun started baking.

And work he did. Who needs weights when you've got hundred-pound dryers and two hundred–pound washing machines to push around? The sweat was worth it because all the work he did in Suborney paved the way for the work he'd do in New York—or wherever he got stuck trying to get there, like his mom always said. Dolman showed up at eleven, looking like he'd slept in his car. He leaned against the barn door eating a jelly donut that left powder on his Wolfman Jack beard. His hair, long like it was 1973 instead of 1980, looked three-days greasy.

"How the fuck are you?" he asked Tommy.

"Not bad for a workingman."

"Ah, don't give me your workingman bullshit. Heag wants me to get the rig back to him by one. Can you do it?"

"Yeah, sure. With your help or without." Tommy lowered a washer onto the forklift, then climbed behind its wheel. "Hey, you get laid last night?"

"Just drunk. It's one or the other these days."

"Is that supposed to be my moral lesson for the day, boss?"

"It's Sunday, ain't it? Moral lesson day?" Dolman wiped powdered sugar off the jean jacket vest he always wore. "You see the news last night? Think that sick guy'll make it out of Iran alive?"

"If he doesn't, I probably won't either. Your hero Ronnie Reagan'll send me over, and I'll come home in a pine box."

"You want this country to keep rolling over for every raghead who doesn't like us?" Dolman kicked the door behind him with his heel. "Get it done by half past twelve, and there's a whole day's pay in it for you."

"Yes sir!" Tommy said, saluting like the marine he'd never be. "Done by half past fucking twelve, sir!"

* * *

The Sunday regulars gathered at noon for coffee at Pete's, some coming back from church and some pretending that they'd once again slept too late to make it. They wondered aloud about the man Phil Luder saw last night while calling in his dog, the man who looked like a Mexican but didn't walk like one. Who'd come to Pete's counter that morning, not ten minutes after Tommy left, to buy a can of beans and a loaf of bread with nickels and pennies.

"How'd he look?" asked Wally Ogrean, the ex-navy captain who'd taught Tommy how to shave and used to be the local badass before his hips went bad.

"Homeless," Pete said. "One side of his face all smashed in—it looked like cottage cheese."

"He said he came for the church?" asked Tami Willer, who sat in Wally's booth.

Pete nodded. "I'm guessing it's not for the junk inside."

"That's where he was heading when I saw him," said Phil, who shared the other booth with Ron and Kate Ulin. He adjusted the green VFW cap he only wore on Sundays.

"Last thing we need is somebody dragging that damn church back from the dead," said Sam Kurtep at the counter. When he noticed Ron and Kate Ulin frowning, he flashed them an insincere smile. "Not that there's anything wrong with churches. We just don't need people waltzing in here and taking over ours uninvited."

"Last year was bad enough," Tami piped in, and they all murmured in agreement. The summer before, a tent commune from Michigan had rolled into town on its way to Colorado Springs, where every born-again seemed to be heading like planes into the Bermuda Triangle. There were so many kinds of born-agains all the sudden, while a few years earlier it was only Baptists and Pentecostals. The Michigan people strolled in preaching love, love, love, and singing plantation slave songs. They sat cross-legged in tight rows on the high plains grass, praying for Jesus to liberate us all from the desires that poisoned us.

They did such a good job in their three weeks of camping out on Carl Mangetti's land that they liberated Carrie Olds—the last teenager in Suborney other than Tommy—from her family and took her with them when they moved on. Everybody figured their head guy,

Mike, was sleeping with at least three of the women in the camp, which wasn't Jesus-like in any of their eyes. They would've liberated Tommy, too, if Mike had anything better than half-assed answers to his questions about God. Nobody liked using the word *cult*, but it fit. Losing Carrie Olds barely hurt, since her family rented and they'd only been in town a year. But when she left, they all felt that losing Tommy, a child who belonged to the soil they once tilled, would have been a tragedy.

Tommy, the fatherless boy they pitied and loved and fed sometimes, until he started playing that awful broken saxophone. Until he started calling his mom a slut, then tried making a slut out of every girl he got his hands on. Until those ragheads took the hostages and Tommy said he'd never serve his country—that he'd rather burn himself alive in an American flag than get shipped off to die in Iran. Before that they were willing to put up with his bullshit, even after he quit football, but disrespecting the flag was inexcusable. Now that he was almost eighteen, their pity had hardened into an unacknowledged species of hate, the kind one holds for a national traitor, and they counted the months until Tommy left town. If the new batch of Jesus freaks took him, fine. If Dan Stannard married his mom and he ran away screaming, fine. When the good citizens of Suborney heard the cowbell clang against Pete's front door, they turned toward Tommy without a smile between them.

"What'd I do *this* time?" he said, raising his hands slowly as if a cop had told him to.

"Who's that man you talked to?" Tami asked him.

"Talking's natural, Mrs. Willer. It's why God gave us mouths."

"Don't act up," Wally said, and Tommy dropped his hands. "He came in here this morning, said he talked to a teenage kid by the church last night."

"What'd he say I told him? All the big town secrets?"

"What's he doing here?" Kate said. "He's got no business grabbing hold of that church."

"Says he owns it," Tommy told them all. "Wants to get it going again."

"You expect us to sit here and let somebody like *him* walk in and start up a church?" asked Cam Yorney.

"What's wrong with starting up a church?" Tommy asked. "You guys *say* you're Christians, right? Most of you, anyway." He threw a dirty look at Sam.

"We just don't want you getting sucked in by the wrong kind again, Tommy," Kate Ulin told him, using every ounce of grandmotherliness she could muster.

"We don't need Commie Jesus freaks," boomed Wally. "They'll go for you like they went for Carrie."

"Do I look that easy to fool?"

"Shit, Tom-Tom," said Sam. "Somebody says the word *Jeeeeee-zusss* just right, and you'll get brainwashed before they even know your name. Just 'cause we got an empty church, it don't mean they're welcome here."

"Can I go now?" Tommy asked them all. "Or do I have to keep putting up with this shit?" He turned to Sowell. "I know you're not feeding me lunch."

"Not after you lied to me. What'd that guy say to you?"

"He's fixing up the church, and the junk's got to go. Dolman's gonna kick like a mule."

"Better not kick too hard," Phil said, "or this guy'll snap him in half. How's a decent man get a face like that?"

"Somebody hit him with a brick," Tommy said.

"Any other secrets you got about him?" asked Tami. "Sounds like you know more than you're saying."

"That beats saying more than I know. I saw the guy for five minutes. His name's Richard Thorpe, and he got hit in the face with a brick. That's it."

"See?" said Tami. "You saw him before we did, but you didn't tell us."

"I see lots of things before you do, Mrs. Willer. Might blow your mind if I said 'em all. Afternoon, everybody. If you want to know what I think, turn on your radios at one o'clock."

Then Tommy was gone without his lunch, down a street he couldn't even call a street. Where to go? Where to sit and just *be*? In New York he could find a million places to hide but never for long—that was the problem with New York. The problem with Suborney was having nowhere to hide. If he ever did find one, though, he could hide there forever.

* * *

Both Dan Stannard's truck and his mom's had left the house, which meant freedom. Tommy called up his semi-girlfriend, Sherry Medina, and arranged to meet her at the mall in Widefield that afternoon, then called up Justin Stannard's show on 620 AM KJML (King Jesus My Lord). *Reverend* Stannard—the older brother of Dan and therefore Tommy's potential step-uncle—ran a born-again roll-your-own church in Colorado Springs called LifeBound that had been among the first in town to conquer the airwaves and preach Christian social activism. People who loved God needed to stand up for America and get themselves elected, said Reverend Stannard and people like him on KJML and a dozen other stations too. For school board, county clerk, dogcatcher, anything, so there'd be more of *us*, less of *them*. So we could stop innocent babies from getting murdered and be a strong country again before it was too late.

They said crazy stuff, especially about how God loved America best of all, and it drove Tommy nuts. They got God mixed up with the American flag, and he didn't think God would like that too much. Why would God always take America's side in every war? Why would God want Ronald Reagan to be president instead of Jimmy Carter? Why would God—and this is what Tommy asked himself at a Widefield High School football game one Friday night last fall, with scouts from Wisconsin and Arizona State in the stands watching him—want one football team to win more than the other if both of them prayed to him equally hard before the game? God wouldn't care, Tommy figured, if he loved everybody equally like all good Christians said. So he stopped covering the tight end slanting across the field and dropped to his knees, praying while his man scored the winning touchdown.

Everybody hated him after that, and he had fresh questions about God that only Reverend Stannard seemed smart enough to answer. The guy wasn't as sin obsessed as most radio preachers, at least when he was talking to Tommy. He talked about Hell plenty, sure, but with Tommy he got gentle—practicing his uncle voice, probably. Tommy called five minutes early to make sure he was first in line, then washed off his chest and armpits in the kitchen sink. He replayed the scene at Pete's in his mind so many times that he missed Reverend Stannard's intro.

"Blessed Sunday to you, Mr. Sandor," the man said, his voice low and round. Nothing like the whine of his wayward younger brother, who couldn't stop committing the delicious sin of adultery with that fine piece of unmarried flesh in Suborney. "You keeping out of trouble?"

"Depends on who you talk to and what they call trouble. I just got one question today, Reverend. Then I'll hang up, 'cause I don't want to argue like last time."

"Appreciate that, for our listeners' sake."

"Let's say God's law and man's law are the same," Tommy started in. "Like with murder. How do you know which law you're really listening to? It'd be easy to fool yourself into thinking you're follow-ing God's law when you're really following man's, right? Okay, I'm hanging up now, appreciate your thoughts."

"I've got two ideas for our caller," Reverend Stannard said. "Inten-tion and the fruits of our labor. If our *intention* is to follow Jesus, we're more likely to follow God's law, and we're also better able to tell the difference between what God wants and what *we* want. This is *always* hard because we're so mired in human sin that we can't see our lives the way God sees them."

"Uh-huh," Tommy replied, even though he wasn't on the phone anymore, as he put on deodorant to get ready for Sherry. He grabbed his silver transistor radio from his bedside table, turned it on, and telescoped out its antenna. He left the big radio in the kitchen on so his mom would come home to the sound of KJML, which she couldn't stand.

"Because we're blinded by sin," the Reverend continued, as Tommy headed for the junkyard, "it's hard for us to be certain of our own intentions. I'm sure every single one of our listeners has thought they were doing what God wants, only to turn around later and realize they've been serving themselves. The fruits of our labor matter because we can't tell right away if we've been acting on God's behalf or our own. Say, for instance, a young man like our caller is interested in a young woman and pursues her. If the fruit of that labor is love and marriage and a strong Christian family, then it's a good bet that the young man's been acting on behalf of God all along. If the fruit of that labor is mere sexual *entertainment*—which is destroying America from within—then you can be *positive* that he's been following man's—"

Tommy turned off the radio before he reached the junkyard fence because his question had already answered itself in some dark, ancient space within his body where words didn't dare go. He didn't want to think he was using Sherry for "mere sexual entertainment"—and he couldn't be since she'd never let him have actual sex with her. By the fence on the far side of the yard, he kept a car that he'd pieced together from junkers: a '71 Chevy Vega Coupe with a '73 Camaro engine, plus eighty-six extra welds so its chassis could carry the weight. No hood yet because he still had to cut a hole for the top of the oversized carburetor. Brand-new racing tires on it just the week before, a set of A70-13s from an MG Midget somebody totaled. Tommy fired the Vega up, sniffed for anything burning, and finally headed out of his shithole town.

He'd gotten up to 140 a few times on empty back roads, but today he drove like an old lady to keep the bored, speed-trapping cops off his ass. Down Road X to Marksheffel Road to Fontaine Boulevard and finally to the half-dead strip mall in Widefield, the closest place to find kids his own age. There used to be a big grocery store, but now there was only a pizza joint, an Armed Forces Recruiting Center, and a Baskin-Robbins. Plus a big empty parking lot where kids went to drink beer, smoke weed, and try to get laid.

Tommy parked in front of the pizza joint and saw Robin Cullen and Pam Elvers, cheerleaders who had crushes on him before they even got breasts. They would've given anything to suck him off last summer, when he was still an all-state linebacker. Both girls wore halter tops, plastic sandals, and tight white shorts. They'd never leave home—Tommy would bet a million on it. They'd try living somewhere else, get scared, then come back and marry whoever could stand them.

"Look, it's Tommy the Commie," Robin said, jerking her chin at the Vega. "Your mama lets you drive that thing?"

"Your mama lets you dress like a whore?" He pointed to Robin's slice of pizza. "Hey, you buying me that?"

"Only if you buy me two. One for me and one for *Jeeee-zus.*"

Tommy grabbed the pizza from Robin's plate, stuffed as much of it into his mouth as he could, and stepped inside to get three more slices from the stoner dropout behind the counter. He came back out to find the girls looking at his engine, then handed Robin her slices. They saw Sherry heading over on her bike and called her a wetback, and when Tommy yelled at them for it, they slouched off to eat in Pam's car. He waved Sherry over and French-kissed her right in front of them because Sherry was the only girl Tommy knew who was worth kissing. Fucking was another thing—he'd done that with a bunch of girls, a few women too. But kissing was only for Sherry.

"You taste good." Sherry stepped back and licked her lips. She was too tall and blonde for a Mexican girl, too dark-skinned for a white one. The kind of girl New Yorkers would see fifty times a day without batting an eyelash but who made Colorado people ask, "What *are* you?"

"That's just the pizza," Tommy said. "You don't know how I really taste."

She whacked his chest. "Is that your lame try of the day to trick me into giving you head?"

Five minutes later he parked the Vega in their secret spot off Bradley Road, hidden under some trees in the middle of a dry creek. Zippers undone, hands everywhere. He begged Sherry to let him inside her, and she said no, like always. They brought each other to manual orgasm hurriedly, eager to talk about being half–one thing and half-another—though Tommy, without a father, didn't know what half of himself even was. How could anybody call it "mere sexual entertainment" if they talked about stuff like that afterward?

"My mom says I can get a scholarship at Wichita State for being half-Mexican," Sherry told him. "She looked it up."

"Kansas? That's worse than this dump."

"It's college. It can't be worse. And there must be other half-Mexicans there if they're giving away scholarships."

"Where do I go to find people like me?" Tommy slid sideways with his legs out his window and put his head on Sherry's lap.

"How about Freaktown State College?" When she lunged down to kiss him, he felt like a boy who didn't get enough mother-love. And it was true—anybody who looked at him and Connie could see that. Connie loved him, sure, but she held some of her love back from him, punishing him for everything his father wouldn't give her. So he held some of his back, too, just to punish her. Sherry traced designs on Tommy's neck and let him take that mother-love from her, even though he never gave her the father-love she'd been missing. She pulled him up, and they kissed again, and he tried to give her what he thought father-love felt like—the straightforwardness inside him, the steadfast love that would never leave a woman behind—and for that moment they were both perfect.

Two people who didn't fit their world. Two bits of nothingness that made one.

* * *

When he got home at sundown, Tommy found his mom's Chevy LUV idling in the driveway. She stood in the kitchen packing road trip snacks into the big Tupperware bin she only used for visiting her mom in Sidney, Nebraska. The left side of her face, its skin drooping, looked ready to cry. The right side looked ready to bite some small animal to death.

"Grandma's not doing so hot," she told him. "Fluid in her lungs. I've got to go up."

"Me too?"

"Not yet. I'll call if it gets worse. Can that junker of yours make it up to Sidney?"

"Junker? I'd be up in three hours."

"It's a four-hour drive." She sealed the bin and put her hands on Tommy's shoulders, then stood on tiptoes to put her forehead to his. "Be good while I'm gone." He pulled away because he'd felt other foreheads against his own, the foreheads of girls and women he'd been inside of, and he didn't want his mother bunched up with them. She slid her hands down to his forearms while she kissed his cheeks, then left, honking twice as she pulled out of the driveway.

Tommy took a shower and pretended to soap up Sherry Medina, fantasizing that they'd just found out she was pregnant. There was no way he'd dump Sherry or their kid—he'd rather chop off his fingers live on national TV than abandon them. But that would mean no college for Sherry, definitely no med school, and shittier jobs than they both deserved. It would mean a big city, too, where skins like their baby's got born every day. In New York, Tommy could be a graveyard shift security guard who played sax between his rounds at a fancy Midtown office building, then came home at sunrise to snuggle with Sherry and the baby.

But him, a father? What bullshit. He had too much hate for his own father to be a decent one himself. Too much anger for his mom to treat a woman right. As soon as it got dark, Tommy pulled on his jeans and his work boots—Red Wing Irish Setters that he'd bought with his own money—and headed for the church with his sax.

"Hey Tommy," Julie Parness called from her porch, a swirly blue glass in her hand.

"Hey Jules." Tommy stood the case on end and leaned against it, talkative this time. "My mom's gone, you know that?"

"Yeah, she said to make sure you don't have too many orgies. One or two, tops." She finished what was in her glass. "Who's that guy you talked to at the church?"

"Richard something. Only saw him once."

"And what the hell's an intentional community? That's what he told Tami he's building."

Tommy shrugged and blew her a kiss, and Julie returned it as he moved on. He stopped at the corner of Mangum Street and Road X to put the reed in his mouth, sidestepped Sam Kurtep's dog shit, and looked at the cross and the Reagan banners at the Fiddler house. He inspected the edges of Tumbleback Road to see what junk had blown into town since last night, when the water and the wind came for him and only him.

There was a half-crumpled movie poster in a language he didn't know, with a blond guy in a Hawaiian shirt talking to a parrot. A three-foot square of plastic sheeting with masking tape and red spray paint at the edges. A plastic Luke Skywalker soda cup. He didn't knock at the church doors this time—since he wanted to surprise Richard Thorpe, who'd be poking through the junk—but there was nobody inside. He put his sax together, ready for the music to blast out of his lungs and wow the best sax men in New York, who'd come at first because Drake begged them to but now came for Tommy's music itself.

But he had no music inside him, only a heavy, dead sense of all the

Tommies he'd never be. All of them were dying inside him at once without even taking a final breath, and he felt like the last pieces of his boyhood were leaving his body forever. Why? Was it the touch of his mother's skin against him, so soon after the touch of Sherry's? Was it knowing how rotten and selfish the fruits of his labors were? With every exhale, more of his boyhood disappeared. The singing five-year-old who saw Jesus, the fifteen-year-old who once stood at perfect attention for an hour saluting an American flag, the stud linebacker.

Those boys had escaped into the air like steam, and the only thing left for him was to become a man. Not that being a man would feel any better. All it meant was carrying the heavy silence of those dead selves around for the rest of his life. Carrying the weight of all the possibilities he'd already lost, the ones he was losing that very second, and the ones he'd lose tomorrow without ever knowing they were his to begin with.

Go outside, Drake told him. *Now you're ready. Let the notes come.*

Tommy sat on the front steps, the sax bell resting on his knee. His insides were as empty as what lay outside him—unbroken plains for six hundred miles north and south and east and mountains to the west that he couldn't even see. A night sky that offered only ghosts who wouldn't speak their names. He breathed in, finally ready to blow, but then heard voices from the fields near the Perrin house. In the darkness he saw silhouettes moving toward it: four men with poles on their shoulders that held up a bundle, like a picture he'd seen once of four slaves carrying a queen. One of them had to be the tallest man he'd ever seen. A short one stood in front of them all, dragging something on a rope.

"*Ah ah ah ah aaaaaah!*" sang a girl's high voice, thin but clear. No real words. Patient and soft, like he got with his sax if he didn't rush himself. She sang her line again, and Tommy held his breath, waiting.

"*Give thanks to the skyyyyyy!*" the others sang in response. They called back and forth with the girl until they reached the front steps of the Perrin house and fell silent.

One of them knocked on the door, and it opened from inside. The men let down the bundle, and the tall one picked up something and carried it in. Then the one who'd been dragging something—a stout old woman, Tommy could finally make out her silhouette—turned and looked straight at him down the road. She lifted a hand up by her shoulder and left it there for ten seconds, twenty, until Tommy's hand came up and hovered in front of his own shoulder. When her hand went down, his went down, like she had his arm on a string.

She turned and went in, and the door to the Perrin house closed behind her. Tommy's hand went to the bell of his sax and traced out the engraving on its surface, *S-E-L-M-E-R*. Then he did it backwards, *R-E-M-L-E-S*, thinking about the dead man whose saxophone it used to be. Had to be a dead man, from the looks of that Buick. Could have been Drake from the Lower East Side of New York, getting within inches of his son before God laughed and pulled the plug on his life.

Tommy kept his fingers against the sax bell, still tracing those letters as the sky doubled in breadth above him, holding even more songs than stars. *My hands are not my own*, he told himself. *My song is not my own, my breath is not my own, my life is not my own.*

•

3

Everybody else in Suborney knew that Tommy had Jesus problems before he did, and because of him, they all feared the abandoned church coming back to life. A tough, crazy kid like him who was messed up about Jesus—not knowing how to follow him or even which version of him to get behind—could cause a lot of trouble for everybody. It was hard to blame Tommy for being confused because he'd been going to church with people he wasn't related to since he first caught the Jesus bug back in Bird City, Kansas, where he was born and raised on a goat farm. During a summer fair a five-year-old girl named Jane Marie sang a song about how her friend Jesus walked with her wherever she went, and a four-year-old Tommy climbed onstage uninvited to dance along to her father's banjo. After that all he wanted to do was play with Jane Marie, whose parents wouldn't let him because he was a bastard. Instead, he'd go outside and make forts with Jesus, feed the goats with Jesus, hunt for bugs with Jesus.

He'd seen Jesus three times in one day, Tommy told his mother, doing regular people things. Following birds around, making a nest for napping in the tall grass, sitting on a fence and staring up at clouds. Connie wasn't a big fan of Jesus. She'd grown up going to a Lutheran church with her mom, and she never hated it but never loved it either. After she had Tommy, it was the people who shouted most about loving Jesus who hated her most for having a bastard son, and before long she expected a dirty look to come her way whenever somebody in Bird City said *Jesus* or *God* within twenty feet of her.

But Tommy kept on talking about Jesus, and when he pestered her enough about going to church, she let him go with the Sneads, their Methodist neighbors from two farms down. The Sneads didn't hate her for having a bastard because their own daughter had one, but they never got too close because they didn't like how she wouldn't go to church when her own son asked her to.

Jesus, make my mom come to church, he'd say at the end of his bedtime prayers. When he first came to Suborney, the dead church thrilled him because his mom had no more excuse not to go—they could almost walk there holding their breaths! But by then it had been shut down for nine years, and Connie hadn't been inside a church for almost eight. Tommy kept bugging her about Jesus so much that she let Ron and Kate Ulin bring him to their church in Fountain, a ragtag gang of born-agains called Gracehouse that met beneath an Interstate 25 overpass every Sunday morning, rain or shine.

Connie didn't keep track of the Jesus gap between herself and Tommy as it grew wider. She'd started off feeding the Sneads lunch after church and did the same with the Ulins during her first year in Suborney. She eventually let the lunches drop off, and when she'd ask Tommy how church went, he'd just say, "Fine." When he turned nine, the Ulins blessed his head with oil and he cried his brains out in front of the whole congregation, begging God to send him a father. After that he organized a children's choir that took him away on Wednesday and Friday nights—though Connie drew the line at letting him work Saturday mornings at a soup kitchen up in Colorado Springs.

Then puberty hit Tommy early, and his muscles came in, along with so many questions about his dad that Connie almost ran away from home to avoid them. On his fourteenth birthday she told him about Drake, the blond tenor sax player from the Lower East Side who stole her flighty sixteen-year-old heart at the Red Willow County

Fair in McCook, Nebraska. Right away Tommy started looking for girls whose flighty hearts he could steal, and by fifteen he'd found a couple. The Gracehouse people didn't like that and said he was a dirty sinner, and they all laid hands on him and tried to heal him.

He made himself scarce at church after that and looked for Jesus out on the plains instead. Jesus wasn't calling him a dirty sinner. Jesus only told him to straighten out his life and stop bullshitting himself, but the Gracehouse people wanted to make an example of him, just like his teachers and his football coach. He let the Ulins drag him back to the underpass after he quit on that touchdown play, but he fainted in the middle of a blessing and never returned. Tommy stuck himself inside of every girl who'd let him, and when the Ulins tried to reel him in again, he said he was done looking for Jesus. How could you look for something that was spying on you? Always watching, with a sly smirk on his face that said, *I know you, Tommy Sandor. You'll come around.*

So the good citizens of Suborney felt they had a perfect right to keep a close eye on Tommy now that another Jesus commune was in town. They were scared of what Tommy joining a cult would look like but universally agreed that it just might be better than the direction he was going. No friends his age, acting like he was black with all that stupid jazz, fucking that wetback girl, talking trash about America and the flag. Acting like he came from New York City just because his father did. A little Jesus wouldn't hurt him, they believed. Might even give him some direction. But not *too* much Jesus. Not the contagion they feared coming into town on the bashed-in cheek of Richard Thorpe, which few had seen but all had imagined.

✳ ✳ ✳

Nobody answered when Tommy knocked at the door of the Perrin house at sunrise, though he heard something like a cat yowling. It still smelled like mold, thanks to years of rain that sneaked through the roof. The windows were covered in burlap from inside, which they hadn't been when he walked by a week ago to look for Wesley's ghost. Tommy put his hand on the doorknob but couldn't turn it.

"Thorpe, you in there?" he called. Another sound came from inside, halfway between a raccoon's growl and a baby's cry, but still nobody answered. Tommy took the long way home to drop off his sax and pick up his radio, walking past Joe Mandari, who was up early to water his plants and totally ignored Tommy, as usual. Walking past Mrs. Culp, whose first name he wasn't sure anybody in town knew, who slept in her living room recliner with last night's messy blob of knitting on her lap. He cut down Jefferson Street and walked past two empty houses that nobody owned anymore—houses he could sleep in, maybe even play his sax in, once Thorpe and his gang took over the church.

Where did they come from, and why did they walk at night like that? On the door handle at Pete's gas station hung a plastic bag with two bagels, the cream cheese and ham already on them, and a note that said, NOTHING TO DO, CHECK BACK LUNCH TIME. Tommy walked to his Vega and ate in the driver's seat, listening to KJML so he could get enough arguments going in his head to keep him occupied until Dolman showed up and gave him real ones. One Moral Majority clown pretty much said everybody was going to hell except the people who joined his church, and another one seemed like he wanted to set a world record for saying *Jesus* and *America* the most times in a single sentence.

Once he got sick of the radio, Tommy leaned way back in the driver's seat and fantasized about being in New York with another day full of busy, busy, busy ahead of him. Giving lessons all morning to rich teenage snots on Park Avenue, then doing an audition at Rockefeller Center. He'd see his girlfriend at the edge of Harlem for lunch—not Sherry Medina but a New York version of her, half-this and half-that and a quarter something else. Enough of everything for people to say *She's one of them* but not enough of anything to make them say *She's one of us.* Her name was Celia, and she wanted to be a jazz singer. She talked about how tough it was to make rent, then suggested they could save money if they moved in together.

"I could handle that," the flesh-and-blood Tommy in Suborney said aloud, and he and Celia started making plans to shack up. Her studio in Harlem wasn't big enough, and his in Alphabet City wasn't safe enough. Maybe somewhere close to the Williamsburg Bridge, so he could play on it every day like Rollins? They celebrated by pulling each other into orgasms that left them dizzy and gasping, and Tommy had a hard-on when he heard car tires crunching the dry, scrubby grass beside him.

It was Dan Stannard, who acted like the sheriff of Suborney even though he was just a state patrolman. Acted like he dropped out of a John Wayne western to give the poor town hope. Stannard lined up his driver's side window with the Vega's, then cut his engine. The sun was barely up, and he already wore those mirrored aviator sunglasses the state patrol guys loved so much, though not even those could make him look like a real cop. He looked like a guy who should have been teaching junior high biology.

"Isn't it a bit early for shades, officer?" asked Tommy.

"Your mom's worried about you," Stannard said, taking off the sunglasses to show Tommy how sincere he was.

"I should be worried about *her*, with her taste in men. How's my grandma?"

"Still trouble with her lungs. Your mom might be there awhile."

Tommy made his eyes puppy soft. "But what does that mean for you and me?"

"Nothing. Stay away from those new people, will you?" Stannard fired up his engine and slid his shades back on. "They're thieves. Their grand pooh-bah guy's been to jail, probably still belongs there."

"You've been to jail too. Embezzlement's a sin and a crime, ain't it?"

"Not like arson and manslaughter. Some people get back on the right side of the law in jail, and some don't. Remember that."

"Aye, aye, captain." Tommy made his wrist limp and gave Stannard a fake salute as he drove off. The whole *I'm-gonna-be-your-stepfather* thing would've been easier if his mom screwed some big-ass cop who could knock his head off without even trying. It would be just like in the movies, and the movies would tell them both how to act. Instead, his mom had to screw an embezzler who reformed in prison and begged his way onto the state patrol, even though the felony should've kept him out. But he begged and begged, *Please oh please*, probably the same way he begged his wife in Colorado Springs for a divorce. Probably the same way he begged Connie Sandor to let him under her skirt.

Slimy, weak, greedy. Not the kind man Tommy could ever call *father* or even *dad*. He put on his leather gloves, got out of his Vega, and stretched under the big, crisp sky that covered him like a cocoon. Quarter to eight, he guessed from the sun, because the pink in it had all been drowned out by yellow. Time for this workingman to climb the fence and start his working day.

✳ ✳ ✳

At eleven thirty the sun decided it was truly summer—time to turn up the heat full blast and bake the patch of dirt called Suborney, Colorado, into complete submission. It wanted to keep old people inside, sitting in the dark with their fans on and their lights off. Wanted to fry the whole town like an ant under a microscope because it was used up, done needing to exist, and only clung to the earth out of stubborn habits that needed to be broken.

But Tommy kept on working in the sun because he wanted it to know he could. He finished loading up the Garson brothers' scrap dumpster with fenders, bumpers, hoods, and whatever else he could tear loose from the junkers that were already getting stripped down and parted out. He felt like Jack "Hacksaw" Reynolds of the LA Rams, another linebacker he used to want to be, and he filled that dumpster higher than he had to because he liked the Garsons, with their chewing tobacco and ZZ Top beards and truckers' wallets and stories about growing up on Guam. Then he headed for the office, ready to tell Dolman he was taking lunch. But Dolman had left early for his own, and Tommy found a black guy a couple years older than him standing at the counter with his hands in his pockets. A tall, lanky guy with jeans and a yellow T-shirt and a messy Afro that looked like he'd cut it himself.

"Are you Dolman?" the guy asked.

"Shit no, I'm Tommy. Dolman's AWOL. What do you need?"

"Tarpaper and shingles, that's what they sent me to get."

"Well, we got some. What's your name, where you from?"

"Benjy Harms, from Philly." Benjy stuck his hand out, and Tommy shook it, wishing all the redneck bigots of Suborney would walk in and freak out at the sight of black skin touching white. He headed to the yard with Benjy and hopped into the first pickup he saw. Heagren kept a bunch of them around, barely running, and parted them out when their engines quit.

"You with that Thorpe guy?" Tommy asked as Benjy climbed in beside him.

"Yes sir. You the one he met?"

"Yeah." Tommy rolled off into the maze of scrap. "A guy shot his wife and kid in the house you're living in, you know that? Then forgot to shoot himself."

"We heard about that."

"I was ten. I played with Wesley till sundown that night. Last kid to see him alive."

"Let's pray for him then."

Benjy bowed his head, closed his eyes, and folded his hands. Tommy figured he might as well pray for Wesley, too, which he'd pretty much quit doing, so he stopped the truck hard. *Caving in to the Jesus freaks already*, he told himself in Sam Kurtep's voice. *Didn't even put up a fight.* He tried to pray like he used to with the Sneads back in Bird City, holding his breath with his fingers woven together in front of his chin. Instead, he remembered chasing Wesley around the kitchen island on another night, when they were seven and he'd slept at the Perrin house because the snow stranded his mom at work. When Tommy held his hands open in front of his shoulders like they did at Gracehouse, Benjy grabbed the closest one and said, "God, please take care of Tommy's friend Wesley."

Tommy held Benjy's hand tight and almost cried but instead laughed at himself for doing the same thing he did last summer—flirting with the new Jesus freaks as soon as they got to town. He would've gone with Mike and his Michigan gang last summer if they'd had the slightest idea who Jesus was, but they turned Jesus into some free-love hippie who never asked a damn thing of anybody. And that's one thing Tommy knew about Jesus—he asks you for something. For everything, once you really let him in. Tommy ended up hating Mike and that bunch almost as much as he hated the born-agains who wanted him to go kill for Jesus in the desert. Their Jesus was squishy, saying everything they wanted him to and nothing they didn't. It was bullshit religion—no religion at all really. He quickly prayed that this new bunch didn't have a bullshit Jesus, too, then squeezed Benjy's hand and let it go.

Enough Jesus, Tommy told himself. He pulled up to a covered stall that had two pallets of shingles and six rolls of tarpaper in it, then opened a roll for Benjy to inspect. Benjy might as well have been looking inside somebody's stomach.

"Some of you people know how to use this stuff, right?" Tommy asked.

"Yes sir," Benjy said.

"What's with the *sir* shit? You're older than me."

"It's to keep us respecting people." Benjy pulled a bunch of crumpled, dirty-looking singles out of his pocket. "How much you want for this stuff?"

"You can work that out with Dolman. Help me load this, I want to go eat lunch."

They loaded everything into the truck bed and headed to the Perrin house, where people milled around outside. A Mexican guy with a stump instead of a right hand. A greasy guy with half his teeth gone. The tall guy, stooping over to talk with the old lady. Tommy pulled up to the porch, and she walked toward his window while the men started unloading.

"Afternoon, Mr. Sandor," she said. She looked seventy, older than his grandma. She wore a plain yellow sundress with a man's white collared shirt over it, plus a red sun hat that she knocked off whacking at a fly on her neck.

"Same to you, ma'am," Tommy told her. "How'd you know my name?"

"I've heard you on the radio, clear over in Kansas."

"That so?" *They came for me*, he told himself, though he immediately dismissed the idea as selfish. "Guess that means you know I've got some stuff on my mind."

"Come up here and talk any time," she said. "We've got stuff on our minds too."

The tall guy slammed the tailgate and shouted, "That's a fact!" Then he gave a thumbs-up, and Tommy drove back to the yard to find Dolman at the open gate, shouting at him.

"I just watched you sell tarpaper to a nig—"

"No sir." Tommy hurled himself out of the truck, itching for a fight. "You just watched me *give* tarpaper to a kid named Benjy Harms. You want money from him, go get it yourself."

"Want to go, you little fuckwad?" Dolman held up a fist. "I made it through prison, I can take care of you."

"First two shots are free. Do it, man. You'll feel better."

Tommy bumped Dolman's chest with his own and stuck his chin out, ready to take the punch—praying for it almost, so he'd have an excuse to tear the shit out of a man twice his age. But Dolman bumped back and laughed like it was all a game, and they flipped each other off as Tommy shuffled toward Pete's gas station. Halfway there he broke into a run because he felt light inside—so full of light that every step might spring him into the sky. There was something different about this batch of Jesus freaks. They were meatier than the Michigan people, tougher, and didn't need to sell you on themselves. They made things happen but didn't crow about it first. Pete's cowbell clanged, and Tommy stepped inside to find the shelves half-bare.

"What the hell happened here?" he called to Pete, who was on his knees rearranging things so it looked like he still had food to sell.

"Look in the register," Pete said back. Tommy opened it and saw the tray stuffed full of dirty, crumpled dollar bills. The change slots overflowed.

"Was it that Thorpe guy?"

"No. An old lady with whiskers, plus the tallest fucker you ever saw."

"They're moving into the Perrin house. Just gave 'em tarpaper and shingles."

"Gave?"

"They'll be back buying plenty if they want to fix that place up. Dolman can nickel-and-dime 'em."

"That's all he'll get, nickels and dimes. Hey, pull everything you can eat from out back, will you? Get prices on it, put it wherever it fits."

While Pete sorted the money, Tommy went to the storeroom and labeled all the food he saw. At first he added ten cents to the old prices, figuring it might earn Pete enough money to give him a raise. Then he thought about the mountain of change in the register, about the crumpled bills in Benjy's hand, and he wondered what these new Jesus freaks did to get that money. Begging? Not their style. He started taking ten cents off the old prices instead.

"What are they like?" Tommy asked Pete.

"Not half-bad. Talk like normal people, not *Jesus* this and *Jesus* that."

"Stannard says they're thieves—one of 'em did time. They say why they're here?"

"The tall guy says they're like the Catholic Workers, just without the Catholic part."

Tommy nodded like he understood and labeled a flat of tomato soup cans. Some at eighty-five cents, some at seventy-five, some at sixty-five. Then Pete came over and gave him a ham and cheese sandwich on a bun with the edges ripped off.

"Didn't I throw those buns out yesterday?" Tommy asked.

"They bought up all my bread. I don't know how many more people they've got coming, but they bought enough food for a hell of a lot more than I saw."

"I don't know what kind of work they think they'll get around here," Tommy said. "Nothing to pick, nothing to build."

"Maybe they'll build a playground for all the kids," Pete said back, and Tommy pictured Suborney flooded with children—some his own, even. They'd stop playing and run to the big church when the bell in the old steeple finally rang again. *How about now, Mom?* he heard himself saying. *You ready to go to church with me now?*

* * *

"This Thorpe guy's no picnic," Stannard said from Connie's stove, where—at her request—he heated up three cans of chili to make sure Tommy ate supper. "Sixteen years in the Nebraska State Pen. Burned down somebody's house, cold-blooded. A guy died 'cause of him."

"Aren't name checks illegal without probable cause?" Tommy said as he quartered a head of iceberg lettuce so he could tell his mom they ate vegetables.

"I'm glad you learned something at school."

"I learned it on the streets, man." Tommy raised his fist in a Black Power salute, like that picture from the 1968 Olympics.

"You and your jazzman bullshit," Stannard said. "Let's go up there after supper. No gun. Deal?"

Tommy nodded, closer than ever to letting Stannard be his stepdad. But Danny Boy would never be good enough for that, never strong or true enough. If the guy told him *Do this* and Tommy asked *Why?* then the best Stannard could ever say is *Because I'm the guy who fucks your mother*. Not good enough, never would be. Tommy lopped the pithy stems off of all four quarters of lettuce.

"Your mom's worried about you," Stannard told him.

"That's her job, isn't it? What she says, anyway."

"She doesn't want to give you that thousand bucks 'cause she's got money to burn, you know. She wants you to get out of here and do something with your life."

"Like be a football star? A marine? Bet you didn't know you're the one who made me drop the marine thing, did you?" Tommy wiped his mouth with a napkin. "I overheard you guys one time, when she said she was worried about me, and you said the marines were good at straightening out 'little shits like Tommy.' Remember?"

"That's enough."

"That was when I decided. If you wanted me in the marines, there's no fucking way on earth I'd join up."

"I'd like to eat in peace," Stannard said, trying so hard to bite his tongue that his face twisted up. Tommy took his chili and lettuce and headed to his bedroom, eating as he stared up at the New York subway map. Fuck New York. Just another place, like his mom always told him. He imagined himself ripping that map down a dozen times, and each time it revealed a different word on the wall behind it that told him some secret, absolute truth about himself. The words always faded before he could even tell what language they were in, though. Tommy heard dishes in the kitchen—Stannard cleaning up after himself for once—and a couple minutes later the man knocked on his bedroom door.

"Let's walk," Stannard said. "No use freaking 'em out with the patrol car."

Tommy grabbed his tenor, figuring he wouldn't come back to the house before he went to the church and played. As they neared Tumbleback Road, he ran over and left it on the steps. When Tommy caught up, Stannard bunched his lips as he stared up the road at the Perrin house.

"You scared of those Jesus people, Sheriff?" Tommy asked. "Or just the ghosts?"

"Don't *Sheriff* me, sonny."

"Don't *sonny* me, Sheriff."

They walked on, their strides caught in the same rhythm for a moment. If Tommy had been twelve when Stannard started screwing his mom, he'd probably want to be a state patrolman by now. But the bond never took. He remembered hearing Stannard come in his mom's bedroom on his seventeenth birthday—it pissed him off so much that he stole her Chevy LUV and leaned against it in a dive bar parking lot, waiting with his shirt off. The woman who came over to check out his muscles told him she was forty as he left her apartment, which meant he'd fucked a woman older than his mother. It seemed like fitting revenge at the time, for his mom and Stannard both. Maybe himself too.

When they got close to the Perrin house, all its years of bad vibes hit them at once. Stannard didn't even know that Suborney existed back when Ike Perrin lost his shit, but now he knew the story well enough to hesitate when he reached the flagstone walkway. He climbed the steps and knocked, while Tommy, not wanting the Jesus people to see him next to a cop, stayed at the bottom. Stannard hovered in the doorway, listening to silverware clank against dishes inside, then knocked again half a minute later. The door opened and an ax-faced woman with straight black hair and bangs poked her head through it.

"We're just having a meal and a prayer," she told them. "You're welcome to join us." She looked like a college kid at first but seemed older the longer Tommy looked at her. The tight corners of her mouth said she'd spent a long time holding back what she wanted to say.

"Just ate, thanks," Stannard said. "We were—"

"A prayer and a song," she said. "Then we'll be right out." As she

43

closed the door, Tommy saw a sneer cross Stannard's face. Having a radio preacher for a brother must have made him loathe the kind of Jesus freaks he'd seen before, with all their memorized verses and their shouts of *Trust Jesus!*

"You get too much Jesus from your brother, don't you?" Tommy asked, and Stannard nodded. "You're like my mom, except I'm the one she gets too much Jesus from."

When Stannard got tired of waiting and stepped off the porch, Tommy circled the house to see what it still needed. The water worked—he'd turned on the main and tried both outside spigots two weeks earlier, out of curiosity. It needed new glass on half the windows, probably a ton of fresh drywall. The kitchen door had no steps down to the ground. He remembered how that kitchen used to look inside, with its checkered linoleum floor and its yellow fridge and oven. Wesley's mom used to put marshmallows on toast in that oven, then melt them down.

People should live here, Tommy thought, *to make up for the ones who died here.* When he came back around to Stannard, the singing started—the girl's voice he'd heard the night before. High and broken and not coming out of her straight but as true as any sound he could make himself.

"*Ahh ohhhhhh,*" it sang, and then a half-dozen voices sang, "*Ahh ohhhhhh*" right back. The girl's voice came again, tripping upward and dropping down for a long last note. "*Ah ah ahhh ohhhhhh.*"

In the silence that followed, Tommy's fingers searched for those notes on an imaginary sax. It was the same scale that had run through him on the night he met Thorpe at the church, and his head throbbed with joy at finding other people who used it. At finding other people who felt the same way about music as he did—that you had to let it roll through you, fill up your body until you couldn't keep it from soaring out. Another voice came, and Tommy felt sure it was the woman who had opened the door.

"*I am   of dust and bone,*" she sang, and the other voices sang it back.

"I'm done," Stannard called, walking off. "Had enough of this shit in my life."

The girl's voice came back, and the broken soul–ness of it shook Tommy up so much that he almost fell to his knees. Then he found the notes in his fingers, and his feet raced him to the church so he could put his sax together.

"*I am   of dust and bone,*" the people inside sang as he ran, their voices drifting toward him on a brand-new wind. Tommy sat on the church steps and pointed the bell of his sax toward the house, and when he closed his lips on the mouthpiece, his fingers knew what to do:

$$D\flat \quad G \quad G \quad B\flat \quad C \quad G$$

The house waited for one more breath to fill it. Then it sang the words again, trusting that Tommy would send them back whole.

4

Tuesday, July 8

Tommy rolled out of his own bed at sunup and headed for the Perrin house, striding up the front porch steps like he did when Wesley was alive. The front door swung open before his hand touched the knob, and behind it stood the old lady. Her sundress looked the same as yesterday's but baby blue this time.

"Who are you people?" asked Tommy. She raised a finger and stepped away while he peeked into Wesley's old living room, full of knapsacks, sleeping bags, and boxes and cans from Pete's store. On the biggest wall was a half-finished mural of Mary watching Jesus preach. Her white robe trailed on the ground, and her hair was pulled back under a blue scarf. She held two dead chickens by the neck and listened while her son talked to a half-dozen people with blank ovals for faces. Jesus pointed a finger at the ground, his mouth in the middle of a word. *Here*, Tommy thought. Or *This* or *Now*.

A whole pile of color sample jars from paint stores sat underneath the mural, next to an apple crate with a clay pitcher and an empty wicker basket on it. A man's big laugh boomed from the kitchen, and when the old lady came back to the front door, she handed Tommy a soft, worn-out business card that said, THE SONS AND DAUGHTERS OF JESUS AND MARY. The other side was blank.

"No address?" he asked.

"We tend to move a bit."

"What do you people want here?"

"We heal people who need healing, and we bring dead churches back to life." She opened the screen door and took back the card. "And we don't think Jesus wants you to fly out to the desert and kill *anybody*."

Tommy nodded, reassessing her. She knew exactly what to say to let him know she was on his team. "Are you that Thorpe guy's mom?"

"Only in a manner of speaking. But you can call me Mother Meg, like he does." She leaned against the doorjamb and let Tommy study her face—the whiskers Sowell had talked about, the tight lips that showed how sharp her tongue might get if you pissed her off.

"Who's that girl I heard singing?" he asked.

"Why don't you come in and meet some new people, Tommy?"

"Why don't you tell me who was singing, Mother Meg?"

His attempt to sass her didn't even raise a smile. In the kitchen five people stood at the island Ike Perrin had built in the middle of the room, eating peanut butter on old bread as they introduced themselves. He recognized Brother Benjy. The tall guy was Brother Zypanski, the Mexican with the stump was Brother Beto, and the greasy guy with missing teeth was Brother Worrell. The woman with the long black hair and bangs was Sister Melanie. Every one of them was closer to his age than anybody else in Suborney.

"When do you start fixing up that old church?" Tommy asked.

"When everybody knows it's time," Melanie said. "No hurry."

"I'm the only one who uses it. Shouldn't I be part of *everybody*?"

"Of course," said Mother Meg, popping back into the kitchen before Tommy even knew she'd left, then slipping out again.

"Where's the girl who started the song last night?" Tommy asked the others.

"Sleeping." Melanie held out a slice of bread slathered with peanut butter, and Tommy took it. "Who's that cop you came with? Your dad?"

"Shit no, that's my mom's boyfriend. He's state patrol. My best friend got murdered here, you know that? In the second bedroom, back in the corner."

"We know," Zypanski said. "That's where the girl is."

Tommy nodded, wondering what Wesley's ghost might think about sharing his room. The poor kid would probably take any company he could get, especially with his best friend too scared to visit. Tommy took a bite of bread and chewed it to mush, and the Jesus and Mary people watched him swallow.

"Just 'cause I help you doesn't mean I'm one of you," he told them. "But I can tell you what needs doing in this town. Lots of people here who can't help themselves. Or won't."

"Appreciate that," said Worrell, his voice sloppy from the missing teeth.

"And there's people who don't *want* to be helped," Melanie piped in. "You know who they are too."

Tommy looked from face to face, studying the Sons and Daughters of Jesus and Mary. They weren't like the Baptists, who turned their noses up at him for not knowing his Bible, or the Pentecostals, who told him he'd burn in hell, or the Gracehouse people, who said he smelled like sin. They weren't like the wackos who called in to KJML begging Ronnie Reagan to fly them to Iran the second he got elected so they could kill for Jesus like they'd always dreamed about.

"That cop says you're thieves," Tommy told them. "Says he looked you up."

"Shouldn't bother," Sister Melanie said. "We'll tell him all he wants to know. Are you a thief, Tommy?"

"A couple times. It's never been my big thing."

"Well, don't start," Brother Zypanski told him. "We take a little vow, 'Thou shalt not take what ain't thine.' It's the eleventh commandment."

"Actually, it's the eighth," Tommy piped in.

"That's a joke," Brother Worrell said. "We've got lots of eleventh commandments. And we've got work for you, if work's what you like doing."

Tommy flexed his arms and popped the rest of his bread into his mouth. Worrell and Zypanski waved him out the kitchen door, which had a thirty-inch drop where the back steps used to be, and past a freshly strung clothesline already full of clothes. Underwear, T-shirts, Mother Meg's yellow sundress, Thorpe's army camo shorts. They headed out to the leaning-over shed where Ike Perrin once kept his junk, which they lifted up by the corners while Tommy slid bricks underneath it to make it level. They stepped inside to break up its crumbling, oily plywood floor, letting Tommy do most of the stomping. They piled up the broken plywood, then asked him to walk them over to the junkyard and help pick out stuff for the house.

"Why'd you walk here at night instead of driving?" Tommy asked.

Worrell cleared his throat. "Less likely to get, uh, apprehended by guys like your stepdad."

"Hell if he's my stepdad." They walked past Ginny Caslow's house. She had a shrine for the hostages, like the Fiddlers did but smaller, and Tommy wondered if she was dead because her sign still read 242. "She's got boards for back windows. Spiderwebs so big she's scared to sweep 'em down."

"Got to have somebody in town telling us the score," said Zypanski. "Or we can't do much good."

"Is that what Sister Melanie did in your last town?"

"*My*, how perceptive our boy is!" Worrell whacked Zypanski's arm. "It was two towns ago, actually. Little spot called Bird City, Kansas."

"No shit!" Tommy jumped up and down. "I was born in Bird City! Lived there till I was six, on a goat farm."

As they neared the junkyard, Tommy thought nonstop about Bird City—a place he wished he'd been old enough to truly know. He wanted to call Grandma's house and tell his mom how the church people had been there, which might soften her up a bit about them.

Tommy remembered the goats they had in Bird City, but he couldn't remember the name of the last people in Suborney who had them—a skinny old woman always dressed in black and her potty-mouthed daughter who drove a milk truck. Wilkinson, Tarkeson? He used to play with their goats until they left and even milked them when the daughter let him.

"Who's this, Tom-boy?" called Dolman from behind the big gate, which he'd unchained on time for a change.

"Brought you a couple thieves," Tommy said back. "This is my boss, Ed Dolman. Did three years for thieving in the Colorado State Pen."

"Let me tell my own damn story." Dolman jutted his chin at the men. "You with that church bunch?"

"Yes sir," Zypanski said. "Lots of us got on the wrong side of the law."

"Then I guess you can't have Tom-boy here. He's squeaky clean."

"We make exceptions for people with enough anger to fill a blimp," Worrell said.

Tommy headed out to the yard and waved for them to follow, and when they wouldn't come, he climbed onto the roof of a red '63 Ford pickup to survey the yard. So much junk that nobody needed anymore, and that was just the junk from Colorado Springs. How big was Denver's junkyard? New York's? Before he could think too much about it, Worrell and Zypanski came out laughing with Dolman.

"You guys can ride with me," Tommy called, lowering himself to the wheel through the open window. "Unless you don't get in cars 'cause Jesus didn't."

"If you're in a car," Worrell told him, "you might be tempted to get away fast, so you might be tempted to take what ain't thine."

"Twelfth commandment?" asked Tommy.

"We'll catch up with you." Worrell slapped the side of the truck, and Tommy drove off. Once he got to the corner where they kept the lumber, he could see the Perrin house. Should he call it that anymore, now that the Jesus and Mary people lived there? He climbed the chain link fence to the only spot in Suborney where he could see Pikes Peak—except for the top of Lester Hill and the rickety old church steeple that might crumble underneath him. He looked down at the town, too, seeing what work needed to be done so he could tell the Sons and Daughters who to help. He saw his mom's house and wondered what help it needed, other than him getting the hell out of it.

That would take care of everything, right? Then he pictured his mom on the couch, crying loud over problems he couldn't know but keeping the TV even louder so nobody else could hear her sobbing.

* * *

Connie hadn't made it all the way to her mom's house in Sidney the night before and in fact hadn't left Colorado at all. She'd slept at a motel in Sterling because she couldn't decide whether to keep going north to Sidney or head east to Nebraska City, where she could scour the town to see who'd ratted her out. There was no way in hell Richie Thorpe came to Suborney by chance—not after sixteen years of sitting in prison and planning his next move. Richie came for her and Tommy—she had zero doubt about that because there was nothing else worth coming to Suborney for.

She woke up groggy because the night had been hard. Connie kept peeking through the blinds, sure that Richie had a network of spies watching her every move. Thieves, like the ones Dan Stannard said were with him now, who he'd put under his spell in prison. Thieves who knew everything about her life—when Dan slept over, where she kept her keys at night, who in town would check up on her and who wouldn't care if she died. Connie made the motel bed, pulling the sheets taut and folding down the greasy comforter because she was a neat, organized woman. Even if she skipped out on her troubles and became somebody else again, she'd still be organized about it and not leave messes for anybody else to clean up.

Except for the Tommy mess, of course. She left her key in the room and climbed into her truck to face the same dilemma as yesterday. Nebraska City was a far longer drive than Sidney, six hours instead of forty-five minutes, and she'd have to explain the delay to her mother and her boss at work. Connie pictured Nebraska City sucking her in like quicksand, imagined a sidewalk opening up and swallowing her to the middle of her thighs. Then she couldn't run away, and everybody on the street would get in her face and say, *Is that Jeannette Holmquist?* They'd notice the tiny egg-shaped scar on her cheek that she got from falling out of a tree on her twelfth birthday, and they'd know it was her.

We know who you've been running from, sweetie, they'd say, so consolingly that it made her want to retch. *We've been counting the days till he got out, just like you.*

But maybe she didn't need to go all the way to Nebraska City to learn who ratted her out. Her mom might have been feeding Richie information the whole time he was locked up or helping him find out about Suborney without even knowing it. She might have known who Richie's spies were all along, like the creepy guy in silver overalls Connie used to see in Bird City, hovering around the edges of the goat farm. Connie chickened out on Nebraska City and showed up in Sidney just in time to see her mom through the living room window, buttoning up her high-necked blouse for opening time at Wexler's department store. Trish Sandor, who spent her first forty-six years being Ada Holmquist, watched her only child walk up the concrete pathway but still made her knock on the door.

"You could've unlocked it when you saw me coming," Connie said when Trish opened up.

"Not with your lover boy on the streets."

"He's on *my* streets, not yours." Connie slipped past Trish and plopped down onto the brown vinyl couch, and the air seeping out of its cushions echoed her sigh. "You swear there's not a single person you told?"

Trish took a pack of cigarettes from the windowsill, pulled one out, and gaveled it against the glass in front of her. She fiddled with it instead of smoking it, knowing she'd win her willpower battle with tobacco the way she'd won all the others: by outlasting her weakness, not giving it anything to feed on. Anybody who met Trish would know where Connie got her straight spine, her way of getting through life without best friends.

"I'm not changing my name this time," Trish said as she waved to someone walking down the street.

"You might not have to. I might not even change mine."

Trish tiptoed across the room so softly she seemed to be gliding, then loomed over her daughter. "You want to stand and fight with *him*? He'll snatch Tommy away from you like nothing. The man's a murderer."

"No, he's not," Connie said. "I was with him when that fire started, I told you."

"You told *me*, not the *judge*." Trish slid her cigarette back into its pack and saw her daughter for what she truly was: too bony, too wiry, too twitchy in her muscles. Restless and easy to knock off of whatever she tried to do but strong and stubborn enough to keep at it even after the game was lost. "You've got to call your son," Trish said.

"Give me the phone."

"The cord won't reach out to—"

"Just give me the phone!" Connie jerked up off the couch and hustled into the kitchen. She wrapped the phone's curly cord around her wrist and punched random numbers until the phone yowled at her like a miniature siren. "Hi Tommy! Hey listen, I lied to you all those years about your father. He's really the Jesus freak with the fucked-up face you met a couple nights ago. Sorry! Love you, see you soon!" She handed the phone to Trish, who checked to make sure nobody was actually on the line. "Is that what you want me to do?"

"You act like it's all in Richie's hands," said Trish, hanging up.

"Isn't it? He's got the truth. I've been lying. Looks pretty black-and-white to me."

Connie leaned against the fridge and slid down until she sat on the floor, digging the point of her chin into her knee. She pictured Richie Thorpe calling her out in front of everybody in Suborney at that dirty old church he was fixing up. He'd have a bonfire and yell at them for living unclean lives or whatever preachers like him yelled at people for.

"And *you!*" he'd shout, pointing a thick finger at Connie. "*You!*"

The calling-out could happen slowly, too, with whispered rumors stitched together here and there until everybody in town knew about her lie. Then they'd start burning crosses in her yard, leaving dead animals on her doorstep, or doing whatever Jesus freaks do when they turn against somebody. They'd suck Tommy in, of course—he'd be such easy prey. He'd be so ashamed of her that he'd leave town before senior year even started, giving up his thousand dollars and blindly following Richie wherever he went next. Connie would have so much egg on her face that she'd have to leave Suborney too. A fresh name would be nice, though it wouldn't help keep Richie off her scent. If he'd found her in Suborney, he could find her anywhere. She could call herself Linda Samsino, picking her own name this time instead of letting her mom do it. Any judge would understand that she wanted to get away from the crazy ex-con who stole her son. From the man who'd tracked her down and trapped her and would do who knows what if she let him find her again. She looked up at Trish.

"I'm losing my son to a cult, Mom. How do you think that feels?"

"Like losing my daughter to a white trash thief. Now you'll see what you put me through."

Connie said nothing and went to stare out the living room window. Up and down the street, yellow ribbons for the hostages hugged the trees. Two boys younger than Tommy walked down the sidewalk in baggy army surplus clothes he once lusted after but wouldn't be caught dead wearing now. Across the street a homemade banner hung between two telephone poles, saying, PRAY FOR AMERICAS HOSTEGES. Connie imagined Richie Thorpe next to her, making some wisecrack about the bad spelling, but she couldn't picture how he'd look now. All she had to go on was her own son's face, plus secondhand descriptions of Richie's bad cheek. She pictured him, standing so strong that a neutron bomb couldn't even move him, with a face that didn't care how ugly it looked. With his followers saying, *Yes ma'am* and *No ma'am*, paying for everything with dirty dollar bills like they didn't believe in money at all.

"Tell your son," Trish said. "Look your lie in the face."

"Easy for you to say. It's not your lie."

"It sure in hell is. I helped you make it. Don't you *ever* forget."

✳ ✳ ✳

Brother Zypanski and Brother Worrell followed Tommy around the junkyard and bought things from Dolman with crumpled-up dollar bills—a toilet, a sink, copper pipes, a ton of two-by-fours, plywood, windows—and Tommy drove it to the house for them. He laid down a new plywood floor for the shed, which at twelve feet by twelve was as big as his bedroom at home. Tommy headed inside to tell them he was done but heard people praying, and he didn't want to get anywhere near praying because he might turn into a puddle on the floor crying for Jesus. Instead, he drove to the church and poked around for junk they could use at the house.

A kitchen table with chairs that didn't match. A coffee table and a love seat. A couple dressers, a coffee maker, some pots and pans. He didn't know what they needed or wanted since they came to town with nothing and seemed like they'd leave with nothing too. Tommy put some handpicked junk in the truck, figuring he'd tell Dolman later on and pay for it himself. If he cleared a bit every day, he guessed he could stretch out how long they let him play his sax there. Then Dolman would be happy, the Jesus and Mary people would be happy, and Tommy would be—well, Tommy didn't know what he'd be. Fucking up his life for good probably. He heard Thorpe's rattle coming up the stairs.

"You're like a rattlesnake," Tommy said. Thorpe had tan shorts on this time, and his United Farm Workers T-shirt was yellow. "I can tell when you're coming."

"This?" Thorpe swung his right leg, making the sound, then gave out a big *Huh-haaaaaaa!* that sounded like a donkey braying. He pulled a chewing tobacco tin out of his back pocket, and inside were two little red dice with the letters M-A-R-Y on their sides, instead of dots, plus two black ones with J-E-S-U-S.

"You make those in prison?"

"Lots of time on your hands in prison. Made 'em for a friend of mine who died."

"Same guy who hit you with the brick?"

"Yes sir. Mother Meg's son, if nobody's told you that yet."

"Did he die 'cause you killed him?" asked Tommy.

"No sir. Never killed anybody in my life."

"Not meaning to, anyway. Isn't that why they call it involuntary manslaughter?"

Tommy stared at Thorpe like he had him over a barrel, but the feeling didn't last. Thorpe just showed the right side of his face for five seconds, and that was enough to let Tommy know he could handle a thousand times more abuse.

"How many times did he hit you with it?" Tommy asked.

"Seven."

"And you let him?"

"Took me that long to turn the other cheek. I've got a favor to ask you, Mr. Sandor. I'm looking for a ride up to Denver. Got a mission there, downtown by the viaduct."

"Right now?"

"Or tomorrow," Thorpe said. "Whenever you're ready." Then he walked off without saying goodbye, which Tommy figured he'd have to get used to. Thorpe headed to the Perrin house, and twenty feet up the road he stopped to pick up a broken kite in the tall grass.

"You know that stuff keeps blowing back in, right?" Tommy shouted.

"Not the point!" Thorpe shouted back. He picked up a milk bottle, a soda can, some newspaper he chased down. It was the right thing to do, and Tommy wanted to be next to him, picking up junk and keeping God's world beautiful.

God's world. Tommy sneered at himself. *Listen to yourself, freak. Stop swimming in this shit while you can still climb out of it.*

5

Wednesday, July 9

After a bad night with her mom—shouting and swearing, three glasses broken in the sink—Connie hopped onto Interstate 80 toward Nebraska City, figuring out what she'd say to Richie Thorpe, the man who took away her father and gave her back a son. She pictured his wrecked face hovering in her windshield like a rotten Halloween pumpkin.

"You think you can waltz in here and *take* him?" she asked the face, and it let out that deep *Huh-haaaaaaa!* of Richie's that always hit her like a bark. "It's *my* town. It's where I raised him."

I'm not the first man to come and take what's mine, am I?

"Since when is he *yours*? You never laid eyes on him."

He's always been mine. Always loved me, like I loved him.

All the Jesus stuff Richie had apparently picked up in prison would make him harder to talk out of things than ever since he'd be convinced he had God on his side now. How ridiculous to think of that low-life thief running a church! Connie almost got plowed over by a red Chevy Blazer as she tried to pass a truck hauling cantaloupes, so she erased Richie's face for safety's sake and thought about Tommy. She imagined him slouched over in her passenger seat like he'd done on so many other trips to Sidney, every breath a bored, defeated sigh. Maybe Richie had already gotten hold of him, shaved his head and wrapped him in orange robes like the Krishna kids she saw in Denver once.

Jesus cults don't dress like that, though she'd seen some dressed in loose white robes as thin as gauze. They sucked in teenagers with promises of a perfect, holy life away from the sins of their parents, then turned them into robots—loving Jesus and praising Jesus until they couldn't get through a sentence without saying the guy's name fifteen times. What if Thorpe brainwashed Tommy into his cult and never even told him "I'm your father"? Turned him into a Jesus robot and had the last laugh when her own son came to her door one day, offering her some stupid pamphlet?

"Do you know about hell, ma'am?" Tommy would ask, not even recognizing his own mother. Richie would stand behind him, grinning and knowing that he'd won.

* * *

As Connie drove east to Nebraska City, her son drove north to Denver in his Vega, its air conditioning shot and its hatch full of food from Pete's store. Brother Worrell and Sister Melanie sat in back stuffing baggies full of hard-boiled eggs, peanut M&M's, and dollar bills for the mission. Up front Tommy told Brother Thorpe how he tricked out the car. The 350cc Camaro engine, the transmission that howled in first gear, the extra chassis welds. Tommy couldn't afford the Don Hardy Supertwister conversion kit he'd heard about, so he cannibalized parts from the yard and put them together in May with help from Paul Lenshaw, who was in town while his mom finished dying.

"This thing's street legal?" Worrell asked after Tommy half-skidded through a turn.

"Yes sir, Officer. Got insurance on it too."

"Feels heavier than she should be," Thorpe told him, swaying side to side. "She'll skid all over but won't roll."

"That's my baby." Tommy took the next bend extra fast to test that idea. The Vega shimmied, but all four wheels hugged the pavement. "You learn about cars in prison?"

"No sir. My daddy was a race car driver."

"*Was*? Is he dead or just done racing?"

"Just done racing, I think." Thorpe shrugged. "Uncertain of his whereabouts."

"Runaway dad, huh? I got one of those."

"That so?" Melanie piped in, and Thorpe quickly grabbed her eye in the rearview mirror. Then Tommy told them about Connie's fourteenth birthday present to him: the story of Drake, the blond tenor man who stole her flighty teenage heart. She'd come to the fair with goats to show but left with a baby in her belly who Drake never knew about.

"At least she kept you," said Melanie. "A lot of girls these days wouldn't."

"Yeah, I guess she's not too bad. Didn't kill me when she had the chance."

They hit the last empty road before Colorado Springs, and Tommy put the pedal down. Eighty-five, 95, 105. Fence posts, broken-down shacks, fence posts, telephone poles, cows. Scrubby brush and weeds, fence posts, blur of red-tan earth. Broken-down tractors and tillers. A hundred and ten, 115, 120. Melanie and Worrell grabbed onto what they could, but Thorpe winked like it was nothing.

"I don't know what you're proving, Tommy," Melanie said. "Or to who."

"Ever been this fast?" Tommy spoke only to Thorpe.

"Sure. Been faster."

"Is that cheek of yours the real reason you don't believe in driving? So you can keep that side of your face away from people?"

"That's a good theory," Worrell shouted from the back. Then Tommy pushed the engine up to 130.

"How come you Jesus people always pick me?" Tommy asked. "Do I look easy to fool 'cause I'm bored out of my fucking mind?"

"Because you look lost and you sound lost!" Melanie shouted over the engine's roar and the air that chiseled through the poorly sealed windows. Tommy looked at Thorpe, who cocked his head and raised his good eyebrow, so Tommy guessed it was true. He took his foot off the gas, and soon he was down to a legal speed. A good citizen on the right side of the law, driving to help his fellow man.

He learned about his passengers, starting with Thorpe's sixteen years and two days in the Nebraska State Penitentiary. Then about Worrell's three times behind bars in three different states and the way Mother Meg found him asleep in his own puke in Topeka. Then about Melanie's problem with pills and shoplifting at her fancy college in Iowa and the parents who wouldn't take her back in. About the day she heard the Sons and Daughters of Jesus and Mary singing with Tessy in a Bird City parking lot and decided to start singing with them.

"I always loved to sing," she said. "Then that day I said, 'Oh well, might as well sing for God instead of myself.' How about you, Tommy? You ever sing for God?"

"I play sax for God. That count?"

All three of the Sons and Daughters gave him a thumbs-up at once. Soon enough they were in Denver, and Tommy followed Thorpe's directions to the mission. It was in a block of decrepit warehouses at Fifteenth and Wewatta in Lower Downtown, the oldest part of the city. Close to the Platte River and the viaduct that loomed over it, where people didn't walk unless they were drunks or junkies looking to hide out with their own kind. Abandoned buildings everywhere, plus some half-broken ones that nobody bothered demolishing. The air smelled like piss and cement dust, and the only people on the street staggered like they had to ask themselves which foot hit the ground next.

A woman with an orange face and a gray scarf wrapped around her head dragged an empty dog leash behind her. A stick-thin man in gym shorts and a suit jacket waved his arms as he shouted. Tommy had no idea what he'd say to them if they stared him in the face. He was scared that the darkness in them might call out to the darkness in him and make him want to destroy things. Scared that the Sons and Daughters might strip him of everything he knew and trusted until he was out on the streets with his soul and nothing else.

"Those your mission people?" Tommy asked.

"That was Doggie Annie and Pete the Prophet," Melanie told him.

"They all get nicknames like that?"

"Only the ones you can't pray *with*," Thorpe said. "Just pray *for*." He pointed to a red brick building without a door, and Tommy parked in front of it. They opened his hatchback and unloaded all the food onto a blanket that Melanie had spread on the sidewalk. Thorpe climbed the crumbling steps and came back out with a hand-painted plywood sign that he leaned against a window ledge: THE MISSION OF THE SONS AND DAUGHTERS OF JESUS AND MARY IS TO HELP THE POOR IN SPIRIT. Then he turned to Tommy.

"You up for more driving? Just around the neighborhood, let 'em know we're here."

"Looks like they already do." Tommy pointed to a couple of scruffy bums racing up the block with shopping carts. He tossed his keys to Thorpe, who headed for the passenger seat and tossed them right back. Their stout and meaty bodies moved in sync as they grabbed hold of the roof and swung down into the seats.

"You sure she's okay here?" he asked Thorpe as they waved good-bye to Melanie.

"Yep. Brother Worrell's got a knife that'll stop anybody cold."

"Isn't that a concealed weapon?"

"You sound like a cop, with all the laws you know. Maybe you're hanging around that trooper-man too much." Thorpe directed Tommy with hand signals while he blew New York cabbie whistles out the window, and a few faces poked out of buildings at the sound.

"You from New York?" Tommy asked. "That where you learned to whistle?"

"No sir, St. Louis. Lived all over, but never New York."

"Lived all over, even though you spent sixteen years locked up?"

"My dad moved a lot. A thief, always on the run. Not the life I'm after." Thorpe leaned out the window to whistle two last times. "Having a hard time pulling 'em out today. Maybe it's the fancy car."

"You could always make a little wind and rain." Tommy clamped his fingers against his palm and slowly opened his hand, the way Thorpe had done the night they met. "Blow 'em right out of their holes."

"I save that for when I need it. It's not something you do for show."

"It was show when you did it for me, wasn't it?"

Thorpe didn't answer. He looked up through a break in the shabby buildings toward the pint-sized skyscrapers of downtown Denver, covered now by gray clouds that threatened afternoon rain. Tommy stopped the car before the clouds fell out of sight and stared at them, hoping Thorpe would change the weather for him.

"Did somebody teach you how to do that wind and rain stuff," Tommy asked, "or did you learn it yourself?"

"Little of both. Somebody had to teach me I could, then I figured out the rest."

They both looked out at the sky above the city, soaking it in like five-year-olds figuring out how big the world is, until Thorpe told Tommy to head back to the mission. Thorpe thanked him for the ride and stepped out of the Vega, then started hugging and talking to the bums who stood around the blanket eating. One of them, with teeth even more messed up than Worrell's, had greasy blond hair halfway down his back and wore a dirty Mexican poncho with boxer shorts underneath.

"Going to Suborney, man!" he shouted, waving his arms. Tommy got out and said goodbye to Brother Worrell and Sister Melanie, shaking hands with a few bums too, and he made sure not to touch his face afterward. Dirty people, sick people. He knew in his mind that every single person is a child of God, but he didn't want the dirt and scum of certain children of God on his skin. Jesus would shake his head at him for thinking that way, but Tommy stopped at the first gas station he saw to scrub his hands clean. The shame he felt at wanting to wash off the touch of his fellow human beings made him scrub even harder.

Everybody's just as holy as anybody else, because we've all been given God's love. Isn't that what the preacher at Gracehouse said the day Tommy fainted? *We've all been given God's love, and we still have it inside us, even if it's caked over with sin.*

Tommy thought about finding some skank so he could fuck all this Jesus stuff out of himself before he started singing and dancing and praising God every second of his life. Desperate, dirty sex was the only thing that could save him from getting saved. He knew how to linger outside a ladies' night bar and lock eyes with a woman who'd love a night with some big, horny kid who had as much shame to fuck out of his system as she did. She'd buy him liquor, take him to some fleabag motel or dingy apartment with yellow window shades, and take everything he could give her. Then she'd pat him on the back like a good little boy and say, "Go home, honey. You know where to find me if you need me."

And then Tommy would leave her, feeling dirty inside and out. Dirty in the blood that ran through his veins, dirty in the breath that got trapped in his lungs and never found its way out again. What would he do then, if he let the dirt get stuck that deep inside him?

✳ ✳ ✳

Once Connie got to Nebraska City, she headed straight for the place where her old life fell apart and her new life started gluing itself together: the corner of Central Avenue and Sixth Street, where Holmquist TV and Entertainment Showroom once stood. Where, as Jeannette Holmquist, she used to sweep the floors and greet customers and dig up sales numbers while her father bargained on the phone with wholesalers. When she turned fifteen, she started running deposits up to Great Western Bank to learn responsibility—$11,153.47 one time. She was Daddy's little girl, Gregory Holmquist's only child, and they had a plan. Business major at Stanford, an MBA from the University of Chicago, then back to Nebraska City to start creating their nationwide appliance center empire.

But she wasn't sixteen for long before she lost her father's trust by falling for a nineteen-year-old street hustler. A man—and Richie was definitely a man by then, though Greg refused to call him one—who made his living the same way his father did: gambling, petty thievery, racing cars for money on back roads or homemade tracks. A man with a crooked smile and sunbaked skin and crow's-feet even at that age, with hair as blond then as Tommy's. And that damn neck just like Tommy's, a giant coil spring that could bounce back from any blow. A man who never listened to the threats from Connie's father when he walked into Holmquist TV and Entertainment Showroom asking after her.

"You're not welcome here," Greg would say every time Richie walked through his door. They were the Holmquists then, before their prized young daughter got knocked up and Greg died in the showroom fire and Ada picked the name Sandor out of a Chicago phone book. The cops arrested Thorpe two weeks after the blaze, but by then Ada and Jeannette Holmquist from Nebraska City were Trish and Connie Sandor from McCook, even though they'd never been to McCook. They moved to that semi-abandoned goat farm outside Bird City, Kansas, telling everybody they were second cousins of the last owners. Eight months later Thomas Gregory Sandor was born on the path between the house and the barn.

Connie parked in front of where the TV showroom used to be and leaned the achy small of her back against the hot hood of her truck. There was nothing left of the store, not even the pile of bricks it had turned into after the firemen and the bulldozers were done with it. Just the asphalt of the parking lot, cracked and dry and overgrown with weeds, and a pile of dirt where the bricks used to be. How does a building made of brick burn down? How does a man who has a wife and daughter to love run into a burning store four times just to save his precious *stuff*?

Connie Sandor didn't have any more answers in 1980 than Jeannette Holmquist had in 1962. She waved to a woman with a toddler stumbling beside her and a baby in a carriage. Amy Salles, if Connie remembered right. Four years her junior. Played the violin to please her mother but never got good at it, and she was so in love with her 4-H sheep that it almost hurt to see them together.

"Hot one," Amy said as they passed. Her eyes darted confusedly over Connie's sandals, Colorado license plate, and too-open blouse.

"Burning hot." Connie could tell it wasn't Amy who'd ratted her out. She leaned back further against her hood, soaking the engine's heat into her muscles, until Will Tannerman, who used to take her deposits at the bank, did a double take at her on his way across the street. He might have half-recognized her, or he might still be the kind of guy who had to check out every pair of legs he saw. He headed for the diner catty-corner from the showroom, which used to be Abel's and then Branch's and now called itself Gorham's. He opened its door for Mrs. Michniak, who used to come to canning parties at the Holmquist house every October. She used a cane now and didn't have the energy to notice the out-of-towner watching her from the little blue truck.

Mrs. Michniak put one hand on the diner's wall and inched toward her powder-blue house on First Avenue. Connie wanted to offer her a ride home, but that would be pushing her luck. All she wanted in Nebraska City were people's first glances at her. If they'd helped Richie find her, she'd see it right away. Somebody in Nebraska City had to know that the Holmquists became the Sandors; otherwise, they never would have been able to sell their house and collect their insurance money. But her mom never said who and never would. To protect everybody involved, she used to say, though it was

Jeannette—the whip-smart girl who'd dropped her pants for the first man who tried getting into them—who really needed protection.

Jeannette? she wanted somebody to say as she stepped up Central Avenue. *Jeannette Holmquist?* Somebody who used to be a friend at school or a neighbor. She wanted to hear the name she'd grown up with and recognize who spoke it, to turn around and smile involuntarily like a person whose entire life wasn't a lie. Kim Darden, who used to fantasize with her about all the crazy things they'd do together after they blew town—to Omaha, Minneapolis, Chicago, even New York. Becky Scheifle, who'd spent hours on her bedroom floor practicing with a stolen French-English dictionary for when they ran away to Paris.

Connie remembered her own escape fantasies and felt sorry for Tommy, who had the most desperate and elaborate escape fantasy known to man. So damn specific, with the names of sax men who might know his father and the clubs where they played and even the subway stations that would take him there. She wished she had the guts to tell him about Richie—just flinging out the truth casually, the way she might mention a sale she heard about on TV. But she couldn't do that because her whole life was built around the lie of Drake, and that meant Tommy's life was too, and she couldn't let herself imagine how he'd explode once the lie stopped holding their lives together.

Because Tommy was the exploding kind. Whatever name she'd given him, he was a Thorpe underneath. He'd destroy things when he found out the truth—hell, he might know it already. Maybe Thorpe walked right up to him and spat the truth out and her house on Mangum Street had already burned to the ground. Or been smashed to gravel-sized bits with a sledgehammer—that would be more Tommy's style.

Connie stepped back from the curb at Ninth and Central for a huge woman driving the decrepit blue Cadillac that Eric Moulton swore he'd fix up someday. She stepped past The Fort, where she used to window-shop for cowgirl clothes that her dad said she was too classy to wear. Stepped past the Otoe County Courthouse, past the bank where she used to drop off her father's deposits, past the movie theater on Eleventh Street as workmen rolled out new carpet in the lobby. Past one of their old houses, the third biggest in Nebraska City for a while, now getting a new red tile roof. Past the diner where she and her parents used to have Sunday brunch after church, then eventually instead of church.

Connie stood by the diner's front door, looking at the menu and trying to remember the old name of the place. Small's maybe? Now it was the Red Feather Café, and she recognized people ambling out of it. Doreen Degrette, two years ahead of her in school and always bragging about how she'd blow town and never come back. Teri Crofter, a year behind her, who carried a baby in a sling. Girls she used to swing with at the playground were now women she could sit in the shade with there, watching their children run, climb, shout. Not Tommy, of course, but a new baby with a new man. Maybe with Joe Bolstead, the last boy who chased her before Richie caught her. Though he was a stick compared to Richie, a nobody.

"Jeannette!" she heard a woman behind her shout, and she froze. It turned out to be Carissa Torswain, a prude even when she and Connie were ten, calling to her own toddler. She gave Connie's lipstick and cleavage a judgmental glare, but there was no human recognition. Connie felt like she'd been stripped out of Nebraska City's collective memory, intentionally removed from it by a magic spell. Some of the old ladies who volunteered with her mom at the library might know her, she thought. And if she hung around long enough to catch a church bingo night, they might know her there too.

But Connie didn't want to stick her face into somebody else's and say, "Don't you know who I am?" She wanted to be discovered, recognized out of the blue like a traitor. To be exposed where her lie was first born, so she could see how it felt when the truth was laid bare. Because that's what waited for her in Suborney, sooner or later. The bare truth and Tommy torturing her for it.

She walked all the way to the end of Central Avenue, past the fertilizer plant, to the spot by the Missouri River where she and her friends used to throw rocks at the black snakes swimming below. Where in eighth grade she dared a boy named Teddy Fansen to catch one bare-handed and repaid his bravery in the woods with seven slick kisses and a peek beneath her bra. Connie headed down South First Street, over the creek and the railroad tracks to where Fourth Corso became State Highway 2. She walked, laughing, past Drake's Bar—her inspiration for the name of Tommy's made-up father. She crossed more tracks and walked up Third Rue to Fifth Terrace, then looped down to the tree house between the road and the creek where she and Richie Thorpe used to make love.

And it really was making love, not just teenage lust-fucking. That's why she'd kept the baby. She'd loved Richie's wildness, his carefree grace that could live on bread and water and still be grateful for it. Grateful in a way that her father never was, even with all the *stuff* he gathered, all the *stuff* he gave her. She kept Richie Thorpe's baby and didn't regret it, because at seventeen Tommy Sandor was already twice the man than any other Connie knew. Indomitable thanks to the wildness of his father and strong in himself because his mother cultivated that wildness. Because she molded her son into someone who could carry twice the weight of most grown men and never chickened out on anything.

Except the football thing, of course. But still she was proud of Tommy, and she'd stay proud of him no matter how viciously he turned against her when he found out the truth about Richie. She stared at the tree house where he was conceived, now overgrown with some foreign-looking vine she'd never seen before. The place where she'd taken Richie's seed and grown it into a man who knew right from wrong and straight from crooked.

Not that a liar like you knows straight from crooked, she heard Richie mumble. A grown-up Richie she'd never met, his words so gravelly that they rattled her chest.

"I never could've kept him," Connie said to the tree house, not knowing if she meant Richie or Tommy. Was it worth going back to Suborney at all now? She could bypass its impending humiliations and keep heading west on the straight line of her life: from Nebraska City to Bird City to Suborney to the next point south and west. She'd figured out the geometry of leaving herself behind years ago. The line would eventually lead her to San Diego or Tijuana, and she could save herself the trouble of creeping west every time Thorpe found her by jumping all the way out there in one move.

But she had to face Tommy. At least once in her life, she had to see his face when he found out what she'd been protecting him from all those years. What she'd hidden from him so he'd grow into a solid man, instead of a crook, a thief, a gambler. *I saved you from the worst you could become*, Connie imagined telling her son as she stepped closer to the tree house. *You go spend the rest of your life figuring out why if you have to.* Then a man in a yellow tow truck pulled up and said, "Help you find something, Miss?"

"Nothing, thanks." Connie let the man look her up and down. Her face and clothes belonged to Colorado, not to Nebraska City. She was an outsider, not a native daughter returned. She knew this man—Carl Tenney, who ran through three wives before he got sick of women altogether—but he didn't know her or wouldn't let on. "Just wishing I had a camera, that's all."

"Well, you don't," Carl said. "Shouldn't take pictures of what's not yours, anyway."

Then he drove off, and Connie headed back toward downtown, her skin sticky from the muggy summer air, and on the way she saw the ugly cinderblock house that Richie and his dad used to rent the top floor of. Such a dingy rathole that he never let her see the inside of it. No electricity, he'd told her with pride. It looked like nobody lived there now, and maybe it still didn't have electricity. There wasn't even plywood to cover the broken windows and nothing in the yard but dirt and chickens.

Then she heard a slap against a wall, and a flash of arm pulled a throw rug back inside an upstairs window. A dust cloud billowed out, reached high into the air, and dissipated. Connie held her breath until the dust settled, then walked to the hole in the fence where she first told Richie she was pregnant. A hole exactly like it used to be, no bigger or smaller. Where he'd fallen to his knees inside the fence, clutching her hand in both of his with the jagged metal between them.

"I want to be your husband," he'd said then, kissing her hand eight times, ten times. "I want to be our baby's father. I'll learn to work honest."

"I can't," Jeannette Holmquist said.

"Can't 'cause you don't think I can be a husband or can't 'cause you don't think you can be a wife?"

"I don't know, Richie. Let me go."

"You can't let go of daddy's money, that's it." He pulled her arm closer to him. "You better not get rid of my baby, Nettie."

"I'd never do that."

"What'll you do, then? Give it up and let somebody else raise it?"

"I'll raise it, I swear. Let go of me, Richie."

Jeannette yanked her hand back hard, getting it clear of the fence, but Richie wouldn't let it go. She kept pulling away, and he pulled back against her, so that when he finally did let go of her hand, his arm shot backward through the hole in the fence and caught on the metal. He got blood—a quick, inky river on his wrist that he licked off, laughing. The blood kept rising up to his skin, and he kept on licking it clean.

"Just what I need," he told Connie. Was she already Connie by then? Yes, although she didn't know her new name yet. Because that was the moment she shed the skin of Jeannette Holmquist—when she knew that Richie Thorpe, this man licking his own blood and laughing about it, could never be her husband. He was too much of an animal, too elemental, to ever be kept inside of anything she could call a family. Richie kept licking his own blood with the same look in his eyes he got when he came inside her, when he made the wind knock dead trees into the river, when he tried to teach her how to shift the wind herself. Then he squatted and rocked back and forth, sucking on his cut wrist and humming. Five rising notes over and over, the last one longer than all the others put together.

"What are you doing?" Connie asked him.

"You'll see," Richie told her. "Go there."

He said nothing more but kept humming those five notes. Connie smelled his blood so strongly that she could feel it filling her own mouth, and she started toward home gagging and almost puking. She smelled smoke right away and denied that Richie had caused it, denied that he could make fire with only blood and sound and will. Halfway home she heard the sirens, and she ran through the bugs and the thousand centuries of fertile, murderous human sweat that hovered around the Missouri River. Down to Central Avenue and Sixth Street, where Holmquist TV and Entertainment Showroom stood burning. Where she watched her father running out of the building with his safe in a cart.

"Dad!" she shouted, but he didn't hear her. He set the safe down on the sidewalk and ran back inside with the cart. He came out with the accounting books his daughter helped him balance, then with his most expensive stereo equipment.

"Dad!" Connie called again, standing as close to the flames as she dared. He glanced at her once, as if she could never understand his need, then ran back inside for more stuff and never ran out again. Smoke inhalation. A peaceful death, some said. The worst pain you can imagine, others said. Like all the weight in the universe is pressing down on your chest.

Now, 17 years and 357 days later, Connie Sandor—born Jeannette Constance Holmquist in Nebraska City—climbed into her blue Chevy LUV, across the street from where the TV showroom had burned, and slipped out of town like the thief her son's father was. Nobody had recognized her; hardly anybody had even noticed her. She might as well have never been there. She'd slipped back into town to be Jeannette Holmquist for a moment, then slipped back out to be Connie Sandor until that name expired. Just like her first one had.

6

Friday, July 11

Connie took her time getting home, spending Wednesday night poking around in Omaha and Thursday night at a motel in Limon. It was only an hour and a half from Suborney, but she didn't have the guts to face Tommy. When she got to work on Friday morning, the big boss, Bill Rocher, pulled her into his office to say good luck and God bless. Bill's son, Darren, didn't believe a word of Connie's reason for missing time and kept pressing her for details. She wouldn't let him near the mystery between her legs, so he kept poking at every other mystery he found on her.

"That's not *really* why you were gone," Darren said, not quite cornering her by the copy machine as she collated new lead sheets for the sales team. People who might need office building remodels, sheet metal warehouses, enhancements to meet new safety codes.

"Not now," Connie told him, though before the hostage crisis she might have made up a story about a Saudi prince whisking her away on his private jet. But nobody laughed at Arab jokes anymore.

"Top secret lover?"

"Go away, Darren. Or I'll tell Daddy you're being slimy again."

After lunch Connie made a mistake on an order for fireproofing to line an elevator shaft. She spent two hours fixing it, then Bill sent her home. At the Albertson's in Security she bought three steaks, a bag of spinach, and a watermelon, and at Loma Liquors, next door, she got a six-pack of Michelob. Friday was usually Tommy's night to help cook, and if he helped enough, she'd give him one. Tonight she'd let him have all six if he just didn't talk about Jesus or Richie Thorpe. At home she slapped the steaks onto a cutting board and banged the meat with a tenderizing hammer like she was destroying the good side of Richie's face.

"Sure as hell I lied to him," she practiced telling people. "You've seen his dad. You think any mother in the world wants her son turning into *that*?"

Then Julie Parness came over, claiming to be worried about the banging but really just wanting somebody to drink with. Connie took the vodka tonic she offered, knowing it would help her lie about her mom. Her first two sips worked perfectly—she seamlessly interwove random details from *Marcus Welby, M.D.* into a plausible medical story. Then it was Julie's turn to talk.

"You missed all the fun," she said. "Got six or eight of those Jesus yahoos in the Perrin house now. Don't worry, Tommy's not one of 'em yet."

"He wouldn't join a cult without me there to watch," Connie replied. "Excuse me, I meant a *commune*."

"The old lady who runs it says to call it whatever we want." Julie whacked once at each steak and sat at the kitchen table. "Hard-working bunch of people, though. Smoked out the Hallseys' wasp nest and tore down Maggie Gander's shed before it killed somebody. Tommy's been walking them around town, pointing at stuff. They swarm in, and it's done in ten minutes."

"Like piranhas." Connie threw the steaks in a bag with Worcestershire sauce and brown sugar, then shook them. "You see that guy with the mashed-up face yet?"

"Enough to say 'Nice day,' but I couldn't get a good look." Julie raised her drink and her eyebrows. "Hunk of muscle on him."

"He's a preacher, Jules. Probably unavailable."

Julie made a sad face, and Connie wished she had the guts to tell her that Thorpe was Tommy's father. Then the fact would be all over Suborney by the end of the five o'clock news. A single slip of the lip, and she'd beat Richie to the punch, get rid of the secret that he *thought* he could hang over her head.

"Is Tom-Tom acting different?" Connie asked Julie instead. "*Jesus* this and *Jesus* that, like he did with those people last summer?"

"This is a different kind of bunch. They're working or praying or getting into somebody's car to go work someplace else. I saw Eddie D driving 'em around a couple times."

"Ed Dolman's the second easiest person in this town to brainwash," Connie said. The rest of the drink hit her the wrong way and got her thinking that Richie might punish her best by hanging around in Suborney but never telling Tommy who he was. Not making him Jesus-crazy like the cults on TV but turning him into a decent, humble young man who prayed all the time and worked his ass off helping other people. Who married some decent, humble Jesus-loving girl who'd kneel with him five times a day to pray, *Dear God, please open up Connie Sandor's heart to you*. And all that time Richie Thorpe would be nothing to Tommy but the traveling preacher who turned him toward Jesus. That would be the worst torture Connie could imagine Thorpe inflicting, and she kept stewing about it long after Julie left.

"You want to know who your dad is?" Connie practiced telling Tommy. She shook the marinade bag again and thought about spitting into it. "Find out who killed your grandpa. Then tell me how much you like your new Jesus buddies."

The words came out with too much hate, and she searched the house for Tommy to make sure he hadn't heard them. She even checked for him outside, but all she saw was the Jesus freak with messy teeth that Pete told her about, waving to her as he walked by.

Does he know? she asked herself. *Do all of Richie's people know?* Then Dan called and dutifully asked about her mom before inviting himself over for supper and sex. He hadn't felt her come in days, and the poor man needed to feel her come more than anything in this world. It was good he didn't have the balls to divorce Holly because that officially kept him Holly's problem. Connie closed the bedroom door behind her and hoped Dan would show up soon—that way Tommy would see his truck in the driveway and avoid the house altogether. But she couldn't predict Tommy anymore, not even at her best moments, and Richie's arrival had thrown her barometer way off. The boy might blast his damn saxophone in the hallway while she and Dan screwed, for all she knew. Or pray.

Connie stripped to her panties and crashed in her bedroom until four minutes after five, when Tommy came up the back steps with the same heavy walk Richie used to have. She threw on shorts and a T-shirt from The Who's *Tommy*—her son always treated her more gently when she wore it—and stepped into the hallway.

"Grandma's still alive and kickin'?" Tommy asked, almost bumping her shoulder as he walked past her to the bathroom.

"Heck of a way to show concern." Connie stared at his eyes, just as far apart as Richie's used to be. At his neck zits, in the same places where Richie's used to be.

"Well, you didn't call, so I figure she wasn't dying." He cupped his hands where his breasts would be and wobbled them up and down. "Free-ballin' tonight, I see. Sheriff Bullshit coming over?"

"Oh, give it a rest." Connie ditched the formerly lucky T-shirt and put a bra on. The shower turned on and off four times before she gave up wondering what Tommy was doing in there. Dan showed up in his state patrol uniform and nibbled at her neck, needy as ever, while she threw salt and pepper on the steaks. Tommy stepped out of the bathroom with nothing but a towel on.

"This isn't a locker room," Connie told him.

"Top o' the morning to ya, Officer." Tommy ignored his mom and threw a fake smile at Stannard, flexing to show off his stomach muscles.

"You joining us for supper?" Stannard asked him.

"Only if I can talk about anything I want. No forbidden subjects."

"Watch out for Tom-Tom tonight," Connie told Stannard. "He's got tons of lip to give. Nothing *but* lip, sounds like."

"I'm just speaking the truth. People who don't want to hear it shouldn't talk to me."

"I'm waiting for the day you can see me and your mother together without putting on some kind of act," said Stannard, his mask of calm already melting.

"Awww, da big sca-wy state patwolman is jealous!" Tommy went to his bedroom and shut the door. Connie kissed the top of Dan's head and smiled vapidly, as if Tommy's misbehavior were the only thing wrong with her life.

"I know he's hard," she said.

"I never thought he wouldn't be." Stannard poured his Michelob into a glass, which Connie considered an intolerably effeminate affectation. "Will you still give him that money if he drops out and joins the marines?"

"Sure, but not if he joins a Jesus commune. Did you find out who they are?"

"The old woman's son was in prison with that Thorpe guy. Died in the joint. Couldn't find out what he was in for."

"Your brother ever hear of this bunch?"

"He said he's heard of them and they do good work, but they're too hippie to be on his side. They fixed up a bunch of churches between Lincoln and here. That's where the Nebraska State Pen is."

"I see" was all Connie could say. In his room Tommy blasted a jazz tape that sounded like a sheep getting hacked to death, so she went outside to tend the steaks. Dan followed her.

"Justin said Tommy called his show today and asked what 'Honor thy mother' meant. Wanted to know if it was more complicated than just doing what your mom tells you."

"Did he talk about how his baby brother's sinning with the flesh again?"

"Since when do you care? It's just a radio show."

"Right. A radio show where your brother called me the 'Whore of Babylon.' *Twice*."

"It's got to be water off your back." Stannard sipped his beer. "You're just not used to it yet."

"Maybe I don't want to *get* used to it," Connie said.

"It'll be fine once Holly's out of the picture."

"That might not change anything," she said. "You know it."

"What's that supposed to mean?" Stannard turned to her sharply, his brow furrowed, and noticed he still had his holster belt on. As he stepped inside to hang it on its nail, Tommy's jazz got startlingly loud and then turned off.

"Yup," Tommy said as he came into the kitchen, with clothes on this time. "Nothing says 'peaceful family' like a loaded handgun by the door."

"Having a good day?" Dan asked him. "Find anything worth saving at the junkyard?"

"No sir. But Ed Dolman decided *he* was worth saving. When I left, he was still talking to some guys who want to help him do it."

"Gee," Connie shouted through the screen door. "I wonder who they'll try to 'save' next."

"They've got a funny name," Stannard said. "I didn't know Jesus and Mary were a couple. Didn't know they had sons and daughters."

Tommy put his hand to his heart. "If you're a child of God—like your brother says we *all* are—then you're either a son or a daughter of God. Therefore, you're a son or daughter of Jesus, who's God, who's the son of Mary. Therefore, we're all sons *and* daughters of Jesus *and* Mary." He bowed like a circus clown looking for applause.

"Sounds like the brainwashing's going pretty well so far," Connie said, coming inside with the steaks all plated up. "Remember that TV show last winter, with the dad dragging his son out of that apartment in Chicago? The kid who crossed his arms on his chest, pretending he was dead?"

"They call it 'nonviolent protest,' Mom. Martin Luther King, you know? Or is he too black for you to remember his name?"

Connie's lips got as tight as razors. "Remember when his dad broke down and couldn't drag him down that last flight of stairs, 'cause he couldn't handle his son's head thunking against the steps?"

"Yes ma'am."

"Well that won't be me, guarantee you. I'll drag you out all the way—I don't care if you bang your head so damn much you forget your name."

"Simmer down, people," Stannard piped in, and before Connie could spit out a response, the front doorbell rang. Tommy jumped up, rushed to the window, then zipped back to the kitchen, laughing.

"It's for you, Mom!" he told her. Connie rinsed her hands, prepared to meet Richie Thorpe and get the whole charade over with. She opened the door to see Sister Melanie, dwarfed by Brother Zypanski behind her. Melanie wore a dirty gardening hat and apron, while Zypanski wore a Kansas State football T-shirt with engine grease all over it.

"Mrs. Sandor?" Melanie asked. "We're introducing ourselves to everybody in town."

"It's Miss. I'm afraid I'm not in a position to give any—"

"We're not that kind of church, ma'am," Zypanski told her. "We serve God by helping people who need it. So if you need any help, let us know."

"Or if you know somebody who needs help," Melanie said, "but can't find a way to ask for it. They're the ones who need help most."

"Let 'em in, Ma!" Tommy called. "It's Brother Z and Sister Mel!"

Connie let them in and walked back to the kitchen, growling at Tommy with her eyes as they crossed paths. He low-fived the guests like he'd known them for ages, pointed out his favorite pictures of himself on the living room walls, then pulled them into his bedroom to show off his sax. In the kitchen Connie cut a bite of steak and blew on it like too-hot soup.

"I don't see how this ends well," she told Dan, who sat staring like a dumb fish. He wasn't husband material, no way in hell. A man who could be her husband would say *something*. Connie instead listened in on what spilled out from Tommy's bedroom. Laughter. Then "That's a hunk of bull!" Then "Bird City, yeah!"

"Maybe you're not part of the ending," Stannard finally told her.

"How's that?"

"He turns eighteen, he picks somewhere else to be, and he goes there. If you don't try hanging onto him too tight, maybe he keeps in touch."

"Did you hear that on TV? Or is it your many, many years of parenthood talking?"

"Connie, let's—"

"Let's talk about things like they really are. My son's in his bedroom with two total strangers from a *cult*, and you give me some 'live and let live' bullshit?"

"I didn't say that." Stannard chewed. Connie walked, slow and calm and with perfect posture, down the hallway to Tommy's room. Melanie honked out a note on the sax that sounded like a dying duck. She handed it to Zypanski, who held down all the keys and tried to blast it like a foghorn. He'd never played a sax before, so it came out like a scream, thanks to the messed-up D key. He handed it back to Tommy when Connie came over.

"We hear you know Bird City, Mrs. Sandor," Melanie said.

"It's Miss. Yeah, Tommy was born there. Did he tell you that?"

"Yep," said Zypanski. "We were there for a couple months this spring, fixing up a dead church on Bressler Street."

"Some people there didn't even know it used to be a church," Melanie added. "Had all sorts of trash in it."

"Then I guess you'll know what to do with the trash in ours. I hate to kick you people out, but I need to get this boy fed."

Melanie and Zypanski were nice as pie as they invited Connie and Dan—"Officer Stannard," they called him—up to the church house anytime. If they needed anything, or if they just wanted to pray with another human being, there was always somebody around. Zypanski banged his head on the doorjamb on his way out.

"That was interesting," Stannard said.

"Tallest motherfucker you ever saw, huh?" Tommy asked him.

"Thomas Gregory Sandor," Connie blurted. "Do you think he wants you calling him that?"

"He calls me a bastard. They all do. And I'd bet he's fucked a mother or two along the way, before he got turned on to Jesus. So yeah, he's probably a motherfucker."

"Thomas! I do *not* want my son using that word in front of me, or anybody!"

"Why not? It's a useful word, like if you're talking about some-body who's fucking your mother. Mother—" He pointed his index finger at Connie, then his middle finger at Stannard. "Fucker."

"*Out!*" Connie hissed, pointing at the back door. "I could've given you up for adoption, but I didn't."

"You could've done worse," Tommy said. "And I'm grateful you didn't." He balled his fists and thunked his chest. "So *glad* to be alive. So *fucking* glad you let me live."

"You will *not* talk to me like that in the home I made for you." Connie shook. She felt like nothing more than a red, angry face and a rock of pain in the middle of her gut.

"Relax, lady." Tommy pretended to smooth her feathers, then went to the bedroom to fetch his sax. He stepped back into the kitchen to grab a paper towel, wrapped his steak in it, and took a Michelob from the fridge. "Just saying the truth, that's all."

"I don't hear any truth. All I hear is a teenager throwing his life away."

"Maybe it's just the way your ears are tuned, Mom. Change your ears, and maybe you'll see who I'm throwing it away *for*."

"*Jesus, Jesus, Jesus*, right?" Connie threw her hands up and covered her eyes. She waited for the back door to snap shut, then counted out Tommy's steps until long after they faded. She sat at the table and stacked her plate on his and lifted her knife and fork to cut another piece of meat. It felt as if she'd forgotten everything—who she was, who the uniformed man at her kitchen table was, how she'd ended up in this place. Forgotten even simple things, like how to cut a slab of dead mammal into small enough bites to eat.

"That boy," she said, finally popping some meat into her mouth. She was ready to chew it until Dan Stannard spoke. Ready to count how many grindings of her molars it took for him to say something that mattered. If he didn't step up and act even *remotely* husbandlike by the time she got to a hundred, she'd give up on him once and for all. Connie couldn't stand being with a man who didn't know how to say the right thing and fill up the silence inside her. Because there would be so much of it, she knew. That same old silence, renewing itself forever.

7

Saturday, July 12

By day 250 of the Iran hostage crisis, the people of Suborney had stopped worrying about Tommy falling into a cult and started thinking that the Sons and Daughters weren't half bad. They never preached, never guilted you, never talked about hell. The town already looked better in little ways that mattered, with stray junk getting picked up everywhere and broken things getting fixed. The windows on Paul Ozell's house finally slid open. The canoe that Janice Sauter wanted to fix and sell was patched, then given in tears to her stepson. Even people who couldn't leave home had heard about the fresh paint on the Perrin house and the old church—the same paint that was on Julie Parness's house now, courtesy of Brother Benjy.

"I wouldn't mind them in that church," Janice said.

"They can't be all bad if they fixed that damn guardrail on the bridge," said her husband, Rob. "The county sure in hell wouldn't."

"Not a single thing missing from my house," said Ginny Caslow after Brother Worrell cleared her cobwebs and Mother Meg cleared the stacks of newspapers obscuring her bed.

The Sons and Daughters cleaned, swept, washed, mended, picked up. They asked for nothing but the chance to work some more, and in return the people of Suborney gave them change and dollar bills. They used it to buy enough food to keep them working the next day, then to buy food for whoever had less than they did. Like Mrs. Culp, who'd been living on Minute Rice and packets of instant oatmeal for who knows how long.

"They're not bad people," said Julie, who sat at Sowell's counter that afternoon drinking rum-spiked coffee with Sally Kurtep while Tommy stocked the shelves. Pete and Carla would be up in Colorado Springs all afternoon with their son, so Tommy manned the store.

"Give 'em time," Sally replied. "Remember how sweet those dirty hippies looked before they suckered Carrie in?"

"Nobody's getting suckered in this time except little Tom-Tom," said Julie.

"Little?" He popped his head over the shelves. "What am I getting suckered into now?"

"Just the Jesus thing." Sally reared her head back and rolled her eyes. "Ohhhh, *JesusJesusJesusJesusJesusJesus!*" Then she let out a big, scaly laugh.

"You know it's just a matter of time," Julie said. "You're like a kid waiting for the right circus to blow through town. Waiting for the right kind of Jesus fever."

"They're pretty laid-back about Jesus." Tommy punched out the bottom of a box and folded it. "All they say is the more good you do for people, the more you understand him."

"You believe that?" Julie asked.

"Yes ma'am. You don't?"

"Julie's got too much booze in her blood to know what she believes," Sally said.

"And Sally's got too much man-hunger," Julie shot back.

"You ladies go at it," Tommy said. "I'm in the storeroom if somebody gets hurt."

He reorganized boxes while the women bickered, thinking how pathetic it was that he knew exactly how long they'd fight before they laughed it off. Too long in Suborney. Had to get to New York. But he couldn't leave because he finally had people to hang out with, somebody new to *be*. Showing the Sons and Daughters who needed help in town made him feel like he had a reason from God to be in Suborney, at least for now. Tommy put canned corn and green beans on Sowell's list of things to order from the wholesaler, then wrote, *They don't eat meat* next to *Spam* and *chili*. He crossed out *They* to write *We*, but lost his nerve and wrote *They* again.

"Every damn night!" Sally shouted at the counter.

"You find me something better to do, and I'll do it," Julie barked back. It made Tommy remember what Melanie had told him on the Perrin house porch the night before, when he shook so hard after his fight with his mom that he couldn't eat his steak and hurled it into the weeds for some coyote to finish.

"Anger happens when you forget you're a child of God," she said.

"Bastard child of God, that's me." He sighed hard, and she set all five fingertips on his heart, breathing with him. He hadn't tried to touch her, hadn't wondered how she looked naked, because God was on the porch with her, pulling little Tom-Tom out of his darkness. Reminding him that there was no separation between himself and the woman next him, between himself and the sky and the wind, between himself and the dead wood he sat on. Then Melanie slid her fingers down a few inches below his heart.

"Is that where my soul lives?" he asked her.

"You don't *have* a soul, silly. You *are* a soul."

Back in Pete's storeroom, Tommy touched that same spot on his chest. Trying to heal it, trying to pull the anger out so he could bury it somewhere else. He stayed that way until laughter spilled out from the counter and the cowbell rang.

"I'm taking another coffee for the road, Tom-Tom!" Sally called. "I'll bring the mug back tomorrow. You're out of creamers too."

"Okay!" Tommy yelled to her. Then he thought back to that scene on the porch.

"So it's that simple?" he'd asked Melanie. "Remember I'm a soul, forget everything else?"

"Yep. Everything's that simple, unless you decide it's not. Find what's clouding you up, then sweep the clouds away." She'd made a slow brush with her hand.

"What if my love is what's clouding me up? Doesn't God want me to hang onto that?"

"You don't *own* your love. It's God's—you can't trap it like a raccoon in a cage."

Zypanski overheard them talking and said, "Don't trap the raccoon of your love, man!" Then everybody else at the house picked up on it, put their hands on each other's hearts and said those words and laughed. Even Beto, who almost made people piss their pants. It ended with Tommy and Zypanski standing by the part of Lester Hill where shouts echo against it, seeing who could make those words echo the longest.

He almost had the balls to sleep on the living room floor with the rest of them that night. Not quite. In Pete's storeroom his heart pumped hard and slow, like it only had a few more beats left. Tommy stepped outside, his mouth so dry that he couldn't swallow, and his saliva felt as thick as chewing gum. He leaned against the dumpster and pictured his heart as a coconut about to crack open from the inside, and he wanted to be all the things in the world that ever were, all at the same time. Every animal, every stone, every branch.

Then Jesus slipped his fingers inside Tommy's chest, wiggling them to tease that coconut shell apart. If Tommy wanted to love everything in God's world, like any believer would say he was born to do, then that meant loving every*body* too. His mom. Drake in his dingy yellow room, sticking a needle in his arm. Dan Stannard. The football kids who spat when they saw him. Himself.

"Hey," somebody called. Tommy opened his eyes to see Dolman a foot away from him. "You okay there?"

"Just thinking," Tommy said back.

"I bought a sandwich and a Snickers. Left cash on the counter. Keep the change for the collection box, okay?"

"Sure. Those people are for real, right? Not full of shit, trying to get what they can?"

"Sure in hell hope so," Dolman said as he walked away.

The earthquake in Tommy's chest started up again. Jesus kept breaking layer after layer of the crust around his heart, slow and calm, and it surprised Tommy how little he fought it. All the swearing he did, all the girls he chased and fucked—they didn't matter to Jesus right now. Only the crack in the shell around his heart did.

"That's just him at work," Melanie had told him the night before, her hand resting on his chest. "All day, every day, everywhere."

Like it was that simple. Like it could ever be that simple. Like a bunch of strangers could waltz into his town and give him Jesus and ask for nothing back in return.

* * *

Tommy closed the store at 5:00 p.m. sharp, then headed home to find a note from Julie on the fridge: YOUR GRANDMA'S SICK AGAIN. NOT CANCER. YOUR MOM'S THERE ALL WEEKEND. Then the phone rang, and Julie was on the other end.

"C'mon up to the Fiddler house, Tommy. Party for the sick hostage, free beer."

He turned on the news and saw that Richard Queen, the hostage the Iranians had released, was alive and sort of well in Switzerland. He walked to the party and saw that people had tied bundles of flowers to the yellow ribbons on their trees and taped newspaper pictures of Richard Queen onto their windows. Half the town was gathered at the Fiddler house, piling flowers at the foot of the cross and thanking God for Queen's release. Tommy listened, freely drinking Old Milwaukee. Sam Kurtep pulled the party onto his lawn by grilling sausages for everybody, and three cases of Bud showed up. Then somebody bitched out Carter for getting our servicemen killed back in April without even firing a shot at those damn sand-nigger towelheads, and the whole thing turned into a Ronald Reagan rally in no time. Tommy rolled his eyes when Tami Willer teared up talking about him.

"You're telling me you wouldn't vote for him if you could?" Tami asked.

"Why? So I can fly to the desert and die for him?"

"It wouldn't be *him* you'd be dying for," said Wally Ogrean. "It'd be your country."

"Shouldn't *I* pick what I die for?"

Tommy got a bunch of dirty looks, then shut his mouth and lurked around, listening to people's bullshit. How they'd kill the Ayatollah with their bare hands if that damn faggot Carter would only let them. How every American owed it to their country to be part of the fight, whether that meant slinging machine guns over their shoulders halfway across the world or writing their congressmen. Delbert Morin, who fought in World War II and had a plate in his head to show for it, half-cornered Tommy by the big white cross.

"What do you say? Do you love your country enough to die for it or not?"

"Can't I love my country enough to *live* for it?"

"Tommy's too special to go fight for his country," said Cam Yorney, whose son got throat cancer from Agent Orange in Vietnam and died trying to sue the government for it. "I remember when you wanted to be a marine."

"Don't you think God wants you to serve your country?" asked Tami, and in a flash it went from Delbert Morin cornering him to half a dozen people. A mini-mob.

"You're sure it's my country I'd be serving if I went over and died in the desert? 'Cause I'm not sure. Might be dying for a bunch of guys in suits, with briefcases full of cash."

"Somebody get Tom-Tom a flag to burn," shouted Sam Kurtep, bringing over a platter of sausages and buns, and while everybody

89

laughed, Tommy slipped away. He grabbed four cans of Bud and headed for the Jesus and Mary house but couldn't see anybody on the porch. They wouldn't let the beers inside anyway, so he took the long way home to avoid the impromptu rally and called Sherry Medina.

"Come out to my place," he said. "I don't feel like parking today."

"What's in it for me?"

"Two beers. My mom's in Nebraska again."

"You're not answering my question."

"Let's play house, Sher. I'll put on a French maid outfit, the whole bit."

Sherry promised to come over after supper, so Tommy put on his mom's rubber gloves and cleaned the house. He wanted Sherry to think somebody respectable lived there, just in case he knocked her up and they got married. He waited in the living room, freshly showered and bare chested and wearing clean jeans, until Sherry's rusty Ford Maverick pulled into his mom's parking spot. She knocked on the door even though it was already open for her. When they kissed, her hands dug beneath his jeans and fumbled with his belt buckle.

"What got into you, tiger?" Tommy asked her.

"I got my period. Now's your chance. You might not get another one."

Tommy kissed Sherry hard and pulled up her T-shirt, got her bra loose. He imagined them in New York together, with her in med school and him working nights. Every Monday and Thursday she'd have a couple hours free, and that's when she'd let him inside her. Just enough to keep them together until things evened out.

"Skin to skin?" Tommy whispered in her ear. "No rubber?"

"I'm not *that* stupid. You better kiss me like that when you're inside me."

"Oh, I will." Tommy let his lips warm up Sherry's neck and ears. Did Jesus like him doing this to a seventeen-year-old virgin? He ignored the question. Their clothes came off in the living room, but

Sherry wanted to be on a bed for her first time, so she climbed onto his back and let him carry her to his room. When Tommy fell face-first onto the mattress, she kissed his shoulder blades and rubbed her pubic hair against his ass. Then she rolled him over, propped up on her elbow, kissed two fingers, and ran them from his forehead to his navel.

"You're a serious girl," Tommy said.

"It's a serious thing. Don't we need a towel?"

Sherry went into the bathroom to take out her tampon and settled on the old black towel that Tommy fetched from the hallway linen closet. Her legs poked straight out, and her knees clamped together.

"This won't work without your legs apart," Tommy said.

"And it won't work if you don't put a rubber on."

Tommy reached into his bottom dresser drawer to pull one out, but when he ripped open the packet, Sherry spooked a bit. Her legs jerked, and when he tried to tease them apart, they pulled back together.

"Who else have you done this with?" she asked him. "Sandy Finholm?"

"Yeah."

"Katy Turkett?"

"Maybe." Tommy put on the condom. "Why?"

"I want to know what's different about me." Sherry pulled a stray hair out of her eye, and Tommy's erection started to wilt.

"What's different about you?" he repeated.

"Yeah. Why am I different from everybody else you did this with? Why me?"

Tommy got his face next to hers, but that didn't help him answer. He brushed her cheek with his palm, and instead of saying anything, he blubbered at her. She started crying and pulled his head toward her, jamming his mouth against her collarbone.

"Why me?" she said. "You can't even say?"

Tommy still couldn't come up with an answer, so Sherry pushed him away. She wiped her tears, hopped out of his bed, and scowled her way to the living room. He followed, the condom dangling from his fallen penis, and watched her get dressed.

"I believe in God, you know," Tommy told her.

"I'm sure God's glad you couldn't say a single nice thing about me when I asked."

"I think you're—"

"Too late. You better throw out the trash in your bathroom, or your mom'll know you had a girl over."

"I'm sorry, Sher."

"Yeah, me too."

You're special because we both know we're nothing, he thought of telling Sherry as she pulled out of the driveway. *So we can fuck like we're the last two nothings on earth.* But that wasn't the answer. He pictured a different Sherry, an older one with less hope, who saw him as a machine to give her orgasms and nothing else. She was greedy, coming six or seven times for every one she let Tommy have, and he loved that greed as much as he loved her butterscotch skin.

You know that's not the way to go, said Jesus's voice. Tommy pictured him sitting at the kitchen table with Mary, their hands dirty from work and their white robes in need of a wash. They had to have fresh robes drying on the line, like the Sons and Daughters did. They slathered peanut butter on stale-looking bread, getting ready to head back out and work for God. Simple. Everything's simple unless you cloud it up.

"Did I do the right thing?" he asked them. "I'm supposed to love a girl before I do that, right?" He heard nothing back. When the phone rang in the kitchen, Tommy stepped in to answer it. No Jesus sitting at the table, no Mary. "Hi, Sandor house."

"Hi Tommy," Connie said from her mother's bedroom in Sidney. "House hasn't burned down yet, I guess?"

"Nope, still here. How's Grandma?"

"Looking like a blood clot. Not cancer, that's all we know."

"That's what Julie's note said. What's up, why'd you call?"

"I'm sorry I got so mad at you yesterday. But you're getting hooked up with people you don't even know, and I'm scared."

"You don't know 'em either," Tommy said. "All you know is secondhand from your boyfriend. Your *married* boyfriend."

"Oh, hell. I don't want to hear another lecture."

"Then hang up. You expect me to keep my mouth shut about it for a thousand bucks? There's this thing called right and wrong, Mom. A thousand bucks means *nothing*."

"People fall in love when they're married to other people," Connie said. "Happens every day."

"Doesn't mean it *has* to. It happened 'cause you're weak. 'Cause Danny Boy's weak."

"Seriously, Tommy. Why don't you have some cheerleaders over while I'm gone? Talk to Julie—she'll get you the booze. It'd be better than all this Jesus stuff."

"This *Jesus stuff* isn't going away, Mom. This *Jesus stuff* is what life's about, not screwing thy neighbor's husband."

Connie slammed the phone into its cradle, then picked it up again and got a dial tone. She set it back down slowly, the way she should have the first time, then looked around her mother's bedroom, thinking that she ought to see pictures on the walls, on the dresser, on the nightstand. Pictures of herself as a child, of her son with a dog and a father. But there was nothing, all because she wouldn't marry Richie Thorpe and help him live a regular American life. What would he look like on that wall, without his time in prison? With a clean, undisfigured face and a nine-to-five job? How would he look standing next to Tommy, with a few more sons for good measure? They could've cranked out six or seven, every one of them as strong as an ox.

"Never would've worked," Connie told herself, shaking her head.

"What wouldn't have worked?" asked Trish from the hallway.

"What the hell?" Connie hurled the phone at the door. "You're spying on me?"

93

"Somebody's got to watch out for you, girl. Never could watch out for yourself."

* * *

At sundown Tommy stood in the kitchen, wrapping the long, curly phone cable around his wrist as he talked himself out of calling Grandma's house to apologize for being so mean to his mom. Part of him said she deserved it for her adultery, and he couldn't let that part of him go, even though Jesus and Mary wanted him to. Sadness filled him up from inside like the marrow of his bones was turning to cement. He wanted to feel the same oneness with the world that hit him by Pete's dumpster, but instead he felt like a dried-up old man. Maybe it was from living in Suborney too long and being around too many dried-up old people with all their hopes gone.

He walked up to the church more slowly than usual, surprised that Julie wasn't drinking on her porch but instead was on the phone inside, bitching to somebody about Carter and the Ayatollah and World War III. He stuck close to the creek to avoid Sam's house because he could hear the old men still gathered there, drunkenly boasting about what they'd do to the Commies and the niggers and the wetbacks and the faggots once Reagan was president. He didn't want them to spot him and say, "Hey, you Commie faggot, how come you're not signed up for the marines yet?"

"He ain't no marine," one of them would say, and Tommy would knock the old fart out with an uppercut. Three seconds later he'd have a gun to his temple. "Go ahead," he'd tell whoever held it. "Go right a-fucking head and end this waste of a life." Then he'd give the smirk they all hated, and somebody would pull the trigger, and it would be over—his teenage bullshit would turn into the endless weight of manhood for a second, then turn into the endless silence of death. Would Jesus be waiting for him? No clue.

When Tommy reached the creek, he saw the Sons and Daughters standing in a circle in it, with the water up to their knees. Not saying a word, just cupping water in their hands and pouring it out, one person at a time, over each other's heads. Mother Meg baptized Brother Beto, who baptized Brother Worrell, who baptized whatever Zypanski had in his arms. The singing girl, it had to be. She baptized Brother Thorpe, who baptized Brother Zypanski, who baptized Sister Melanie, who baptized Mother Meg.

That's how you get clean, Tommy told himself. *That's how you keep love growing inside you—you water it.* His marrow started loosening, and the creek began to rise. Up to the Sons and Daughters' waists, up to their ribcages, and they all held onto each other as the water swelled. Zypanski lifted the singing girl above his shoulders, and Tommy wanted to bring that water down before he drowned them all. But he didn't know how, couldn't even be sure he was the one raising it.

Up, up, up. Sister Mel shouted, "Help!" Their feet were off the creek bottom, and they hung onto whatever they could, while Tommy thought of the dryness and deadness that he feared so much about being a man. The husks of all the Tommies he'd never become, stacked up and ready to burn at even the thought of a spark.

Down, he told the water. But nothing worked until he remembered the shame he'd felt when he couldn't tell Sherry he loved her. Isn't that what she'd been looking for? Tommy pictured himself saying "I love you" and kissing her forehead, then saying "Let's wait" and covering up her naked body with a sheet. His marrow stilled, and the creek started dropping down. Lower and lower, the more settled he felt his marrow getting, until it was back to normal.

"Hoooooo, baby!" shouted Thorpe, and Sister Melanie whooped. Tommy swore he heard his name mentioned as they went back to baptizing each other. Haphazardly this time, scooping up handfuls of water and laughing as they dumped it onto each other's heads. Tommy ran home, barely able to get a breath in past the top of his lungs, and tried to move water in the sink and the bathtub. But it wouldn't work—the water needed to be natural, touching God's earth, for him to move it.

Like God has anything to do with this, he told himself. He focused instead on his marrow, on controlling the precise feeling of its rise and fall. Or was it a thickening and loosening? What were the signs that came before the change—was it the tingling in his lips, the tightening in his fingertips? He coursed through his whole body looking for the trigger, but the only word that came up was

marrow
marrow
MARROW

People can't feel their own marrow, can they? He wished the Sons and Daughters were there with him because they'd know how to make him feel okay with this new thing he'd learned about himself. Brother Z would play dumb and get him laughing. The others would make Moses jokes, tell him that his power came from God and that he had to ask God how to use it right.

Did they know what I could do before I did it? he wondered, remembering how they laughed and said his name when the water went down. *Did my mother know, and that's why she's always been so worried about me?*

Tommy went outside to see if he could make it rain like Brother Thorpe did, and he clamped his hand together slowly until it cramped up. Nothing came. He pictured Thorpe beside him, knowing that he was ready to learn. The two of them would sit together atop Lester Hill, playing with Suborney like it was a board game. They could dry it out for a few hours, drive all the town's water so deep into the earth that it would feel like Death Valley. Then Tommy could bring the creek up so high that the water was at everybody's door, and Thorpe could bring the rain down on top of it until all the houses unmoored from the earth and sailed away, wiping Suborney off the human map forever.

Then everybody in town who hated Tommy would say, "Okay, you win." After that he'd make the water recede, and Thorpe would dry the ground with wind like nothing ever happened. They'd leave just enough moisture behind for everything to grow, grow, grow—taller than anybody dared to believe it could.

8

Sunday, July 13

Before dawn Tommy wanted to find out whether he could move a bigger body of water than the creek and whether his trick worked outside of Suborney. So he headed for Big Johnson Reservoir, fifteen minutes away on Bradley Road. On his way to the Vega, he saw Janice Sauter, who stood in her front yard filling up a birdbath with a watering can.

I'll take care of that for you, he felt like saying. *Put in a drop, I'll do the rest.* Instead, he just waved. All he could think of was where the water came from when he made it rise and where it went to when he made it fall. If water was finite, then making it rise in one spot had to lower it somewhere else. But what if it wasn't finite? Then he could raise Suborney Creek and irrigate all the dry, unused fields around it. Wheat would grow like never before. Corn, hay, broccoli, melons.

"Thanks, Tommy!" all those old farmers would call, looking up from their hoes and shovels. They'd work the land by hand and horse, like people did before engines, and everything would grow up strong from the ground because they trusted God, trusted Tommy to make the water come.

He parked on the shoulder above the Big Johnson, half a mile from the spot where he and Sherry would probably never fool around again, then hopped the barbed wire fence. Let the owners shoot him, he thought, whoever they were. He headed past the cow pies, toward the water, keeping an eye out for rattlers. Down the embankment and past clumps of yucca plants, their big seedpods starting to blacken in the sun. Tommy drew a line a foot above the water's edge with his boot heel, then squatted just above it and stared at the center of the reservoir.

"Watch this," he told an imaginary Thorpe squatting beside him. He knew his marrow wouldn't do its job if he was being a show-off because Jesus didn't like show-offs. He wanted to see Jesus walking on the water but instead saw him on the far shore with Mary, throwing out a fishing net. They both gave Tommy a big, slow wave, and that was enough to get his marrow moving. He shut his eyes and pulled back the muscles between his shoulder blades so hard that his neck popped. It felt like God was pulling him up, up, up, by a fishhook at the base of his skull.

Let it go, Jesus said. *No use carrying it.*

Tommy didn't know what Jesus was talking about, but the water rose past his line in the dirt to soak his boots and the seat of his pants. Across the reservoir a white dog barked, and even in the half-dark he could see that it was chained to its little house and couldn't get away. The barks turned to yips, and it jumped on the doghouse for safety as the water rose to Tommy's ankles. He tried everything to still his marrow and keep that dog from drowning—thinking about Sherry, about Drake shooting up in his apartment, about the people he'd let down when he quit football, about all the dead Tommies inside him.

Nothing worked. The water came up past his knees, and he scooped some up to baptize himself, but that didn't stop the rising either. The only thing that changed his marrow was thinking about his mom, alone and crying about him. Then the dog's yips felt like they came from just behind him, and everything went white, and the water crested and dropped.

Yeah, he could move bigger water than the creek. Yeah, he could do his trick outside of Suborney. The water kept on going down even after the dog stopped yipping, and Tommy didn't want to find out how low it would go. The reservoir could keep shrinking until the land was parched so badly it never bounced back. Or it might be connected to him forever now that he'd claimed it, drying out when he felt like shit and rising up when he felt halfway happy. He walked up the embankment to his Vega without looking back at the water, figuring that if something bad happened, he'd hear about it on the news soon enough.

Tommy took off his soaked boots and jeans and drove home into a sunrise that was more red than pink, wondering if there was a desert so dry that he couldn't find any water there to move. That might be a good place for him to stay out of trouble. But with his luck he'd spit in the sand one day without even thinking, and the water from it would grow until it swallowed him up. Maybe he'd be better off someplace that had tons of water already, where he could learn more ways to control it—turning it into ice and steam, making waterfalls and hurricanes. A place that had so much water, it wouldn't make a difference if he screwed up and added more or took some away for good. Minnesota maybe. He'd fooled around with a girl from up there sophomore year, an army brat who moved again six months later.

"Land of ten thousand lakes," she called her home state more than once, like she knew his secret before he did. "You should go sometime."

＊ ＊ ＊

Tommy headed home to Suborney and got ready to drive back up to the mission, a team effort he'd organized with a patience and precision no one expected of him. Jeff Heagren had sold a 1973 Buick Riviera—a prized junkyard possession that he'd never parted out—to a guy in Denver, transport included. Tommy would get fifty bucks in cash, which he'd already promised to the mission, for driving it up. Dolman had preloaded the flatbed with all the drywall and two-by-fours he could scrounge from the yard. Zypanski, Worrell, and Benjy joined Tommy in the cab of the flatbed with screws, drills, nails, and hammers, ready to fix up as much of the mission as they could before they had to bring the truck back.

"You got a team name for us, Mr. Sandor?" asked Brother Zypanski on the drive up. "You football guys are always making team names."

"He's an army guy too," said Brother Worrell. "Isn't that what I hear?"

"I was gonna be a marine, man. Discipline. No soft living."

"Oh, we got that covered," said Zypanski. "No personal cash-ola and only two sets of clothes, the one you're wearing and the one you're washing."

"Sometimes I swear I'd break somebody's arm for a third pair of boxers," Brother Benjy said. They talked about how the Sons and Daughters lived, with everything communal and no alcohol except for communion wine. No screwing around—though you could get married. They all admitted that being around Sister Mel, who was the smartest and most beautiful female any of them were ever likely to know—those cheeks, those hips, that straight back—regularly drove them apeshit mad with desire.

"God puts tests in your way," Worrell said. "Wants to see if you'll keep crashing into 'em or if you're ready for another lesson."

"What's *my* lesson?" asked Tommy.

"What do you keep crashing into?" said Zypanski. "Your mom, maybe?"

"Is it that obvious?"

"Big as a blimp," Worrell told him.

"You and your blimps," Tommy replied. They dropped off the Riviera and headed to the mission, and he raced out as soon as he parked with his hammer at the ready. The other three hung back, standing in a clump while Tommy climbed up to unstrap the drywall and two-by-fours. He noticed them staring and stopped in mid-motion.

"Shouldn't we remember who we're working for?" Worrell asked him. Tommy still wasn't used to praying before he worked, like the Sons and Daughters did, and he dropped to his knees waiting for somebody else to start it.

"Your plan, your prayer," said Zypanski.

Tommy hadn't led a prayer since Gracehouse, and his first try came out a mumble. He cleared his throat and thanked God that he had two hands to work with, then thought of Beto and added that one hand was plenty good enough. The others muttered an *Amen* and hopped onto the flatbed to unload everything. As soon as they stepped through the mission's empty doorframe, they found a pair of green plaid boxer shorts on the floor.

"Want to try 'em on?" Worrell asked Benjy. "Won't tell, I swear."

They worked and sweated until the time came for Justin Stannard's show, when they drove to Union Station so Tommy could ask his usual opening question from a pay phone. The others sat in the illegally parked flatbed waiting for one of them to speak his mind.

"I'm so sick of Brother T not telling that boy," Brother Zypanski finally said. "Tell the truth or move on. That's his choice."

"We can't force his hand like that," Brother Worrell told him. "God's working at his own pace."

"This ain't God, Brother Worry. This is Brother T, and he's dragging his feet, and we've got the right to say something about it."

"You want to kick him out?" Worrell turned in his seat, protected from Zypanski's massive frame by Brother Benjy's slim one.

"Never said that. But we can help him do it, like he told us we might have to."

Things got silent a moment, then Benjy piped up. "I feel like Brother T's pulling me away from Jesus right now, not closer."

"That's how Tommy'd see it if he knew," Zypanski told Worrell. "It's a sin to hold the truth back, and Brother T knows it."

Benjy held out his hands and the others clasped them, and they prayed for things to work out between Thorpe and Tommy. Prayed that the father wouldn't hold onto the truth for too long and that the son wouldn't fill with hate once he heard it. Justin Stannard's show was about to start, so they turned on Tommy's transistor radio. They'd learned about him from listening to KJML all the way from Kansas—about the jazz he loved, the sex he kept having, his mother's affair with Justin's brother. Connie's lie about his made-up saxophonist father irritated them in particular and justified the long walk with Thorpe to Suborney. A fool's errand, the Sons and Daughters they left behind said, and the longer they stayed in town without the truth coming out, the more right those words felt. They'd been asking themselves louder and louder—and they knew with absolute certainty that Thorpe did the same—whether withholding the truth from Tommy now was just as bad as the lying Connie had done to him his whole life.

The truest thing Thorpe could have done was to stride into Suborney and say, "Tommy Sandor, I'm your father." But none of the Sons and Daughters expected him to do that—not even he was that strong. The compromise Thorpe had settled on, the collective lie that he'd asked them to participate in, was to let the boy know him as a man first, then as a father. It wasn't ideal, but they forgave Thorpe for his weakness. He needed a way to get inside his son's heart before he sprang the news, simple as that. Those who walked to Suborney with him had agreed to his plan and pledged to stand by Tommy, to make sure that he wouldn't feel alone when the truth broke. Some nights, especially when Brother Thorpe hid himself away to ask God to forgive his cowardice and deceit, keeping that promise felt like a too-hard task.

"Can't you see it, Tommy?" the men in the flatbed wanted to ask him. "His face is your face. His shoulders are your shoulders." Inside Union Station, Tommy got to ask his question.

"I know Jesus is the one you're supposed to lose your life to," Tommy blurted out as soon as Reverend Stannard greeted him. "But how do you start losing it to Jesus if you've already lost control of it? Like everything's running away from you, and you want to give your life up to God, but you've got no life left to give. 'Cause you've already let it slip away into whatever kind of nothing is out there. Okay, I'll stop jabbering. Peace, Reverend."

"God's Peace to you too," Reverend Stannard said. Then Tommy ran to the cab of the truck and climbed in. Brother Z's hand opened next to him, and Tommy took it.

"—you seem to be getting at," the Reverend continued, "is the difference between losing *control* of your life and *giving* it to God with your full agreement and intention. If your life is spinning out of control—with hate, drugs, sex, lies, greed—then you can't *give* your life to God because you've already given it to something *other* than God. After you stop giving your life away to things that can't give life *back* to you, then and *only* then can you have a life left to give to God at all."

"Amen," Brother Benjy said.

"And it doesn't matter if that life is perfect or not. God doesn't care if your life is perfect—he cares that you *give* it to him. Think of it like a bird, Tommy. You might like to think of your life as a magnificent eagle, and God would love it if someday you have an eagle to give him. But right now, the way you've been talking when you call in, I'm guessing that the life you can give to God—and I mean *after* you take it back from whatever else you've spent it on—is going to look more like one of those birds people rescue out of an oil spill. Can't fly, eyes glued shut, barely able to open its beak. But God doesn't care. As soon as you get that life back in your hands, you *give* it to God. You—"

"Enough already," Tommy said, pulling his hand from Zypanski's to turn off the radio. He started up the flatbed and headed back to the mission, where he worked in abstracted silence until all the drywall was up. Tommy was hard to be around the whole afternoon, and the Brothers didn't feel any of his usual exuberance pulsing out of him. They left him alone until they got south of Denver and onto open highway, when his shoulders relaxed a bit.

"I like what Reverend Stannard said about that oily bird," Zypanski told him. "Think I've been that bird a few times."

"Yes sir," said Benjy. "Been that bird."

"And we'll all be it again a few more times before we're said and done," Worrell added.

"Yup," was all Tommy had to say. He couldn't tell them why he kept so quiet—it was his marrow, migrating back and forth between liquid and solid ever since Justin Stannard talked about that damn bird. As the highway cleared before him, Tommy saw himself as he actually was: full of mother rage and father rage and fear of what he might become or never become. He saw himself clutching something to the center of his chest, a little oily hatchling bird with its mouth gaping open, then held it out in absolute trust for two pairs of ancient, dirty, work-worn hands—Jesus's hands and Mary's hands, both reaching toward him from tattered, once-white robes.

Cheesy. So damn corny, like a cult would do if it started putting recruiting ads on TV. Couldn't he come up with a better Jesus and Mary than that? Couldn't he come up with a better picture for his own soul than a half-dead fucking bird?

9

still Sunday

"I'm a big girl," Connie said, looking at the sandwich, the can of RC Cola, and the apple that sat on Trish's kitchen table. "You don't have to pack me a lunch."

"Just saving money you might need if you move," said Trish.

"If I do, I won't move here. He's been here already, I know it."

"I didn't say a damn thing to anybody." Trish left the kitchen, unwilling to be accused again. Yesterday Connie had interrogated her mother's two closest friends to see if any religious crazies had wormed their way into Trish's life, and this imposition would not be forgiven easily, if ever. Trish leaned against the doorjamb with her arms crossed on her chest like her husband used to. Poor Greg Holmquist, who died thinking he had a wife named Ada and a daughter named Jeannette. Who may never have said the words *Trish* or *Connie* or *Sandor* in his life.

"Put your arms down," Connie told her. "Quit trying to be Dad."

"I didn't like you talking to my friends like that," Trish said. "I told you it wasn't me. But when you get your mind set, nobody can tell you anything. Even if you don't know what your mind's set *on*."

"Aren't you going to tell me what I *should* get my mind set on? Wouldn't be like you if you didn't." Connie stuffed the food into her purse. "Should I tell Tommy you picked out his last name? Should I kiss and make up with Richie?"

"You're not stupid enough to fall for him again."

"Then what *am* I stupid enough for? Getting pulled into his cult, till I'm Sister Jeannette? Richie's got me over a barrel, and you don't get it. He rigged the game."

"So figure out what you'll say if Tommy finds out first," Trish said.

"No shit. Why do you always save your lectures for right when I'm leaving?"

"Because it's the only time I can ever talk sense into you. Call before you come next time, and careful what lies you tell about me."

"Funny," Connie said. "Most people say not to tell lies about them at *all*."

Trish shoved the can of RC Cola at her, and they gave each other two quick nods: their long-standing sign of assent that they would hold onto whatever lies were necessary, at any cost, to keep their secrets. Then Connie was in her blue Chevy LUV, headed back to Suborney. Fifteen minutes later she crossed the Colorado border, where she wanted to turn around and finally stand up to her mom. All she'd ever be in Trish's eyes was a smart girl who turned dumb the moment Richie Thorpe gave her the eye. Who climbed out her window every night to make love to a common criminal in a tree house with who knows what kind of animals living in it. A smart girl who let her blood get too hot the first time it was tested.

What did that smart girl have now? A whole life built over the wreckage of a single mistake. A child, born of that mistake, who was almost old enough to set himself loose on the world. A boy so much like his father that it made her ache to watch him move.

"Oh, Tommy," she sighed to herself. "What are we gonna do?"

Five miles into Colorado, Connie saw a billboard with SUPPORT OUR TROOPS and a big yellow ribbon hand-painted on it, and she wished Tommy would finally join the marines. Then he'd be out of her hair for a few years, however long it took Reagan to get the

Arabs back under our thumbs, and when he came back, he wouldn't care who his father was anymore. He'd be messed up by war, with a million other things to worry about than Drake and the wild, drugged-out black men he played sax with.

But what a terrible way to think about her own son! Wanting him to risk dying in a war or coming back with parts missing, just to avoid telling him the truth! Connie pictured Tommy methodically banging his head against a wall in a bare white room filled with light. A military hospital. Banging hard and incessantly but not blacking out because the wall was padded. He reached an arm through the bars on the inside of his window, trying to break its glass so he could slice his wrists open with a shard. But he couldn't reach—the glass was just far enough away.

I did this to him, Connie thought to herself. The image of her son locked in a padded room wasn't Tommy after he came home from a war with Iran. It was Tommy now, locked away from what she kept him from knowing out of spite for Richie and herself. She had enough spite stored up to burn down everything she knew. Sidney, even with her mom stuck inside it. Suborney, with herself stuck inside it—maybe Tommy stuck, too, and *definitely* Richie. Nebraska City, where the lie was born. Bird City, where the lie set itself in stone.

Connie reached Sterling, Colorado, planning to hop onto Interstate 76 and head home. Instead, she took the old U.S. highways heading south and east toward Bird City, where she'd given her son to the world. The town hadn't been much back then, probably wasn't much now. There weren't many people to recognize her, so it might be a clearer place to think than Nebraska City. No father of hers had died there, no lover of hers had stood trial there. Bird City, where she decided to love a bastard child without shame. Where she told anyone who'd listen that the man responsible for her pregnant belly was a sax player from New York who'd loved her and left her. Bird City, where the lie about the child was born even before the child himself.

Connie headed there, wanting the same burst of energy that the lie had given her when it was fresh, the same sense that this new being called Connie Sandor could become everything Jeanette Holmquist might have been—even more, because Connie was free in a way Jeanette never could be. Jeannette was rooted to the charred ground at the corner of Sixth and Central in Nebraska City, but Connie could sail through the air, bending her body with the wind until it took her to the spot where she was meant to land.

For almost seven years, that spot had been Bird City. For almost eleven more, Suborney. But she needed another wind soon because she didn't like what waited for her back home. The faces of those half-dead old people who would know the truth about her soon enough, if they didn't already. And she'd have to see the look on Tommy's face when he cornered her and growled, "You lied," then turned into a cross between a bull and a werewolf. He'd tear down the whole house with his bare hands, tear down the whole town. He'd tie her to a tree and make her watch, turning to her occasionally to say, "You did this to me!" before destroying something else, someone else.

But the worst would be Richie Thorpe's face, grinning big when he took Tommy away from her in front of everybody. Just walked up and said, "He's mine," and stole the one thing that anchored Connie Sandor to the world. She'd lose Dan Stannard too—he'd purse his lips and shake his head as he yanked out the nail he hung his holster belt on. Acting disgusted by her lie, when in truth he was ashamed of himself for thinking he really wanted to marry her in the first place. Ashamed that he could never stand up to Richie Thorpe, never beat him in a fair fight over a woman.

"Like Richie still wants you," Connie told her rearview mirror. "He wants his Mary, Mary, Mary."

Then Connie's future turned into a soap opera romance in which she took Richie back and earned his love again. It worked at first, but being boxed up in prison had made him need freedom even more than he used to, which made him run from the soft prison of her succulent, still-fertile body. Nonstop sex and fighting, until sex was fighting too. Back when Richie was first in prison, Connie used to let herself fantasize about him that way because no other man measured up. In Bird City she used to picture him walking up her long driveway in the middle of winter, wearing a bright-red parka that popped out from the snow. Hot breath shrouded his face, and from afar she felt the hands that once made her feel absolutely here on earth, absolutely supported.

She'd indulged in such fantasies until Tommy started walking, then cut them off abruptly when the creepy guy in silver overalls showed up near the farm looking like a botched copy of Richie. That's when she started mapping her escape route from Bird City, because he and his spies might follow her for the rest of her life.

Not that all her planning made a difference now. The second Richie said, "I'm your dad," Tommy would jump into his arms like a five-year-old. Then he'd look back at his mother and laugh, a big, open-mouthed *Huh-haaaaaaa!* just like Richie's, as if father and son had been plotting this moment for years. What if they'd been sending each other letters the whole time, pulling luxuriously at the noose around her neck and taking glee in how tight they could make it without her noticing? Ron and Kate Ulin could've ferried their letters—or somebody from that underpass church.

Connie let her imagination get to her and had trouble staying in her lane, then made an illegal pass and almost ran into a big green semi. She knew she'd go home to Suborney to face the music, at least for a while, but couldn't decide whether to stick around and let Tommy and Richie humiliate her in front of everybody before she left town for good. Maybe she deserved that. Or she could bolt right away and let Tommy pick up the pieces. But part of her wanted the public confessions and confrontations that awaited her in Suborney because she'd done nothing against life, nothing against the God that Richie claimed to love so much. She'd kept her promise to have the baby, instead of aborting it with some back-alley doctor. She'd raised a good son in miserable circumstances, when lesser women would have let him turn into a monster. She'd let Tommy go to church, even though she didn't believe herself. Her only crime was loving an untamable man and being the soil where his seed grew. She'd nurtured that seed as best she could, better than most women could. Who was that a crime against? Tommy? Richie? Herself? God?

"Just look at Tommy," she'd tell the people of Suborney, circled tight around her. "Look at the man I made him before you hate me for it."

Seeds need soil to grow in, don't they? Why should the soil feel shame? But she had one thing to be ashamed of: lying to Tommy about his father. She could have lived the truth and told the world, "I'm bearing the son of a criminal who can't be tamed." She could have moved to Lincoln—under her real name—and brought Tommy to visit Richie in prison so father and son could know each other, love each other.

Instead, she made up the pathetic, weaselly Drake, who didn't even deserve a last name. Connie had to go back to Bird City because that's where her lie was born and the only place she could undo its curse. In Bird City lived the Connie Sandor who could turn her back on anything and leave it behind, and she needed to find that decisive place in herself again. "The pivot point," a high school science teacher she'd dated used to call it. The place where you can make any decision, create any future.

The driving got easier once Connie knew what she wanted in Bird City. As she reached its outskirts, she wished Tommy were sitting next to her—a Tommy who'd never been to Suborney because she'd never felt any reason to run away from Bird City in the first place. Because there was no creepy guy in silver overalls lurking around the property. Because nobody asked her questions like how long she'd lived in McCook before moving to the goat farm and did she go to school there with Sylvie Baker or Chad Knowley? Did she have any people back around Omaha? Because her face looked awful familiar.

She would have stayed if the questions hadn't started, if that blurry

Polaroid hadn't shown up one day—one simple piece of evidence, tucked beneath her front porch doormat, that proved she was being watched. It showed a smiling, Jesus-loving Tommy holding a black baby goat with a white spot on its forehead and a red bandana around its neck. She remembered picking up the Polaroid, then turning around to see if the man in the silver overalls was watching her. He had to be the one who took that picture, who came up to her house and dropped it by while she slept inside with her front door unlocked. One of Richie's spies. And how many were there?

Leaving Bird City was an instantaneous decision, made seconds after she saw that picture. Connie moved them, based on nothing but blueprints, to the little house on Mangum Street in Suborney, Colorado, with four hundred dollars in cash and her first month of mortgage paid. She simply packed Tommy into their beat-up white van and told him, "I can't wait to show you the new house!" She told him how excited she was for her new job, even though she hadn't found one yet. Connie wanted to go back to the days when she could pull off a move like that. Back to her days at the goat farm, where she clung so deliciously to her pivot point for almost seven years, able to spring in any direction that circumstances required.

That farm. What a beautiful farm. The skin on the back of her hands perked up as she steered around a familiar corner, waiting to see the twin willow trees and the twin red barns. But when she turned onto the driveway she once knew, Connie saw no house or trees or barns at all. Not even a fence. Nothing but an asphalt paving crew putting down a brand-new road.

* * *

After Tommy dropped off his drywall crew at the Jesus and Mary house, he went home for his sax and grabbed his sleeping bag, just in case he had the guts to spend the night with the Sons and Daughters. It felt like an inevitable next step. He stood on the front steps of the church, the bell of his Selmer pointing up to the porch where he used to play marbles with Wesley Perrin, and he honked out variations on the two songs he'd heard the mystery girl singing. Why hadn't he seen her yet? Tommy played riffs on the scales for *"Give thanks to the skyyyyyy!"* and *"I am of dust and bone,"* periodically going back to the simple refrains before attacking their scales again like a rabid bebop wolf.

He played until he didn't have any more notes left in his sax—he even turned the instrument upside down to see if anything dropped out of the bell—then cleaned it and left it in the church and hoofed his way past the gently blowing debris on Tumbleback Road to the Perrin house. Tommy still called it that sometimes, even though the house belonged only to Jesus and Mary now, because he still loved Wesley like a brother. He figured Jesus and Mary would understand. By the time he got there, nighttime prayers had ended, and Brother Thorpe was the only one left on the porch. He lay in a sleeping bag at one end, propped up on an elbow and reading a battered little green Bible in the dim light of a stinky kerosene lantern. Tommy quietly set himself up on the other end of the porch, where he and Wesley had once built a racing ramp for their toy cars, and as he climbed into his bag, the Sons and Daughters in the living room snuffed out their candles.

"How come you're out here?" Tommy asked. "Everybody else is inside."

"Might be leaving early," Thorpe said. "Plus they say I smell bad."

"You're like the invisible man. Nobody knows when you're coming or going."

"You keeping tabs on me? Spying for your state patrolman buddy?"

"Never." Tommy rolled over to face the plains, hoping he'd see Jesus and Mary waving at him again and telling him he was doing the right thing. Instead, he heard an up-too-late winged grasshopper clicking its way through the air.

"Remember I said God might like you playing that sax?" asked

Thorpe. "I think he'd like what you did tonight. Even with the crazy parts."

"That's bebop, man. Some people say it's the devil's music."

"Music's only the devil's if you play it for him."

"I don't, in case you're wondering."

"I know who you play for, Tom-Tom. Isn't that what they call you around here?"

"Yes sir," Tommy said. "You can call me Brother Tom-Tom if you want."

"When everybody knows it's time," Thorpe said, and just like that, the words were gone from their conversation, like the notes were gone from the saxophone. Tommy, in his mind, turned Thorpe upside down to make sure no more words fell out of him. Thorpe, in his mind, let the words *My son* drop from his mouth with a hundred different intonations. *My son, my son, my son.* Every single one of them loving, gentle, wanting forgiveness.

10

Monday, July 14

Before sunrise father and son silently piled into the living room to break morning bread. Melanie passed Benjy the wicker basket that held yesterday's leftover chunks. Beto poured a splash of wine into his mouth from the pitcher, then handed it to Mother Meg. The whole thing didn't seem religious at all, just a bunch of quiet people having bread and wine. It wasn't like Gracehouse, with everybody trying so hard to speak in tongues. It felt more like hanging out with the Sneads right after church in Bird City—just looking at the world and finding God everywhere and being silently glad for it.

As guest of honor, Tommy got a bonus chunk of day-old bread and the very last drops of wine. Then they prayed in a circle, asking God to let them know him better this day. Asking Jesus and Mary to walk before them so they could learn which way to go. After singing a long *Amen* they gathered in the kitchen to eat English muffins with margarine and honey while Mother Meg gave them their jobs for the day. She'd go with Benjy and Beto to a women's shelter they were helping set up in Colorado Springs; Sister Mel would stay home with the singing girl; Z-pan and Brother Worry would go to Widefield and help fix the water-damaged flooring of an old folks' home; Brother Thorpe and Tommy would start clearing the church, keeping an eye out for what the women's shelter might need. Ed Dolman, she announced, had given his okay.

Thorpe and Tommy took white plastic trash bags and picked up blown-in junk as they walked to the church. A newspaper from Wichita that either blew all the way to Suborney on its own or hitched a ride in a car. A glow-in-the-dark Frisbee chewed up by a dog, a Peter Frampton album snapped in half. A pair of red boxer shorts with white Santas on them, which made Tommy think of Brother Benjy.

"How come the Sons and Daughters only have two pairs of clothes?" he asked.

"Two's the lap of luxury," Thorpe said. "I bet Jesus only had the clothes on his back."

"So we're supposed to live like Jesus, even two thousand years later?"

"When he said 'Follow me,' I don't think he just meant north and south." A hard wind came up from their right, and Thorpe covered his bad eye. He saw Tommy noticing. "Sometimes I can't close that eye all the way. Muscles get jammed up."

"That's a metaphor for something."

"Metaphor? What you talkin' 'bout, son, with your fancy book learnin'?" Thorpe had to put on a hick accent to let himself say *son*—a word that had been burning a hole in him ever since he'd confirmed Tommy's existence. Early in his sixth year in the Nebraska State Penitentiary, a Polaroid came to him of Tommy balanced on the fence of a goat pen. It was a beacon that kept him sane for six more years, until he stupidly lost it in the prison laundry.

"Well," Tommy said, "if you can't close your eye, then you have to keep looking at God. And when God looks back, you can't shut him out. See? Metaphor."

"You oughta git yourself one of them radio shows."

Tommy put on his best DJ voice. "Welcome to Angry Teenage Jesus Freak Hour with your host, Tommy Sandor. Your home for bebop and continuous religious confusion."

Thorpe laughed and ditched the accent. "Reverend Stannard'll hook you up, I bet."

"*Reverend,*" Tommy muttered. "Who made him a reverend, huh?"

"He's got a lot less hate in him than most radio preachers," Thorpe said. "And a soft spot for you too."

"Sure does. How about you, Brother T? You got any hate?"

"None I want to live with a second longer. You?"

Tommy didn't answer. They said a quick prayer on the church steps and launched themselves into the junk, looking for things the women's shelter might need. A Wesleyan church and an Assembly of God church had gotten together to start it at an empty house on East San Miguel Street, and Thorpe figured that if those two could play as a team, the Sons and Daughters would gladly pitch in. Tommy loved the way news moved around among believers like that, like a secret code in wartime. Some old lady needs help but is too proud to ask for it, and word gets to the Sons and Daughters, and soon they're at her door taking care of her. They dug out three bed frames for the shelter, plus two dressers, a kitchen table, a blender, a waffle iron. Tommy found the porch swing that used to be at the Perrin house and convinced Thorpe to put it back where it belonged. Thorpe found a webbed yellow lounge chair like the one Mother Meg had in Lincoln, and he earmarked it for her.

"Did you live with Mother Meg when you got out of prison?" Tommy asked.

"Yes sir. She was a second mom to me. Visited me even after Nick died."

"What happened to your first mom? She dead?"

"Oh yeah. When I was twelve."

"Then you went off traveling with your dad, right? He was a thief, always on the run?" Tommy tapped his temple. "See, I remember stuff."

A memory flashed into Tommy's mind—him seeing Thorpe walking past the house on Mangum Street on the day his mom got her truck—but it had to be fake because Thorpe was in prison then. They worked until they ran across old curtains so dusty that they sneezed dozens of times, then took a break on the church steps where they'd first met.

"Need a shower and a change of clothes after this," Thorpe said, scraping caked grime off his forearm with a fingernail. He felt tempted to write something on it but could only come up with MY SON. No, too obvious.

"Yeah. Plus, I gotta go to work sometime." It was a half-assed excuse, since Tommy knew that Pete and Dolman had given up depending on him.

"Your mom like you doing all that work? Doesn't leave much time for being a kid."

"She doesn't care, and I don't care right back. Seen her with too many boyfriends to respect her."

"Maybe she's seen you with too many *girl*friends to respect *you*."

"I haven't slept with a girl since you people came to town. Had a chance, didn't take it. Knew Jesus wouldn't like it."

"One less sin to scrub off," Thorpe told him, scratching at the grime on his arm again. Then Tommy went home to get a change of clothes and ran into Dolman, who was on his way to the yard.

"You're really letting those people take that stuff in the church?" Tommy asked him. "I thought you were starting a store with it someday?"

"Look at me." Dolman stopped and pointed at his face. "Do I look like I could run a business? Those guys are out there helping people like I don't have the balls for. Least I can do is help *them*."

"Why not join up?"

"Too selfish to give up my stupid stuff. I was an altar boy once, you know that? Altar boy gone bad when he started smoking dope in Boy Scouts. Give 'em all the junk they want, man."

Dolman started walking on, but Tommy grabbed him by the elbow. The light around them suddenly felt ancient, like they were two brothers on the road in Bumfuck, Israel, in the days when Jesus walked the earth, deciding whether to follow him or not. *Is he for real? Would he lie to us?* Tommy dropped to his knees and prayed without words until Dolman broke down crying and stumbled away. The light had taken them over and stripped them down to the nothingness at their cores. Isn't that what God wanted?

When Tommy stood up, it was 1980 again, and he walked home to find his mom's Chevy LUV still in the driveway. He felt ready to apologize to her, or at least be civil, and thunked up the back steps just as Connie grabbed her purse from the kitchen counter.

"Howdy, ma'am!" Tommy bounded in to kiss her cheek.

"Howdy." Connie pulled back from his grimy body. "Mind telling me where you slept last night?"

"On Wesley Perrin's porch."

She deflated. "You don't know those people, Tommy. There are *convicted* felons in that house."

"There's one in your bed too."

"Oh, don't start on him. And that one with the cheek, he spent sixteen *years* in prison. Can you trust somebody who spent that long locked up?"

"God's trusting him with a church," Tommy said. "Don't see why I can't trust him enough to sleep on the same porch with him."

"On the same *porch*? You don't know what that man's done."

"Yeah, I do. Involuntary manslaughter. He burned down some guy's house."

"Not his house," Connie said, her face flushing red from telling too much of the truth. "Dan said it was a store. He looked it up."

Tommy slipped past Connie into his room for fresh clothes, and when he got out, he saw her standing by the front door with her fingers to her temples.

"You okay?" he asked, touching her shoulder gently because that's what Jesus and Mary wanted from him. Connie put on her usual mask of fake calm.

"You coming to supper tonight?" she asked.

"Sure. No meat, okay? We don't eat it."

"*We?* Oh, Tommy." She shook her head and let out a big sigh, then headed to her truck, wondering if tonight would be the last supper they ever ate together. After that she'd have to hear all those people blab on about *JesusJesusJesus* if she wanted to see her own son. Then he'd lecture her about how his real mother, everybody's real mother, was *MaryMaryMary*.

As she drove to work, Connie thought about the day ahead to try keeping her mind off Tommy. Piles of filing, the college girl horning in on her turf, Darren's condescending flirtations. Every mother loses her children someday, and plenty lose them to fathers who swoop in after ignoring them for years. Richie hadn't exactly ignored Tommy—praying to pictures of him was probably more like it—but the idea was the same. He could swoop in any second now, finish off his little ambush and claim his prize. Connie pictured Trish in the half-seat behind her, protecting her from that moment with the .38 she bought herself the day Richie got out of prison. She'd told Connie to do the same and even offered to pay for one.

"You'd better know what you'll do when he shows up at your door," Trish had told her over the phone that day.

"Maybe he doesn't care anymore. You don't even know for sure he's coming."

"I damn well do. So do you."

The imaginary Trish pointed her pistol out the window, aiming at one sheet metal cutout of Richie Thorpe after another. Boom, shot through the heart every time. Sometimes the cutouts were painted to make him look like an Old West gunslinger, sometimes like the street trash he was, sometimes like a family man holding two young kids by the hand.

"Your turn," Trish said, and when Connie reached back to take the gun, she felt Richie Thorpe's hand around her wrist exactly like she'd felt it by that chain link fence eighteen summers ago. That same grip, daring her to pull back against it.

* * *

Thorpe was back to work at the church by the time Tommy returned, so their showers had to wait. They separated useful junk from dead junk until the heat of midafternoon, when they dug out an old braided rug with three half-mummified cats inside it. Then Thorpe finally led the way to the Jesus and Mary house to get clean.

"Maybe I'll see that singing girl today," Tommy mused.

"Not with all that dust on you. She's got breathing problems. Name's Tessy, by the way." But Tessy wouldn't be there, Thorpe remembered—she'd gone off to the doctor with Sister Melanie, driven by an unnamed benefactor. They washed their hands and faces enough to eat some peanut butter and bananas, then Thorpe jumped out the back door to make sure the hose was warm enough. The inside shower leaked, so the Sons and Daughters showered outside with a patched-up hundred-foot hose they left uncoiled to warm up like a snake. Afternoon showers, a rare luxury because they were usually out working somewhere, meant more hot water. Thorpe stripped down and tapped at the cracked-open kitchen window while Tommy rummaged for more food inside.

"You can still talk to me," Thorpe called up through the gap. "If there's anything you want to talk about."

"Is there stuff you can only say naked?" Tommy cranked the window open wider.

"All I've got to say when I'm naked is, 'Thank you, God, for the flesh and blood you gave me.'" Thorpe turned and flexed his upper back, its ropy musculature thatched by a roadmap of scars, as if he'd spent years whipping himself with barbed wire. He stepped onto the four-foot square of paving stones that served as a shower and turned on the spigot, hosing himself down with too-hot water.

"So how'd this church get started?" Tommy asked. "You cooked it up in prison with Mother Meg's son, right?"

"Lots of time on your hands in prison." Thorpe turned the spigot off and lathered up with a communal bar of Ivory soap. "He got me praying my first month in, but we didn't start calling it a church till eight, nine years later."

"Is that before he bashed your face in or after?"

"After."

"Where'd he get the brick?"

"Asked a guard who didn't like me. You ready? Almost your turn."

While Thorpe rinsed off, Tommy went outside and stripped down, setting his clothes next to an old-fashioned washboard and basin. Then Thorpe dried off with a communal towel, put on a pair of communal flip-flops, and unpinned his fresh clothes from the line. Tommy stepped over to the patio blocks and wet himself down.

"You're a boxer shorts man, I see," he called to Thorpe.

"Only way to hang, sonny."

Sonny didn't come out the way Thorpe had hoped—too forced, too calculated. Tommy soaped up, wondering whether he could hack full-time life with the Sons and Daughters. Would he last a year with all that self-denial? Or just long enough to scare the piss out of his mom? He watched Thorpe put on his black cutoff shorts and yellow United Farm Workers T-shirt, toss over the flip-flops, and hang the towel on its nail. Father and son didn't look at each other, not even to say, "Your body is my body," and Thorpe hung his head at his own failure. It was wrong, this too-patient plan of his. Not honest enough, not right with God. Tommy rinsed off too slowly, and the water in the hose turned cold before he finished.

"Thank you, God, for the flesh and blood you gave me," Tommy said after yowling at the cold water, and he flexed his muscles just like his father had. But Thorpe didn't see it because he'd gone to the clothesline to pin up his son's fresh clothes as if they'd been hanging out to dry with everyone else's. He knew Tommy would like that.

"Toss that hose over when you're done having fun," Thorpe called as he headed for the shaving stand and washbasin. He shaved with a communal razor while Tommy dressed by the clothesline, then wetted down his dirty clothes when it was Tommy's turn to shave. He almost cried when his son smiled at him with lather where sideburns would be, lather on his chin where a patch of scruff would be.

Don't say it yet, Thorpe reminded himself as he scrubbed his shorts clean with a hard-bristled brush. Then he bit the inside of his cheek, cursing himself for letting another chance at the truth slip by.

"How much of this Sons and Daughters stuff did Mother Meg's son come up with?" Tommy asked, pulling on a white V-neck and ruffling his buzz-cut hair dry.

"Most of it."

"What was he in for?"

"Ask her."

"Did he teach you to make it rain?"

"Maybe."

"Damn, you're full of answers today," Tommy said. "Will you teach me how, if you guys ever make me Brother Tommy?"

"Not sure I need to. I saw you move that creek, didn't I?"

Tommy couldn't meet his eye and instead watched Thorpe walk inside. He felt his own leg muscles twitch every time Thorpe's feet lifted from the ground, but instead of embracing it as biological kinship—which his body knew, which his breath knew—his mind wrote it off as mere emulation. Young male gorillas all want to be silverbacks, like that movie he saw in biology class said. Tommy wanted to learn Thorpe's silverback vibe because he'd need it for his band someday. He'd need to get New Yorkers behind him, and New Yorkers don't follow anybody but the strongest. Tommy took the laundry soap and brush and scrubbed needlessly hard at the thighs of his jeans, then hung them on the line between Melanie's clothes and Zypanski's.

"Brother Tommy!" he hooted to himself in imitation of Z-Pan's big voice, and he said it again in Melanie's soft, imploring coo. "Brother Tommy?" Then he watched a gray truck heading east on Tumbleback Road, a direction hardly anybody drove except locals and lost people. He didn't recognize the truck or the little yellow livestock trailer it towed. Tommy saw Benjy in the passenger seat, then saw two goats in the trailer—Nubians, a kind they'd had a few of back in Bird City, with chocolate-brown coats and long noses and floppy ears. The truck stopped in front of the house.

"Goats, man!" Tommy shouted inside to Thorpe. "We got goats!" He ran to the trailer, where Benjy tried to coax the animals out by poking them with a broomstick. There was an old billy about his age and an extremely pregnant nanny that Tommy guessed was twelve. The sweaty man behind the wheel didn't cut his engine or say a word.

"You know anything about goats?" Benjy asked as Tommy grabbed the broomstick.

"Shit yeah. Born on a goat farm. You gotta give 'em a little more hell than that. C'mon, you ol' stink bombs. Let's get you out of this rattrap."

Tommy pushed down hard on the broomstick, wedging it against the nanny's rump. She had chunks missing from both ears and ragged hooves and was so pregnant that she looked ready to drop. She came out easily, but the billy—a good 'ol boy whose looks and frosty attitude would scare off people who didn't know goats—caused a ruckus. Tommy had to yank his horns while Benjy worked the stick.

"Get your ass out of here, Billy Boy," Tommy said. "You want to live to eat another day or turn into dog food?"

When the man behind the wheel met Tommy's glare in his rearview mirror, the billy came out as if he'd heard the magic word. Tommy shut the trailer gate, and the driver pulled away fast and pissed. When the nanny nuzzled Benjy, he jumped.

"Herbivore," Tommy told him. "Can't eat you."

"No goats in Philly, man. Gimme a break."

Tommy went to the shed that he'd helped fix up, the only place private enough for the nanny to squeeze out her kid. He'd have to put up a gate and cut some windows so she could stay cool, but it would work. The billy followed Tommy and started trying to eat his boot.

"He likes you," Benjy said. "Must know a goat man when he sees one."

"Could you get me some food and water, Brother Ben? Anything handy?"

Benjy headed for the house while Tommy crouched in a sliver of shade to let the goats nuzzle him and sniff his pockets. He loved their acrid smell, the muscular solidity of their bodies. Try knocking a goat down, and you'll end up on the ground yourself.

"You stand strong, don't you?" he said, pushing the goats away hard and feeling them come back even harder. "Glad for what God made you, even if it ain't much?"

❊ ❊ ❊

Connie stopped at the gas station for the makings of what she called a Jesus freak potluck: canned foods Pete said they liked (creamed corn, meatless chili, kidney beans), carrots and apples, and day-old bread. Baby Ruth bars, apparently Richie Thorpe's secret vice, would be dessert. She bought some Michelob to test Tommy, thinking free beer might keep him at home. But who was she kidding? She'd already lost him and had to fight to get him back. Had to kneel down in the muck and brawl with the people who took him.

"I'm working for God now, Mom!" Connie said, in a voice that sounded nothing like her actual son's, as she opened up the cans and spitefully poured them into one big pot. The phone rang, and she guessed it was Dan, so she let it ring through to the machine. Tommy burst out of nowhere and flung the back door open.

"Goats, Mom! They've got goats! Up at Wesley's house. C'mon!"

Connie shook her head, but when Tommy grabbed her elbow, she knew he could toss her over his shoulder and haul her there. She kept pace with him for half the length of Mangum Street but ran out of steam, and when he looked back at her over his shoulder, she wobbled herself like a rag doll to show him how tired she was. He doubled back to her, wrapping an arm around her waist and pulling her against his meaty shoulder. It was exactly how Connie wanted Richie Thorpe to see her. *Mother and son are one*, their intertwined walk would tell him. *You can't break in.*

"That better?" Tommy asked once their legs fell into rhythm.

"Perfect." But it didn't last. Tommy tried to speed up again, and Connie wriggled out from under his arm, so he threw up his hands and plowed ahead.

"Those church people get any money from you yet?" she called after him.

"Yes ma'am. Put it right in the collection box. They don't even have to steal it."

"Don't 'ma'am' me—I'm your mother."

"All the more reason to show you respect, isn't it?"

Tommy tossed her the smartass smirk she couldn't stand, and Connie worried a bit less about him turning into a Jesus robot. He was still Tommy underneath, obnoxious as ever. He started jogging toward the Perrin house, but she kept her own pace so she wouldn't sweat. "Sweat means nerves," her father used to say. "Nerves mean you're scared of people seeing who you really are." Connie looked up at the late-afternoon sun and felt the pivot point moving into place inside her, the long lost piece that made her capable of letting the wind blow her anywhere.

"You twist in the wind," her mother used to tell her before she became Daddy's little businesswoman. Her mother never understood that this was her gift, her way of holding all possibilities inside her simultaneously. If she waited for the right wind, she could trust that it would lift her up and drop her where it needed her to go next. She rejected Richie in July of 1962 because she had to twist in the wind and see where it would send her, and that's why she came back to Suborney in July of 1980 too.

Connie saw the goats tethered to the front porch nibbling corn-cobs that Tommy's cult buddies held out for them. She counted seven people clumped in a half-circle around the goats, one her son and another—she recognized his stance and the cut of his ass—Richie Thorpe. Thicker now, even more full of muscle. Still with the chip on his shoulder that she knew so well from her son.

"Hey Mom!" Tommy called. They all turned and looked at her sideways, like they knew exactly who she was. Thorpe, with a grimy wetback hat on, threw her a single glance before turning away, almost frightened, to take his turn with the cob.

"Pleased to meet you, ma'am," Worrell said. "We hear you know your goats."

"Raised a few," Connie told them, pointing at Tommy. "That two-legged one too."

"Meanie," Tommy said back. "This gal's gonna kid any minute. See that tail?"

Connie stepped through the half-circle and checked out the liga-ments near the nanny's tail. When Thorpe stepped back to give her room, the billy butted him in the thigh and gave everybody a laugh. Tommy grabbed the billy's horns and tussled with him.

"I'm guessing tomorrow night," Connie told them. "She won't kid unless she's used to the place. You got somewhere to put her?"

Everybody looked to Thorpe for an answer, and when Connie looked, too, she finally saw the bashed-in cheek that people talked about. It made him look like something from before humans, come to make humans strong again. Connie's hand flinched toward her own cheek, and she knew she was in a deeper game than she could handle. She couldn't beat Richie because he had nothing to lose—he'd already lost his face, so there was no telling what else he'd be willing to give up.

"Tommy thought that shed might work," Thorpe said, pointing. "But you're the one who knows goats, ma'am."

"*Knew* goats. I haven't had any since we got here when Tommy was—how old, Tom-Tom?"

"Six," her son replied, scruffing the billy's back.

Connie latched onto Richie's eyes, which didn't offer her even the vaguest recognition. What her own eyes offered him she couldn't name. He had the upper hand because he'd been preparing for this moment for years, not for a week, like she had. Sixteen years in prison, plus every second since he got out. She couldn't beat him, but she wouldn't just give Tommy away either. Richie would have to tear him away.

"Will the shed work, ma'am?" Thorpe asked her.

"Sure. Get some hay on the floor and a gate up. Keep her outside in the shade when the sun's high, and keep the billy *out* once she stops walking around."

"Can we count on you for help if there's problems?" the tall one asked.

"I'll check in tomorrow. She won't kid in the heat of the day, not this time of year. Why'd you folks get a pregnant nanny if none of you know how to take care of one?"

"Somebody had to get rid of them quick," Thorpe said. "Would've slaughtered 'em."

"Well, that's kind of you." Connie knew it was time to get face to face with the enemy at last. She stepped around the goats and held her hand out to him. "I'm Connie Sandor. I guess I'll be seeing you around."

"Richard Thorpe." He hadn't gotten used to the idea of shaking women's hands yet since it wasn't something men did much of before he went to prison. But he let her squeeze his and pump it twice before he pulled it back. "Fine son you've raised there."

"Thank you," Connie said. "All on my own. No father."

In the half-second after their hands separated, their minds slipped toward the last time their skins touched, to that night by the fence in Nebraska City. But that tunnel back in time was blocked, filled in with concrete and blood. Connie shook a few more hands and strode off, certain that Richie had gotten hold of those goats to punish her. To tell her, "I know everything you've loved and everything you've done since the day you took my child from me." She looked back to see Tommy sitting on the billy like a bronc rider. Thorpe stood next to him, whooping and waving his hat like a rodeo cowboy.

"Yee haw! Get 'im, sonny boy, go go go!" Richie shouted.

Sonny. Connie noticed the word and wondered how many times Tommy would need to hear it before he got the message. "How could that child not know?" she asked the sky on the way home. "How could anybody look at them next to each other and not know?"

✳ ✳ ✳

Tommy decided to sleep outside with the goats that night, but Thorpe insisted on putting the honor up to a vote. Tommy was the only one nominated, and everybody voted for him on the condition that he didn't complain when they called him "Goatmaster." He set his sleeping bag by the shed's new makeshift gate, then tethered the billy far enough away so he wouldn't get butted and nuzzled all night. He wrestled with the billy a bit, then went into the shed and hugged the nanny. She'd be fine—the windows he cut let plenty of air through.

"It's gonna be all right, sweetheart," he told her, thinking back on all the goats he'd seen kidding in Bird City. "Millions of goats have done it before you. Done it a few times yourself, I'd guess."

Tommy got sad thinking about the goats back in Bird City because he and his mom had run off in such a hurry and never gone back. Did anybody take care of those goats, or did they just starve to death? Being around goats again gave him a dream for his future that didn't involve getting stuck in Suborney or dying in Iran or trying to chase down a New York father who might have OD'd on heroin years ago. He could go back to Bird City for a while, see if anybody needed help with the kids and grandkids of the goats he'd grown up with. He could even raise some water for the farmers out there if the land was dry.

"Goat-*mas*-ter!" sang Mother Meg and Sister Melanie from the lantern-lit porch, but they were gone by the time Tommy walked up the steps. He saw Brother Zypanski ducking through the front door with a bundle against his shoulder: Tessy, wrapped in a blanket with her face half-covered. Her legs dangled by his ribs, with clubfeet too stubby to ever stand on, as Zypanski sat on the freshly installed porch swing.

"She can get scared sometimes," he said, rocking the swing as gently as he could. "So I'm going to sit here and let you come up slow. Isn't that right, baby girl? Aren't you a scaredy little monster?"

Tessy mewed as she reached up to Zypanski's chin, her spiky fingers bunching up like a talon. She looked barely bigger than a cocker spaniel. Her elbow bent like a regular one, but it was as thin as a baby's. Tommy had never been around a creature so deformed, so wrongly made. A creature who made you put your money where your mouth was if you ever said, "We're all God's children" or "All men are created equal." Tessy moved her hand to Zypanski's mouth, and he pretended to bite her fingers off, which got a giggle out of her.

"She's got a regular giggle," Tommy said, finally sitting on the swing.

"Sometimes. She's a mess in the body, but not in the soul."

"Is she your daughter?"

"Somebody shoved her into a stack of pallets to die, and I'm the guy who pulled her out." Zypanski leaned down to kiss her. "So I guess that makes her my daughter, yeah."

Zypanski told the whole story once Tommy put his hand close enough for Tessy to touch it. Eight years ago he'd been walking back to his apartment at four in the morning in Omaha, after a night of drinking and drugging, when he heard Tessy cry. She sounded more like a regular baby then because the parts that pressed against each other now hadn't grown yet. He pulled the pallets off until he saw this naked thing, only one limb out of four fully shaped.

"It was a test," he said. "God wanted to know if I gave a shit or not, so I said 'Yes sir, I *do* give a shit.' So I picked her up and took her home. Ain't that right, Tess?"

Zypanski hugged Tessy so hard that she gurgled, then he handed her to Tommy and stepped inside. Tommy had never held a child before, let alone a severely deformed one. But he'd held baby goats and figured he ought to hold Tessy like one. He settled her into the crook of his arm, then pulled back the blanket to see her whole face. It looked like somebody had twisted it sideways—her jaw didn't close all the way, and the bottom half didn't line up with the top. She had a cleft lip and a stub of a nose, with the tiniest nostrils Tommy had ever seen.

"Hey," Tommy told her. "Nice making music with you." He lifted the blanket more and saw a spine so out of whack that her hips and shoulders didn't line up any better than her face. Tessy reached out her half-good hand to him, and Tommy kissed it like a prince.

"We don't know how long she'll be with us," Zypanski said through the window. "So we love her while we can."

"Love her while we can," Tommy repeated, staring into Tessy's spongy-wet eyes, and his jaw and intestines trembled. His head spun in widening counterclockwise circles, and his hands dripped with sweat where he held her. She opened her mouth, took in a loud breath, and started to sing.

"*Ah aaaaaah ah ah ah aaaah aaaaaah.*" It came out clear and perfect, and then she nodded at Tommy, trying to get him to sing it back. She repeated it, then thunked his chest twice and looked up at him. When she caught his eyes, the words came to him like his mouth wasn't his.

"*I come to seek the an-gels,*" he sang, and Tessy nodded. She sang her tune without words again, and Tommy sang his words back to her in a soft, high voice he didn't know he still had. The voice of the boy in Bird City who chased dragonflies with Jesus and counted leaves on trees with Jesus and never wondered why. Being with Jesus was something you did because you were alive, that's all. Anybody could do it. Tessy sang her line again, and the other Sons and Daughters, huddled inside by the window, sang Tommy's words back to her. Round and round it went, with Tessy and Tommy and the people inside, until everybody knew exactly what side in life they stood on.

II

Tuesday, July 15

Before work, Connie drove up to look in on the goats — and on Tommy, though she couldn't find him anywhere. She checked the nanny's rump and decided it still wasn't time. Yes, her tail ligaments were too receded to feel, and she'd gotten nuzzly like goats do before they kid, but she didn't have any discharge yet. That would come tonight when it cooled down again, and Connie tried to remember what she'd need for the delivery. Iodine for the umbilical cord, buckets and towels, something sweet for the nanny.

"Anything else you need, you just say so," Connie told the goat as she closed the shed gate that Tommy had made. "Been a while for me, not so long for you."

The Perrin house door gently closed, and Connie saw Richie ambling toward her, looking older and younger than she did at the same time. Older from the hard years of prison, younger because he hadn't been dragging around a mountain of lies like she had. Connie had always been a solo mama bear, shielding her son from the deceptions of strangers without a husband to help her, and she clung tightly to that role as Thorpe approached. She lengthened her neck like she always did when dealing with people who wanted things from her. The drivers and the loaders, some of them as thick around as Richie, wanting to know why this paycheck was smaller than the last one.

"Thanks for starting my shift," Thorpe said as he leaned, a respectful distance away from her, against the gate. "Tommy just came in to get me."

"I see a goat, I want to take care of it. Living on a goat farm does that to you."

"Looks like you came a long way from that goat farm, ma'am." Thorpe gestured at her clothes, her too-good shoes. She dusted off their toes with the back of her hand.

"Don't call me 'ma'am.' You can call me *Miss* Sandor, if you have to call me at all." She watched the nanny try to stand, then give up. "So are we going to pretend we don't know each other face to face, too, or just in front of other people? I need some rules, Richie."

"You make the rules, Nettie. You always—"

"Number one is you can't call me that anymore. It's Connie. Say it."

"Connie." Thorpe put a tiny snarl into it, then shifted an inch closer to her.

"What do you want with Tommy?" she asked, checking around for spies. "Don't say it's just to let him know who you are. You could've done that a week ago."

"I want to be a father to him. Like I always did."

"I'm not sure you know what being a father means."

"Probably something different for every man. My way of being a father'll be different from your dad's."

"Don't even bring him up." She whirled around at him. "You kill—"

"I didn't kill him, *Connie*. You saw him run into that fire."

He watched her hand flinch back for a slap and wanted to grab her wrist to stop it, but he'd promised the Sons and Daughters to be an absolute gentleman with her. Promised Nick Rachmann to never lay a hand on her because most teenage girls in the world would have run away from a man like him, just like she did. Thorpe watched Connie turn her eyes back to the nanny and felt the barrier between them—something that seemed like he could reach straight through it but might swallow up his arm if he tried.

"You haven't told him who you are yet," Connie said. "I'd see it in his eyes if you did. Are you laying out clues for him till he figures it out himself?"

"I got no plan except being a father. God wants—"

"Do *not* throw that word around like you own it, Richie. You knocked up a sixteen-year-old virgin. You think God wanted that?"

"From the looks of Tommy now, I'd say yes. Probably wanted his mother and father to get married, though."

"Is that what comes next? Happy ever after?" Connie laughed and pushed back from the gate, pasting on her least sincere smile. "Well, enjoy our little town! If the heat doesn't get you, the brush fires will. But you're on good terms with fire, if I remember right."

She hopped into her truck and waved goodbye to Richie with a teaspoon hand like the queen of England. Connie looked behind the shed as she drove off to make sure that nobody had overheard them, but his people had to know the truth already. They were helping him put the squeeze on her, squatting in her town and torturing her with their super-Christian sweetness until the shame got to her and she puked out the truth.

"You know that Thorpe guy with the cheek?" she'd ask Tommy casually one day. "Well, he's your—"

Connie couldn't finish that sentence, not even in her imagination, and as soon as she left Suborney, she felt trapped in her truck. Once she hit Highway 87 going north, she rolled down her window and undid her seat belt because the only solution to her problem that she could see was to hit something bigger than her and get flung out onto the road. Let some state patrolman find her there with one last breath on her lips. Let it be Dan Stannard—she didn't care. It would serve him right. That weak, piece of shit man who couldn't even save her from herself.

* * *

"So are you Brother Tommy yet?" Connie asked after her son insisted on praying before supper that night. She grilled up some lamb chops, which used to be his favorite, but instead he ate a huge bowl of steamed broccoli with olive oil and tons of pepper. "Would you even tell me if you were?"

"You know how cults work, right? I have to give them your house and bank account first, *then* maybe they'll make me a brother."

"Ha, ha. Is that what that Richie guy's saying? Their grand pooh-bah?"

"Mother Meg kinda runs things. You should come up and eat with us, Ma. Work with us. See the difference between us and what you're so afraid of."

"I'm working with you already, aren't I? With the goats?"

"That's a start." Tommy cut off a bite of lamb and put it in his mouth out of habit, then gently spit it into a napkin. "I just wish we could talk about God together—that's what it comes down to. You always treated God like some kind of disease you were waiting to pass on through me."

"Not always," Connie said. "It was easier when you were younger."

"Why? Because you think God is kid stuff, like the Easter Bunny?"

"I didn't say that."

"Then what changed?" he asked. "Why's it harder now?"

Because your dad runs a church, and he's got me cornered, she thought of saying, but the words stayed in her mouth. "When you were young it was sweet," she said instead. "Now it's more— aggressive. I guess that's the word. All that stuff I hear on the radio doesn't help."

"Ah," Tommy said. He chewed his broccoli in silence, leaving Connie to mentally try out excuses for why Jesus pissed her off so much now. She had to be prepared for Tommy to push her on the question, and he'd surely point out that the Michigan people last year hadn't bothered her nearly so much. Maybe he'd put two and two together and realize *Aha! My mom hates Jesus because my father loves Jesus, so my father must be Richie Thorpe!*

Then, like he was reading her mind, Tommy wrapped her right hand in both of his.

"Remember that day in Bird City?" he asked, twice as calm as she'd ever seen him. "When I first got the 'Jesus fever,' like you called it?"

"Of course."

"Well, that's how I want to live the rest of my life. Nothing separated me from God. Everything was—" He pulled back his hands and wobbled them in front of his chest like he was polishing a giant snowball. "It was all *one*, and I was part of the *one*." His hands fell back to the table. "I want that for me, and I want to tell people about it so they can have it for themselves. Can you still love me if that's who I want to be?"

My son is a man, Connie thought to herself, and she smiled as she told Tommy, "Let me think about it." Then they went to the living room to watch the six o'clock news and eat mini ice cream sandwiches on the couch. It was day 253 for the hostages, and Richard Queen was in serious but stable condition. Jimmy Carter was still the weakest president in American history, and Ronald Reagan still waited for his chance to save the country. In Detroit they went crazy for him at the Republican National Convention, saying, "Let's Make America Great Again!" every thirty seconds. Connie knew she'd vote for him, and now she just wanted him to shut up until he took over. But she couldn't say that in front of Tommy, just like she couldn't say, "Did you ever wonder why your Jesus buddies picked Suborney?" or "Don't you think it's weird how they fixed up a church in Bird City too?"

How much did Tommy know? How much was he hiding? The anchorman talked about a hit-and-run up in Denver that killed a mom and her twelve-year-old son, and during commercials Tommy cleaned up in the kitchen. He hummed some church song over and over, and Connie counted the notes to make sure it wasn't the same song Richie had hummed that night by the fence in Nebraska City. It had seven notes instead of five, so it couldn't be.

"I see your cult's teaching you some manners," Connie said when she saw him drying dishes. "Why couldn't I do that?"

"I'm going up, Mom. Want me to bring anything for the nanny?"

He was turning into a dependable man, the kind who took responsibilities and kept them, and for that Connie Sandor took a moment to be proud of him. Of herself too. Whatever Tommy turned into after Richie got his claws in all the way, she could be proud of turning him into a son worth stealing in the first place.

"Anything I should bring up, Mom?" Tommy asked again. "For the goats?"

"No, I've got everything. Let me get some grubbies on. I'll see you up there."

"Sure." But Tommy didn't move. "Sheriff Bullshit's not coming back, is he?"

"Probably not. Does that make you happy? Never having to call him 'Dad'?"

"The only guy I want to call 'Dad' is probably sticking a needle in his arm right now."

"You don't know Drake was like that."

"And you don't know he *wasn't*. I'm not the one who chased Stannard out, am I?"

"Would you be happy if I said yes?"

"A week ago," Tommy told her. "Not now."

"Not now that you're on Jesus's side, you mean?"

"Yeah, pretty much. Jesus isn't real big on 'hate thy neighbor.' See you up there."

Ten minutes later Connie Sandor was walking past the abandoned church carrying a blue plastic bucket in each hand. She wore cuffed jeans, cheap orange flip-flops, and a white V-neck T-shirt of Tommy's that she'd pulled from the laundry basket. She wasn't walking to meet her destiny, she told herself, just walking to make sure that one more kid goat came into this world alive. One bucket had towels, and the other had dental floss, molasses, udder wash, sponges, iodine. She tried making a checklist, remembering what order to do things in, but it would be easier to let her hands do the thinking. Tommy heard her coming and popped his head out of the shed.

"She's almost there," he said. "Face on her hooves, ass up."

"Well, that's a pretty picture." Connie looked at the sky and figured she'd coax the kid out by sundown. Nannies who kept pushing after that always ended up pushing all night. Thorpe, out of view at first, stood up next to Tommy and opened the shed gate for her. Connie stepped back at the sight of them side by side.

"I should let your mom handle things," Thorpe said.

"It's all right." She handed him the buckets. "Would you get us some warm water, please, Mr. Thorpe?"

"Yes ma'am. Already on the stove."

"Not too hot. Half and half it." She watched Thorpe walk away, gauging how prison had changed his gait, then stepped into the shed. The nanny felt her close and bleated. "Hey gal." Connie scratched along her spine. "It'll be just like last time. You're a pro."

She kept scratching while Tommy stroked the nanny's head and whispered to her. When Thorpe came back with the water, Connie started mixing the udder wash so she could scrub down the nanny's vulva. The goat had to be thirteen at least and must have birthed eight or nine kids, so she knew that once the scrub-down happened, it was time to get to work. Connie washed her with the sponge, and sure enough, the nanny's water broke.

"You know the drill," Tommy told the nanny as Thorpe leaned back from the gate at the smell.

"You're not a farm boy, are you?" Connie asked him.

"Not even close," Thorpe said.

Connie kept washing down the nanny, even though she didn't need to anymore. "This is your son being born," she wanted to tell Richie. "This is your Jesus and Mary and Joseph in the manger. Anything more you want from me?"

* * *

Just before sundown, after Richie walked off to who knows where, Connie reached inside the nanny and pulled a kid out by its legs. The Sons and Daughters named him Sir Thomas and wanted to hold him right away, but she said to wait until he walked away from his mother. They had to be satisfied with standing at the gate and watching the nanny lick the kid clean. Occasional whispered *Amen*s slipped out of people's mouths.

"Are they praying *for* the goats or *to* the goats?" Connie whispered to Tommy as he helped with the cleanup, but he didn't acknowledge it. As she stepped through the clump of Richie's people to head home, the tall one caught her eye.

"For Tommy's mom," he said, "in thanks for the life she's brought into this world, we all pray."

After the long *Amen*, Tommy prayed extra hard for his mom the way he used to when he first started: holding his breath, clenching his jaw, clasping his fingers together so tightly that his knuckles went white. Then the prayer turned to hate for his mother, but that hate squirted out from between his folded palms like a bar of wet soap. He couldn't hold hate, wasn't meant to. For a delicious second his bones and muscles felt like they hung free on his spine—no hate, no weight, no burden to carry. *No use carrying it*—hadn't Jesus told him that by the reservoir, those exact words? Tommy took in one big breath and tracked it through his arteries, through his capillaries. *How long can you keep it flowing, Brother Tom-Tom?* he asked himself. *God's love, going where it wants to go without you getting in its way?*

Then they all smelled smoke on the air coming from the north, and Connie stopped walking. Not nearby, not frightening, but like an unwatched campfire that might cause trouble later. Tommy and Connie had been through enough brushfire seasons to know it wasn't a controlled burn—usually with those, if they were close enough to smell, they were close enough to see. Connie figured it was Richie starting a practice fire, getting ready for the one that would come for her and her alone.

"Is it close?" Melanie asked.

"Five or ten miles, I'd guess," Connie told her. "Probably won't make it here, but you might want to get your clothes off the line before they smell like ashtrays."

Zypanski's face flopped like dough, and he ran toward the house, and the others glumly went to gather their clean clothes. Connie stepped back into the shed and picked up her forgotten buckets.

"Coming home to celebrate?" she asked Tommy. "Got a couple Michelobs left. You can have 'em both."

But Tommy shook his head. A curt little wobble that said, *These are my people now.* Connie gave him a fake smile and headed home, swinging those buckets like a younger, freer self. It wouldn't be long before she was that free, she knew. One way or another.

* * *

After nighttime prayers Tommy set up his sleeping bag by the shed again, wondering why Thorpe had skipped out and where he'd gone. Sister Mel, who knew the answers to both questions, slipped out the back door after nighttime prayers to find him. She knew her way east by heart to the bottom of a small, sandy arroyo that would be a stream bed if enough rain ever came. There she found Brother T inside his usual twelve-foot square scratched onto the earth, with a tiny fire glowing in the middle of it. The Brothers and Sisters all knew about the cells he drew when he went to pray alone. About how he made one whenever he needed to bind himself in, prevent himself from acting too rashly. But Melanie, who made sure to catch his good eye as she approached, wanted him to be *more* rash.

"How long are you going to torture that boy?" she asked, squatting just outside the cell's border.

"I don't know. I'm a coward."

"Just say the word, and I'll let it slip." She didn't like the tone of her own voice as she said it. Too much like her old, bitchy self, too much like *Miss* Sandor. "I can't stand his mom, but I don't like what you're doing to her. Come out and say it—it's better for everybody."

"I don't know how to do this, Mel. Don't know anybody I can ask either."

"Tell him at morning prayers, how about? Just say, 'Tommy, there's something I've been meaning to tell you.' We'll all be there with you, like we said we would."

"What if he runs?" Thorpe asked. "Then I lose him again."

"And if you don't tell him, he'll never be yours to lose at all."

Melanie dropped from squatting to kneeling but only lasted long enough for a quick prayer because she knew that Brother T needed to be alone. She reached her palm toward him, and he reached over to touch hers briefly, and once she walked away, he pulled the thick, smoky air as far as he could into his lungs. It stung him like ten thousand pinpricks, and he thought of Tessy—how long her lungs would last, whether he should have brought her along at all, what might happen to the Sons and Daughters if she died and the child welfare people said they never should have had her in the first place.

He tried to think of Jesus and Mary but couldn't focus on them long enough. He was too caught up in the world, in the foolish and botched pursuit of his son. And he was *so* close now—done with the search really. All he had to do was say the word, like Melanie wanted him to.

"I'm your father, Tommy," he tried to say, but the words wouldn't slip past his lips. Instead, he managed to say, "Help me make the rain, Nick," and held his hands up by his shoulders the way they did together in prison. He and Nick used to pray so hard that water droplets covered their ceiling, then fell down in the most delicious mist they'd ever felt. Thorpe wanted to feel it on his face again, the inexplicable mist that nourished him. He wanted to sit like he did with Nick in the middle of that dim cell—mouth open, palms upturned in thanks, breathing only when he had to—and wait for God's rain.

It fell down over his cell etched in the dry dirt, not touching anything beyond its borders. A gentle rain, unsteady, just enough for him to know that he could still call the water down. Enough to put out the fire, not much more. He wanted to make it rain with his son too. Just once. *Praise God. Please, God. Let me make the rain with my son.*

12

Wednesday, July 16

By the time Mother Meg gave out jobs for the day, Benjy had already gone with Thorpe to clean up a dead man's house in Fountain. She'd stay with Tessy, trying to keep the air in her room wet so her lungs wouldn't suffer from the brush fire's leftover smoke, and Melanie would stay with Mrs. Culp, who had fallen the day before. Zypanski, Beto, and Worrell would clean out the church, picking out more things for the shelter.

"Mr. Sandor can do goat patrol," she said. "And help me with lunch, once he's done earning profits for The Man over at his junkyard."

"No ma'am," Tommy told her. "Ain't no profit, ain't The Man, ain't my junkyard." He ate a second breakfast as he helped out at Sowell's, then headed to the yard to find a note from Dolman saying, WITH HEAGREN IN SPRINGS. Tommy knew it was a lie—Dolman was ferrying junk up to the shelter on Heagren's dime. He finally had a key, so he didn't need to climb the fence anymore, and once he opened the gate, Tommy drove a junker truck to the southwest corner of the yard to watch Suborney Creek trickle by. He wanted to see if he could still move water, but it had to be useful to somebody. Even something stupid, like raising it up near Sam Kurtep's house so it could wash the dog shit off the road and back onto his lawn where it belonged. But if he tried to move the water an inch, it might move a mile instead. No control yet. Not enough practice. So he did nothing.

Mother Meg would probably ask about the water at lunch. What else could she want with him? To tell him that his new job from God was to make his mom see the light of Jesus, even if it meant getting kicked out of the house like that Pentecostal kid at Widefield High who tried converting his parents? That kid ended up moving to a Jesus commune in Oklahoma, but Tommy wouldn't need to bother moving because the Jesus commune had come to him. When he thought about trying to convert his mom, the water jumped half a foot to remind him what he could do.

It was a slow morning at the yard, with just two customers who didn't find what they wanted, so Tommy decided to finally put the hood on his Vega. He sawed a rectangle where the carburetor would stick up, then filed down the edges until he could run a finger around it and not even feel a bump. At noon he checked his fluid levels for no particular reason, put a BACK SOON sign on the gate, and locked up. He strolled into Wesley's kitchen to find a cheese and tomato sandwich sitting on the island but no Mother Meg. Then Wesley's door closed, and she headed toward him.

"Thanks for lunch," Tommy said. She put her elbows on the island and watched him chew like he was a baby and she'd just fed him his first solid food. "Do I make you miss your son?"

"Anybody who's walking and breathing does."

"I'm sorry he died."

"It was best for everybody."

Tommy nodded and took another bite. Mother Meg stood behind him and slipped a hand under his shirt, settling on a spot between his neck and left shoulder that always felt tight. A place where he knew his body would fail him someday, like Wally Ogrean must have known that his hips would fail him. Her hand hovered over that spot, heating up the air between their skins with fast circles.

"What lives there, Tommy?" said Mother Meg. "Ask yourself."

Then she rubbed and kneaded the spot until they both felt something hard and crunchy beneath his skin. To Tommy it felt like one of those goat head burrs that got stuck to his jeans when he walked the fields. Mother Meg pulled on it slow and steady, then tightened her grip and tugged harder because the burr fought to stay inside him. He felt something tear off deep in his shoulder muscle, where the burr's roots reached, and inhaled sharply as his skin softened and opened up.

"Yesssss." Mother Meg breathed in long and slow and mumbled something Tommy couldn't understand.

"You got a special prayer for doing this witch doctor stuff?"

"Shhhh. Do you want this out of you or not?"

The burr felt more stretchy and stubborn now, and she flicked his skin hard before pinching him again. As the burr came closer to the surface, she rolled it the way Tommy rolled zits when they didn't want to pop. Tommy wondered if Jesus wanted that burr out and pictured him coming to take it, walking toward them with a gleaming white robe like he wore in those goofball born-again velvet paintings. But the robe looked rattier as Jesus came closer, with splatters of blood and mud. Tommy panicked when he saw Jesus's bare, dust-caked feet and his greasy, matted hair. He was constantly dirtied from his job on earth, helping out those poor humans who couldn't help themselves. Tommy felt hopeless and dirty, and the burr pulled back inside him.

"Why'd you do that?" Mother Meg asked. She struck his skin with her sharp fingernails as fast as a rattlesnake, grabbing the burr and pulling it back from its hiding place, and Tommy swore he felt her fingers inside his skin. Pain shot all the way down to his intestines, and something snapped loose, and he smelled a mix between mothballs and wet clay. He didn't know he'd shut his eyes until he opened them to see Mother Meg holding a smooth yellow chunk of what looked like sulfur in her palm. Nothing like a burr at all.

"What's the hell's that?" He tried to take the chunk, but she closed her hand.

"Your hate." Mother Meg laughed. "You want more out, get on the floor."

"Shit yeah." He knelt down, then rolled onto his back and rubbed at a knot on his right pectoral muscle, opposite his heart. "I've been on this floor plenty of times, with Wesley Perrin. You know about him?"

"We pray for him every day. His mom and dad too."

Mother Meg set her fingers to work on the knot. They pressed and circled, discovering its contours. Then they pinched and pulled, not gentle at all, until Tommy flopped on the floor and had to fight just to suck in half a breath. After a solid minute she pulled out another yellow chunk, this one the size of a pea, and the mothball smell made him pass out momentarily. When he came to, she set both chunks in his hand.

"What am I supposed to do with these?" Tommy asked.

"Burn 'em," Mother Meg said. "Take a walk, dig a hole, start a fire, drop 'em in."

"Is that what Brother Thorpe's doing half the time?"

"Ask him yourself."

"I will." Tommy knew just where to burn his hate: east of the junkyard, at the bottom of a sandy little arroyo where he used to play with Wesley. "Can I get this stuff out by myself, or do I have to come to you?"

"You can do it. But it'll take longer, and you'll get greedy, so it'll hurt like hell." She walked across the kitchen and pulled a deck of raggedy blue playing cards from a drawer. "You ever hear of tarot, Mr. Sandor?"

"Sure, there's a chick at school who's way into it. Becca."

Tessy mewed from her room, so Mother Meg checked in on her while Tommy got up and finished his sandwich. The spots on his shoulder and chest felt like giant mosquito bites covered with cigarette burns and doused with alcohol. He set the chunks of hate on the island and watched them like they would move on their own. Mother Meg came back, shuffling the deck faster than Tommy had ever seen a human being shuffle. She set a card in front of him on the island, face down.

"Is this how you make your money?" Tommy asked. "Like Brother Thorpe's dad?"

"I'm not above it when I see a fool who needs to come down a peg. Pick it up."

"Becca's tarot cards are twice that size."

Mother Meg glared, and Tommy turned over a two of hearts. Then she set down the nine of hearts and the jack of clubs, both face up.

"The two says you're a man of humble beginnings but heir to a throne. The nine says chicks dig you so much, you have to beat 'em back with a stick."

"That's not tarot." Tommy mock-poked her shoulder.

"Oh, let an old lady have some fun. The jack means you've asked yourself who you are so many times, you can't even think of one straight answer."

"That's me," Tommy said. Mother Meg shuffled the deck into another blur, then pushed it toward him with three cards sticking out.

"Did you win this house in a poker game?" Tommy asked, pulling the cards free. Four of spades, eight of spades, queen of spades. "The church too?"

"*Spade*'s another word for 'shovel.' Three spades in one pull means you have to dig hard for everything, and the queen means there's a woman above you who's in your way. The four means you're digging for truth, and the eight means you're digging for water." She caught his eye. "But you don't need to *dig* for water, do you?"

The next time she shuffled, Tommy picked out a seven of clubs, a five of diamonds, and a ten of hearts. "I wonder what kind of bullshit you'll pull out of those," he said.

"Five and seven mean you have to go back into your past and find what's not there anymore. The ten means you have to go on a trip to find it."

"Back to Bird City?" he asked. Mother Meg sighed and rolled her eyes, then set down three more cards.

"King of clubs means you need to go to a state that's right next to yours. Three of spades means you need to go to a town named after that state, a town on a big river. Ace of diamonds means you need to find out what happened tomorrow."

"Huh?" He felt as stupid as his face must have looked.

"What happened tomorrow in Nebraska City, Nebraska? Aw heck, Tommy, they told me you were smart."

"Am I picking up your secret stash of dirty dollar bills or what? Are you even telling me why I'm going?"

"Nebraska City, Mr. Sandor." Mother Meg shoved the chunks of hate closer to him. "Figure it out. Don't leave till tomorrow comes, and don't leave till you burn your hate."

❋ ❋ ❋

Tommy sat at the edge of his bed in his underwear, wondering which things he owned were worth taking with him when he left Suborney—possibly forever. Once he found out what happened tomorrow in Nebraska City, whatever the hell that meant, would he keep driving until he got to New York to find his father? Fuck that dream.

"I'm joining the marines, Mom," he shouted, though she wasn't around. "Happy?" The recruiter said he could join at seventeen if his mom signed a form. Why not? Suborney would throw him a party, and he'd get blown to bits fighting for Ronnie Reagan in the desert, then come home in a pine box draped in the American flag that people said he hated so much.

Tommy felt a crunchy spot on the outside of his left thigh, but it took him ten minutes of rubbing and kneading just to get a grip on the hate inside. It felt like a pencil eraser, and he twisted it between his thumb and middle finger. He tugged and squeezed until his leg felt on fire, then closed his eyes and shouted as he pulled out long, lemon-colored hate with roots like a weed still embedded in his skin.

Tommy kept pulling, wanting to know how deep inside him the roots went, but they wouldn't give. *Too greedy.* Mother Meg had warned him about that. What if those chunks of hate were all that held him together? Tommy imagined pulling hate out of himself all day and night, littering the floor with it, then not being able to stand up because his hate had been the only solid thing inside him.

He got scared and flexed his leg to make sure it still worked, and the roots broke off. Tommy cursed and stood up, his leg hurting so badly that he punched it to drive his hate back inside him. When he finally banged the pain away, he passed out on his bed, sleeping hard until he heard a knock at the front door. He got dressed and found Sherry Medina there.

"What happened to you?" she asked as he let her in. "You smell like a campfire."

"Didn't think I'd ever see you again." Tommy bent sideways over the spot on his thigh where he'd pulled out the hate.

"Well, I give a shit about you." Sherry plopped onto Connie's spot on the couch. "It was nice having a boyfriend, even if everybody hated him."

"Was I that bad?" Tommy sat on the other end of the couch and wondered if this would be the day they finally did it—when he felt broken, unsure of who he was. It would be love that stripped off their clothes, not lust, so Jesus and Mary might not mind so much.

"Really, Tommy." Sherry wrinkled her nose at him. "You don't smell good."

"I gotta go to Nebraska. Church stuff."

"Church stuff? How Jesus-y are you getting?"

"Things are different, Sher. I don't regret all the stuff we did, but I don't want—"

"I'm not here about the stuff we did," she told him. "I just want to know you're okay. You disappeared."

"And I might disappear even more." Tommy felt something moving in the tendons above his right knee, and his hand slid there as if to nab a crawling bug. What kind of hate lived in that spot? Was it for somebody specific or just floating free? Sherry put her hand over his for a moment, then stood bolt upright at the sound of an approaching engine.

"Just my mom coming back from work." Tommy took hold of her dangling hand and kissed it—just like he'd kissed Tessy's, a simple human love without greed. Sherry stood up to watch Connie check out her rusty Maverick, then sat back down next to Tommy and held his hand like they were old people watching TV.

"Who's this?" asked Connie when she came in, and Sherry introduced herself. Tommy added that she was a straight A student who'd already arranged a free ride through college. Sherry said a quick goodbye and made Tommy promise to be in touch when he got back, then Connie sat down in her still-warm spot on the couch. She put on a fake, ditzy smile and stuck out her breasts—evidently her best Sherry Medina imitation.

"I'm waiting for the barrage of questions, Mom."

"Oh, you'll get it." Connie dropped her chest back to normal.

"I didn't knock her up. Never even slept with her."

"Sure."

"I *didn't*." The tone of her *sure* drove Tommy instantly apeshit. "And if I did knock her up, I'd marry her. She knows that."

"Good for her. What's this trip she was talking about?"

"I'm going to Nebraska City," Tommy said. "Pick up something for the Sons and Daughters."

"Like what?" Connie felt her hands shaking and jammed them under her thighs. "A bag of drugs?"

Tommy smiled and said nothing. He liked being the one with the secret, even a made-up one, especially since it made his mom so nervous. Sweat rose from her upper lip, and her jaw started to tremble, and without another word she holed herself up in the bathroom, even sliding the latch shut. Connie sat on the closed toilet seat and felt like Wile E. Coyote in a Bugs Bunny cartoon, concocting evil plans while a one-ton iron block hung suspended over her head by a thread. If Tommy went to Nebraska City, he'd know everything. People there still knew about the fire. She heard Tommy scurrying around in his room and swearing underneath his breath and felt a sharp pain on the right side of her abdomen. Appendicitis? It couldn't be, hers got taken out when she was fourteen.

"What's the matter, Tom-Tom?" she asked him through the door.

"You know I hate it when you talk to me from the bathroom." Tommy slammed his own door and wrapped his chunks of hate in a bandana that he slid into his sax case, along with a change of clothes and his red windbreaker.

"What the hell's in Nebraska City?" Connie called extra loud.

"Don't talk to me from the toilet!" Tommy shouted to get the sound through both closed doors. He looked through his closet, but he didn't need anything there except the sixty dollars hidden in his winter coat. He yanked on a stuck dresser drawer, looking for his condoms so he could throw them away somewhere. Connie gathered up enough spit to swallow an emergency Valium, then knocked on her son's door.

"Smells like you've been smoking something," she said.

"Nope. Staying clean for dear old Ma, remember? You sound scared."

"My son might be running drugs for a cult, for all I know. You know any mom in the world who *wouldn't* be scared right now?"

Tommy opened the door and rolled his eyes. "We're not a cult, and we don't do drugs. We're an alcohol-free Christian intentional community—except for the communion wine."

"So it's *we* now?"

"It's *we*, Mom. Where've you been?" Tommy grabbed his sax case and tried to get past her, but Connie stood firm in the doorway.

"Are you going to Nebraska City to fetch more goats?" she asked him. "Fetch a few more thieves whose souls need saving?"

"You're only fighting me 'cause I feel God and you don't. You can start feeling God, or you can get the hell out of my way."

"That doesn't sound like somebody who loves God. Why Nebraska City? If you're so desperate to get out of here, just go to New York already. I'll give you your money now."

"Here's what I think of New York." Tommy ripped down the subway map and saw nothing behind it—no secret window, no clues to his true self written in unfamiliar languages. He crumpled it into a ball the size of his fist, then threw it at his mother's crossed arms.

"Don't *throw* shit at me." Connie kicked the balled-up map back at him. "Look at what those people are doing to you. You're only hurting yourself."

"Do I look like I'm hurt?" He flexed a bicep in her face. "Huh? Do I?"

"I'm not letting you through this door, Thomas Gregory Sandor. I don't care how full of muscle you think you are. I'm your mother, and you're seventeen. You are *not* going to Nebraska City for those people."

"No." Tommy said, instantly calm. "I'm going to Nebraska City for *me*."

He turned and headed for his window, using the sax case as a battering ram and smashing its bottom pane. He cleared away the shards and climbed through the frame, hopping down to the ground and turning to smile at Connie. She came right to the window, so he could almost whisper to her.

"Don't worry, Mama, we'll fix it. Us Sons and Daughters are handy that way." Then he winked—that damn Richie Thorpe wink, which she'd fallen for the first time she saw it—and was gone.

* * *

After she checked in on the goats at six o'clock, Connie tried another strategy: *love thy enemy*. Isn't that what the born-agains believed, at least officially? Except the Iranians, of course—apparently, they didn't deserve our love anymore and deserved to be killed. Oh, and the blacks and gays and liberals, too, while we were at it. Clean up the country. She couldn't stand that strain of born-agains any more than Tommy could, with *lovelovelove* dripping out of their mouths and *hatehatehate* itching to come out through their trigger fingers. Now that she'd stopped sleeping with Dan, she felt even less compulsion to try understanding them for his brother's sake. She was the Whore of Babylon, after all.

The nanny and kid were fine, happily suckling together. Connie willed the Valium to kick in even further as she walked from the goat shed to the front door of the Perrin house, pushing its pearl-white bubbles of calm into her fear-tightened muscles. She knocked on the front door, and it opened quickly. The woman with the long black hair and bangs, who Connie hadn't liked from the get-go, tightened her lips and cocked her head sideways.

"I'm not here to take him back," Connie said before Melanie's thin lips could open. "I wanted to tell you the goats look fine and to see how my son's living."

"You're welcome to come eat with us. We're just digging in."

She followed Melanie through the living room, which had a garish Jesus and Mary mural on the biggest wall and folded-up sleeping bags all over the floor, and heard Tommy's voice coming from Donna Perrin's kitchen. It looked bare except for Ike's island, covered with beans, corn, carrots, bread, bananas, and smashed muffins that looked like they'd been in the trash. Richie stood in line, spooning food into a red-striped bowl from a set Connie had tossed into the church two years ago. Tommy stood two spots behind him.

"Evening," Thorpe told Connie, giving her the same half-smile that he used to toss her back in Nebraska City whenever they met in public. Not soaking her in like a poor orphan staring at a pot of gold, the way he did when they were alone.

"Glad you let me in," Connie replied. The one-handed Mexican gave her another red-striped bowl, and she got behind him in line. She reached for the light switch and flicked it, but no light came. "My son knows how to jack the wires. Don't you, Tommy?"

"Illegal and immoral," Tommy said back as he surveyed the food before him. Melanie got behind Connie with a paper plate.

"First things first," Melanie told her. "We want to get that church fixed up, then we'll worry about turning the lights on."

"Well, you have your priorities," Connie said. "That's admirable."

Mother Meg made the introductions, and a cheer went up when she said that Connie hailed from Bird City. Connie opened her mouth to say, "Actually, I'm from Nebraska City," but she didn't have the guts. And they knew the truth about her anyway—she could tell from their faces. They'd circle around her and shuffle in to squeeze her to death if Richie gave the order, right then and there.

"Actually, my mom's from McCook," Tommy filled in. "We moved to Bird City when I was a bun in the oven."

She nodded at him the way she nodded at her mother, as if they'd both shared in the creation of the lie and were equally invested in its safekeeping. Once bowls and plates were full, Zypanski wheeled the island toward the sink, and everybody sat in a circle with their dishes on the floor to hold hands. Because Connie was next to Beto, she had to hold his stump of a wrist. It was Benjy's turn to say grace, and he thanked not only God for the food and the beautiful world they got to live in but also Connie Sandor for helping with the goats and for raising a good kid who stayed out of trouble.

"Which most of us had a hard time doing," Benjy added, and everybody laughed before the *Amen*. Tommy added a prayer for the Perrin family, and they polished off their bowls in three minutes. When Zypanski stood at the island to mash up leftovers for Tessy, Thorpe asked Connie to tell them about the Perrin family. She did, keeping it superficial until Tommy piped in that Ike hit Donna in the ribs so much that they were always bruised.

Then Tommy took over the conversation and talked about playing football with Wesley until after sundown on the night of the shooting, with him pretending to be Steelers linebacker Jack Lambert and Wesley pretending to be Vikings quarterback Fran Tarkenton.

"Then we punched each other in the chest a couple times and said, 'Good game,' like always," Tommy said. "And that was it. Three in the morning, everybody heard the shots."

He fought back tears harder than Connie had ever seen him and stood up to get more food. Thorpe got up to stand in front of him and punched him in the chest twice, and Tommy nodded hard before returning the punches. Then he put his head against Thorpe's shoulder a moment, biting back tears until he couldn't. He cried until he got sick of it, soaking half of Thorpe's dirty shirt. Richie sat back down and looked at Connie with a softness his eyes hadn't possessed years ago. A gentleness that came from defeat and loss and longing.

See that? those eyes told her. *It's what our son was missing, and now he's got it.*

She let her own eyes be just as softly accepting and wondered if she was fated to throw herself back into Richie's web. Connie knew she could drop all her lies in an instant—come clean in five seconds and end all the fighting between who she was and who she told the world she was. *Follow Richie Thorpe and you'll know exactly where you belong*, the walls around her said. *Because you'll be with him, and he belongs any damn place he plants his feet.*

But Richie was her past, not her future. She could swallow a bowl or two of pride, but going back to him would mean swallowing tubs of it every day. It would mean facing the lie she told her son, and she'd rather make a new lie. Build a new name and a new past, then hold out her arms until the wind took her somewhere new.

13

Tommy got up at four in the morning and hustled to the arroyo, knowing in his marrow that Thorpe was his father. But the knowledge wouldn't rise past his throat, and it pooled there like bile he couldn't throw up or swallow back down. He walked double time to keep up with the self he was turning into. A freak who could pull hate out through his skin. Water Boy, who could make creeks rise and fall.

He slid down the bank of the arroyo and sat between two yucca plants, then pulled down his jeans to see the spot where he'd broken off his hate too soon. A tight lump rose on his thigh, like the boils he got on his neck sometimes. Mother Meg would take care of it when he got back from Nebraska City, Tommy thought, though he didn't plan to ever come home. If he did, he wanted Suborney to be gone—the whole damn town, burned or drowned or packed up and carted off in the night. He pinched the chunks of hate out of his handkerchief and dug a hole with his boot heel, then knelt and dropped them inside it and prayed. *Lead me to my father, dead or alive.*

Tommy lit a match, and the chunks slowly caught. He leaned down to breathe in their smoke, which smelled like metal shavings and cinnamon, and they burned to ash in another minute. Then he headed for the Jesus and Mary house, where Mother Meg waited for sunrise in her yellow lounge chair.

"How'd it burn?" she asked.

"Fine. I can go now, right?"

"You ought to say goodbye to the goats first."

Tommy blew one goodbye kiss to her and another to the Brothers and Sisters still asleep inside, then headed for the shed. He found Thorpe crumpled in a corner, opposite the nanny and kid.

"You're nowhere or you're everywhere," Tommy said. "How'd the goats treat you?"

"Barrel of laughs. I hear you're going on a trip."

"Yeah, Nebraska. Going to see my grandma."

"Don't lie, Tommy. We're the ones you don't have to lie to, remember? That's what you said, once upon a time." Thorpe stood and leaned against the gate, face to face with his son. "Hope you find what you need there. You're coming back, right?"

"Do I look like a kid who knows what he's doing?" Tommy turned to look east, as if Nebraska City were flying straight at him and he had to duck.

"Need any cash?" Thorpe reached into a pocket for a thick wad of singles. Some were dark around the edges, as if they'd been dipped in mud.

"Thanks." Tommy stuffed the wad into his pocket. "How'd they all get dirty?"

"Buried treasure." Thorpe winked.

"Who buried it? Is that what I'm supposed to go find out?"

"Maybe, Mr. Sandor." Thorpe scratched at his bad cheek. "God's got plans for you that I don't know about, and I wouldn't understand 'em if I did."

Thorpe watched his son walk off with the broad, loping stride he thought was all his own. He could've told Tommy everything, but it felt too late. His son was better off finding his own truth in Nebraska City, like we're all meant to. Mother Meg came out to the shed and saw Thorpe hunched over the gate.

"Happy now?" he asked her.

"If you wanted to make me happy, you would've told him a week ago." She put a hand to the back of his neck and stroked it. "How about yourself? You happy now?"

"When have I ever been happy? I took a man's life, and I won't give my son his. You think I've got a chance in hell of being happy?"

* * *

Tommy got to Nebraska City at two in the afternoon, worried that whatever he was supposed to see happening today had already ended. A trial? A public execution? He looked around for a parade or street fair, and when he saw nothing, he went to the public library and asked the smartest-looking person he saw to help him. That turned out to be Mrs. Petorak at the reference desk, a tall, sixtyish lady with shoulders like a man's and gray hair that matched her polyester suit.

"I need to find out something that happens today," Tommy blurted out.

"That's hard to say." She looked him up and down, then settled on his face. "There's still quite a bit of today left."

"Somebody sent me here. They said it already happened, so maybe it's another year."

"What's your name? When were you born?"

"Tommy Sandor, 1963."

"Sandor?" Mrs. Petorak drew in a sharp breath through her nose, then seemed to stop breathing entirely. "Not a name from around here."

Tommy tried to look behind her eyes, but her face went stony and he couldn't read it. She didn't like him or his kind—that's all he got from her. She motioned him to a table and started bringing over big red binders of newspapers, three at a time. He flipped backward through each year's compiled July to September *Nebraska City News-Press*, laughing at the stupid goings-on of a stupid nowhere town, even though his own town was twice as nowhere and five times stupider. New sewer pipes. A boy standing on a horse. Old people celebrating their fiftieth anniversary. From the way Mother Meg talked, he focused on the big headlines, but by 1972 nothing earth-shattering had shown up in the July 17 paper—or on the two days to either side of it.

"Where are you from?" asked Mrs. Petorak, bringing him three fresh binders and whisking off the others.

"Colorado. Somebody sent me here. I have no idea what I'm looking for."

Kids in Nebraska City got scholarships to fancy colleges, won wrestling tournaments. The fire department had a party. The edge of a tornado took down a house under construction. As he went back in time, the pages got thicker, yellower, louder. Nebraska City seemed more and more like a country town, where people farmed and made babies and didn't have time for nonsense.

Then he got to 1962, with its columns jammed so tight that he could barely tell the stories apart, even with the thin black lines between them. Feed prices, sales on dishwashers, boys building a fort out of scrap pallets, girls getting their lambs ready for a 4-H show. On July 17 the lead story was about a girl winning a clarinet scholarship. But on the next day, the main headline read, DEPUTY KILLED IN FIRE. Underneath was a picture of his grandma looking as sour as always but with her head down and a knuckle wiping at her eye. Behind her firemen rolled out hoses, and further back a two-story building sprouted fingers of flame.

Deputy Sheriff Gregory Holmquist of Nebraska City, 44, died Thursday night in a fierce blaze at Holmquist TV and Entertainment Showroom on Central Avenue. Fire and police from as far away as Syracuse and Lincoln have come to assist in determining the cause of the fire, which Roy Rydinger of the Nebraska City VFD suspects was caused by arson.

"Anybody who's been inside that store knows there wasn't enough combustible material around to cause a blaze that strong,"

Rydinger said. "We're lucky there weren't other buildings around, or we wouldn't have had enough men to keep it from spreading. I'm calling this arson until somebody proves me wrong."

Holmquist, originally from Omaha, had served as a deputy sheriff in Nebraska City since his honorable discharge from the U.S. Navy. The Purple Heart–decorated veteran is survived by his wife, Ada, and daughter, Jeannette, 16.

"Somebody did this," said Ada Holmquist. "Somebody meant to." But Police Chief Paul McCarron would not go so far.

"We're investigating arson," he told the *News-Press*. "I can't say anything until that's verified. We've never seen anything like this, and we'd be fooling ourselves if we pretended we could handle it alone."

"Jeannette Holmquist," Tommy spat out, slamming the book shut. "Bullshit." His hands got sweaty, and he couldn't swallow. The truth wasn't supposed be so damn easy to find, and it wasn't supposed to make his brain crack apart. He reopened the book, and his fingers flipped to July 18. It was his grandma, all right. Her face matched what he saw in the few old pictures she had, though nobody ever said those pictures came from Nebraska City. They supposedly came from McCook, where she supposedly grew up. Or Sidney, where her husband, Gregory, supposedly died on an icy road one night when Connie was a baby. Tommy looked up and saw Mrs. Petorak staring at him like a bull about to breathe out smoke.

"Check the next couple days," she told him. "Then skip ahead two weeks."

He flipped through more pages of July 18, wondering where the name *Sandor* came from and why the hell his grandma had changed hers too. Wondering why the hell Mrs. Petorak, who wouldn't stop staring at him, already knew what he wanted to find out. She must have been one of Grandma's bingo buddies or knitting buddies or pie-making buddies. No wonder she hated his face so much—he was to blame for Ada leaving.

Who else in Nebraska City would hate his face like that? Maybe everybody. The air around him got stuffy, and he felt surrounded—a little army of Grandma's lost friends, plus some of Mom's, all circling in to crush him. The newspaper book swam in front of him, and his eyes took forever to settle on anything. In an ad for Holmquist TV and Entertainment Showroom, a smiling Gregory Holmquist—his hawkish face nothing like Tommy's own—said, *"I GUARANTEE IT!"* in a cartoony caption. On the next page a kid named Eddie Turley dove into a swimming pool. The kind of straight-arrow kid that Tommy might have been if he'd grown up a Holmquist in Nebraska City instead of a Sandor in Suborney. Maybe Eddie was a marine now, a linebacker who'd turned down a full-ride scholarship for a chance to serve his country.

NO NEW EVIDENCE IN BLAZE, said the headline for July 19, and there was another picture of the TV store—only a skeleton now, billowing smoke and dust. The next day the smoke had cleared, and Tommy's grandma stared at it with a teenage girl beside her. There was a caption under this picture but no headline above it.

Ada Holmquist, widow of late Deputy Sheriff Gregory Holmquist, stands with their daughter, Jeanette, in front of the fire-ravaged Holmquist TV and Entertainment Showroom. For public safety reasons the building will be demolished tomorrow.

His mom's face—the same one as today, with freckled cheeks and thin lips and the sharp muzzle she got from her dad—pressed hard against Grandma's shoulder. Tommy swore a bunch, drawing Mrs. Petorak closer. He did some quick math and realized that he was in the picture too, underneath Jeanette's white blouse, seven months from being born.

Deputy Sheriff Gregory Fucking Holmquist. Tommy flipped to the TV section for the *I GUARANTEE IT!* ad but couldn't find it. So he flipped back to stare at the man in the last ad, who didn't look any more like a deputy sheriff than Dan Stannard looked like a state patrolman. So it made sense that his mom would go for a cop who didn't look like a cop. He should call her "Jeannette" the next time he saw her, just to watch her jump.

"Nothing more happens till August," said Mrs. Petorak. "The first week of it."

"How do you know this shit?"

"Big news at the time. Still is, to some of us."

Tommy flipped to August 3, then saw a mug shot with the face he'd been looking for all his life. A father, finally. Actual flesh and blood. A face as hard as a brick, with anger drilling out through its eyes. A fuck-you smirk. That blond, buzz-cut hair and bull neck, the same neck he'd admired in so many mirrors.

"Fuck," Tommy barked, slamming that face with the side of his fist. The headline said, SUSPECT APPREHENDED IN HOLMQUIST FIRE.

Richard Curtis Thorpe, 19, originally of St. Louis, Missouri, was apprehended yesterday in Chadron. He is being held on suspicion of murder and arson for the July 17 fire on Central Avenue that killed Nebraska City Deputy Sheriff Gregory Holmquist.

"We have the suspect in custody and a signed confession," said Otoe County District Attorney Michael Bandori. "This should not be a difficult case to prosecute, and we expect to move forward quickly."

Thorpe, a driver on the amateur stock car circuit in Nebraska, Iowa, and South Dakota, was acquainted with the Holmquist family. Prior to this incident, he had no criminal record other than a series of traffic violations. His father, Eldon Thorpe, has several gambling arrests in the area but no convictions, and two of his brothers are known to have passed through Nebraska City. Police Chief Paul McCarron stopped short of assigning a motive to the blaze.

"We're aware that the suspect knew the Holmquist family, but that's all. We've got a confession, but all it says is what he did, not why."

Ada Holmquist reported that Thorpe had never worked at her late husband's store.

"He's a murderer, and I'm glad they caught him," she said. "I'll be at his trial, and I'll be there when he pays with his life."

Some doubt remains as to the charges that will be brought against Thorpe, however, because witnesses tell the *News-Press* that they saw Gregory Holmquist enter the burning building of his own volition multiple times to retrieve his belongings, some of which were found outside the store. District Attorney Bandori did not comment on possible charges.

"We have a suspect who confessed to a felony," he said at the courthouse yesterday. "And we will prosecute that felony."

Tommy went back to staring at Thorpe's mug shot. Only nineteen years old but with a dead man hanging over his head already. Scared and defiant. Zits in the same places his son had them now. Tommy stared so hard that he didn't notice Mrs. Petorak looking over his shoulder until he felt her breath.

"There's one more picture," she said when he looked up. "August 21." Then she went back to her desk, head down like Tommy didn't exist. He found the page and saw another picture of his father, this time in a trim leather jacket leaning back against a car without a hood. Arms crossed, head tilted back to let loose a big *Huh-haaaaaaa!* Blond hair, sideburns that didn't really show yet. Pointing at him from nearby was a sharp-faced man in jeans and a white V-neck T-shirt with a pack of cigarettes rolled under his sleeve.

GUILTY PLEA IN HOLMQUIST FIRE, the headline read, and Tommy scanned the rest of the article without registering the words. He only absorbed the ones beneath the picture, and as he read them, he lost all feeling in his body. Everything but his eyes spun around.

Richard Thorpe, who pleaded guilty to arson and involuntary manslaughter in the Holmquist TV and Entertainment Showroom fire of July 17, is shown with his father, Eldon, at an unnamed racetrack. The whereabouts of the senior Thorpe are unknown.

Eldon Thorpe was partly in shadow, his deep-set eyes darkened by it as he pointed at Richard. He stood much taller than his son, though he wasn't nearly as thick around. It made Tommy wonder what his grandmother on the Thorpe side was like—it took a tough woman, probably a hell-raiser herself, to love a man like Eldon and raise a boy like Richard. Other sons too. Men who roamed, who disappeared for months at a time without needing a reason. Tommy looked at his father leaning against the car, at his grandfather's pointing finger. "You're next," that finger said, and Richard stood up to win his race or die trying. Tommy felt his father's jangling walk, a walk that knew where it was going even if it wasn't welcome there. He imagined his father strolling out of the picture, cocking his head back like he was about to get into a ring with somebody. A boxing match before the race—or a knife fight.

Then Tommy couldn't take it anymore. The feeling came back to his body, and it got sluggish all the way through because knowing who he came from gave him an even heavier load to carry than not knowing. He got worried for his marrow and what it might do to the town where he was conceived, especially with the Missouri River so close by. So much damage he could do. He slammed the big red book shut and brought it to Mrs. Petorak at her desk.

"Do you know who I am?" he asked her.

"You're a murderer's son." She hated him so much that she couldn't even blink. "I knew your grandmother before she went away. Lots of us did. Now it's time for you to go away too."

✳ ✳ ✳

Tommy immediately started looking for a Nebraska City girl he could knock up and leave behind, preferably a girl whose father had a business he could burn down. He'd knock her up, go to jail, and claim his bastard kid when he was damn well ready—after eighteen years, one-upping his own father. He saw girls in passing cars who would do. Not taut, hatchet-faced ones like his mom had been, but ones with pale, round, vacant faces. Girls dumb enough to fall in love with a ticket out of town and stick around long after he ditched them, waiting like old dogs for him to come back and be a proper husband. He walked down Central Avenue toward the river and a banker-looking man stepped aside, giving him wide berth. Tommy wanted to ask him if he knew about the fire eighteen years ago today. If he'd known the man who died in it, the wife and daughter who disappeared and changed their names. *Huh, fucker?* he pictured himself asking. *You know who I am too?*

Tommy kept hustling toward the river, passing a woman a few years older than him who pushed a baby stroller. She looked dumb enough for him to knock up and leave, though maybe her baby's father had beaten him to the punch. Tommy didn't want that kind of girl after all. He wanted today's version of Jeanette Holmquist, smart and capable and never letting anybody look down on her. A tough girl, though she was scared enough to need a man of the law around to protect her. Tommy stopped at the corner of Central Avenue and Sixth Street to stand in his grandfather's parking lot, the showroom nothing now but a pile of dirt. To stand where his grandfather, whose name he carried, had died in a fire set by the man whose face he carried.

Richard Thorpe, whose face could stare at the child he never knew but say nothing. Whose face could plot and plan to trap that child without once having to say, "I'm your father," then claim him when the moment came. Whose face Tommy wanted to pull toward his own and wash with tears.

Tommy kept staring at the pile of dirt. "Witnesses saw Gregory Holmquist enter the burning building of his own volition multiple times," the newspaper said, which explained the *involuntary* part of Thorpe's manslaughter sentence. He finally left the pile of dirt behind and walked down Central Avenue toward the water, past the fertilizer plant, and to the banks of the Missouri River. There he saw black snakes swimming in the water—spawn of snakes that his mother must have known, his father must have known. He thought about trying to raise the river, but with the way he was feeling, it might not ever stop.

"My daddy wasn't a sax player," Tommy told the snakes. "My daddy was a race car driver. How the fuck do you like that?"

Tommy figured Thorpe was the kind of man who'd spent a lot of time near railroad tracks, so he walked there next along the banks of a lush, deep creek that smelled like rotting vegetables. Nothing like the scraggly creeks of Colorado. He looked up and down the tracks, four sets of them curving through each other, and found a shack by the rails nearest the creek. He could picture his father and Grandpa Eldon gambling there, taking money from low-rent scum like themselves or maybe from rich people like Greg Holmquist who couldn't keep their hands off the cards. Gambling debts, that would be one good reason to burn somebody's store down. Tommy walked over, ready to shoulder open a door and find some half-dead drunk on the floor, but there was no door and nothing inside but an empty wooden cable spool.

He looked outside to see if anybody was watching him, then knelt to pray. All Tommy could say was "JesusJesusJesusJesus," like the people who made fun of him, and when he couldn't say the name anymore, he let himself cry. As he headed back toward the river, his walk turned into a prayer—whispering "Jesus" to himself with every inhale and "Mary" with every exhale. He got ready to wade across the creek but then felt like drying it up with his marrow. Why the hell not? It couldn't do as much damage as the whole Missouri River. Tommy stood with his hands open by his shoulders, asking God what to do with the water and with his life, and when he stepped into the creek, it got so low the water didn't even seep through his bootlaces. As he stepped out, it rushed by almost strong enough to knock him over, sending him a *Don't fuck with me* message before settling back to normal.

At the crest of the creek's bank, Tommy stood twenty yards from the vine-riddled tree house where he was conceived and thirty yards from the hole in the chain link fence where his mother had spurned his father. He knew nothing of these places that had formed his life and fate, but he stood there nonetheless, rooted to the one spot where he could see both. He counted the months between the fire and his birthday to double-check that his mom was pregnant when his grandfather died. Had Gregory Holmquist known about his existence? Had Richard Thorpe's brothers?

Uncles, Tommy thought. *I've got uncles. Cousins probably.* He heard a sharp whistle, then turned to see a scrawny man in overalls five sizes too big walking his way. The man's skin was as worn as his overalls, and he had a shotgun on his shoulder.

"What you want here?" the man yelled.

Tommy stuck his hands in the air. "Looking for Eldon Thorpe."

"You one of his sons?" The gun came across his chest.

"Grandson. Never met him. He have a bunch of sons?"

"Hell if I know. Been fifteen years since he left, easy. Probably dead ten times over."

"Or in prison."

"Cops never catch a rat like him. If you're looking for that money he stole, don't bother looking for it here. Every inch of this dirt's got dug up ten times."

"Did you know a guy named Richard Thorpe?"

"Knew 'em all. Used to race across the river." The man jerked his chin east. "One of 'em still owes me a hundred bucks."

"I don't have that for you, sorry." Tommy tried out the charming smile he'd seen Thorpe use, but the scrawny guy didn't smile back.

"Then move along like you never set foot here." He pointed the shotgun at Tommy's crotch, then waved it west. "Town's that way."

"Gotcha." Tommy walked backward a few paces. "Did you know Greg Holmquist?"

"That chunk of shit was as bad as them Thorpes. Don't let anybody tell you different. Chunk of shit and a liar. Deserved what he got."

The scrawny man spat, and Tommy turned to walk downtown, following the same route that Jeannette Holmquist had taken on the night his grandfather died. All he could think about was fire, fire, fire. Burning buildings to the ground, filling people's lungs, scorching them down to ash. Then he pictured a fire in a barrel by a roadside at the edge of a good-for-nothing high plains town even shittier than Suborney, without even a junkyard to its name. Three men cooked some animal they'd shot and skinned or maybe found dead in a ditch.

They didn't know what time it was, didn't care about days of the week or how long they'd worn their clothes. They didn't need women, didn't even need each other. His grandfather Eldon and two of his uncles, whatever their names were. Criminals and nothing more, ripping people off or racing cars or playing poker, then hiding their money in the ground for when they needed it. Men like snakes, who could eat once a month and live through the end of the world on nothing but ancient canned beans that nobody else had the stomach to touch.

And you're one of them, Tommy told himself. *Scum of the earth, the kind nobody can scrape off.* He walked past the pile of dirt on Sixth and Central again, trying not to think of his grandpa Holmquist choking to death while he fetched his stuff. Instead, he thought of his father—who was just as much of a liar as his mom, despite his *I work for Jesus* bullshit—and wanted to race back to Suborney and burn both their houses down. Maybe burn down the old goat farm in Bird City on the way, erasing all evidence that he'd ever had a home so he could join those Thorpe men by the roadside. Men who'd still be standing long after the neutron bombs dropped. Long after the rest of the world had decided that life was too much and closed its eyes in defeat.

Tommy walked and walked, aimless. When he got to Eighth and Central, he saw a Pontiac Firebird idling next to his Vega, and the driver stepped out to look it over. Tommy ran uphill and shouted until the Firebird guy saw him.

"You like my car, bud?" he called when he got close enough.

"Shit yeah," the driver told him, getting out. The Firebird was a 1973, painted a dull, flat black all around. Its driver was as blond as Tommy, maybe a couple years older, and they shook hands in the street. A wide receiver type, long muscled and slim in the waist. The kind of guy Tommy wouldn't want to see rounding the corner at him, but who wouldn't want to see Tommy coming straight for him either. "You ever race this thing?" the guy asked.

"All the time," Tommy lied. "Mostly on the streets, back in Denver."

"We got a little track out there." He pointed east, over the river toward Iowa. "Asphalt, banks, lights, the whole show. We're running tonight. Just go over the bridge, take a left, you'll see it. Got six guys coming out regular."

"Racing for money?"

"What else do you race for?" The guy got back into his Firebird, and Tommy wondered if they were Thorpe cousins. He had a face like Grandpa Eldon's, didn't he? "Come by around sundown," he called. "Just say Brock sent you."

Then Brock peeled out, burning rubber, and Tommy didn't think he was a cousin anymore. He was a hack, a showoff with no real balls. Why burn rubber for show in a car you're going to race that night? Tommy Sandor would outrace Brock and everybody else who showed up at that track because Tommy Sandor had nothing left to lose except the fake self he used to be. A self that stood empty now— only a thin membrane of skin drained of what he might have been, ready to fill with what he had no choice but to become.

14

still Thursday

Tommy sat down to eat at a mostly empty diner called Gorham's catty-corner to the remains of Grandpa Holmquist's showroom. He sank into a turquoise booth by the window and watched the pile of dirt as if it would start reconstituting itself any second, becoming a store again so Richard Curtis Thorpe could burn it down again. So Tommy could watch his grandpa run in and out of the flames, carrying whatever he thought was worth more than his life.

"Don't go back in!" Tommy would shout from the sidewalk. "I'm your grandson!"

Grandpa Greg would sneer at him, hating Tommy because of who his father was, and rush back into the burning store. His mother would have been smarter to tell him the truth when he turned fourteen instead of bullshitting him about the imaginary Drake because then he would've grown up picturing that fire every day of his life and loathing the man who'd set it. She should've shown him Thorpe's mug shot every July 17 and said, "This is what you'll turn into if you don't listen to me." Then maybe he would've wanted to be a doctor or a lawyer. A TV salesman or a deputy sheriff.

Instead, Connie had lied, giving him a fake father he wanted to become and a real one he couldn't help becoming. Tommy should've been grateful because her lie gave him two tickets out of town when most kids don't get any. He felt like calling somebody—Sherry, Pete Sowell, Dolman, even the football coach he'd quit on—to say that he finally knew who he was and would stop acting like such an asshole to everybody. He couldn't call his mom, though. Fucking liar. Sleeping with one guy after another, showing off her legs and cleavage. If she wanted somebody to love, she should've loved the man whose son she raised.

"Beer?" asked a waitress his mom's age who might have been Jeanette Holmquist's best friend in high school. Strawberry blonde hair, too much blue eye shadow, chapped hands, no ring. He ordered a burger and a Coke and watched her walk away rubbing her left hip. Exhausted, probably a single mom. Tommy wondered whose kid she raised alone and what lies she'd told the kid about its father. Wondered how many women lived those kinds of lies and how many sons and daughters were better off for it like he was. If he'd known the truth all along, he would've been in trouble constantly because his dad was a jailbird. His grandfather Eldon would've been one, too, if the cops could ever make a case stick.

Thanks for the lie, Mom, Tommy thought. Then he snorted to himself and, deep inside his marrow, shifted indiscernibly from being the son of a tenor sax player to being the son of an arsonist, a thief, a man some called a murderer. *But I'm still gonna get you for it. Watch out, Connie. You too, Jeannette.*

✳ ✳ ✳

Tommy gassed up and checked his tires for the races that night, then walked around looking for a church that the Sons and Daughters might have fixed up. He found an abandoned one on Thorpe's side of the tracks, up the hill on Fifth Terrace past Fifth Rue. An empty, piss-smelling, garbage-filled rectangle of brick with the window frames gone and the walls ripped open for the copper. Why hadn't Thorpe's gang been there? Saving it for him probably. He started sweeping garbage out with his boots, piling it up by the door until an old woman with tennis balls on the feet of her walker stared at him from across the street.

"Just cleaning the place up, ma'am," Tommy told her before she could say anything. The woman nodded and moved on more deliberately than Tommy could imagine: lifting her left foot forward, shuffling her right to meet it, pushing her walker ahead half a foot. Ten minutes later another woman came out, this one as big as him with a bathrobe still on at suppertime and snaky blonde hair going dirty white. She walked to the end of what, before its paving stones got stolen, used to be the church walkway.

"Who are you, and what the hell are you doing?" she said.

"I'm Brother Tommy, ma'am. A church shouldn't be a trash can. You got any lawn bags I can use?"

She huffed off, muttering, and Tommy tried to picture the church full of people back in the day. Tried to picture Thorpe and Grandpa Eldon in there singing and praying, plus two uncles who didn't have faces or names. Praying for what? To drive faster, rip people off better, evade the cops? What a joke. Tommy dragged an empty bomber of Schlitz and a shit-caked baby diaper toward the door with his foot, and when he got there, the big woman handed him a bunch of lawn bags, a rake, and a snow shovel.

"I'm guessing you want something for doing this," she said.

"No ma'am." Tommy started filling a bag. "Not asking for anything."

"But you'll take a few bucks and food if I ask you enough times. One of those?"

Tommy nodded, and she left, replaced by an imaginary Eldon Thorpe in the frameless doorway. *Easier ways to earn your keep*, Grandpa Eldon mumbled, shuffling a deck of cards even faster than Mother Meg had, but Tommy still couldn't see his eyes. They stayed permanently in shadow, like in the newspaper picture, and his voice was half–city boy, half–southern twang. The newspaper said Richard Curtis Thorpe was born in St. Louis, but that didn't mean Grandpa Eldon came from there. It didn't mean he'd ever set foot there. He could have knocked up some teenage girl who went to St. Louis and gave birth to a bastard, giving the boy his father's last name so they could find each other later. Then the big woman filled the doorway again.

"Take these," she told Tommy, and when he came over, she had four dollar bills in one hand and a warm can of Coke in the other. He stuffed the bills into his back pocket one at a time so they'd crumple, then opened the can of Coke and toasted her with it.

"Thank you, ma'am. Anywhere I should put these bags when I'm done?"

"Leave 'em outside the door. Make it look like somebody gives a damn."

Tommy nodded and felt like saying, "God be with you," but he wasn't a preacher and never would be. He was just a young man who cleaned up dead churches, who gave his sweat so that people could have places to kneel together and pray. The woman thanked him quickly and left.

"Nebraska City's clean and ready, sir," Tommy imagined telling Thorpe when he got back to Suborney. He'd be their scout, the one who drove through America looking for the next abandoned church to fix up. Looking for the next teenager whose life they'd blow apart once they showed the world his truth.

* * *

At sundown he drove up Fourth Corso, which led him to Route 2 and over the Missouri River into Iowa, and found the racetrack. It was homemade—a paved, elongated figure eight surrounded by cornfields—and his headlights showed him the veins of jet-black tar where the asphalt had been repaired. Both loops of the figure eight had steep banks, with guardrails and tripled chain link fencing to keep cars from running off. On the side facing the river sat a bank of empty bleachers, and in the middle of one loop was a pit surrounded by concrete dividers. Three cars already waited there. A diesel generator powered big lights that looked like they'd been stolen from a high school football field.

Tommy had never raced anybody before and didn't know a damn thing about it except that he was going to win, because racing and gambling were in his blood. He'd gamble tonight, with his life if he had to. Win for the line of men who'd given him his muscle, his tenacity, his ferocity. Win to become Tommy Thorpe. He stilled himself long enough to pray that he wouldn't die and drove into the pit, where five people flitted among the cars. They all seemed under thirty except for one guy, stooped over like he was eighty, who checked Tommy out as he pulled up next to Brock's Firebird.

"Mind if I take a couple spins?" Tommy asked him. "New track for me."

"Knock yourself out," the guy called, and Brock poked his head out from underneath his hood. His girlfriend popped hers out too—blonde, a cheerleader type—and Tommy knew he'd win. Any guy who brought his girl to a pit didn't have real balls, just the ones his girl told him he had.

Tommy laughed at himself for thinking he knew a damn thing about racing, then hopped onto the track and took the banked first loop at sixty to learn its contours. He took the second at ninety but slowed way down because the Vega skidded, just like Thorpe said it would—"She'll skid all over but won't roll." Tommy gunned it to a hundred on his way through the figure eight's center, and when he hit the first loop again, he jammed his steering wheel to the left and burned rubber, drifting across the bank and taking up as much space as he could. The bank was so high that it took all his gut muscles to keep him in his seat.

When he passed through the pit again, he slowed down and waved to the people jeering at him. Tommy took the next loop at 110 and jammed the wheel again and barely braked at all on the bank. The tires shrieked as he drifted through the loop, the sax case thunked all over his trunk, and the burning rubber made his eyes half-blind. If he had anything but new tires on the Vega, he'd have no chance. Tommy pulled into the pit next to Brock, and the old man came toward him.

"You sure you oughta be out here?" he asked Tommy. From closer he didn't look that old, maybe fifty, but he moved like every bone in his body had been broken five times. A track junkie who couldn't pull himself away, who raced against himself when nobody was looking because he'd promised someone to never race another man again.

"That's my decision, isn't it?" Tommy said back.

The man looked him over. "I know you, don't I?" His face was as much of a jumble as his body. Stitched up everywhere and with one nostril smaller than the other.

"Don't think so." Tommy wondered if this man was another friend of Grandma Holmquist, but the thought made him laugh aloud. "I'm Tommy Sandor, from Denver."

"Ray Colton." The man didn't offer a shake. "If you say you know what you're doing, I'm not saying you don't. Brock give you the scoop?"

Tommy shook his head, so Ray told him that the challenger had to race everybody head to head in reverse order of their last finish. He'd lay down the first bet and start off with three laps against Cliff in a Datsun 280Z. If he won, he'd take the pot and go four laps against Doug in a Mustang. If he beat Doug, he'd get Brock in the Firebird. Last race was five laps and all money down.

Tommy took out the wad of bills that Thorpe had given him, plus the twenty-eight dollars left of his own and the four bucks he'd earned cleaning the church, and he counted them out under Colton's flashlight. He laid down forty-three singles before he ran into a hundred-dollar bill, and he laughed, Thorpe style—a big *Huh-haaaaaaa!* that made Colton glare at him sideways. They counted out $197, and while Colton limped over to Cliff's Datsun with the cash, Tommy checked out Brock's girlfriend. She wore Bermuda shorts and a pink polo shirt with the collar flipped up.

"What's your daddy do for money, honey?" he asked her once he got face to face, thinking she could be the Jeanette Holmquist of 1980. The girl who'd get knocked up by a wild thing from out of town and move someplace she'd never been, become somebody she'd never dreamed of being, just to get away from her bastard child's crazy daddy.

"Back off my girl," Brock told him, brandishing the screwdriver he was using to tweak his carburetors.

"Just making friendly conversation. What else do you expect me to do in this shithole town?" Tommy turned to the girl. "You ever been to Denver?"

"No, but I've been to London and Paris. Brock, will you get this guy off me?"

"Sorry, baby." Tommy held up his hands and backed away. "I won't make you breathe in my stink anymore. I won't stare at your pampered little ass."

"You fuck off!" Brock shouted, stepping closer with the screwdriver this time, and Tommy laughed as he walked to his Vega. He laid back on his hood with his legs open wide, then turned to see the girl glaring at him.

"None of that shit here," Colton told him. "Save it for the track."

"Careful what kind of trash you let in here," Brock called to Colton.

"*You* told him to come." Colton turned to Tommy and said, "Strap in, bud. You got three laps with Cliff—let's go."

Tommy left his sax case in the bed of Colton's truck and climbed nonchalantly into the Vega, as if heading off to buy groceries. He lined up next to the Datsun at the white stripe in the center of the figure eight and waved to Cliff, who revved his engine and stared at Colton's green flag. Tommy said a quick "Help me, Jesus," though he wasn't sure how Jesus felt about racing cars for money, and the flag sliced down. He jumped hard and slowed, while the Datsun started out smooth. The Vega had enough horsepower to pull even on the straightaway, and after that it was a question of who took the loop harder. Tommy started into it at 110 again, pushing himself and his machine to the edge of control, and sure enough, Cliff lost his nerve and braked when he heard the Vega start to skid on the bank.

Just like that it was over, like an arm wrestling match on ABC's Wide World of Sports. Tommy only had to stay in the middle of the track and head into the turns ahead of Cliff, and round one would be his. After three laps Colton waved the checkered flag, and Tommy zipped through the figure eight again, wanting to learn the track better because Doug and his Mustang would be tougher to beat.

"Want to step out?" Colton asked Tommy when he got back to the starting line. "Next one's four laps."

"Just getting comfy," Tommy said. "Let's roll the cash, all of it." Then Doug's Mustang pulled up, its window open.

"You drive dirty," Doug told him. The guy looked older than Brock, with a bushy brown beard and arms as thick as thighs. Tommy shrugged, with nothing smartass to say back, then wondered what advice Thorpe would give him. Nothing probably. Ignore your own bullshit and win the race.

Colton chopped the green flag down, and Doug, not wanting to make the same mistakes as Cliff, took the first loop hard and stayed in the middle of it. He did exactly the same for the first two laps, with the Vega tight on his tail, but on the third lap he went in too fast and had to brake. Tommy ripped past him on the outside, not caring that he sparked against the guardrail, and came out of the loop so fast and out of control that he wasn't sure he could stay on the track. Everybody in the pit saw him barreling through the crossover and jumped back from the concrete dividers.

Tommy didn't slow down because he knew that Doug wouldn't lose his balls like Cliff had. Sure enough, the Mustang was on his ass right away, jockeying. On the next loop he kept the Vega dead in the middle of the track, pulling the steering wheel until he skidded sideways and Doug couldn't pass him. Then he yanked hard the other way and stuck to the inside, coming onto the straightaway so fast that he couldn't even pretend to be in control. But Doug didn't crap out, and he stayed on Tommy's tail until Colton waved the flag. Tommy coasted around one more time, and when he got back to the starting line, Brock was already there.

"All money down," Colton said, and Tommy opened his window to nod. "Five laps for fifteen hundred then. Try not to kill yourself for it."

"Fifteen seventy-six," Tommy told him. "Don't gyp me with your shitty math."

Tommy looked at the Firebird and saw Brock's middle finger sticking up at him, so he blew the guy a kiss and rolled up his window. That much money would buy a lot of cans for the mission, a lot of paint for the church. He didn't just want the money, though; he wanted to show Brock what real balls meant. Show him the desperation and strength you get from not having a place in the world, from not being on anybody's radar except your own.

You were always on my radar, Thorpe's voice told him. Then the flag dropped, and Brock jumped in front, hogging the middle with his wide, low-slung Firebird. Brock knew the track and knew his enemy's tricks now, so Tommy hung on his tail for the first two laps and looked for a chance to pull a move. When a gap showed up, he'd have to squeeze through it like a man with nothing to lose, which he was. Because a guy like Brock—with a girlfriend and a day job that could pay for his tricked-out car—had so much to lose that he couldn't squeeze himself down small enough. But Tommy could because he was a man who came from nothing. He could squeeze himself down so tight that he was only hands on a wheel and feet on pedals.

On the first three laps neither of them got going fast enough to even have fun. Then at the start of the fourth, just after the tight center of the figure eight, Brock glided a foot off the center line and gave Tommy enough room to pull even and take the inside. They stayed that way heading into the first loop, which Tommy took as hard as he could, even though he was half an inch from dropping off the asphalt onto the dirt. He skidded again and couldn't control it, and the cars bumped back ends, slowing down both drivers as they tried to get out of the loop with momentum. Somebody had to be first when they came back through the crossover because the Vega and the Firebird were too wide to fit side by side through the heart of the figure eight, unless they slowed down to almost nothing. Tommy hesitated as he bumped the Firebird's tail, and Brock made him pay for it, taking the nose for a second. Then Tommy moved to bump him hard near the back wheel, and Brock tried to slip out of it, giving Tommy the hole he could squeeze himself through that Brock couldn't.

He barely had enough asphalt to whip ahead of Brock by the starting line, but he did it somehow and took the middle to start the last lap. Brock got desperate, and as they rushed into the next-to-last loop, he tried to cut inside. But Tommy jammed the wheel, taking up the whole width of the track going sideways in a cloud of burning rubber. When Brock tried to shoot a gap that wasn't there, his wheels caught dirt, and he spun out off the track.

It looked nondramatic from there on out, with only one car left standing. But Brock hopped back onto the track going the wrong way and headed for the last loop, looking like he wanted to run the Vega off, and from then on it was a game of chicken. The Firebird sped up, and Tommy kept the Vega dead in the middle of the track, knowing that Brock would flinch first because he could never match a kid like Tommy for desperation, not even in his dreams.

Sure enough, the Firebird braked, and Brock's involuntary flinch made it veer leftward. When Tommy's Vega caught its tail, Brock overcompensated. The Firebird hit the concrete just right and jumped into the pit, then rolled three times before it found its wheels again. When the Vega crossed the finish line, Colton didn't even bother waving the checkered flag.

"Do something!" the girl screamed as Tommy got out. Inside the Firebird, Brock's head hung over to the side. Everybody rushed over to him except Colton, who held Tommy's sax case in one hand and a paper grocery bag in the other.

"You're a Thorpe, aren't you?" he asked, dropping his load at Tommy's feet. "You drive just like one. Craziest motherfuckers I ever saw."

❊ ❊ ❊

Tommy left the Vega outside the track just in case Brock died and the cops had to track him down—they'd charge him with involuntary manslaughter, of course—and he started walking home. He trudged over the bridge across the Missouri River, through the stretch of Nebraska City where his father and grandfather and uncles used to live. *A bunch of Thorpes*, he heard voices say, as if Thorpes were something decent folk had the right to spit at. He went past the spot on Central Avenue where his grandpa Holmquist died, then past where Route 2 met Route 75, then out of Nebraska City entirely. Forever probably. He stuck to side roads, like the Sons and Daughters did, and wound up walking west on County Road I. He headed south to look for County Road J, then walked along the edge of a creek to see if there was a County Road K too.

"Damn alphabet roads," he muttered when he found it. Tommy switched hands on his sax case and started his next hundred paces, certain he could walk all the way to Suborney like that. Heck with fifty paces—that was for losers. He'd do it to prove that he deserved to be Brother Tommy, deserved to wake up every morning like Sister Mel and Z-pan and help people too weak and too lost from God to help themselves.

Brother Thorpe, though? To hell with him. Tommy had nothing to prove to him. He'd take over the church and excommunicate the lying bastard. Or maybe Thorpe and his mom would make up and crank out a bunch of little brothers who Tommy could help out with. Teaching them how to raise goats, play sax, and scrounge through junkyards. How to race cars, play football, and quit on things once they stopped believing in them.

When Road K ended, Tommy popped open his sax case. He took his time putting the instrument together, waxing the cork on the neck and wetting the reed for longer than he had to. He was more patient than any previous version of himself because the empty plains would be his Williamsburg Bridge, the place he made himself a genius like Rollins. Tommy wouldn't be walking to New York, like he'd thought, but maybe he wasn't supposed to. He clamped his lips on his mouthpiece and stood—his feet planted dead in the center of where County Road K and South Fifty-Second Road intersected—to fill his lungs and wrap his lips around the mouthpiece.

"*I am of dust and bone,*" he said with his sax, louder and louder until he could picture the Sons and Daughters hearing it from who knows how many hundred miles away. They'd sit up in their sleeping bags and say, "Hey, that's Tommy," and sing the words right back to him. Even Brother Thorpe, who he had to forgive. Even Brother Thorpe, who he had to punish.

15

Connie woke at dawn and put on a rumpled sundress to go check in on the goats, only to find two people sprawled on the floor instead: a man with ratty hair and a greasy Mexican poncho and a tiny Chinese-looking girl with metal rings all across her lips. Connie found Mother Meg on the ground outside the kitchen door, awake but still in her sleeping bag, with the billy nestling by her feet. The nanny stood nearby, with the kid tugging at her full, heavy udders.

"Just you against the wolves?" Connie asked.

Mother Meg sat up. "Doesn't seem like wolf country to me."

"Have you ever been to wolf country?"

"I spent my whole life in Alaska before I came down here to take care of my son."

"Is that preacher guy your son? Reverend Thorpe? Whatever he calls himself?"

"He's somebody else's son. I just love him like one." Mother Meg unzipped her sleeping bag and stood. Her solidity made Connie feel like a waif. "If you're looking for yours, he went to Nebraska to figure things out. Didn't say much about it."

"He never did anything without telling half the world." Connie's head spun at the thought of everything Tommy might learn in Nebraska. "At least before you people got hold of him."

"He got hold of himself, *Miss* Sandor. He started asking what God wants him to be. Don't you ever ask yourself that?"

"I came here looking for my son, not to get preached to."

"Well, you either ask what God wants of you or you don't. Guess you don't, even though you're sleeping with a preacher's brother. *Married* brother."

"You can't help who you love, *ma'am*."

"But you *can* help who gets inside you, most of the time." Mother Meg popped her head through the kitchen door and gave a sharp whistle. "I don't know how long you want to keep pretending we don't know who you are."

"Doesn't matter who I am, not to me and not to the law," Connie said. "You're a cult, you've got my son, and I want him back. He's a minor. The law's on my side." She stroked the nanny's head. "You better milk this old girl soon, or she'll get infected. She's making too much."

Mother Meg nodded, and Connie walked home wondering what exactly Thorpe and his gang wanted from her. To crawl into one of their circles on her knees and start singing? To say, "I was a child and I made a mistake and I should have let Richie marry me"? A pair of white four-by-fours stuck out of the ground in front of the old church, signposts without a sign. She walked up the brand-new steps and opened the door to find the church emptied out and half-drywalled. A sign leaning against some used two-by-fours read:

THE SONS AND DAUGHTERS OF JESUS AND MARY
A COMMUNITY OF WORSHIP AND THANKS

The letters were plain black and so perfect that she leaned down to look at their edges. So patient, so sure. Everything she wasn't. She heard a thunk and a rattle and turned to see Richie in the doorway.

"What are you doing here?" she asked him, though she knew it was his church.

"Brother Beto did that." He jutted his chin at the sign. "Only got one hand, but he sure knows what God wants him to do with it."

"Is that all you talk about now? What God wants?" Connie was sick of the God talk Richie brought to town, sick of the ways it made people blind. And not just her son.

"Not much else *to* talk about, the way I see it."

"Then tell me why *God* sent Tommy to Nebraska City. Sounds more like you fine people sent him."

"Don't you think there's things a boy ought to know?" Thorpe asked her. "If his mother won't tell him, somebody's got to. I've kinda got an obligation as his—"

"Don't call yourself his *father*, Richie. You didn't change a single diaper or put a single meal on the table."

"Never had a chance." Thorpe felt his body clench and stepped toward Beto's sign, praying as he had all through prison that Jesus and Mary would keep him from taking vengeance on the woman who'd spurned him. He'd promised to not hurt her, not destroy her. "I *always* wanted him. Wanted to give him brothers and sisters. Do you think that could ever go away?"

"I guess not. But either you're going away, or I am." Connie tried to stare him down but quickly looked at the floor, at the rough boards they would soon sand down and varnish. They'd slap some paint on the walls, start praying and singing *Hallelujah!* in no time. She pictured herself walking around outside the church, trying to get a glimpse of Tommy through the windows as he sang, because pretty soon that might be the only way she'd get to see him. "What do you want from me, Richie?"

"If I knew, I would've knocked on your door and asked you."

"So instead you hijacked Tommy, and now you're waiting around to see who he picks? Do you expect me to let him go, just 'cause he thinks God's calling him?"

"Nobody expects that from a mother. Especially if her son is all she's got."

"But if I had God, it wouldn't be so hard to let go of him. Is that what you're saying? If I had God, this would be *so* much easier."

Thorpe shrugged but didn't answer. Connie hated him for ambushing her, for smearing her lies in her face. Why the hell else would he send Tommy to Nebraska City if not to learn about the enormous lies of Jeanette Holmquist? The girl who made one stupid mistake and thought she'd paid for it by giving up her whole life to raise a fatherless boy, only to learn that her whole life wasn't enough.

"Do you think you can trick people into loving God, Brother Thorpe?" she asked him. "Think you can back them into a corner till all they can talk about is God, God, God?"

"I've been in that corner," Thorpe told her. "Lots of freedom in that corner."

"Well, don't think you can trap me there. I can't say what I'd do if you try."

"I can't say either. Well, you have a good day."

"You too," Connie mumbled back without wanting to, and as Thorpe headed down the steps, she closed the church door behind him. Light poured in through holes in walls where windows used to be, and would soon be again.

Jesus'll be here soon! she heard Tommy say, like he was four years old again. *Jesus is coming—we made a place for him. Just wait!*

✳ ✳ ✳

Sleep, eat, walk, pray, play sax, look for Jesus. Feel the sun burning his skin, then let cool night fall over him. Think about God with every step because there was nothing but steps now, nothing but God. Tommy had five hundred miles of that routine ahead of him, give or take, on a straight southwesterly line from Nebraska City through Bird City to Suborney. The sun punished the earth and made the air shimmer, spreading pond-like mirages at the horizon of every road. Rain clouds danced slowly, whispering each other's names from a hundred miles away.

Tommy vacillated between hating his mother and hating his father, between believing he was truly waking up to God and truly going crazy. The Jesus fixation he'd picked up since the Sons and Daughters came to town might have been an act to get back at his mother, and Thorpe's might have been the same. If the guy believed in God the way he said, he would've walked straight up to his son and said the truth, instead of laying a trap. Instead of gathering lost but gentle people like Melanie and Zypanski and twisting their minds until they wanted to avenge a woman they'd never met for sins they'd never seen. Tommy couldn't respect *Brother* Thorpe because he was a hypocrite, a spineless sack of bullshit.

"You see *Brother* Thorpe," he practiced telling the Brothers and Sisters with a growl in his voice, "you tell him I got something to say."

No feeling lasted long as he walked. The monotony of the plains—farm, fence, house, cow, truck—demanded that he change on the inside, and he did it continuously. He'd fantasize about yelling at his mother until she cried, then get lost in his memories of the things they did together. Taking care of goats, playing in the creek, camping and canoeing at Jackson Lake, shoe shopping, the time she found him a trombone for fifty bucks.

It was hard to hate her when the good memories came, and they kept cycling through with the anger he felt. Every once in a while Tommy felt the lightness inside him that he'd always wished for and sometimes prayed for: the complete harmony between who he was and who God wanted him to be. Having a father and *knowing* that father let him feel like himself, not like all those fake Tommies he'd tried so hard to believe in. The sun's relentless rays burned the marine and the linebacker out of him and left only the child of God inside, cooked and warm and ready to step out of the coconut shell he'd built around himself.

This child of God Tommy didn't question every breath. He walked past the *Why? Why? Why?* he'd always bumped against and into the *Here, This, Now* that Jesus had been pointing him toward ever since he was a little boy. It was right in front of him, everywhere he turned, and it made him feel like his body was made of nothing but light.

"Why couldn't you see it?" he shouted over his shoulder at the old Tommy, who followed a few paces behind him with his eyes to the ground instead of the sky. Tommy reached a hundred paces and switched hands on the sax case, his shoulder muscles so tight they'd squeezed the water out of themselves and turned brittle.

No use carrying it, he remembered Jesus telling him, and Tommy laughed as if Jesus had meant the sax all along. No, he was carrying something heavier: the hate that had hardened inside him, waiting to be pulled out and burned. The old hate for his mother, plus the new hate for Richard Thorpe, plus the hate for himself. Jesus and Mary would tell him to stop making any more before it hardened inside him and he got stuck halfway across the plains, like a pillar of salt from the Bible.

Walk, play sax, sleep. Hitch a ride here and there. Pray, walk, eat, sleep, play sax, sleep. Hate his mother, hate his father. Love his father, love his mother. Skirt the edges of fields, the barbed wire fences. In Wymore, Nebraska, he played in front of a burger joint with his case open, and before a cop shooed him away, he'd earned enough spare change for a burger, fries, and a shake. He dipped into his racing money to buy a thick army camouflage hat to replace the Australian one he'd left in the Vega, even though his skin was already long past sunburned. Tommy played sax by the railroad tracks, then found some shade to nap in by the Big Blue River. He started walking the second he woke up, like he figured the Sons and Daughters did. No dawdling, getting their praying done on the move. He played at the corner of 581st Avenue and 708th Road, which he was sure had to be the highest numbers to ever name human streets. He laughed because he was lucky to only have twenty-six letters for road names that could haunt him, while some people had all the numbers in the world. There could have been some other teenage fuckup out there, playing his desperate sax to God where 10,903rd Street met 12,257th Avenue.

"Hey brother!" Tommy called to his imaginary counterpart, loosening his ligature before he blew. In Steele City, Nebraska, he dug four post holes for an old man whose son was stuck with a sick kid. It earned him nine dollar bills, two bananas, and a can of Dr. Pepper. Later Tommy walked over the Little Blue River and raised it to test himself, but he got scared of stealing water from some farmer downstream and let it fall. He skirted the Kansas border until he got to Mahaska, where he helped two brothers attach a lawn mower engine to an old bike.

When he tried to play his sax in the town park, two mean old ladies stared him down before he even got the reed into his mouth. So he bought two Snickers bars at a gas station and played on his way out of town, then followed the railroad tracks to Narka. He bought an awful microwave hot dog at another gas station, then washed his face and armpits in the bathroom. He checked out his hair, wondering when the roots would start turning dark like his father's. By the cash register a girl his age stacked up piles of pennies on the counter. She had a round face and curly orange hair, and she looked smart enough for college but too lazy. She didn't wear a ring, which meant she was fair game for knocking up and leaving behind.

"Anyplace to sleep in this town?" Tommy asked her. "Maybe get a shower?"

"You'd have to ask around. Nothing like a motel, though."

"That thing make collect calls?" He pointed to the phone outside.

"All phones make collect calls." The girl pointed at the case. "What you got in there?"

Tommy set the case on the counter and opened it just long enough for her to see the gleaming brass, the mother-of-pearl keys, and the paper bag full of money sticking out of the bell. Outside he dialed the operator and asked her to call Trish Sandor on Toledo Street in Sidney, Nebraska. Collect, from her grandson, Tommy.

"Hello, Tommy," Trish said when the operator clicked off. "Been awhile."

Ada Holmquist? he wanted to say. But no, too soon. "Just checking up on you, Grams. Sorry I didn't visit when you were in the hospital."

"Oh, I probably would've tried to act better than I felt. Where are you?"

"Dinkhole town in Kansas. Narka, I think."

"Narka's a funny place to end up," Trish told him.

"Yeah. I started driving to New York, then my car broke down. Feel like a dumbass."

"Well, it was a dumbass thing to try. You're safe? Do you need money?"

"I'm safe, Grandma. Doing okay on money too. Walking home, hitching some rides."

"That doesn't sound too safe. Do you want me to drive down and pick you up?"

"No, it's good to walk. Serves me right for driving a car I couldn't trust." He licked his lips, done with lying.

"Does your mom know where you are?" asked Trish.

"We're not really talking." Tommy watched a cop pull up and walk into the store. "Don't you ever worry about her? Running around with this guy and that?"

"You've got to remember she's still young. She never got to go out dating. She—"

"Had me instead, right?"

"Now that you're grown, she gets another chance at it. Try to understand."

They said goodbye, and Tommy wondered how to get back at Grandma. She'd changed her name too, good ol' Ada. The cop walked back outside with a giant slushie and glanced at the phone like there was nobody standing by it at all, like the creature before him was something less than human. Just a dirty Thorpe, not even worth looking at.

❊ ❊ ❊

Tommy followed County Road D until it stopped, then headed south to Republic. There he helped a guy with a bad back named Frank load a pile of bricks from a dead uncle's backyard into a pickup. This earned Tommy a ride to Webber, where Frank's wife fed him eggs and beans and let him sleep on their back porch hammock on the condition that he take a shower and wash his clothes. On Saturday morning Frank drove him to Burr Oak, where the bricks were headed, and Tommy told him he was walking to Bird City.

"That's a couple hundred miles still," Frank said. "Long walk."

"Part of my religion," Tommy said back, winking the way he thought a Thorpe ought to. From Burr Oak he followed the railroad tracks and county roads to Esbon, which was five times bigger than Suborney but had ten times more Ronald Reagan junk. He stopped at the tiny post office to send his mom a postcard. HEY MOM, DOING FINE, JUST TAKING A LONG WALK. LOVE AND PEACE, TOM-TOM. He saw John Wayne's hand-painted face on a billboard next to the word *America* and knew it was really John Wayne that all the Reagan people wanted for president. Somebody who shot the bad guys and never second-guessed himself about it because he knew he was always right. Because he was American and stood for freedom.

Near the railroad tracks on his way out of Esbon, Tommy saw a girl, fifteen and pouty, driving an almost brand-new white pickup. Her town's Jeanette Holmquist for sure—snotty, too good for where God had plunked her down. Looking at the muscly arms of the guy with the black sax case and wondering if those arms were strong enough to drag her out of town.

That's not the way to go, Tommy, said a voice he wanted to sound like Jesus's, though it actually sounded like Pete Sowell's. Then the whole world fell silent, and all he could hear was his father, his flesh-and-blood father, blubbering over the son he never got to call his own. Blubbering on the floor of Wesley Perrin's house with the Sons and Daughters gathered around him, worried that his child might never return. Tommy closed his eyes tight and pictured himself kneeling next to Thorpe, crying with their arms around each other's waists. Then real tears came, for he didn't know how long, and when they stopped, he saw Jesus walking toward him down the tracks. A Jesus with muscle, sweat, gravity.

You're getting it, Jesus told Tommy without moving his mouth. *Keep on walking till you find the next soul who needs you, then keep on walking for more.*

Tommy bowed his head, and Jesus came over to set two cupped palms over his skull. Then Jesus hummed something that sounded like a Tessy song, and Tommy crumpled to the ground, his face at Jesus's feet. Red and dusty feet, so tough they didn't even notice the rocks in the rail bed. So callused from almost two thousand years of walking that they might as well have been Vibram soles on Red Wing boots.

Jesus squatted down to make a cross on Tommy's forehead with his thumb and headed east down the railroad tracks. Tommy followed until Jesus turned and pointed him west toward home. *I've seen him*, Tommy thought, and the world brightened. This beautiful world, blessed and cursed in the same breath, had all its parts in just the right balance for a moment. *I've seen him.* A perfect, frictionless moment of weightlessness and ease when Tommy Sandor knew he could walk like this forever. When he knew he could tear back the curtain that separated the world he saw from the world that always *was*.

❖ ❖ ❖

On the railroad tracks outside Bellaire, Kansas, Tommy's last sax reed split, and there was nowhere to buy a new one. Not even in the next town west, Smith Center, which was big enough for its own bank and library. He borrowed ten dollars of his racing money to buy a good fishing knife, then found a broken willow branch to carve into a reed. At the town park he settled under a cottonwood tree and got to work.

"What are you making?" asked a boy, ten or eleven, who'd been drawn with two younger brothers to this road-hardened man with brick-red skin.

"A reed for my saxophone." Tommy pointed at the case. "You guys mind asking your mom for some water, in a cup or jar she can live without?"

The oldest boy nodded, and they ran off, returning with a plastic cup of ice water. Tommy sipped it, then put the willow in it to soak.

"What's that for?" the middle brother asked.

"Making it soft so I can slice it." Tommy opened the case and pulled the split reed out of its sleeve. "Has to look like this, almost thin as paper."

The boys wanted to hear the sax, so he put it together and blew even though the reed barely let him squeak. The kids loved it, so he kept blowing while they pressed the keys.

"How come you're here?" asked the middle brother when Tommy stopped for breath.

"I'm walking home from Nebraska City, where my dad came from. Didn't know who he was till a couple days ago."

"I don't know my dad either," the oldest boy said. "Mom says I wouldn't want to."

"It's good to know, when you're old enough to handle it. Don't let anybody tell you different."

"Pete! Zack! Joey!" called their mother, as if smelling Tommy's sedition from afar, and she scolded them as they filed through her front door. He left Smith Center, holding the sax case in one hand and the plastic cup in the other because the willow had to get a lot softer before he could whittle it down thin enough. He passed by a giant irrigation sprinkler and tried, half-jokingly, to raise the water in it. The sprinkler soaked him from head to toe, teasing him like a friend or brother. He walked along another railroad track, counting the slow-moving cars, and finally found a shady place to sleep a hundred yards from a field that somebody was plowing with a finicky tractor.

Tommy woke up dreaming of railroad tracks so hot that they burned his fingers to ash, which gave him an idea. He set the wet willow on the track and sliced it down with his fishing knife until he nicked his finger. Then he kept walking, slower this time, switching the cup and the sax case every twenty-five paces for a while and licking the blood off his finger before he started up again. It would take weeks to get back to Suborney at this rate, Tommy thought, which maybe wasn't so bad. Thorpe might have moved on by then, tired of waiting for the prodigal son to return. Or Thorpe and his mom might be back together, with another kid on the way already. Or his mom might have skipped town, leaving nothing in the house but a note stuck to the kitchen table with a bloody knife.

WISH I NEVER HAD YOU, it would say, or I SHOULD'VE THROWN YOU IN THE TRASH LIKE THAT CRIPPLE GIRL. Nothing she would ever say because she loved him and wasn't a complete fuckup as mothers go. And Tommy knew that even if his mom had thrown him in the trash ten times, he would've been found ten times. He knew it so sure that he sang it to the sky —

*I know that some-*one would *have found* meeeeeeeeee.

Tommy waited long enough for the Sons and Daughters to sing the line back to him from Suborney, then sang it again. He saw himself as an old man with a beard, beaten down by the weather and with feet as tough as Jesus's were. So strong within himself, so used to the hardness of the world, that he could walk through a sandstorm and come out looking just the same as before.

Is that who I'm supposed to be? he asked. No answer from God, as usual. Or maybe the answer had been there all along, like those microscopic creatures in his skin and saliva that he'd heard about in biology class. Tommy sat by the railroad tracks and waited for a train that didn't come, then hitchhiked to Phillipsburgh and nearly broke down in front of the Phillips County Hospital. A sign on a big white house nearby said ROOMS, so Tommy dipped into his race money and rented one. He paid extra for a bathtub and spent the night soaking in it, pulling out chunks of hate from all over his body and falling asleep until the water chilled him and woke him up. Pulling hate from his neck, from his beltline, near his left hip, even from his hands. Some of it was buried so deep it took half an hour of pinching and pulling to get at. He'd drain cold water out, run the spigot as hot as he could, pull out more hate, and fall sleep until the water cooled again and he shot up against the tub's edge like somebody was trying to drown him.

Just before midnight a car hit a bicycle outside. Tommy stepped out of the tub and saw the yellow chunks of hate on the floor, like useless rock some poor miner thought was gold. He went outside to watch the ambulance drama and worked on his reed at a little metal table on the rooming house's creaky wraparound porch. A tall old man in a brown three-piece suit came out too—a vest and everything, plus a fedora with a yellow feather in its brim. He poured what looked like milk of magnesia from a blue bottle into a white teacup. He sipped it down, waved to Tommy, and went inside.

The man looked eighty-five or ninety, and Tommy figured he'd end up like that if he didn't get back to Suborney and straighten out the mess between his parents. He'd be stuck all alone, with his own kids too disgusted by him to ever visit. Maybe with his own kids already dead. He'd take a room someplace where he didn't have to talk to anybody, and he'd dress up like it was another time, only eating what he needed to stay alive. He'd work on his sax reeds all day, never getting them quite thin enough to use, and at night he'd pull things out of his body that no living creature should ever have inside of it. Those chunks would sit piled up in a closet, dreaming of fire, and when the right spark came along they'd set themselves aflame, taking the whole world down with them.

16

Sunday, July 20

The Sons and Daughters of Jesus and Mary started their first Sabbath day in their newest church with ringing. Ed Dolman clanged a broken clapper against the three hundred–pound brass bell they'd retrieved from the bottom of the junk pile, which now—because the tower was too rickety to ever hold it again—sat on a makeshift stand built of rebar and scrap four-by-fours. He stood beside the front steps, letting each ring dissipate until he felt like making another one, and it sounded to him like he was calling people to a funeral. Maybe it was a funeral, Dolman thought, for the self he'd grown sick of. A man too proud to believe in mercy and finally ready to burn the crust of shame that surrounded him so he could see what survived inside.

The ring faded, and Dolman struck the bell again. A new Ed Dolman who didn't mind being the first thing in Suborney not named Tommy Sandor to get suckered in by a pack of Jesus freaks. A new Ed Dolman who didn't have to steal anymore because he needed nothing but God's love, and God's love belongs to everybody. "God is free," he told himself as he struck the bell once more. "You can't steal God because God is free, God is free, God is free."

"Good say, sir," Thorpe told Dolman as he walked up the steps with a basket of dried-out bread crusts and a pitcher of wine. A few people from town came, some holding the handwritten notices that the Sons and Daughters had passed out: COME CELEBRATE LIFE WITH US AT 11:00 AM SUNDAY AND BLESS OUR CHURCH. Dolman rang the bell again and thought of how his dead mother and father would feel if they could see their fuckup son humbling himself to something, even if it was just a church full of people nobody else wanted.

Because God wants you even when nobody else does—especially then. Tim Fiddler drove Wally Ogrean up to the front steps, and Brother Zypanski carried him inside, lifting the town tough guy like a sack of potatoes. Ron and Kate Ulin walked past the bell, smiling at Dolman for the first time since he got arrested. Jim Ahearn, who nobody saw anymore, strode up to shake hands with Brother Worrell.

"Glad you folks did this," Jim said. "A town ought to have a church."

Six more locals showed up, and everybody got in a circle on the sanded but unvarnished floor. Sister Melanie read from the Gospel of Luke about how believers will all be betrayed, by brothers and parents and friends, and Brother Worrell read from Saint Paul about how God chastens us the way fathers chasten sons. Then they went around the circle with everybody saying where they'd found God that day. In the smell of the earth. In the skin of a shriveled old hand. In the sound of a grandchild's voice.

Then Mother Meg asked people what they wanted to pray for. The hostages. Peace inside us all. Tommy Sandor coming home safe. The sick and the dying and the lost. After each one Mother Meg or Thorpe said, "We all pray," then started an *Amen* that lasted as long as people could sing it. They lost themselves in the physical fact of praying together, lost track of the boundaries between each other. Mother Meg picked up the plate of bread and walked across the circle to Wally Ogrean, who opened his mouth and let her drop in a crust. She gave him the plate, and he shuffled over to feed Brother Zypanski, who walked over to feed Kate Ulin, who walked over to feed Sister Melanie, who walked over to feed Ed Dolman, who walked over to

Brother Benjy. Once the basket sat empty, they passed around the wine the same way.

Then they sat on the floor again, feeling the lost weight of what they'd given up inside themselves to make room for what their mouths had taken in. They gave up pride and righteousness clung to out of greed. Gave up nameless wants that flew out the church door and dropped to the ground, expired. They gave up the cobwebs inside them that once blocked the light.

Meanwhile, Connie filled her tank at Pete's gas station in case she had to escape Suborney. She was hustling out to Narka, Kansas, she'd tell anybody who asked, to get Tommy out of some trouble she didn't want to talk about.

"Heard from that boy of yours?" Pete asked as he rang her up.

"Just a phone message," she lied. "He told me about God's light, that's all. You think he's ready to shave off his eyebrows and give out little Bibles on street corners?"

"These folks don't do that. You're the only one pissed off at 'em, seems like."

"Are you on their side now?" Connie took back her two dollars and change. "They brainwash my son and send him who knows where, and you say they're not so bad?"

"I think he sent himself. Try to be objective about it."

"What's objective about people taking away your son? You had a kid and lost him awhile, remember how that felt?"

Connie stormed outside, letting Pete feel her outrage at the Jesus freaks for brainwashing Tommy and at the people of Suborney for not helping her stop them. Later on, when whatever storm that needed to break over her had come and gone, she'd want everybody to remember her anger slowly building up until it popped. Whatever a woman did after her son got stolen by a cult had to be forgiven. If Connie kept talking about Tommy from that angle, then whatever she ended up doing wouldn't have to be about Richie Thorpe in the eyes of Suborney, of the law, of the world. She'd just be a mama bear, taking her son back from the creeps who stole him.

Perfect logic, no matter where it led. The increasingly familiar pain in her abdomen stabbed at her twice, and she grunted at it in acknowledgment. Had to get herself to a doctor when Tommy came home. If Tommy came home. Connie drove east toward Kansas for the hell of it, into the open, empty plains, where she kept an eye out for her son. He'd either be stumbling home like a deranged hobo or strutting home like he knew every secret. Marching into Suborney with an army of lied-to teenagers, all wanting their lied-to years back.

* * *

Just as the good people of Suborney walked and shuffled and hobbled out of their brand-new church, Tommy made it to the edge of Bird City, Kansas. His Red Wing boots hadn't let him down, and neither had the reed he'd made for his Selmer. He'd played on street corners and parks in Norcatur and Oberlin, in Atwood and McDonald, blowing full tilt and showing people a kind of music they never knew existed. Angelic choruses like Tessy sang, followed by scolds and yowls that sounded like the cries of some extinct animal dragged reluctantly back into life.

It was the best he'd ever played because he'd finally learned to use those bad keys to control the in-between notes, the grunts and yowls and bellows that felt like they rumbled up from beneath the earth's crust. He played on his knees by the U.S. 36 sign that announced Bird City, the place where God gave Thomas Gregory Sandor to the world on March 14, 1963. A gift, a curse, a burden, a hope. A cop stopped on the wrong side of the road and rolled down his window.

"What the hell are you doing?" the cop said. He looked like what Tommy wished Dan Stannard had been, with a fat, angry neck that spilled out over his collar. Somebody who'd slug him at the first sign of back talk and give him a reason to leave home.

"Just playing some music, Officer." Tommy stayed on his knees.

"I was born here, figured I'd play a little song to thank the town. Am I hurting anybody?"

"What do you want here?"

"To do God's work, Officer. Help whoever needs it."

"You in that church where people don't drive?"

"I am, sir."

"Well, keep your hippie Jesus to yourself and get your work done quick."

The cop rolled up his window and took a U-turn. Tommy went right back to playing, ready to keep kneeling by that sign until one of the Sons and Daughters heard him and took him to the church they'd brought back from the dead. He'd recognize Brother Beto's mural in the living room, and he'd know where everything was in the house because Mother Meg would've organized it.

Tommy glided up and down a scale that he thought sounded Arab. It reminded him of a movie he saw in seventh grade, back before every red-blooded American was supposed to hate Arabs. In the movie a man sang from the top of a tower, calling his town to prayer. Hadn't he been doing that with his sax all along, calling people to prayer? Tommy laughed, wondering what the people back in Suborney would do if they caught him thinking a halfway decent thought about Arabs. Then he thought about his Thorpe blood, whether it would tell him to stand and fight or just walk on.

Walk on, he knew, because Thorpe blood rolled through the world at night to the rhythm of hearts and lungs and feet. Tommy honked a low E♭ and eased his way up the keys, stopping to revel in broken sounds halfway between notes and in sounds that weren't notes at all. He worked up to a shriek he'd discovered that was way higher than where the Selmer supposedly topped out, a sound so piercing it could even call the dead to prayer. *As if the dead aren't praying already*, he thought.

The sax fell silent, wouldn't let him blow another note. Tommy saluted a station wagon full of kids who waved at him while their parents scowled. He cleaned his sax with his old blue bandanna tied to a fishing weight, stuffed the money bag back into the bell, and headed down Bird Avenue toward town to look for a phone booth. It was one o'clock in Colorado. Time to make a call.

"Hello, Reverend Stannard," Tommy practiced saying, jangling the fistful of quarters in his jeans pocket. "You got a little time to talk?" But first he called home.

"It's Sunday afternoon, Mom," he told the answering machine. "Time for Justin Stannard's show. You might want to listen in this time."

Connie didn't hear it right away because she was outside tossing Tommy's stuff, which fit into three heavy-duty black trash bags, into her truck bed to drop it off with the Jesus freaks. The tape player and the headphones and the hideous jazz cassettes. The jeans and the white T-shirts and the crumpled New York subway map and the stolen library books about John Coltrane and Charlie Parker. The brand-new deck of cards and the pocketknife collection. No drugs or porn at least. As Connie heaved the last bag in, Dan Stannard parked his patrol car behind her truck.

"Don't worry, I'm not leaving," she said as he stepped out. "It's all Tommy's."

"Do you *have* to do this?" Stannard asked.

"Yes. It'd make things easier on me if you swept his room while I'm gone. Don't get any ideas just 'cause it's empty."

Stannard nodded and watched Connie start her truck angrily and struggle past his patrol car with a squealing ten-point turn. She drove up Mangum Street looking for Tommy, hoping to intercept him before the Jesus freaks did. She could tell him everything—what his father could do with fire and how she needed to protect him from it even if he had that same power inside him. *Especially* if he had it. But if Richie's gang got to him first, they'd parade her through town, hanging her by the hands and feet from a junkyard two-by-four like a sacrificial pig. Tommy would lead the way with one end of the beam on his shoulder, shouting, "See what a liar looks like, right here!" Thorpe would carry the other end, wiping away crocodile tears and mumbling about how none of this would have happened if Jeanette Holmquist had only said yes to him eighteen tears ago. No fire in Nebraska City, no dead grandfather, no lies in Bird City or Suborney. No flag burning jokes from Tommy because he'd love himself enough to love his country.

On Road X Connie waved to Sam Kurtep and even to Ed Dolman, who knelt in his driveway working on the Harley he'd been fixing up for years. At the church she saw the black kid on a ladder, holding up a can for the one-handed Mexican who painted red trim around the brand-new windows. The kid waved, and the Mexican raised his paintbrush as she drove past—both of them killing her with kindness today so they could bury her in shame tomorrow.

"All you gave me was lies," Tommy would growl at her when he came back. "I'll lock you inside that house and burn it down with nothing but the lies you fed me." Connie drove onto the Perrin house lawn and took a big breath that came in like icicles and left like shards of glass. Melanie stepped outside with the same annoyingly sweet smile as always.

"Morning!" she called cheerily from the porch steps, but Connie didn't buy the act.

"This is for you." Connie pulled the first bag out of the truck bed and flung it to the ground. "I figure you'll see him before I do." The second bag went down.

"We don't know where he is either," Melanie said.

"You're telling me he hasn't called you?"

"We don't use phones, ma'am. We're just as worried as—"

"*Don't* give me that. He's not your son. You don't know what worried means."

"When did you turn on him?" Melanie cocked her head back, squinting one eye—a gesture she no doubt picked up from Richie, who'd used it all the time back in Nebraska City.

"Excuse me?" Connie stiffened up, the third bag still in her hands. *The second Richie showed his face here*, she thought of saying, but that would give too much away.

"You turned on Tommy. You come here looking for him, but I don't see any love from you at all. You're just mad, and you're passing it off as mother love."

"What do *you* know about mother love? And don't give me some bullshit about how your *Mary* is everybody's mother. This is my *son* we're talking about. If you don't have one, you don't understand." Connie hurled the third trash bag across the yard.

"I *did* have one." Melanie's sweetness dropped away. "And I know how it felt to lose him forever, not just for a few days. So don't go telling me I don't know what mother love is, just 'cause I can't call myself a mother now—*Miss* Sandor."

After Melanie stalked back inside, Connie strewed Tommy's stuff all over the yard and on the porch steps too. She went around to check on the goats and saw the nanny pushing her kid away hard enough to hurt it. The nanny's udders were distended, so full and tight and infected that she wouldn't let the kid anywhere near her.

"Take care of your damn goats, people!" Connie yelled. She shooed the billy away to look at the kid—hungry and scared of its mom but otherwise okay. Connie cooed to bring the nanny closer and squeezed a bunch of milk onto the ground so that mama could stand her kid's pulling. As she drove home, her mind slipped back to Tommy, whose Jesus obsession made her push him away just like the nanny pushed away her kid. If the boy ever came back, he'd be all Jesus, all the time, and she could picture herself twitching every time she felt that name rising up to his lips. Connie got so exhausted from all her poisoned thinking that by the time she saw Stannard staring into her son's room, her shoulders couldn't slump any further.

"I said don't get any ideas. I don't need a roommate."

"I don't want to be your roommate," Dan told her.

"Then figure out what you want to be. It's not my husband, we know that."

"I don't think there's a word for it."

"But there's one for me," Connie said. "I'm your *whore*. Your brother said it in front of ten thousand people on the radio."

That got Stannard out the door in a hurry. Connie noticed the flashing light on the answering machine, and when she heard Tommy's message, she felt like her bones were melting. She slumped against her back door with her radio on her lap and rolled the dial to 620 AM to hear him. The clock on her stove read 1:02.

"—believe she never *told* me!" said Tommy's voice. He sounded near tears, which had to be a put-on because he never got that way. "The father she gave me was a lie. How am I supposed to forgive that?"

As Justin Stannard licked his lips, Connie felt a weight descend from her neck and jaw to her abdomen, sliding like a cross between maple syrup and molten iron. It filled her esophagus and pinned her to the inside of herself, so she didn't dare move. She awaited Richie's triumph—the moment when ten thousand people learned about her lie. She would've run if her body weren't weighed down by this change of density inside her. Was this thick, impossible liquid turning into a stake through her heart?

"Might take a while for you to forgive a lie like that," the Reverend finally said.

"I mean, to say the guy's a sax player from New York when he's really some dumbass Okie shitkicker passing through with a rodeo." Tommy blew out hard through his lips. "Come on, Mom. You could've given me a better father than that. A better *lie* than that."

"The thing is to ask what Jesus wants of you right now," Justin Stannard said. "He doesn't need you worrying about her lie—he'll deal with that when the time comes. He wants you to love your mother, understand me? He doesn't want what you've learned to poison your love for her because that'll throw you right off the path that leads you to him. You've been working to get to that path, bushwhacking—"

Connie lowered the volume and felt the liquid inside her stop descending and twist into a thick, primitive fishhook. Tommy hadn't spilled the beans about Richie, but he'd made up a lie of his own, and that made him doubly dangerous. He could—following her own wonderful example—weave that lie into a new family history, a new identity. He might even take up rodeo just to spite her. She turned the volume back up.

"—then I ought to be Tommy Milderbrandt," her son said. "My dad's first name was Derek, not Drake—but hey, at least she used most of the same letters. He came from Enid, Oklahoma, had a dad stationed at the air force base there. I'm going down to find him."

"That won't do a thing unless you let Jesus find you first," said the Reverend.

"I did!" This time Tommy's cry sounded real, and Connie flinched against it. "Jesus doesn't know where I'm at. At least he knew who his father was."

"He knows where *everybody's* 'at,' Mr. Sandor."

"Don't call me that. It's a made-up name—it's a lie. *I'm* a lie."

"You're not a lie, Tommy," said Reverend Stannard. "You're a child of God. Put the phone down, get on your knees and pray, and call me back later if you've still got quarters."

Then came silence. Connie waited for Tommy to hang up, then turned off the radio. She did a quick, involuntary scan of her house, calculating which possessions should go with her and the various options she had for packing them. Her timing would depend on how mad at her Tommy was when he got back—and after the radio call she knew it would be a matter of *when* and not if, because he'd want vengeance.

Mother Meg and Richard Thorpe weren't so sure he'd ever come back as they listened to KJML at the Jesus and Mary house. They sat on the kitchen floor, just like Connie had, and Thorpe banged his head against the doorframe behind him.

"Well, that didn't work out so hot," he said as he turned off the radio. A tear slipped out of him, but it got lost in the cottage cheese maze of his bad cheek. "Sister Mel was right. I should've just come out and told him."

"Give him time," said Mother Meg beside him, wrapping an arm around Thorpe's shoulder and kissing his forehead. "You could've tried it fifty different ways, and maybe they'd all be wrong. You should go see Tessy."

"Yeah," Thorpe said. "At least I know she won't jump out of my arms."

"Give your boy a chance to get *in* your arms before you worry about him jumping *out*. Do it for us, if you won't do it for yourself."

✳ ✳ ✳

The church in Bird City was on East Bressler and bigger than the one in Suborney, with green-gray roof shingles that didn't match the tan brick walls. Tommy laughed at the roof. Knowing how the Sons and Daughters operated, there must have been a whole lot of dirt-cheap green-gray shingles laying around somewhere. The church had a decent lawn, plus the black-and-white sign that Tommy had seen Beto painting another version of in Suborney, plus a big cement vase full of flowers between two sets of glass double doors. He walked up the flagstone steps and peeked in, expecting to see pews, but found instead a bare wood floor and piles of square, purple seat cushions with white Kansas State Wildcat logos on them.

"Wonder where you scrounged those up, Daddy-O." Tommy wished Thorpe were next to him, secretly checking in on the church. His hate for the man had blown away for the moment, replaced by a wish for the kind of camaraderie he used to want from the marines. Feet shuffled on the sidewalk behind him, and he saw a fortyish man with thick glasses and dirty-kneed jeans. His black collared shirt was as stiff as the way he moved.

"Can I help you?" The man shuffled halfway up the concrete path and stopped, unsure of the creature before him. "Are you okay?"

"Just checking out your church, sir. Getting ideas." Tommy pointed at Beto's sign. "That looks like a one-handed Mexican painted it."

"Do you need some food? Water?" The man stepped closer. "Are you okay?"

"You keep asking me that."

"I'm Brother Warren, the caretaker here."

"I'm Tommy Sandor."

"Well, well." Warren breathed deeper and put his hands behind his back. "The mythical beast lives. You want food? Water? A place to sleep?"

"All three," Tommy said. "Any order you got 'em in."

Five hours later Tommy was fed, watered, showered, and napping in a house a block away, which had the same gray-green shingles as the church. He woke to find a pair of gym shorts and a United Auto Workers T-shirt hanging on the doorknob, then walked through the house looking for Brother Warren. Beto's mural covered the biggest wall in the living room: Jesus walking on a dirt road, tall and straight, next to a blue-robed Mary. In front of him stretched a scrubby desert, but the land he'd passed through was green and lush.

The backyard of the church house looked as green as that part of the mural, full of flowers and surrounded by an eight-foot hedge. Warren knelt before a statue of Mary holding a baby Jesus that sat in a hole carved out of the shrub. Tommy opened the back door, ready to joke that praying to statues would get you tarred and feathered by the Pentecostals back home, but instead he knelt on the grass beside Brother Warren. Tommy stared at the statue to keep his mind focused, but he didn't quite know how to pray. So he stared at the grass by his knees and thought *Thank you, God, for the grass and dirt you gave us*, then *I'm scared my whole life is exploding*. Brother Warren took a deep breath and sat back on his heels.

"What were you praying for?" Tommy asked him.

"Not sure. I don't ask myself that anymore. Probably you." Warren stood and wiped off his knees, which kept their grass stains anyway. "You're welcome to stay out here, but I'm going over to feed the Laingers."

"I'd like to do that."

"I'll need a couple minutes alone to say who you are. They're touchy."

"When did you meet my dad?"

"Let's feed the Laingers." Warren held out a hand and pulled Tommy up to standing. "Plenty of time to talk after that."

The Laingers lived in a tan house on Demick Street, its living room piled high with labeled boxes—the things, Warren whispered, that they planned to parcel out to their now-distant children when they died. Mrs. Lainger wouldn't look at Tommy's face or say a word to him, and she barely moved from her seat at the dining room table. Her husband sat on a fat lounger and wouldn't come to the table at all. They ate beans and rice and bread slathered with margarine. Mr. Lainger had a box in his throat from cancer, but he made sure to say a raspy, robotic "Thank you" when Tommy brought over his food.

"Pretty glamorous, isn't it?" Warren said as they walked back to the church house twenty minutes later.

"Are all our churches in towns where half the people are dying?" Tommy hadn't intended the *our*, but he liked how it came out. He could still be one of the Sons and Daughters, even if he never talked to Richard Curtis Thorpe again in his life.

"Just works out that way." Brother Warren spit at the curb, then startled as if he'd let an old self slip out. "Are you glad your dad found you or just as pissed off as before?"

"How'd you know I was pissed off before?"

"We all heard the legend. Like Bigfoot." Warren waited for Tommy to laugh, but it didn't happen. "I'm glad he found you. Maybe now he can stop living in pain."

"Where'd you meet him?"

"I latched on up in Sidney. His third town, I think."

"Sidney, Nebraska?" Tommy asked. "My grandma lives there. Did you know he was trying to track me down when you met him?"

"No, not till here. Your dad's not the kind to say everything on his mind."

"No kidding." They turned a corner, and Tommy saw a woman pulling weeds in front of the church house. "What did you steal? Don't you have to break the law to get mixed up with this bunch?"

"Back in North Platte I stole money from the city. For three years almost."

Tommy pointed to the woman on the grass. "What did she steal?"

"Better ask her, but I wouldn't make it your first question. She's Clara, by the way."

Clara turned out to be one of five people who gathered for supper at the church house, all of them back from feeding people who couldn't feed themselves, and Warren introduced Tommy as Brother Thorpe's son. He acted gentler than usual with them as they ate spaghetti, smiling and laughing because everybody in the room knew his father. Afterward they walked to the church to pray in a circle on those Kansas State Wildcat cushions and give each other dried-out bread and wine. They sat in silence for the longest time, waiting for Jesus to settle into the room, and once they felt him, they talked about the things they wanted to bring into the world. God's light everywhere. Jesus in every heart. Love between people who'd turned away from it.

"I want to keep seeing Jesus when I walk," Tommy said when his turn came. "And I want to bring my father peace. I want him to stop running."

17

Monday, July 21

"You're the son of that man, I know it," said Mrs. Lori Manconi to Tommy first thing in the morning. Everyone from last night's prayer circle had come over to clean her house, which she'd finally allowed after months of the Sons and Daughters offering. "The one who's always talking love, love, love, when he's got all that hate in his heart."

"I'm sure he doesn't hate you, ma'am," Tommy said back as he pulled her fridge out and watched two mice scurry for a hole in the baseboards. "Plus, his hate doesn't slide down to me just 'cause I'm his son."

"When Warren told me he was moving on, I opened up my heart. Understand? Like I couldn't with him around."

Mrs. Manconi rolled her wheelchair down the hallway. She over-flowed that wheelchair the way her thoughts overflowed her mouth, Tommy thought, and she couldn't spare a word of thanks for the people who cleared out her mouse shit and her cat shit and her half-eaten cans of food. First she had an army of mice, then she brought in an army of cats to kill them, then the county decided they were a health hazard and took them away. Now it was the Sons and Daughters' turn, and they didn't expect her to be any more grateful to them than she'd been to the cats. Tommy could feel exactly how she and Thorpe would raise each other's hackles.

"I try every day," she told the woman who cleaned her toilet. "I just don't have the arm strength anymore."

"Stuff it in as far as you can," said Warren, handing Tommy steel wool and a wooden spoon. "Then check the garage, that's where they're coming in." Tommy filled four holes in the kitchen and threw out a nest made from the paper bags that Mrs. Manconi stashed under her sink. She wheeled behind him, blocking his way.

"You think Jesus is with you just because you *say* he is?" she asked him. "That's Jesus's choice, isn't it? Who he wants to be with?"

"It is, ma'am. He just chooses to be with everybody." Tommy wondered if he could move the water inside a person's body, though he couldn't decide whether to dry Mrs. Manconi up or flood her.

"That's what your father said. 'Even for people who don't believe, he's there with you.' But he never proved Jesus was with *him*, not one time."

As she huffed away, Tommy saw Jesus standing by the pantry dusting off an old peach can. Not the real Jesus—his robe was way too white for that—just a figment to help him keep his cool. The fake Jesus shrugged, and Tommy laughed, and Mrs. Manconi got so pissed that she almost kicked everybody out. Warren pulled Tommy to the garage, which was infested with dry cat turds. As they rearranged her junk—including two broken ladders, a paint-by-numbers canvas with only the browns and grays finished, and empty boxes labeled KEEP—Tommy wondered if the church in Suborney was clean yet.

"How come us Sons and Daughters are so in love with junk?" Tommy asked Warren.

"Chaos gets a grip where there's junk, and sin gets a grip where there's chaos."

"Sounds like something my dad made up."

"He picked it up from Nick, Mother Meg's son." Warren knocked over a box and another mouse nest fell to the floor.

"Were you locked up with them?"

"They don't lock up white boys who can't fight. I was on probation."

When Tommy got sick of touching dried cat shit, he found the bathroom without asking Mrs. Manconi first. He scrubbed his hands and dried them in his hair, finding a brownish strand above his right ear and imagining it all as dark as his dad's. Those bristly Thorpe sideburns would look damn good on him someday. Tommy opened the bathroom door to find Mrs. Manconi blocking his way again.

"You've got it too," she said. "Same as him, that unclean heart."

"I'm trying to clean my heart, ma'am. I'm helping people. I'm praying."

"Only God can clean your heart. Isn't that what you people always say?"

"But God cleans those who clean themselves. Don't we say that too?"

"Get this creature out of my house!" Mrs. Manconi shouted. "*Out*, you hear me?"

Tommy apologized to Brother Warren fifty times, then walked a big circle around Bird City looking for the farm where he was born. He searched all over and didn't see anything like the red barns he remembered or the goat pen he'd been born next to. He found a pay phone by a bank and used all his quarters to call his mom at work without knowing why.

"Are you in trouble?" she asked Tommy.

"Actually, I'm in Bird City. Did you know the Sons and Daughters fixed up a church here?"

"I think you mentioned that once, Brother Tom-Tom."

"And they were in Sidney right before that. Isn't that funny, how they're kinda following us around? None of them knew Grandma, though. I already asked."

Connie heard Bill Rocher laugh in the office behind her and knew she had a few minutes to talk. "What are you trying to get at?"

"Nothing. Just speakin' the truth, like God wants me to. About that Brother Thorpe guy, Mom?"

"Yeah?" Connie wanted to hold her breath until she knew which direction to run.

"Watch out for him when you're taking care of the goats. I don't think he is who he says he is."

"I could've told you that," she said.

"So why didn't you? And speaking of not telling—" Tommy cleared his throat. "Um, did you listen to Reverend Standard on KJML yesterday, like I asked you to?"

"Sorry," she lied. "I was at lunch with Deb from work."

"Oh. Does the name Derek Milderbrandt mean anything to you?"

"Is he some country music star? Doesn't sound like a jazz guy."

"He's an ex-rodeo guy. Maybe you never heard of him."

"This conversation gets weirder and weirder, Tommy. And I have to get back to work. When are you coming back? Are you sleeping inside at least?"

"Yeah, in a spare room at the church house. They feed me. I do some work here and there. I'm learning to pray. Don't you think that's a good thing?"

"Depends on what you're praying for. If it's to make your mother's head explode, maybe not." She remembered feeling staked down against her kitchen door by the liquid in her own body and wondered if Tommy had prayed for that. "What do you want? You didn't call just to say you started praying."

"I wanted to say that when I come back, I promise I'll be a better son. It's what I'm praying for the hardest."

"That's nice to know." Connie didn't ask whether he meant being a better son to his mother or to his father. "You should know I brought all your stuff to Wesley's house."

"That's okay, I'm giving most of it away. Listen—"

"I *am* listening. It's all I've been doing with you lately."

"No you're not. I keep telling you I want to live in the light of

God, but you never want to hear it. Is there something inside you that can't stand the light of God, Mom?"

"I'm hanging up now. Whatever you're going through, I don't think I can talk to you till you're on the other side of it."

"What if I never am? What if all I ever want is the light of God?"

"Then at least pray for the light of God to turn you into a Tommy I can stand, not some Jesus robot. I'm scared of what's happening to you."

"I'm scared for you too, Mom. It's not—" He stopped himself.

"Not *what*?"

Tommy breathed in slow and blew out hard. "When I was a kid, I belonged wherever I was. Just me in the world, you know? When did I lose that?"

"Your fourteenth birthday," Connie said. "When I told you who your father was."

Tommy let out a Thorpe *Huh-haaaaaaa!* and hung up. Connie listened to make sure her boss was still jabbering, then punched in her mother's number. After ten rings the answering machine kicked on.

"He knows," Connie said. "The people who got hold of Tommy were in Sidney. Richie was probably fixing up some damn church right under your nose. Did you—?"

Trish picked up the phone. "You think I know everything that happens here? There's six thousand people."

"What did you know, and when did you know it? There's a noose around my neck, and I want to know if you're helping me get it off or if you helped Richie put it on me."

In Sidney, Trish sat heavily on the rocking chair that she kept in her kitchen. Oak with baby-blue cushions, one of the few things she'd brought with her from Nebraska City.

"Mom?"

"I'm tired," Trish said. "I want to see my friends. The ones I grew up with, not the ones I have now."

"Did you tell Richie where I was? Answer me."

"I never told anybody anything. I'm tired, sweetie. You're better off handling this mess without me 'cause I'm not strong enough to keep you from falling into it. Don't have the grip I used to."

✻ ✻ ✻

That night everybody in the world was Connie Sandor's enemy. She watched reruns of *Dynasty* and *M*A*S*H*, plus part of a movie of the week about two brothers in the air force, but they didn't take her mind off the thing she felt growing inside her—a glop of metallic venom forming where her abdominal pains had hit, where the fishhook had been. It hadn't hardened yet but wasn't quite pliable anymore, and on her couch she squeezed it down to make sense of its contours. It felt like metal from outer space, stranded inside her and reconfiguring her whole bloodstream as it grew and changed shape, looking for its final form.

Where did the venom come from? From her love for Tommy and Richie gone bad? Whatever its source, she knew it needed to get purer and stronger before she could use it. She needed to concentrate all the energies inside herself that had previously been dispersed in the back alleys of her muscles, her organs, her bones. Then she had to pull them toward her pivot point—the very tip of the fishhook, the one place where she could be or do anything.

But it wasn't a fishhook anymore. And it wasn't primitive because as she squeezed down, it grew harder and more refined. It had hundreds of brilliant sides already, like a pearl grown in her own body but cut like a diamond. Some parts of it were still rough, like the meteorites she'd seen with Tommy at the Denver Museum of Natural History, and she had a long way to go before she finished shaping its edges. Connie squeezed her guts down even harder than when she gave birth to Tommy, squeezing that lump of venomous metal like Superman turning coal into a diamond. She held tight for a count of fifty, then huffed out the stale air that had been in her lungs for who knows how long. She sucked in a new breath and held that one too, squeezing down as she counted and turning the shape inside her into a weapon she could use when Tommy came back home. When he stood next to Richie at her front door, with all his Jesus freak buddies and the whole town of Suborney behind him.

Connie only counted up to forty before exhaling this time, and for a moment she couldn't pull a breath in past her throat. Was she strangling herself? Was Richie strangling her from just outside the door? Three times she tried to suck in a breath before one finally made it. She changed channels and watched Flo from *Alice* tell Mel to "Kiss my grits!" for the millionth time, then turned the set off. Everybody on TV seemed slight to her, floating weightless in their puny, invented problems. Meanwhile, she'd almost choked herself to death without even using her hands. Meanwhile, she had to battle a man who'd been tracking her down for Tommy's whole life.

She decided to fight Richie Thorpe for Tommy in front of everybody in Suborney, and she knew they'd all bet on Richie. But the venomous metal made it a more even fight—Richie was Goliath, and she was David, and the thing growing inside her was the magic killing stone. As Connie imagined reaching into her guts for it, a shudder ran from the base of her spine to the crown of her skull. Her whole body flinched three times, and she found herself on the living room floor, on the other side of the coffee table from where she'd first felt the spasms.

Weird. Dangerous. She stepped outside for some air and wound up walking down Mangum Street, sure somebody was looking for her. Tommy? Richie? Dan? Justin? *JesusJesusJesus?* She found Julie Parness on her porch swing and climbed up the steps.

"You got an extra glass handy?" Connie asked her.

"A glass, sure. Don't know how much I've got left to pour in it."

Connie kept an eye pointed toward the bridge into Suborney, barely visible from Julie's porch, so she'd notice if Tommy drove back into town. Then she remembered what her mom said about the Vega breaking down and went back to imagining him on foot. Inside the house Julie plunked ice cubes into a glass and clunked a bottle against a counter. She was the kind of drunk who always had a huge bottle of whatever she craved—gin at the moment—and guzzled it down. Then came two days of promising herself to finally get sober until she broke down and bought a huge bottle of something else.

Connie wondered what kind of drunk she'd be. A hyper-organized one, probably, with bottles lined up by height and color on top of her fridge. Going through them in order, three shots at a time until they were all empty. Laughing at herself for thinking she could ever quit, then blowing a week's pay on fresh bottles of everything.

"Is Tommy coming back?" Julie asked Connie after they clinked glasses.

"He says so, but who knows what he'll be like. He'll probably say he's Mary's son instead of mine."

"He had a girl over here one time while you were up at your mom's. A Mexican. Wonder if him ducking out has anything to do with her."

"That'd be too easy," Connie said, sipping the terrible gin, and Julie kicked the porch to get her swing moving. They slipped into a half-strained silence, a little cocoon that let them feel like part of the world yet immune from having to care about it too much. It was just the world. It passed by. It blew things into your lap sometimes, blew things off your lap others.

"Thanks for this." Connie finished her drink. "I'll set it here by the step."

"No, give it to me. It might scare the shit out of me down there if I go for a walk."

"A walk where? Up to the church?"

"I've been by. Nice seeing what they've done to it."

Connie thanked Julie for the drink again and walked up to check out the church for herself. Behind the new windows, the walls were filled with lantern-light shadows. She heard a woman's laugh, then Thorpe's laugh. Then somebody said, "Bless this place," and she watched the shadows move, pecking the floor like chickens.

"Bless this place," the shadows said. "Bless this place," as if kissing a lover who'd never been kissed before.

Connie wanted to yell at those hypocrites, who wouldn't give a shit about Suborney if she and Tommy didn't live there. That beloved church they fixed up and those beloved people they helped might just as well be in another state. She felt her jaws clench from holding in a scream and opened her mouth wide to pop them, but her jaws kept on getting wider. They felt like a snake's, with the lower one almost detaching itself from her skull. She'd seen a snake in a pet shop once eating a rat three times thicker than itself and a picture of one in South America swallowing a baby deer whole.

"What would *you* swallow whole?" she asked, letting the words out of her mouth even though she hadn't intended to. As soon as the question was spoken, she felt lightness and purpose. The pivot point—she'd found it, right there in her very own jaws.

18

Tuesday, July 22, to Thursday, July 24

On Tuesday morning Benjy, Melanie, and Worrell watched from the church house porch as Connie, dressed for work except for a pair of sneakers, sledgehammered a two-by-four stake into the crusty front yard. It had a hand-painted plywood sign nailed to each side.

"I can help you with that, ma'am," Brother Benjy said, though he didn't move.

"Not everybody believes in your kind of *help*." Connie took a big swing and caught the edge of the stake, splintering it. "And don't start telling me it's God's help because all God's help did is take my son away from me."

"Your son took himself away," Sister Melanie called from the doorway.

"He spent seventeen years without taking himself away for more than one damn night. Then you people show up, and he's gone."

Connie stepped back and checked her work. The sign facing Suborney said, WHAT HAVE THEY DONE TO MY SON? The sign facing the front porch said, WHAT HAVE YOU DONE TO MY SON? Connie kept whacking at the stake.

"Don't ask us about Tommy if you don't want to hear about God," Brother Worrell said. "All we did was tell him where his blinders were so he could take 'em off himself."

219

"What about that 'Honor thy mother' thing from your Bible?"

"There's better ways to honor your mother than doing what she tells you," Benjy said.

"And I'm sure you know *lots* about honoring people." Connie dropped the sledgehammer into her truck bed with a clang.

"We'll leave this up for you," Melanie said, pointing at Connie's sign. "We don't want to stand in the way of whatever God wants you to get through."

"Thanks, *Sister*. All I'm *getting* through is taking my son back."

Connie drove to the church, looking to give *Brother* Thorpe an earful. In the middle of the empty floor sat the tall guy, cross-legged and rocking the ugliest, most deformed human being Connie had ever seen. She was naked except for a T-shirt that looked like a dress on her, and she sang a high-pitched little tune without words. Connie listened closely to make sure it wasn't the song Richie had hummed the night of the fire. Five notes, so it might have been. But this one was in a major key, with no darkness in it.

"*When will my time cooome?*" Brother Zypanski sang back. Tessy clammed up as Connie approached, and he said, "It's okay, Tessy. She's Tommy's mom."

When her eyes met Tessy's, Connie realized that she was on her hands and knees, even though she didn't remember getting there. Just like last night. She couldn't breathe, but neither could Tessy—they stared at each other like they were stuck under a diving bell with the air getting sucked out of it. *Smoke inhalation*, Connie thought. *This is my father dying.* Then Tessy gave a crooked smile, and some air slid down both their throats.

"She's a strong one," Zypanski told Connie as he patted Tessy's back. "Not many people have as much spunk inside them as it takes my baby girl just to breathe."

Connie nodded and crawled out the door backward, keeping her eye on Tessy even though she wanted desperately not to, and she couldn't take in a full breath until she'd locked herself inside her truck. She drove toward Sam Kurtep's house and sat on the rock in the middle of Suborney Creek, where she used to read when Tommy was a boy. While he played in the creek like a regular kid and never asked who his father was, because it didn't matter as long as he knew who his mother was.

We done good, said an imaginary Thorpe, who sat on the rock beside her, pretending to be a hayseed with a long stem of grass between his teeth. He slipped a thick arm softly around her waist, and she wriggled out of it, jumping down from the rock and getting her sneakers wet. Her feet felt nice and cool, and she decided to keep them in the water until the rest of her cooled off too. Then she got another vision: Tommy, baptizing somebody in the deep part of the creek where he used to pretend he was an otter. He spoke softly in a language Connie didn't understand, then sprinkled water over the forehead of someone who rested in his arms, completely still and trusting.

Connie looked deeper into her vision and saw that the *someone* in Tommy's arms was a sixteen-year-old Jeanette Holmquist. A girl who'd put aside her pride for long enough to admit that she needed to be led—she just didn't know where yet or by whom. Jesus? Not for her. Richie? Please. But Jeanette closed her eyes anyway and let herself get dunked into the water by this strange young man. This strong young man, with so much truth inside him.

* * *

Tommy kept walking to the destination Brother Warren had given him: Hugo, Colorado, where Sister Miriam was the church caretaker. After rushing across the plains to get to Bird City, he wanted to stretch out the last leg of his walk so he could show up in Suborney just in time for church—whenever that was. But his legs were used to walking day and night now, and nothing slowed him down but playing his sax and working. In St. Francis, Kansas, he pitched in on painting a Baptist church even though he used to hate Baptists. After that he went through another round of hating his father, imagining huge battles between them with fire and water that filled the sky and overwhelmed the land. Tommy couldn't ever win, so he told himself he needed more practice. He tried playing with some clouds above him, which rained down on his head while he stood at the corner of Road 11 and Road E.

"Gaining on you," he told Thorpe, and their imaginary fight turned into an imaginary training session. Near the Colorado border he found Hugo on a gas station map and meandered toward it, stopping at Bonny Lake State Park and paying for a campsite even though he could have sneaked in. Tommy tried to move the lake just an inch to test himself, but it only glugged and rippled halfheartedly, uninterested in taking commands that lacked all conviction. He couldn't even figure out who to hate, let alone which way to move the water. Let alone why.

"I got no right to play with you," he told the lake, and its movement settled down to a peaceful chug. Down the shore he saw Jesus and Mary, standing in water up to their knees and laughing as they threw out a ratty fishing net. They waved to him again, though not quite as enthusiastically as at Big Johnson Reservoir. Why? When Tommy zoomed in on them, Mary looked like a darker-skinned version of Jeannette Holmquist, with the same short haircut she had in that picture by her father's burned-down television store in Nebraska City. Then Jesus was gone, and Jeannette stood there in a brown corduroy jacket with its collar flipped up against a sudden wind. She threw pebbles into the water one at a time, trying to decide whether to keep her baby or find a doctor to abort it. Whether to give it away once it was born or raise it on her own or stuff it in a pile of pallets somewhere.

His mom threw her last pebble and stepped into the water, as if she'd decided to drown herself, and when Tommy hustled to rescue her, she disappeared. There was only Thorpe down the shoreline, wearing his red United Farm Workers T-shirt and dragging in Jesus and Mary's net. Nothing inside it, no miracles today. Tommy played his sax awhile, wishing he had no imagination at all so he could stop seeing and hearing people who weren't there. Thorpe walked over to him anyway, not grown-up but nineteen and scared because he'd slaughtered Greg Holmquist and didn't know if the baby in Jeannette's womb would come out alive. They made a fire in silence, both afraid of knowing the other, and Tommy finally burned the hate he'd pulled out in the boardinghouse bathtub. He dropped it in one chunk at a time, making green and purple flames and breathing in their scent—like cloves and pancakes and beef bouillon, calling more pain out of his body. A chunk right over his heart came out easy, but one on the back of his knee took an hour to dig out. One on the arch of his foot only came out halfway, even when he gouged at it with a hot knife.

That one'll slow you down, said the imaginary Thorpe, who materialized on the other side of the fire as a grown man but without the bashed-in cheek. Tommy had a ton of questions for him—who'd told him about Suborney, how long he'd known Connie lived there, why he had to fix a bunch of churches on the way instead of walking straight into town and saying the truth. But the figment didn't answer. He only stared across the fire and nodded like a big, dumb fish. Tommy got sick of that nod, so he pushed the right side of his father's face into the fire. Thorpe just sat up and brushed the ash from his face, then turned the other cheek.

"I get it!" Tommy shouted. "Nick, I get it. Turn the other cheek!"

He'd never tasted insanity before, or even the slippery chute that led that way, but Tommy figured this had to be it. And it lived so close to complete acceptance and understanding of his own life, of his own weaknesses. *Why is that?* he asked God. *Why'd you make us that way?* He knelt to pray for Nick Rachmann, who must have seen that same unblinking look from Thorpe a million times before deciding to bash his cheek in and make him turn the other one. That look needed to get knocked off Thorpe's face before he could ever see God.

"You might need it knocked off yours," Tommy heard in his mother's voice, which surprised him because she never had a thing to say about God. "Don't act like it's easy."

He fell asleep as the fire died and woke at the first prods of sunlight. He got walking again right away, even though his foot hurt like hell with that hate stuck in his arch. He walked until he passed out in the shade of a shack, and when he opened his eyes, he saw a man holding a pitchfork six inches from his face.

"What are you doing here?" asked the man, even more sunburned than Tommy.

"Just resting, sir. On my way to my father's church."

The man turned out to be Jon Cowley, a broccoli farmer who gave Tommy a place to shower and wash his clothes in exchange for help fixing a tractor axle. His wife was gone for a few days to take care of her sick sister in Flagler, so Tommy got on his knees with Jon and prayed for both women. They talked about Jesus, and Tommy laid his hands on Jon's head, trying to send God's light between the seams where his skull plates fit together. Jon started to cry, and when he didn't stop after fifteen minutes, Tommy made a meal with whatever he found in the kitchen and fed him until the tears dried up.

Jon gave Tommy a lift to Flagler, and from there he walked toward Hugo on the frontage roads of Interstate 70. He played his sax at the edge of a tiny town called Arriba, and when a Colorado state patrolman hassled him, he resisted the temptation to drop Dan Stannard's name. Tommy hitched a ride to ease his feet, but the college kid who picked him up just wanted help finding dope. His next ride came from a fortyish Kansas City woman who he would have tried to screw a few weeks before. Instead, he told her he was looking for Jesus, which made her laugh.

"You're serious?"

"I've seen him, and he's seen me. Hasn't said what he wants from me yet, though."

"They still make kids like you?" she asked.

"Always will, ma'am. Until there's nobody left."

She bought him a gallon of water and got some ice for his burning neck, then dropped him off at County Road 109 in Genoa. From there he shuffled down County Road 3E and County Road 2T—the kind of street names he was born for—and got to Hugo at seven thirty that night. Tommy found two cops parked by a VFW hall, chatting window to window, and they told him the church was just a few blocks down on Fourth Avenue. Then they asked him what he planned to do there.

"Just some work for my father," Tommy said, pointing up at the sky so they'd know who he was talking about. He stumbled to the church, his brain feeling two sizes bigger than his skull and his tongue five sizes bigger than his mouth. The place was gray stucco and smaller than the one in Suborney, but it had plants growing all around it—even better than the plants in Bird City, like it ought to be in a magazine. He opened the front door and walked up to two child-sized concrete statues on a makeshift altar, one of Jesus and one of Mary, then stretched out beneath them on a gleaming wood floor without pews.

"Oh man," Tommy groaned as he shut his eyes. "The shit you guys stirred up coming to my town." He asked them to forgive him for the hell he put his mom through, and when he closed his eyes, all he could see was horizon in every direction.

* * *

Miriam Podolenz, stout and fifty-one and poodle haired, found Tommy after supper and arranged him like a corpse on the floor. She straightened his legs, crossed his arms on his chest, and splayed his feet evenly, planning to anoint those feet like the sinful woman in the Gospel of Luke did to Jesus. But then Miriam eased off Tommy's socks and saw the bright pink lesion on his arch, oozing yellow pus.

"I'm not anointing that," Miriam muttered. Then she headed across the street to the church house and got the extra room ready. She set a leaky camping mattress on the floor, put duct tape over the spot where she thought the hole was, and huffed and puffed to blow it up. Miriam had no guarantee that Tommy would stay the night, since she guessed he was no more predictable than his father. No guarantee that he wouldn't wake up in ten minutes and stride purposefully across the plains, like Jesus strode purposefully across the desert. Healing whoever he could, like we're all supposed to. Loving what he could while he lived so he'd be ready to love God when he died.

Tommy didn't know much about Jesus yet, she'd heard. He was still a boy that way, just getting to know him. Miriam thought of the sore on Tommy's foot and wondered how she'd heal it. She pictured bugs crawling into the wound, parasites that burrowed through his leg and hollowed him out from inside.

"Not touching that foot," Miriam told herself, and she swept out the extra room even though she'd done it the day before. She and Brother Thorpe hadn't seen eye to eye when he left Hugo, true, but she wouldn't withhold her hospitality from his son because of that. Hospitality, as steward of the church, was all she really had. When Miriam brought the dustpan into the kitchen, she saw Tommy there, back in his boots, washing his face in the sink. She startled, cursing her near-deafness.

"How'd you know this was the house?" she asked Tommy.

"The plants look like the ones in Bird City. I'm Tommy, by the way."

"Miriam. Isn't Melanie doing a garden in Suborney?"

"Melanie's got her hands full of goats." Tommy splashed cold water onto whatever skin he could reach. "How do you talk to each other without phones?"

"We get walkers. They bring the news."

"Where's my dad going next? Is Suborney his last stop, now that he found me?"

"I'm mostly deaf," Miriam said. "Slow down and let me see your lips."

Instead of asking about Thorpe, Tommy asked about food. He wanted meat, regardless of the Sons and Daughters' prohibition on it, and Miriam left to buy him a sandwich. In the living room he stared at Beto's mural, which showed Jesus kneeling next to Mary on a mountaintop and blessing a bowl of food with his hands cupped open, the way he'd set them over Tommy's skull. In the distance sulked a blurry, modern city with smokestacks and highways. Mary stared at Tommy with eyes that said, *Yes, you're exactly where you're supposed to be.* He took a shower and came out to find fresh clothes and a barbecued pork sandwich. Miriam was out tending her garden by the side of the house, and Tommy made sure she could see him long before he spoke.

"Why are we vegetarians, anyway?" he asked.

"Heck if I know. I used to love barbecue. Stay away from me when you eat that, or I'll tackle you."

"What's it like being deaf?"

"I scare easy. The world comes at me real fast."

"When did you meet my dad?"

"In Sidney," Miriam said. "I knew your grandma."

"Is she the one who told him where I was?"

"She kept her mouth shut. But people say things, even when they're trying not to."

"So you've been chasing me down since my dad got out of prison?"

"*He's* been chasing you down. I didn't know about you till he was leaving here."

"Is that why you stayed behind?" Tommy asked.

"I don't like what he's doing to your mom, but he's still a man of God. He gave us all a choice, and I made mine."

"What choice was that?"

"Praying for him to be gentle with her, that's all," said Miriam. "And with you."

* * *

Tommy woke at six on Thursday morning to the sound of Miriam loudly humming a Tessy song. He wanted to get walking again, but he at least owed Miriam his company. She pulled the stubborn hate out of his foot to make walking easier, then laid her hands on his chest and forehead to melt his pain and shame. Miriam asked Tommy to play his sax for her, and she sat by the bell to feel the music. After that she told him how she'd hooked up with the Sons and Daughters. She used to be a pretty good forger and even went to jail for it once, and after that the state garnished her wages so she could make restitution. She got a glorified maid's job at Wexler's, which is how she knew Trish Sandor, and one day on a break she saw people singing out front. Mother Meg got her clapping her hands, and a minute later Miriam was in the circle, singing.

"What was the song?" Tommy asked.

"*Hallelujah, he is com-ing!*" she sang. "*Hallelujah, he is here!* Like that, only better."

She cooked up scrambled eggs with garlic and spinach, then closed her eyes and said grace for him under her breath when she realized that he didn't know how to do it for himself. Tommy asked about his father, naturally, and Miriam told him about the people he'd slowly and patiently lifted out of despair, about the struggles he had over how to reach his son. The people she'd seen him pull into prayer even though their hearts were hard with greed.

"How about the wind and the rain?" asked Tommy. "Ever see him do that?"

"Once or twice. Didn't like it. Seemed like black magic to me."

"No kidding."

When Tommy was ready to leave, Miriam reached into a cookie jar and pulled out a handful of dollar bills that she set on the table in front of him.

"Why do we always have so many singles?" he asked her as they flattened the bills. "And half of them look like they took a mud bath?"

"Your father always knows where to find money if we need it."

"That's 'cause *his* dad stole a bunch. I heard that in Nebraska City."

"I don't want to think about stolen money," Miriam said. Tommy gave her a big thank-you hug and said goodbye, leaving her dollar bills at the door because he had plenty of racing money left. He said goodbye to Hugo, limping west on County Road 2W, and stuck out his thumb when he heard a truck rolling up. A big U-Haul stopped, and a kid around twenty rolled down his window.

"Going to Yoder," the kid said. "I'll give you a ride if you help me unload this shit."

So Tommy went to Yoder and helped unload a truck full of industrial steel shelving. He got twenty bucks and a couple meals for it, then headed to Suborney, thinking of what he'd say when he showed up. Tommy pictured his mom and dad living together in the house on Mangum Street. Pictured himself strolling right through the kitchen door while they watched TV, all curled up on the couch.

"Hey, I'm home," he practiced saying. His father would know from his face that he'd walked the bare earth long enough to understand the one truth he wouldn't be complete without: that there were some things you couldn't get at with words, but had to get at with your feet alone.

✣ ✣ ✣

On Thursday night Tommy walked the straight and darkened roads, cutting south and west, until he found Tumbleback. He reached the Jesus and Mary house at the tail end of bedtime prayers and snuck around to say hi to the goats, bushwhacking his way through the clothes on the line. But the goats were gone, so he tiptoed up the front porch steps and slipped inside as quietly as he could. Everybody was there in the candlelight—even Tessy, stretched across Brother Zypanski's lap, plus two new people he didn't recognize. All the faces brightened when Tommy walked in, and he slid into a gap in the prayer circle between Brother Worrell and Brother Beto. He didn't know what they'd just been praying for, but he sang *Amen* anyway.

"What else should we pray for?" asked Thorpe, who couldn't catch Tommy's eye no matter how hard he tried.

"I'd like to pray for the safe return of Tommy Sandor," Tommy said, which got everybody laughing. The circle broke up, and people converged on him, ruffling his porcupine hair. His return was anticlimactic, but that was probably for the best. Eventually, they all drifted out the front door, chatty and not quite ready for sleep anymore. Tommy noticed his mother's sign and pulled it up, and he would've flung it into the fields if Beto hadn't told him they could paint over it and use it again. After a few minutes, Thorpe finally got his son one-on-one near the porch swing.

"Did you find what you needed out there?" he asked.

"Don't know, Mr. Richard Curtis Thorpe." Tommy cocked his head back like he was daring Thorpe to punch him. "I'm just a dumb kid, ain't sure of much."

"Well, if there's anything I can fill you in on, let me know."

"Like where you were on certain dates and certain times, stuff like that?"

"If that's what you need to know to move on, sure."

"Move on from what?" Tommy asked.

"Whatever personal misery you're stuck in, I guess."

"Is that different from the personal misery *you're* stuck in?"

"Why yes it is, Mr. Sandor." Thorpe took off his picker hat, brushed his itchy scalp, and set the hat back down. "But they share a common border. You have a good night."

Thorpe retreated east toward the prison cell he'd etched onto the earth, too disgusted at his own failure to cry. What had he expected of Tommy after all these years? A cartoon reunion full of angels playing trumpets? *You get what you earn with that boy*, he told himself. Then Thorpe slipped into a kind of darkness he hadn't felt since his last year in prison, when he counted the hours and then the minutes until he could start looking for his son. Back when he detested Jeannette

Holmquist so much that the marble-sized chunks of hate he pulled from his body smelled just like her.

"I let you down," Thorpe muttered as he trudged through the night, talking half to Jesus and Mary and half to Tommy. Maybe half to Connie too. Back at the house, the young people played keep-away from Tommy with a New Orleans Saints football they'd found among the stuff Connie had strewn on the lawn. He and Wesley used to play with it, and he hadn't let anybody else touch it since. But the Sons and Daughters could keep it—hell, they could take it with them when they moved on to the next place, with or without Tommy. With or without Richard Thorpe.

It'll be without one of us, Tommy thought to himself as he intercepted the ball and hurled it as high as he could into the sky. Though he could see them sticking together too. Scoping out towns for the next church to fix up, then walking in opposite directions to pull more Sons and Daughters to it. He could always look for Jesus himself, without the people who helped Thorpe ambush him and his mom. Didn't they deserve a little blame?

It felt like the football hung in the air for twice as long as it should have, as if Tommy had a bionic arm, though he knew he was just slowing down the time inside himself. He saw Mother Meg standing by the front steps with Tessy in one arm and raised his hand slowly in greeting, just as Mother Meg had done to him the night the Sons and Daughters first came to town. Hers lifted back, like it was her turn to be the marionette and his to be the puppeteer.

I'm Brother Tommy, the voice of his new self said as the ball zoomed down and landed between Melanie and Beto. *Have to be. Everybody knows it's time.*

19

At first light Tommy walked back to his mother's house on Mangum Street—he couldn't call it home because it didn't belong to him any more than the Jesus and Mary house belonged to Wesley. His bedroom window was still broken, so he climbed through it and sprawled on his back, bare chested on his equally bare mattress. Connie stepped into the hallway at the sound, completely naked from her morning shower, but rushed back into the bedroom for her bathrobe when she saw Tommy. How long had he been there?

"That you, Tom-Tom?" Connie said from his doorjamb. "You look like one of those firemen in Becky's calendar at work."

"That's a compliment, right?"

"Sure. They're hunky guys, like you." Connie couldn't tell if this creature was a Tommy she used to know or a new one who would never let her understand him. She stared at the lesions all over his torso, some purple and others leaking pus.

"Scratching yourself?" she asked him. "Or stabbing yourself?"

"Bugbites. Got infected." He couldn't tell her about the hate he pulled out through his skin because she'd want to know how much of it was for her. She could never accept the fact that all his hate was one, the same way all his love was one.

"I can smell you from here. Do you even remember what a shower looks like?"

"They're overrated." Tommy rolled onto his side to look at her. "Half the people in the world never take showers. Jesus didn't take showers."

"Is Jesus *all* you can talk about? You can't expect me to—"

"To what? Love me, now that I'm thinking about Jesus more than I think about you?"

"How can you expect me to not be scared? I'm losing my son."

"You lost me when you lied to me. I was in McCook, Mom." Tommy sat up to look in the mirror and see how his own face looked when he lied. "Nobody ever heard of the Sandors or your sax-playing lover boy."

"It was a long time ago." Connie tightened her bathrobe. "People forget things."

"And people make things up, like a sax player named Drake who never existed. If God put a gun to your head and said he'd pull the trigger—"

"Is that the kind of God those people want you to believe in?"

"Hear me out. If he said he'd pull the trigger if you lied, would you still say Drake's my father?"

"No." Connie let the word out slow and whispery, keeping her lips rounded long after the air slipped through them.

"How about a guy named Derek Milderbrandt? Rodeo stud from Oklahoma?"

"Could've been. Is that what they said in McCook?"

Tommy stood and limped to the doorway to stand opposite Connie. He aped her stance: arms crossed, head tilted sideways. "Derek doesn't exist, Mom. I made him up, just like you made up Drake."

"People lie for lots of reasons."

"What was yours, to protect me from who my dad really was?"

"I lied because I didn't know," Connie said. When Tommy's face drained, it told her that this new lie had hit its target. A perfect bull's-eye. And she hadn't even rehearsed it, hadn't cooked it up until the moment came.

"You didn't *know*?" Tommy thunked his head against the door-jamb behind him. "Were you the town slut, sleeping with ten guys or something?"

"Is that better than Drake, or worse?" She laughed the way loose, slinky women did in 1950s movies. Proud, defiant, mannish. "You want names? Tom-Tom? I can't even remember all their names."

"So my mother *was* the town slut, is that what you're saying?" Tommy felt a slap coming, but Connie pulled it back. "Give me a number, Mom. Nine? Thirteen?"

"I never counted." Connie slipped into her bedroom and got dressed. Tommy made some toast and poured two packets of Carnation Instant Breakfast into a glass of milk, then stood in the living room archway to watch the morning news. There was Ronnie Reagan, telling America that we could defeat Communism once and for all if only we stood together. It made him want to change his name, become Tommy Thorpe and live on the run from the government. Instead, he saw himself dying in the desert, close to where Jesus and Mary walked but never seeing them at all. Then his mother came out.

"What'll you do when Reagan sends me off to the desert and I come back in a pine box? How'll you find all my dads to tell 'em if you don't even remember their names?"

"How about all the girls you got inside of." Connie slipped on her work shoes. "Bet you can't remember half their names."

"If I knocked one up, I'd remember her. Get a regular job and everything. Give me a number, Mom. Seventeen guys? Thirty?"

"Stop. You act like I did it for money." Connie headed for the front door, but Tommy's shoulder got there first.

"You think you're getting out of here without telling me?" he said.

"Tommy? What you're doing right now is called felony menacing."

"No, it's called making your mom tell the truth."

"I was a wild girl, all right? That's why I gave you somebody decent for a father."

"Decent? The fucker ran off on me." Tommy jabbed a finger at her. "On you too."

"I lied so you'd want to *be* something." Connie grabbed his wrist, though she had no idea what she wanted to do with it. "So you'd stop whining about not knowing who your daddy was. And now all you want to be is Jesus."

"Jesus is probably the only thing that kept you from killing me before I was born."

"You know I don't believe in that." She threw his arm down.

"But you thought about it, didn't you? Or Grandma did. Bet she found you a doctor, some old drunk with a bottle of bleach and a coat hanger."

This time Connie couldn't hold back her slap. Tommy loosened his neck muscles and let it whip his head toward his shoulder. He straightened up slowly and gave Connie his best Thorpe smile.

"I always wished Sheriff Bullshit did that to me, just to prove he gave a shit. It could've kept you two together."

"All you want to do is hurt me. I raise you into a man, and *this* is what I get?"

"If you cared about me being a man, you should've told me the truth."

"There's lots of truths," Connie said. "You might not want to hear 'em all."

"No, there's only one truth. That's—"

"If you say 'the light of God,' you can kiss your thousand bucks goodbye."

"My thousand bucks?" Tommy laughed in her face. "You think you can buy me from God for *that*?"

"Back off, Tommy." Connie pushed against his chest. "I'm going to work."

"Who's my father?"

"Enough."

"Who's my father?"

"I said *enough*!"

Tommy slid away from the door with plumped-out lips and moping, hopeless eyes—an act if Connie ever saw one—then grinned. "One more thing. When you see Grandma—"

"What makes you think I'm going up there again?"

"When you see Grandma, tell her Miriam says hi."

"Who?"

Tommy said nothing, watching from the front steps and wiping away fake tears as his mother stomped to her truck and backed out of the driveway. In the truck Connie looked from Tommy's face to her hands, which she thought would be shaking but stayed absolutely calm—they didn't even grip the steering wheel too tightly. She looked at her son one more time before she rolled out of view and then crumpled, as if the force that held her spine straight and shoulders back had fled from her body. With it flew her certainty that she would see her son again—not because he would disappear, but because she would. Connie made a list of cities she could move to: Denver, Dallas, Chicago, Phoenix. Another little shithole town like Suborney would do, too, as long as it didn't have a dead church for Richie to fix up.

Once he couldn't see his mother or hear her engine, Tommy went inside and uncapped the blue Sharpie marker that she used for writing dates on freezer bags. He went to the telephone book on the kitchen counter, then lifted it up and wrote, WHO IS MY FATHER? on the yellowy beige Formica where it rested. He put down the phone book, imagining the moment when his mom looked up a number and saw those words. Saw the question that had been swinging inside him for his whole life like a wrecking ball.

"I lied because I didn't know!" Tommy whined, butchering his mother's voice. Connie always left a paperback mystery novel on her white bedside table, so Tommy picked it up and wrote, WHO IS MY

FATHER? underneath it. He looked for places where that question would surprise her the most, wanting it to jump out from everywhere she thought she was safe.

From the shelves inside the bathroom medicine cabinet, behind her Valiums. From the corner of her underwear drawer where she kept her diaphragm and jelly. From the kitchen cabinet where she kept her Cheyenne Mountain Zoo coffee mug. From the spot in the freezer where she hid the ice cream that she binged on when she worried about her wayward son.

Tommy found a carton of chocolate Häagen-Dazs there and wrote, WHO IS MY FATHER? on the underside of its lid. Just to make sure she knew it was him. Just to make sure she knew all those letters hadn't gotten there by chance.

✻ ✻ ✻

As Tommy walked back to the Jesus and Mary house, he saw Melanie on the porch swing, studying him hard and reeling him in with her eyes. It was a different Sister Mel, hard and mean.

"Ready?" she asked when he sat down next to her.

"Where we going?"

"To burn a little something." She held up a folded green bandanna. "Got any?"

"Did you know who I was before you came here?"

"We all knew. The ones who didn't like it didn't come."

"Like Miriam?" Tommy waited for Melanie to nod. "How come Brother T didn't come right out and tell me? How come he had you doing his dirty work?"

"Nothing dirty about it." Melanie stood. "If you don't have any hate to burn, I'll be glad to pull some out of you. God knows you need it."

Melanie stepped off the porch and marched east. They briefly smelled fire, but it came from miles south and disappeared with a shift in the wind. Controlled burn, nothing to worry about. Tommy stayed behind her, watching her stiff back as she pounded the ground like she was stomping a narrow line of grapes.

"How much of *your* hate's for my mom?" he asked.

"Don't make me put a percentage on it."

"Do you think it was right, ambushing her the way you did?"

"I'll tell you what's not right." Melanie stopped and whirled. "Her lying to everybody your whole life, then not telling the truth the second it came to her door."

"What did you expect her to do? Say 'Hey Tommy, it's your real dad, the guy I've been hiding you from! Woo-hoo, we're all free now!'"

"I knew you'd defend her."

Melanie marched ahead. Tommy half-followed, wondering how many conversations he'd been at the center of while the Sons and Daughters worked their way to Suborney. He stopped at a yucca patch where he'd found a dead calf just after Wesley Perrin died, then dug a hole with his boot heel.

"So how long is he planning on torturing my mom?" Tommy called to Melanie, who was looking for her own place to dig.

"Up to her," she said. "All she has to do is say the truth and the torture's over."

"You think Jesus would like what he's doing to her?" Tommy reached into his hip pocket for the scrap of newspaper that held the hate Miriam had pulled out of him. "You must like it if you walked all the way here with him."

"I can't say I *like* it. But life's full of stuff that needs to get done, whether I like it or not." Melanie came over holding a book of matches, and they dumped out their hate, mixing it together. Melanie's looked longer and redder than Tommy's.

"What does my dad's look like?" he asked her.

"I don't think anybody's seen his but Nick and Mother Meg."

"Have you ever been his girlfriend?"

"Slept with him, you mean? We're not that kind of church." Melanie knelt and mumbled a few words, then dropped a match onto the pile. Her hate burned fast, almost getting down to ash by the time Tommy's chunks caught at all. "You don't have to join us all the way, you know. Don't have to give up your car or your girl."

"They're both gone already." Tommy took the matches from Melanie and dropped two more onto his hate. "Doesn't it gross you out how he made you lie to me? Pretending to buddy up to me when you knew *exactly* who I was?"

"Don't think you can turn me against him. Already been tried." Melanie looked away from Tommy, out toward Thorpe's imaginary cell in the arroyo. He'd either be gone from it by now, out looking for somebody who needed help like Jesus wanted him to, or stuck inside that square and waiting for his son to pull him out of it. "If your mom sticks around, I'll be shoving off. She's got to go through whatever God's putting her through, just somewhere I can't see it."

"Hate her that much, do you?"

Melanie didn't answer, but she blew on Tommy's hate to get it burning better. "Maybe I get to see what God's putting *you* through instead," she said. "For a while, anyway. You're lucky you live out here, you know."

"Here? You're serious?"

"You get in a city, you can hardly see what God's putting you through at all. Out here there's nothing else *to* see. So you pay attention."

"That's lucky?"

"Sure is," Sister Mel said. "Some people never know what God's thinking at all."

✳ ✳ ✳

Tommy, his legs accustomed to walking, wandered around for two hours on grazing land that belonged to some faceless corporation while he wondered exactly what God was putting him through. He could see the story different ways, but it was always about a father and a mother fighting over their son—no different than the kids he knew whose parents were divorced, except with Jesus and Mary cheering him on from the sidelines like it was a football game. Who he was supposed to tackle and which direction he was supposed to run with the ball, he didn't know.

He didn't find anybody when he got back to the Jesus and Mary house, not even Tessy. He even checked her room. In the living room he stared at Beto's now-finished mural, with Mary watching Jesus preach and the dead chickens by her side. Among the faces who gathered around them, Tommy recognized Brother Warren and Sister Miriam. He headed to the church and found the people he hadn't recognized from the night before picking up freshly blown-in trash on Tumbleback Road. Aaron was the guy with the greasy poncho he now remembered from the mission in Denver, and Hyun was a half-Korean girl with pierced lips. She came from LA but had been stranded in Wyoming on her eighteenth birthday by a man who drove off while she used a rest stop bathroom. Aaron had his own story, and he liked telling it.

"Been all over the country, man." He jabbed a sheet of newspaper with the tip of a ski pole and stuffed it into his trash bag. "Jail, county work farm in Missouri, rehab in Fresno. You name it, I've done it."

Tommy didn't think Aaron would last long with the Sons and Daughters. He seemed like the type who'd give up on himself too soon and run away to the next thing, adding *Jesus commune* to the list of what had failed him.

"What do you think of all this Jesus stuff?" Hyun asked Tommy.

"Work hard and give more than you take, then he comes to you. That's why we make you do so much walking. The rhythm changes you."

"You've seen him?" Aaron wanted to know.

"Saw him once, on a really long walk. Worth taking one when you're ready."

It was a big day for monsters on the edges of the road: a kid's drawing of a vampire; half of a movie poster that showed a mummy grabbing a woman's arm; a four of spades with a giant human-headed tarantula on the back. Tommy climbed the brand-new church steps, and the brand-new doors opened without even a bump from his shoulder. Inside Beto was painting a mural that showed a Mary who looked exactly like his mom. She walked past that very church holding a little blond Jesus, five or six, by the hand. The mural showed Lester Hill, the trees around Suborney Creek, even the trash on Tumbleback Road. Three goats—the two who came to visit, plus the kid Connie delivered—nibbled at the ground by the church steps.

"That's here," Tommy told Beto. "That's me."

"No." Beto shook his head and pointed his brush at Jesus. "Jesucristo."

"It's me and my mom. I've got pictures where I looked just like that. Plus Jesus was from Israel, no way he had blond hair. And that's *definitely* my mom."

Mary looked different than in any of Beto's other paintings, which made sense because he'd never seen Connie before he came to Suborney. Now that he'd met the Mary in Brother Thorpe's dreams—watched her walk and smile and scold and even pull one goat from the belly of another—he could paint a truer picture.

"Yeah, it's me," Tommy insisted. "Same haircut even."

"Jesucristo," said Beto.

"You act like that's the answer to every question in the world, Brother B. How much is three plus five?"

"Jesucristo."

"Nineteen times seven?"

"Jesucristo." Beto giggled so hard that he had to pull his brush away from the wall. Tommy walked around the edges of Suborney with his heart half-melted and half–stiffened up for a fight. He wanted to lash out at Thorpe for turning his mother into Mary and turning him into Jesus—how could he ever live up to that?

"And who does that make you, Brother Richard the Fake?" he practiced saying. "God Almighty?"

He headed to the gas station to get his mind off things, dodging Pete's questions about what he did while he was gone, and Pete kept him in the storeroom because he looked crazy from all the sunburn and grime. He acted crazy, too, stumbling around like Marty Feldman in *Young Frankenstein*. Things went better at the junkyard, where Dolman let him rap about the Sons and Daughters he met on the walk. Dolman, when it was his turn, talked about finishing up the church repairs and having their first Sunday service.

"They start calling you 'Brother Ed' yet?" Tommy asked as they sat doing nothing by the front desk. "Or do you have to eat a live chicken first, something like that?"

"I'm happy just driving 'em around. But you—" Dolman raised an eyebrow at him. "I caught 'em calling you Brother Tom-Tom a couple times. Guess they must have that chicken all ready for you." Dolman stared at an old hubcap on the wall, silver with concentric rings. It came from a 1955 Dodge, Jeff Heagren's first brand-new car. "Hey, I heard that radio show on Sunday. Heard about the Derek guy."

Dolman looked Tommy in the eye with a forthrightness that had never passed between them before, and Tommy didn't know how to read it. Did the guy already know that Thorpe was his real father? How many other people in Suborney did too? Tommy stared at the same hubcap as Dolman, hoping it could tell him.

"My mom made up the sax player," Tommy finally told Ed. "Said it was to protect me. Might've been a bunch of guys."

"That's some hard shit to learn about yourself."

"That's the problem with life, man." Tommy slapped Dolman on the shoulder, trying out a bullshitting, don't-give-a-shit version of himself. "Asking questions just fucks stuff up. Sometimes you're better off keeping your mouth shut and living without answers."

Don't believe that, Mary told him.

Never in a million years, said Jesus. *Just keep on asking questions till the right one flies out. Then you'll get your answer.*

Then Tommy heard thunder and went to the door, his chest thrust out like he was some ancient warrior who'd just heard the first drums of war. No, he hadn't heard it at all—he'd felt it in his marrow. Water from the sky, calling to the water in him. Far away still, a hundred miles off and gathering over a butte. He gave it a name that only his marrow knew, and he called it closer to him.

20

still Friday

Just after five in the afternoon Tommy felt the thunder in his marrow again, and he walked up Lester Hill in a long spiral to get the broadest possible view of his tiny corner of the world. He would have had a great look at Pikes Peak to the west if it hadn't been for a clump of gray clouds that he thought about pushing away but instead decided to use. Another cloud hung to the northwest, and he asked it to darken, and it did. When he asked them both to converge on Suborney, the marrow inside him said yes, and it happened. Like his marrow and the clouds were made of the same thing, or born of the same thing.

Then Tommy slipped out of time and turned into the clouds' father, calling them home with a single glance. Were they ten miles away? Thirty? Did they speed toward him, gathering every hint of grayness in the sky, or did time slow down so much that Tommy couldn't feel it passing? The clouds floated toward him like jellyfish, leaving tendrils of lightning that lit up the sky. *We hear you*, they said. *We're coming.*

They became one cloud and settled over Lester Hill, streaking the sky above Suborney like daggers. No rain yet, just the promise of it. The cloud was Tommy's child, his grandchild, his grandmother. The cloud would teach him things. The cloud waited for Tommy's word to let its payload fall, and that word would come from his marrow. He opened up his palms, simply and without fanfare, and a few drops of rain fell onto them with a *tip, tip, tip*. Then faster, *tipatipatipatipatip*, as he spread his fingers gently apart and craned his neck all the way back. He didn't have to clamp his hands like Thorpe did to get the rain—which was good to know, though he couldn't tell what that meant. The water drizzled down on his face at first, like any other afternoon shower, until it asked, *Are you ready?*

When Tommy nodded, the rain turned into the kind of marble-sized hail that pummeled Suborney only once or twice a summer. *I did this*, a grown-up voice inside him said, but he wasn't making it come down with his marrow any more than he'd made the music come down with his saxophone. He was only the conduit, the inviter, the host. He shouted, covering the crown of his head to protect himself from the hail as he zigzagged down Lester Hill and collapsed on the church landing. Then he felt his marrow change consistency—it made a slippery rush all through his body, like he felt when he was about to come. Suborney Creek overflowed its banks and covered Road X right up to the church steps, and Tommy looked inside for a place to hide in case he couldn't stop the rising.

He knelt on the steps and prayed, with the hail crashing down on him, punishing him for all his wrongs. Suborney Creek rose even further, and he thought of all the old people in town dying—their corpses floating in the water that he'd brought down from the sky and pulled up from the ground—then begged God to change his marrow again. Not even picturing every old face in town bobbing dead in the water could do it. Not even picturing his mom's or his own.

Jesus can't even stop it, Tommy told himself, and the Jesus in his head told him, *Wait*. By then almost every house in Suborney had a door open. Sam Kurtep watched the creek rise and inexplicably fall. Ed Dolman walked around outside the Jesus and Mary house, making sure the roof and gutters held up under the hail. Ron and Kate Ulin put their valuables on high shelves, remembering how much they lost in 1974 when the creek shifted their house and made its floors crooked.

Connie Sandor noticed the weird weather on her drive home too. The sky had been clear when she left work—escaping early from Darren Rocher, who'd told her three times how much he liked her skirt—but over Suborney she saw dark, woolly clouds. She drove through a burst of hail that crashed down on her roof as she approached the bridge into town, and as she crossed Suborney Creek it swelled, drenching the oily asphalt long enough to make her hydroplane and scrape her fender against the guardrail. The water receded, done taunting her, once she reached the other side.

All of Suborney glimmered with hailstones, as if the town had been frozen solid for years and only now begun to thaw. Connie's wheels spun in them, so she pulled into Pete's parking lot to wait until the hail ended. Too much driving lately, too much gripping the wheel. Suborney Creek went back to normal, then fell even lower—which made no sense at all with so much hail. A last dumping of it pounded her roof, and she jumped when two thunks sounded against her passenger window. It was Pete, on his way back to work after checking on his house, and she waved him in.

"Crazy shit," Pete said as he sat. "A summer's worth of hail in five minutes, then a flood that disappeared."

"We should check in on people."

"I'm sure everybody's fine. The church bunch beat us to it." He wiped the wetness from his face and head and dried his hands on the thighs of his jeans.

"Well hooray for them," Connie said. "Has Tommy come by lately?"

"I get the feeling he's not hanging around for his thousand bucks."

"That's the least of my worries. If I give it to him, he'll probably pass it on to his little gang of felons anyway."

Pete shrugged. "There's worse things."

"You'll end up being one of them," Connie snickered. "I can smell it on you."

"Does that mean you want me to step out of your truck?"

"Step wherever you want, Pete. Just be careful what you're stepping into."

Pete opened the door and held his hand out, checking for hail that didn't fall. "Try to understand him, Connie. I've never seen you this hard, if you want the truth. And Dan Stannard sure in hell won't give you the truth."

"Do you want to be the one who gives me the *truth*, Pete? Want to start sneaking out on Carla in the middle of the night and try slipping your *truth* into me?"

"I didn't say that. But you're headed down a bad road. Everybody can see it."

"Then go tell Jesus all about me. And remember you've got a wife to give your *truth* to."

Connie started up her truck, knowing that Pete was right. She'd been turning into an awful person from the moment Richie came to town, and every inch closer to him that Tommy stepped made her worse. She'd painted herself into a corner, and the best way out was to bust through the floor and escape. Either that or let the good people of Suborney pull her out of it, passing her from shoulder to shoulder. To where? Richie's church, of course, where they'd want to cleanse her lies and heal her.

Sure, she needed healing. Don't we all? But on her terms, not theirs. Pete gave up on waiting for her to talk and climbed out of the truck, then watched Connie spin her wheels in the hail. He wanted to join the Sons and Daughters right away—testify, move into the Perrin house, give away everything he owned—just to show Connie that she was living wrong and hurting her son, herself, the world. But the feeling passed, and Pete headed inside, kicking at the hailstones that clumped up on his steps. He waited two minutes for Connie to get home and called her, then hung up before her answering machine came on.

She needed somebody, anybody, to tell her that her heart was getting too hard. Pete lined the words up in his mouth and called again, ready to apologize, but when he heard her voice on the machine, he remembered how nice her hair smelled while he sat in her truck. He imagined his fingertips against the skin of her bare shoulders and hung up before the beep. Maybe he really *did* want a chance at Connie. That wasn't right for a married man to do or even think. But he had desires like anybody else. Why pretend? Pete dialed one more time.

"I'm sorry, Con," he told her machine. "I know you don't want to talk to me about what's going on with Tommy, but I know Carla would be glad to. She's been through this. I'm not the kind of man you think, and there's nothing secret I want from you."

As Pete hung up, Connie found the first of Tommy's WHO IS MY FATHER? messages scribbled in thick blue Sharpie ink. It was in the junk drawer, underneath the ancient pack of cigarettes that she kept around for when her nerves got shot. Seeing the question jacked her up even more and made her fingers shake so badly that a cigarette wouldn't help. She walked to the bathroom medicine cabinet to fish out her Valiums and saw WHO IS MY FATHER? scribbled there too.

"You know who he is," she said. Connie took her next-to-last Valium, then went back to the kitchen and picked up the phone book to call her doctor and leave a message asking for a refill. There it was again on the kitchen counter: WHO IS MY FATHER? jeering at her, mocking her. Connie kept on combing through the house until she'd found seventeen of them—one for every year she'd kept Tommy from knowing about Richard Curtis Thorpe.

That seemed to be it. By the time she quit searching, the Valium had kicked in. Connie spread herself out on Tommy's empty bed, picturing him as he wrote that seventeenth question mark and stopped, satisfied that she'd get the message. Smirking to himself, putting the cap on the Sharpie, then setting it back in the kitchen junk drawer like it had never left its spot.

* * *

The hailstorm only lasted twelve minutes, but everybody in Suborney had some kind of damage. Tommy did what he could for the worst of it until sundown, without letting on that he'd caused it. The Sons and Daughters must have known, since they avoided his eyes as they helped with repairs and cleanup. They gave him the cold shoulder, and he gave it right back, skipping supper and nighttime prayers and eating leftover meatloaf at home. Then he grabbed a flashlight and his mom's sleeping bag, since he didn't want to fetch his own at the Jesus and Mary house, and headed out to the arroyo where he'd burned his hate before leaving town.

He found Thorpe nearby stoking a tiny fire with brush, and as Tommy approached, he noticed a line etched into the earth. He followed it around—a twelve-by-twelve-foot box. Tommy thought about crossing the line but stepped back when Thorpe looked up sharply.

"You know what this is?" Tommy said. "The cell you locked me in all those years, when you didn't tell me who you were."

"How was I supposed to tell you? I was in a *real* cell. The kind with bars." Thorpe felt the anger in his voice and gentled it for his son, like he'd promised. "I'm sorry, Tommy. A better man would've found a better way."

Thorpe waved, and Tommy stepped over the line, then rolled out his mother's sleeping bag next to his father's.

"How come you're out here alone tonight?" Tommy asked.

"After what happened today, they find my company unpleasant."

"They think you helped me with the hail?"

"Yes sir." Thorpe turned away to hide his bad cheek, and Tommy figured he always did that when he felt ashamed.

"So they're giving you the cold shoulder too?"

"Let's just say they're disappointed in how I've run my little rescue mission."

"Uh, I don't feel all that rescued," said Tommy.

"Exactly." Thorpe laughed and put more brush on the fire. "I wish I had some hate to burn. Wish you did too."

"Next best thing to having a beer together," Tommy told him, sighing. "So am I supposed to call you 'Dad' all the sudden? I can't just keep calling you 'Brother Thorpe.'"

"Your mom always called me 'Richie.'"

"Then I sure in hell won't." They both pointed a finger up at the sky and didn't even need to remind each other that the world was a House of God. "You could've come in the light of day, instead of sneaking around like a spy. Could've sent newspaper clippings to the neighbors and stuff."

"Your *neighbors*?" Thorpe guffawed. "I'm not a big fan of your mom right now, but I'd hate to see how you would've treated her if the whole town knew she was lying."

"So nobody else knows? You, me, the Brothers and Sisters?"

"And your mom. She's kinda central to the equation."

Tommy breathed in smoke and imagined them both in an open, sunlit field by a mountain lake. They used their rhino bodies to build a church from scratch with wood they cut themselves, like people did ten centuries ago when everybody lived off the land. He and Thorpe could live like that for thousands of years, dying periodically and coming back to life whenever God needed more churches. It was a better life than the one he'd have with his Thorpe uncles, eating roadkill and ancient canned beans. He kept the fantasy going until he and Thorpe wore lederhosen and blew on alpenhorns, like they were in a tourist ad for Switzerland.

Tommy laughed, but when Thorpe asked why, he couldn't explain. He got a quick chill—the hail finally catching up to him—and slipped halfway into the sleeping bag. "When's my hair supposed to start going dark?" he asked his father. "When did yours turn?"

"In prison. Stay out, maybe you'll keep the Goldilocks thing going." Thorpe got halfway into his sleeping bag too.

"Why'd you burn down my grandpa's store?" asked Tommy.

"I was mad at your mom for not marrying me when she told me she was pregnant with you. Perfectly logical reaction, right?"

"Doesn't sound like the smartest thing to do," Tommy said.

"What would Tom-Tom have done?" Thorpe asked, chucking dirt on the fire. "O wise, noble Thomas Gregory Sandor?"

"That's not the question," said Tommy, zipping his bag all the way up. "What's wise, noble Tom-Tom gonna do now? That's the one to ask."

❅ ❅ ❅

"Don't shut me out," Connie said, banging on the door of her mother's house in Sidney at eleven that night. "Don't you dare."

A neighbor's porch light flicked on, then another neighbor's dog barked. Trish shuffled across the living room wearing nothing but a mint-green nightdress and slid the deadbolt, slid the chain. "You could've called," she said.

"I did, nine times. You could've plugged your phone in the jack." Connie shouldered past Trish into the living room and flung herself onto the couch. "Have you seen Richie since he got out? He was here in Sidney—Tommy said so."

"I never saw him. Never heard he was here." Trish looked ready for all the browbeatings she'd given her daughter to fly back in her face all at once.

"But he saw *you*. Or one of the jailbirds he had spying on us did. Who the hell's Miriam? Tommy told me she said hi."

"A woman from Wexler's," Trish mumbled, shaking her head and staring at her feet. "She joined a weird church that fixed up the old one on Linden. Connie, I didn't—"

"You *didn't* bother mentioning that when they started fixing up the church by *me*?"

"What difference would it make? If I said they were here, you'd only think I sent 'em to you."

"Well, you *did*, didn't you? Flapping your damn lips with your damn lady friend?"

"She wasn't that close," Trish said. "She didn't even know where we came from."

"*Nobody* was supposed to know where we came from. You let it slip, didn't you? Then you covered your own ass so they could come bite mine."

Connie marched into the kitchen for a glass of water. She expected to find some evidence there—a note on the fridge, a phone number on the corkboard—that Trish had helped Richie track her down. She guzzled the water, refilled her glass, and poured more down her throat until her stomach couldn't take it.

"A greasy guy with his teeth knocked out gave me a flyer at a gas station," said Trish, following her in. "That's the closest they ever got to me."

"Well, now Mr. Greasy No-Teeth is Brother Whoever, buddying up to your grandson."

"I didn't know they were Richie's people. I'd never set you up like that."

Connie sat at the kitchen table and saw two phone numbers scribbled on the back of an envelope. "Whose are these?"

"Guys who can fix my AC. You think they're Richie's numbers? Dial 'em."

"They don't even have phones. Tommy knows we've been lying, Mom. Says he's been to McCook, knows there's no sax player."

Trish shook her head. "You can't give Richie all the power."

"*Give?* You think I'm *giving* him anything? He *took* it from me."

Connie hid in the bathroom awhile, caught between wondering how she'd sunk to this new low and fantasizing about torturing Richie on some medieval-looking contraption. Something with lots of pulleys and spikes that made him scream like she wanted to scream. She'd been right to shield Tommy from him for all those years. But now, with no more shielding necessary, what was she supposed to do? It was too late to go back to that fence in Nebraska City and turn her no into a yes. Too late to do anything but go berserk or slip away.

Connie flipped through a year-old issue of *Good Housekeeping* and wondered how her life would have turned out if she'd said yes to Richie when Tommy was in her womb. She could be on the road with him now, keeping the cops off his back while he gambled or raced some half-tamed car. Or she could keep house while he worked some stupid, hateful job that he kept for the sake of his family—his damn holy family—and spend her nights fucking him incessantly to remind him that there was more to life than the meaninglessness of earning money.

The magazine had a story about taking care of your car's interior and another about fizzy fruit drinks to bring to picnics. Connie pictured Tommy in the Perrin house kitchen, laughing about her with the Jesus freaks and cooking up ways to drive her crazy once she came back to town. Figuring out the most excruciating ways to squeeze the truth out of her.

"Where is it?" Connie asked when she came out of the bathroom and saw Trish staring at the inside of her fridge. "This church on Linden?"

"Just past Twenty-Second. You're going there this time of night?"

"They're soul savers. They'll open for whoever knocks."

"But you're sleeping here, aren't you?"

Connie didn't answer. She headed to the west end of Linden Street and found a plain white church with a pair of knee-high concrete Jesus statues guarding the entrance like lions. She parked in front of the white sign with black letters, painted exactly like the one in Suborney, then walked up the wooden steps and opened the unlocked door. Inside she found a pile of all kinds of Bibles, two wheelchairs, and an empty floor where pews ought to be. It looked more like a dance hall than a church, and she guessed the one in her town would too.

"Hello?" she said, but nobody answered. A flashlight flickered in a window across the street, and Connie headed toward it. A man walked out, shining the light on her as he stepped down the walkway. He wore baggy gray sweatpants and a red-and-white checked shirt.

He looked around sixty, as old as Gregory Holmquist would have been if he'd lived, and he was tall enough that Connie had to crane her neck to look him in the face. He helped her by shining the light on himself, and she saw his broad cheeks, his sharp beak of a nose. His eyes were set so deep, they seemed forever cast in shadow, even with the flashlight shining on him. She saw the crags in his skin, saw the places where the wind had worn it smooth. He'd slept outside a lot, maybe even been left for dead once or twice.

"Help you, ma'am?" he said, his voice low and rusty from disuse. Connie hated him right away and felt the growing weapon inside her fling itself against her abdominal wall, trying to get at him.

"Some people from your church took my son away from me," she said. "I want him back."

"What town, ma'am?" The man moved the flashlight around to inspect her shoulders, her hands, her breasts. "We've got churches all over."

"Suborney, Colorado." Connie turned and pointed at Beto's sign. "They've got the same exact sign there. The same wetback who painted it."

"We don't go around snatching people. They work with us or they don't. How old's this son of yours?"

"Seventeen," Connie said.

"Almost a man, then. Old enough to know what side he's on."

"What *side* he's on?" Connie stepped back and gave out a laugh that sounded too much like Richie's. "He doesn't even know what war he's in."

"At seventeen? Sure he does, just might not have a name for it yet. What'd you say your name was, ma'am?"

"I didn't. But it's Janet, Janet Cole. You?"

"I'm Brother Eldon. Nice to meet you."

"Brother Eldon what?"

"Just Brother Eldon, ma'am. Anybody wants me, that's the only name they'll ever need."

Eldon. Richie's father—it had to be. How many other Eldons were there anymore? The chief spy all along, Richie's outside man while he was locked up in Lincoln. A career minor league criminal who understood what it took to live on the run. Connie could learn a lot from him about disappearing into thin air, but she couldn't ask him without giving herself away.

Brother Eldon mumbled a terse goodbye and headed back to his front door. Connie felt his hand on her nose and mouth, stifling her every protest, even though she'd already crossed the street and reached her truck. He turned the flashlight toward her from his front door, probably to get her license plate number. But didn't they already have that? Didn't they already have everything?

21

Saturday, July 26

As he walked toward Connie's house, Thorpe wished he'd known how to make it rain before he went to prison. Then he could have put out the fire he started at Holmquist TV and Entertainment Showroom before it killed the man he only wanted to frighten. He passed Connie's blue Chevy LUV and smiled at the thought of gripping a steering wheel again. A clean Richie with a smooth cheek, with Jeannette Holmquist laughing next to him as he re-familiarized himself with the pedals, the stick. A Jeannette who'd never hidden herself from him or changed her name. Who'd met him at the prison gate the day he went free, with their son beside her.

Two small clumps of hail, like castoff pearl necklaces, had congealed beside Connie's front steps on a patch of ground that never saw the sun. Thorpe ran his fingers along the wobbly iron railing on his way up the steps and rapped on the screen door, then rang the doorbell too. Connie came over from the kitchen, where she was throwing her stuff into the same big trash bags she'd used for Tommy's. Thorpe's outline filled her doorway, doubly blurred by the frosted glass of its window and the mesh of its screen door. She considered staring at him mutely through the living room window and never opening her door no matter how long he stared back. Instead, she opened it fast and wide.

"You win," she told him.

"Do I? What's my prize?"

"Getting to see me before I go someplace it takes you seventeen more years to figure out. Come in, if that's what you want. Just don't *ma'am* me."

Connie stepped back into the kitchen, covered up Tommy's WHO IS MY FATHER? on the kitchen counter, and kept filling her bags. She tossed in some old knives that she'd wrapped up in towels and duct-taped together—though not her brand-new cleaver, which Dan Stannard had given her, because things he'd bought had no place in her future. She added a teapot she didn't use but loved the look of. Thorpe moseyed inside and leaned against the kitchen archway like Tommy always did, and Connie went through the cupboards above her stove. Tin of cocoa powder? Leave behind. Jar of dried-out honey? Trash. Unopened bag of shredded coconut? For the road.

"I prayed for you every day I was locked up," Thorpe said. "From the beginning."

"I didn't know you were into praying back then, Richie. Didn't seem like the type."

"The first year I prayed the hardest. Prayed you'd keep our baby."

"Well, I did. Raised him for you all by myself so you could waltz in here and snatch him from me." Connie threw a wine bottle opener into the keeper bag, though she didn't plan on drinking another drop in her life. "Every year I flipped a coin to decide if I should take him to see you in the state pen for his birthday or not. Funny, it always came up tails."

"I never hated you. Don't hate me now."

"Then you tell me what else I've got left to fight for my son with, other than hate." Connie handed him a can of tuna fish. "Here, you and your gang can have this."

"Don't eat dead animals." Thorpe handed the can back.

"Well, you can have everything else here when I'm gone. Move into the damn place, for all I care. It's paid for."

"I'm not asking you to love me like you did."

"Don't ask me to love you any *other* way either. And don't start talking about God's love to me—I get enough of that from Tommy."

"Look at yourself," said Thorpe, reaching through the noxious, angry electricity that surrounded Connie and touching his fingertips to her upper arm because that always used to calm her. But this time her skin stiffened so completely that it seemed like the blood had stopped moving inside her.

"You're not welcome here," Connie said, sounding so much like Gregory Holmquist eighteen years ago that Thorpe stepped backward, lifting his hands as if the police had him surrounded again.

He opened the nearest cupboard. Packets of instant honey-lemon iced tea, of skim milk. Things the Sons and Daughters could use or give to people. The tuna too—why not. He set them on the counter, and Connie, without a word, handed him a plastic grocery sack. It was a moment of domestic cooperation they'd never been able to share together, the kind of simple interaction that Thorpe had dreamed of ten thousand times in prison. As he turned to thank her, his hand flinched out toward hers. Connie felt it coming and grabbed his wrist before his touch landed.

"What did you think you could do to me?" she asked him. "Trap me into loving you? Isn't it enough to take my son?"

"*Our* son. I thought you might forgive me for not helping you raise him."

"I didn't need your help." Connie dug her nails into Thorpe's wrist, then shoved his hand away. "Still don't. Don't ask me to apologize for how I brought him up."

"I was going to thank you for it."

"You picked a funny way to do it, running me out of town."

"Nobody says you have to run."

"Nobody *says* it, Richie. But as soon as you spill your little secret, you know damn well they'll all be thinking it. You don't want to just shame me. You want to do it in front of everybody I know."

"That's not how I see it." Thorpe leaned against the counter. "I see it as giving you an opportunity."

"An opportunity to *what*? Save me from myself?"

"To come clean in front of everybody you know. It's a good feeling. Done it a few times myself."

"Take what you want from me and go, Richie." Connie took the plastic bag from him and tossed in an ancient bottle of Fluff that she'd bought for Tommy when he turned eleven but then took away from him because he wouldn't listen. "You can have the mattress your son slept on, make a little shrine out of it."

"Might do that." Thorpe stepped down the hall and knelt at the door of Tommy's near-empty room. With its broken window, it looked as desolate as if someone had died of plague there. He prayed, focusing on a sliver of light that refracted through a forgotten hanging glass star and made a rainbow on the floor. But it wasn't Tommy's place anymore, not the battlefield of his soul. All the internal wars he'd fought in that room had already been won or lost, and he'd moved on to new ones.

"Tell me when you're through," Connie said from the kitchen, staring at Richie as he knelt. "I don't care what you're praying for, as long as you're not praying for me to go to hell."

"I've got no say in where you're going."

"Well, I'm glad we got that straight, finally. You have a nice day, *Reverend* Thorpe. Say hi to *Brother* Tommy for me."

"I will have a nice day, ma'am. A beautiful day, 'cause God let me live it."

"I'm sure God loves you talking about him all the time. I'm sure he never gets sick of hearing his name."

Connie went out to the back porch to look for more scraps of her life to decide on but found nothing worth taking beside her too-big barbecue grill. She looked though her kitchen window and saw Richie standing there like it was his own house, like he'd been letting her live in it all these years out of charity alone. He blew her a kiss, folded his hands together in front of his chin, then rumbled out the front door.

* * *

That morning and early afternoon Thorpe and Tommy did hail damage repair and cleanup while the other Sons and Daughters went their own way. Gus Larnett's gutters, the roof on Mrs. Culp's shed, Mrs. Sauter's cracked birdbath, fallen branches everywhere, glass and clay ornaments shattered on the ground. Tommy cursed himself over the back windshield of Wally and Sara Ogrean's 1969 Plymouth Barracuda, which he could replace with one from the junkyard. But its metal skin, like that of the 1958 Oldsmobile that Delbert Morin couldn't drive anymore, was battered beyond repair.

"Not sure God's forgiving me for those," Tommy said, but Thorpe didn't respond. They kept working in the shared silence of people with too many things to say and not enough words to say them, and they did a few other odd jobs too. The Mukasics let them shovel up the oily dirt from beneath a lawn mower that had died when Tommy was twelve, and they replaced it with the bags of potting soil that Julie Parness had abandoned in her yard three springs ago. They shopped at Pete's for Mrs. Culp, then made her a bowl of potato salad big enough to last three days. They ate with her and prayed with her, and she never said a thing about how they were built alike or how their faces looked the same except for the more refined lips and nose that Tommy's mom had given him. Then they sat on the big, flat rock in the middle of Suborney Creek, not far from where the Sons and Daughters had baptized each other, and slid their bare feet against the cool, slippery rocks of the creek bed.

"Were you scared the night I raised the creek?" Tommy asked. "Or did you know what was going on?"

"Terrified. You were like a five-year-old driving a plane."

"But you knew it was coming, right?"

Thorpe only nodded. Tommy pulled a knife and a hunk of cheese from his pocket and cut some for both of them. "I made some cash back in Nebraska City. A whole bag of it."

"What'd you think of the town?"

"It's a town. I don't have to love it just 'cause I got made there, do I?"

"Wouldn't hurt. How'd you get the money?"

"Your way, on a racetrack." Tommy grabbed an imaginary steering wheel and growled out engine sounds. "Ray Colton says hi."

"Ray Colton?" Thorpe whipped his head and laughed. "I thought he'd be dead fifty times over by now. How much you get?"

"Fifteen hundred bucks about. Want it for the church?"

"We can't have that much at once. Cops would sniff it out, think we stole it."

"We could bury it somewhere."

"More trouble than it's worth, trust me." Thorpe dipped a hand into Suborney Creek and splashed cool water on the back of his neck, then on his face. "I don't know if we'll ever catch up, Tom-Tom. I have a hard time just getting your name out of my mouth."

"Yeah, I got a million questions for you too." Tommy took a bite of cheese to shut himself up, then gave a chunk to Thorpe. "Well, we can talk about all the stuff we didn't do together, or we can get back to work."

"Work it is, sir," Thorpe replied, popping the cheese into his mouth and drying off his feet with his socks. They headed up Division Road past the junkyard, waving to Dolman as he shook hands at the gate with some Texas-looking guy. Before they could find anything else to fix or clean, Brother Benjy ran toward them.

"Brother T!" he shouted. "Boss lady needs you home."

Thorpe shrugged at Tommy and hustled to whisper with Benjy, then nodded and kept walking toward the church house. Benjy jutted his chin at Tommy and ambled over.

"I got something for you," he called, pulling a worn-looking cassette tape from the back pocket of his too-big denim cutoffs. "Ron and Kate taped it off the radio. Thought you and your mom might want to hear it." He handed the tape over.

"They say anything else?"

"They still pray for you. They're glad you're turning back to God."

"Good to know. Hey, did you know who I was before you came here?"

"Your mom fucked you over good, man." Benjy looked around to see if anyone had caught him swearing. "Mine's been lying to me since I was born, but she never lied that bad."

"Do you hate my mom then?"

"I don't hate her. I just want her to tell the truth."

"What the hell does the truth even look like?"

"Maybe this tells you." Benjy pointed to the tape in Tommy's hand, then walked back to the church house. Tommy stood in the middle of the washboard dirt road, waiting for Jesus or Richard Thorpe or even his imaginary ex-father Drake to come along and reassure him that he'd get through this tornado of bullshit someday. He walked home without seeing a soul, then slipped past his mom's truck, trying not to stare at the black plastic bags in its bed.

When the doorbell rang, Connie was poking through her closet, trying to decide if she should let Richie's people have her old clothes or burn them out of spite. She grabbed her cleaver on the way just in case she saw Thorpe's face again, and when she opened the door, she saw exactly that—a younger version of it, anyway. A face like a sledgehammer that knew exactly what it wanted to swing at.

"Hi, Brother Tommy," she said. She kept one shoulder behind her front door and set the cleaver on top of her TV.

"Plan on leaving soon?" he asked, jerking a thumb toward her truck.

"Depends. You coming in?"

"No ma'am." He pointed at the cleaver, visible through the crack between the door and its frame. "Don't want to lose any fingers."

"That's just in case—"

"In case *who* comes by? All my real dads, tracking me down to prove they always loved me?"

"You want names, Tommy? I'll give you the ones I remember."

Connie watched Tommy shrink down, not puffing his chest out at her anymore, and she knew she'd always be able to dance past him from one lie to the next. Sure, Richie Thorpe could be his dad. But so could Frank Martel, Bobby Figerino, Kenny Doak—men who'd never existed, just like Drake and Derek Milderbrandt. If he asked specifically about Richie, she'd say he was just some crazy guy who decided her child was his, even though she'd barely even kissed him, and he spied on her from prison after killing her father. It was terrifying every minute of her life. That's why she'd been so scared ever since he strolled into town.

"Richie Thorpe is not your father," Connie could say if she had to. Crisp, definitive. Those words were six aces up her sleeve. If Tommy kept saying that Richie was his father, she'd insist on a paternity test. By the time the blood work came back, she'd be long gone. She sat on the landing, her face impregnable.

"I want to play you something." Tommy held up the cassette tape. "From the radio."

"Your boom box is up at Wesley's house."

"We gave it away already. But you put that tape player in your truck, right?"

Tommy climbed into the LUV and turned the ignition halfway with the spare key that Connie made him carry. He popped out his mom's favorite Three Dog Night tape, the one with "Mama Told Me Not to Come" on it, and popped in the one Benjy had given him. Connie sat in the passenger seat and rolled down her window so the smell of Tommy's angry sweat wouldn't make her faint. He pressed PLAY and heard Justin Stannard's voice.

"—not remember my brother Daniel, a man as near to me as any living. A man whose sin and shame I carry in my heart, maybe wrongly, because each of us is meant to bear our own sin and shame, not that of our brothers and sisters. But I keep carrying Daniel's out of love for him, and out of fear for him, because I don't know that he has the strength to carry it alone. Not that Jesus would let him carry it alone, of course. Jesus won't let *any* of us carry it alone, not even the ones who say he never lived and breathed."

Tommy stopped the tape. "Can you handle this?"

"I know what sin and shame are. Better than most, some people say." Connie hit PLAY.

"Well, my brother Daniel, even though he's married, is in a sinful relationship with a woman, a slightly older woman with a son of her own from what they call nowadays a 'previous relationship.' A soul I can't stop thinking about, a young man who talks with me on my show quite often, by the name of Tommy Sandor. I can't say my brother and this woman are living in sin because they aren't living together, though according to Daniel's rightful wife, they might as well be. This older woman is not a wicked woman. I've met her, and I repeat, she is not a wicked woman because I can feel the goodness in her heart."

"Me too," Tommy said as Justin Stannard paused to lick his lips. Connie felt the venomous metal move like a snake twisting on the fishhook inside her, maybe at the spot where Tommy had first clung to the lining of her womb. What if that embryo had never stuck? Who would she be now?

"These kinds of things happen every day. Even if they aren't happening in our own families, they're happening in our communities, behind the smokescreens that people wrap themselves in. Smokescreens so thick that you wonder what people might accomplish if they put their energy into the simple pleasure of serving God, instead of keeping up their lies.

"But my brother's extramarital affair isn't my only reason for bringing this woman up. The main reason is this woman's son, Tommy. A hard young man growing up without a father, rudderless in this world. People who know him say that when he was a boy, he was full of love for God's music, for the things of God's world. They say Tommy changed in just over two years—from a child who *knew* that he belonged to God into a pillar of rage. Turning against his mother, against his teachers and coaches, against his own country."

"That's me." Tommy nodded hard at Connie, whose jaw ached from clenching.

"It saddens me to know how much of that change has come upon this boy in the two-plus years that my own brother has been in a sinful, unlawful relationship with his mother. But even more sad and disturbing to me is that she now resists this young man as he tries to turn himself toward God again. As he gives up his possessions to work with a group of God-fearing men and women to serve the poor in his community. To feed the elderly and rebuild a church that's been savaged by neglect.

"And I ask myself why any woman with goodness in her heart would stand between her son and his love for God. Why? I pray to understand this. I ask that you pray for this young man *and* pray for his mother to step out of his way and let her son walk toward the light that he's wanted and loved since the *very* beginning of his life. If you live in the town of Suborney, to our southeast, or in Security or Widefield or Fountain nearby, you might know this young man, this Tommy, and you might know his mother. But if you don't, you may know others in the same situation, be they close to you or hidden from your sight by smokescreens of shame. Pray for them with me, people. It's all I ask. Now I must turn—"

That was where the Ulins stopped recording. Tommy's heart and lungs felt so big he thought they'd grow teeth, jump out of his mouth, and swallow his mom like a shark. Connie looked at him and blubbered for a second, then buried her head on his strong shoulder and wept over all the things she could never let herself become.

"Feel that, Mom?" Tommy asked, ready to hold her until they both breathed their last. "That's the love of God, right here. That's all I want for us."

Connie held her son tighter than she'd ever allowed herself to hold anything. Inside her a door opened, and she heard footsteps—her own—walking down a hall in a big, echoey building.

Then they stopped. Was she looking through the doorway that had just opened? Or had she only taken a few steps toward it and chickened out? Connie didn't know what was on the other side of that doorway except freedom. *A life where you don't have to run,* Richie's voice told her. But as soon as Connie heard those words, the self inside her head started running, faster than ever.

22

At three in the afternoon Connie checked into a sleazy nineteen-dollar-a-night motel in Fountain, then hauled her trash bags inside and lined them up by the bed like a barricade. She didn't know anything about her future except that her lies were catching up to her, even lies she didn't know she'd told. She imagined herself in an iridescent green garden, calmly opening and closing her eyes while a nonchalant lion devoured her, feet first. Connie called the state patrol dispatcher and checked to see if Dan was on duty.

"Ask him to call his side dish," she said, leaving the hotel's number. She turned on the TV and zoned out on golf, a sport she hated, until Stannard called.

"Are you in trouble?" he wanted to know.

"You know that dive motel on 85/87, just past Ohio?"

"Don't tell me you're there, Con. That's for people on the run."

"I might as well be. I'm here till you get here, room 11." Forty-five minutes later Stannard arrived in his own truck at the Big Chief Motel, with its flashing neon headdress that stuttered on and off all day and night.

"This is it for us, right?" he asked as he stepped into the room. He took Connie's silence as agreement. "But you want something from me first. I know that look."

"I need you to talk to Tommy. Find out what that Thorpe guy wants from him." Connie sat on the bed, feeling like a coward for sending Dan to do her own job. But he was stupid enough, and falsely brave enough, to unintentionally goad Tommy into blurting out the truth so she wouldn't have to. "Aren't you going to get comfortable?"

"Here?" He waved a hand around the shabby room. "Like I'm paying for your time?"

"That would be something new." She raised her eyebrows and patted the greasy bedspread beside her, thinking that becoming the Whore of Babylon in real life might make it easier to cut ties with Dan, with Tommy, with the whole world.

"What the hell is wrong with you?" Dan paced around the room, his uniform's shirt blooming with sudden sweat. "First you say you're my whore, and now—"

"Then what *am* I, if I'm not your whore?"

Stannard stood with his back against the door and hyperventilated, staring at her. Connie saw the titillation in his eyes and knew he was working himself up to take her as hard as he could—like something valueless and interchangeable—and she laughed.

"What?" Dan asked her.

"I know why you won't pay me. It'd send you straight back to Kate, wouldn't it?"

"I'm done with all this, Con. I'll talk to Tommy and tell you if he says anything."

Then Dan Stannard was out the door, this man of the law who reminded Connie of her father but offered her no protection at all. Who was merely an instrument. Who could have been her whore just as much as she'd been his.

We're all whores for each other, Connie thought. *It's the way of the world. Amen.* Then she heard Richie's gang singing that *Amen* back to her long and loud and clear, like a gospel choir with a hundred people in it.

* * *

Dan Stannard drove to the church house after supper in regular clothes but with a stray pair of handcuffs in his hip pocket just in case. When he knocked, Ed Dolman stepped out and closed the door behind him.

"You too?" Stannard asked.

"Just praying, ain't staying," Dolman told him. "Not a bad place for guys like us, who got on the wrong side of the law."

"I did my time. I'm right with the law."

"Man's law, maybe. What can I do ya for?"

"You know who I'm here to see."

"You mean the poow wittle wunaway?" whined Tommy, popping his head through the door. "The poow, fatherless boy who needs a big, stwong state patwolman to cawl his daddy?" He stepped out and laughed with Dolman, who headed toward the church.

"No wonder she can't stand you," Stannard said.

"She sent you here to see how the brainwashing's going, huh? Did she give you a little treat for it in advance, or promise you one later?"

"Don't be an asshole. She's scared for you, and you're giving her every reason to be."

"Maybe I'm an asshole 'cause you're both living a lie."

"We're not together anymore. You got your wish. Happy?"

"Yeah," Tommy said. "Maybe you'll hang out with your wife more. When I pray for you, that's what I'm praying for the most."

"What the hell are these people turning you into?" Stannard's fist clenched, and Tommy noticed.

"Just a kid who likes Jesus, Sheriff." The visceral joy of confrontation called to Tommy, tightening his jaw and filling his chest. "Don't get your undies in a bunch."

"Ah, hell. Jesus can't even stop you from being a punk."

"But he might stop *you* from cheating on your wife, if you give him a chance."

"Who the fuck are you? I don't even know why your mom wants you back."

"'Cause I'm the flesh of her flesh, man. You know how good that flesh of hers feels. Mmmmmm, cozy. Mmmmmmmmmmm, deeeee-licious."

Stannard slapped Tommy, who let his head roll with the blow. "That woman gave up her whole *life* for you."

"Turn the other cheek," Tommy said, swiveling his head sideways. Stannard slapped that cheek, too, his hand tightening a bit. "Ooh, give me some more, Sheriff. Don't hold back."

Stannard's hand closed into a fist, but he pulled his punch as it landed.

"Turn the other cheek. Oooh, let me have it, baby." Then came a real punch, and Tommy stumbled. "Ooooooh, make me forget who I am. Make me forget all my lies."

Stannard got a good lick in, and Tommy tasted blood. The next time he said, "Turn the other cheek," it came out slurred and snarled.

"You love this shit, don't you?" Stannard gave him a left hook to the gut, then a right hook to the ribs that knocked him back until his knee hit the porch boards. Thorpe came out to stand in Tommy's place, and Stannard loosened his fist.

"What's all this noise about?" Thorpe asked.

"Just some geezer cop," Tommy said, standing and checking his face for blood. "Slapping me like a woman."

"You can take care of yourself, right? Don't need me?"

"No sir. Don't think the sheriff's got half as much hate as I've got love."

"I'll be glad to take whatever rage and frustration you've got left over, Officer," Thorpe told Stannard. "Unless you want to give it all to the underage plaintiff here."

"Do you have *any* idea what you're doing to this town?" Stannard asked Thorpe.

"Teaching it to pray again. Come see for yourself, every night at sundown."

"You're ripping Connie apart. You took her son."

"I don't see a whole lot of *taking* here," Thorpe said. "Do you, Mr. Sandor?"

"No sir," Tommy said. "I *took* the time to thank God today for the flesh and blood he gave me. Maybe that's what Patrolman Stannard means."

"Right from the young man himself," Thorpe told Stannard. "If we're breaking any laws, Officer, then tell me their names or get off our property."

"*Your* property?" Stannard scoffed and looked past Thorpe to Tommy. "You're a minor, remember that. The law sides with your mom every time."

"But who's God siding with?" Tommy asked. "Is he *for* the man who quit loving the woman he swore he'd love or *against* him?"

As Stannard thudded down the steps, Thorpe and Tommy laughed. "What do you think, Tom-Tom?" asked Thorpe, once the patrolman retreated to his truck. "Can our man of the law feel the love of God or not?"

"No comment, pending further investigation," Tommy replied. He didn't know what TV show he'd picked that phrase up from — *Quincy, M.E.* or *Hawaii Five-O* or *Kojak*. He should remember as much TV as he could, he thought, as he checked for loose teeth. Before he became Brother Thomas and gave it up forever.

✻ ✻ ✻

When the sun sank below the cottonwood trees to the west of his gas station, it meant closing time for Pete Sowell. He'd never been a religious man, and back when the church on Tumbleback Road was first abandoned, he used to go by it with a sneer or even raise his arms with a derisive "Praaaaaaaaise Jesus!"

But he'd heard Justin Stannard talk about Connie and Tommy on the radio, thanks to a phone call from Dolman telling him to listen in, and he figured if he'd ever have a reason to pray—short of his wife or son dying—then the Sandor family imploding before his eyes would be it. As Pete locked the front door, Brother Zypanski loped toward him with a sheet of paper in one hand and a roll of masking tape in the other.

"Evening," Zypanski said. "Got one last flyer, looking for a place to put it."

"How about right here?" Pete slapped his palm on the middle of the glass door, and Zypanski taped it up there. The letters were blocky and awkward—nothing like Beto's fine hand.

PLEASE COME PRAY WITH US.
IT DOESN'T MATTER WHAT GOD YOU BELIEVE IN.
SUNDOWN IN THE OLD CHURCH EVERY NIGHT.
PEACE, LOVE, AND TRUTH,
THE SONS AND DAUGHTERS OF JESUS AND MARY

"I might swing by," Pete said while Zypanski smoothed down the tape. "Did you hear that radio show? You think poor little Tom-Tom can turn it around with his big, bad mama standing in the way like that?"

"Yep." Zypanski tossed up the tape roll and caught it with his thumb. "The only thing standing in his way is poor little Tom-Tom."

"How's his face from that brawl?" asked Pete, since he'd heard about Stannard punching Tommy out.

"Still attached to his thick skull," said Zypanski, shrugging as he moved on. Pete walked home, thinking about how Connie used to laugh with Tommy before the Sons and Daughters came along—laughing even through the flag burning crisis and the quitting football crisis. Pete didn't hear that kind of laughter from Connie anymore, and he thought someone who loved her as a neighbor should help her get it back.

"Think how it used to be," he practiced saying to her. "I know you can get back there." But the more Pete said it, the closer he pictured his face to Connie's. His hands reached for her taut arms, her waist. Carla wasn't at home to stop his train of thought, so the scene kept repeating itself and got steamier every time. He tasted the skin of Connie's shoulder, licked the hollow of her neck while he unclasped her bra. Then a baking sheet fell in the kitchen, scaring him like a teenage boy who'd just been caught jerking off.

Pete skulked over to the church to wash himself clean of his Connie fantasies, which covered his skin like pond scum. Inside people sang a long, slow *Amen*. He hoped they'd been praying for him, and as he tiptoed through the door, he pictured himself standing in the middle of a circle with everybody laying hands on him. But in reality they all looked too zoned out for that, sitting on the hard floor and staring at three burning candle stubs.

Pete crept toward the circle, not quite close enough for people to make room for him because it felt, to himself and to them, like he might bolt any second. Wally Ogrean sat next to Ed Dolman. Julie Parness held hands with Janice Sauter. Tommy pointed Pete toward a gap in the circle between Hyun and Zypanski, who held Tessy beneath her blanket.

"What else should we pray for?" Mother Meg asked Pete as he sat.

"I want to pray for Connie Sandor." Once he blurted it out, Pete felt the stiffness in his chest dissolve exactly the way he wanted Connie's to dissolve. "I'm worried she's hardening her heart to her son, to everybody." Pete glanced around but wouldn't let anyone catch his eye, and no more words came.

"For peace in the heart of Connie Sandor," Thorpe eventually said, "we all pray."

Then everybody sang a long *Amen*—even Pete, who felt miles away from the man he'd always been. A proud man, too in love with being in charge of himself to think of God as anything but the punchline to a joke. The circle waited for another prayer to rise up from it, and Dolman straightened his spine.

"I pray for my friend Pete, that God'll keep opening his heart, like he did mine."

"For the light of God to soften the heart of Pete Sowell," Mother Meg said, "we all pray."

The *Amen* came again, and Pete wanted to cry because tears might wash away all the petty wrongs he'd done in his life. No big ones, no crimes. Just all the nasty things he'd said and thought about people, the times he'd acted hard when he should have yielded. He let his chin drop to his chest and thought of Carla, wishing she were there beside him so they could let all their old fears melt out of their skins. He wanted tears, but they wouldn't come.

Crying comes later, Pete heard a voice say. Too old to be Tommy, too young to be Jesus. *Long way to go before we find your tears.*

❊ ❊ ❊

Nobody noticed Connie's truck driving into Suborney just after dark, and no one saw the defeat in her face and limbs. She could never beat Richie—he had Tommy, he had her surrounded, and it felt like time to come clean. To find the freedom you only get when you're backed into a corner and stop fighting. Isn't that what Richie told her? "Lots of freedom in that corner." Nobody saw her park by the junkyard where Tommy's Vega used to live or slink through the edges of town by flashlight toward Tumbleback Road. Nobody saw the envelope in her hand or the sheet of yellow legal paper inside it that she'd written on so neatly at the grim motel. No one noticed her elegant penmanship.

Richie—

You won't believe me when I say how many times I've thought about how you must've felt in prison. Knowing you had a child somewhere but not knowing if it was with me, if it was a boy or a girl, if it was still alive, if it ever got born at all. I know you're punishing me, and I probably deserve it, but I want it

*to stop right now because I can't keep pretending anymore. I'm
ready to admit who you are to everybody.*

*But Tommy is still pretending, asking me who his father is
even though his father has been standing next to him for weeks.
If you want me to go door to door and tell everybody in town
that I've been a liar as long as they've known me, then that's
what I'll do. But don't leave me hanging, waiting for <u>our son</u> to
make up his mind about how bad he wants to hurt me. Because I
don't deserve that, no matter what lies I told.*

    Let's talk,

    Nettie

Connie had already written FOR RICHARD THORPE on the envelope and licked the seal. She hesitated at the corner of Division and
Tumbleback when some candlelight flickered—six or seven people
were on their way from the church to the Perrin house. She hid in
the tall grass of the ditch to wait them out and didn't feel the wind
suddenly picking up until it had already blown the envelope out of
her hand. She looked for it everywhere—getting down on her knees
and crawling through the roadside weeds—until she got scared that
the people walking up the road could see her. The wind took that
envelope in circles, pulling it farther away from her. Connie combed
through the weeds for it until the candles got too close and then laid
herself flat, as still as a corpse, while feet shuffled past her.

"I pray for Connie Sandor," said Mother Meg.

"I pray for Connie Sandor," said Pete Sowell, sucking up to the
Jesus freaks like she knew he would.

"I pray for Connie Sandor," said her son, whose voice she barely
knew anymore.

"I pray for Connie Sandor," said Richie Thorpe, and when the
Amen sounded, she didn't want to be prayed over by anybody, not
even by her own son and the man who planted the seed for him.
Nobody had a right to pray over her if she didn't want it. She took

back everything she said in that letter, every single word. She didn't need Richie's forgiveness. She needed release, needed to bust through the crust of pointlessness and self-doubt that had hardened on her skin like armor. It was such a part of her flesh now that she couldn't change a thing about herself without a little destruction. Without a lot, maybe.

Connie waited in the weeds until the candlelight at the Perrin house died down, then looked for the letter again. Nowhere—they must have picked it up without her seeing. She walked down Tumbleback Road and slinked into the church to look for Richie, even though she'd heard him walking the other way. Or maybe she wasn't looking for Richie at all. Maybe she was looking for the exact thing that her flashlight found inside: the mural on the wall showing her and Tommy walking hand in hand as Mary and a kid Jesus.

"Like hell," Connie said, and then she checked every corner of the church with her flashlight to make sure nobody had seen her looking. The venomous metal twisted inside her and solidified, not a snake anymore but back to its solid, meteorite form. Not quite its final form, but getting there. She felt herself changing into another person, just like she'd felt herself cease being Jeannette Holmquist by the chain link fence in Nebraska City in 1962. Connie Sandor was slipping away, turning into something she didn't know yet. Wasn't meant to know yet.

Whatever she was becoming, it could take on Richie. This new self wouldn't need to forgive him. Forgiveness was too soft and too weak, too temporary for this new self she would become. She needed something harder and more enduring to pay Richie back for what he'd done. A way for him to remember her that would remind him of what she truly was, not of what he wanted her to be.

Connie shone her flashlight at the mural, at the Tommy/Jesus and the Connie/Mary. How dare Thorpe do that to her and to her son? Making them pillars in his mind that they could never live up to, setting them up so they could only fail. It was worse than blasphemy against the God that Richie claimed to love. It was a crime against her, against Tommy. A crime against life itself.

23

Sunday, July 27

At eight o'clock in the morning, before anyone in Suborney knew that the Shah of Iran had died in Cairo, Richard Thorpe knocked on Connie Sandor's door for a second time. She'd been home for five hours by then, having grown frustrated with the Big Chief Motel's raucous clientele, though her next night was paid for and her trash bags still sat in her room. Thorpe stared at her through the screen door, his sweat-ribboned hat over his heart.

"You've been thinking about me," he said. "Wanting to talk to me."

"What makes you think that?"

"Places people see you going."

"Everybody goes places without other people knowing why." Connie knew Richie wouldn't say a damn thing about her letter, even if he'd read it enough times to memorize it. So she wouldn't either. "What do you want?"

"For you to come to our church. Lots of people in this town are praying for you to heal."

"Funny how they didn't pray for me the first eleven years I was here. Not till you put 'em on my scent like a pack of dogs."

"I'm offering you an opportunity, Nettie. To stop hauling around your—"

"What you're doing is trying to force a confession. Don't forget my dad was a cop, don't call me Nettie, and don't lean your head on my screen door. Bugs get in if it rips."

Thorpe dropped down to his knees. "I'm just asking you to come pray with us."

"Bad shit happens when you kneel in front of me, Richie." Her heart stiffened like a fist. "I'll get this over with and tell everybody in town you're Tommy's father, okay? Just not at your church. It's got nothing to do with Jesus, and that Mary up on the wall doesn't look a damn bit like me."

"Oh?" Richie gave a smirk, the Tommy Sandor smartass smirk that Connie loathed. She slammed the inside door before he could say anything more and hid in her bedroom, thinking how free she might feel if she walked into Richie's church and fixed her lie the way he wanted her to. Thanking Jesus for giving her the courage to confess, of course, then begging Jesus to forgive her. Easy enough to imagine, but she couldn't promise herself to actually do it. She might say yes and chicken out, might say no and slink inside anyway. Richie said he was giving her an opportunity, but it was only an opportunity to let Jesus follow her everywhere she went. Connie wanted the opposite: freedom from scrutiny, freedom to pursue her own mistakes as far as they'd go. Tommy was a mistake, and look how far he'd gone.

Open your heart and let God in, Mom! she heard her son say. *Without God there's no real love!* She grunted at the thought of her son spewing the same brainwashed drivel as thousands of other teenage Jesus freaks. Connie felt her lower jaw muscles ball up again and dug at them with her knuckles, and when the joints popped, she felt her jaw slide forward incrementally. Nothing anybody else would notice. She felt more carnivorous, certain that she looked more like a man, though her mirror refused to confirm this. Out her window she saw Richie kneeling to pray by her truck, with that pierce-lipped, Chinese-looking girl next to him. She closed her bedroom and living room blinds and stepped into her kitchen, then saw Ed Dolman on his knees by her shed. Pete Sowell walked up and knelt beside him, catching her eyes through the glass.

Me too, Pete's eyes told her. *You were right*. Connie pulled the kitchen shades down and looked out Tommy's broken window, only to see her own son kneeling next to the brunette she couldn't stand, with the bangs. At his other shoulder was the Mexican with the stump. She grabbed her purse and keys, then stepped out the front door.

"The big, bad sinner lady is leaving now," she told them all. "Hope you have fun praying to her house. Have a nice day, everybody, and *God* bless this place!"

It felt like a turning point even as it happened: the moment when her annoyance with all kinds of Jesus lovers hardened into something most people would call hate. Connie didn't call it that, but the right word escaped her. Only images carried the mood. First she saw the weapon inside her becoming more defined and adding sides—a thousand at least, reflecting a sharp, hard light that came from an unknown spot inside her. Then Connie saw herself growing impossibly big and Richie's church growing impossibly small, and she kicked it violently into the weeds of Tumbleback Road. Probably at the exact spot where Richie's people had found the letter. That damn, self-incriminating letter.

"Careful out there, ma'am," said the tall guy as he knelt down next to the old lady, and Connie didn't even acknowledge their existence as she stepped past them. Nobody looked her challengingly in the eye, and Richie didn't even glance up when she climbed into her truck, even though she could have reached out and knocked that stupid hat off his head. They only knelt and prayed, and as she pulled out of her driveway, she saw more people walking toward her house.

They'd have to pull their circle tighter, Connie thought as she drove off, because there weren't enough people in Suborney to make one that big. Or maybe there would be. Maybe Richie had more people, waiting in the weeds until he gave the signal. When they got the house surrounded, they'd levitate it with prayers, then make it fall in on itself like a pile of sticks that never had anything holding it together in the first place.

* * *

All Connie could think about while she scouted potential neighborhoods in Colorado Springs was a scene from a black-and-white Frankenstein movie she saw as a girl. The villagers, armed with torches and pitchforks and axes, had surrounded the monster in a house with a thatched roof ready to burst into flames the second somebody put a torch to it. That's what Connie kept seeing: a single torch glancing against the thatched roof of her life and setting it on fire. She kept rewinding the scene in her head and playing it in slow motion, focusing on the face of the villager whose torch started the blaze.

Usually it was Pete Sowell, since he wanted to save her so damn much. Sometimes it was Wally Ogrean, back to being the town tough guy now that he was on God's side, or at least on Richie Thorpe's side. Sometimes it was Tommy, sneaking into the crowd late. A few times it was even herself, after she'd joined the Jesus cult and decided to burn down her old lies. But it was never Richie with the torch, and that bothered her. He always stood off to the side, with his wetback hat and mashed-in face, so proud of himself for finally making her crack.

At a red light Connie checked her watch to time her drive to work from an apartment complex she liked. Colorado Springs was far enough away to move, since she didn't have to run from Richie anymore. He'd still want to convert her, of course. He wouldn't stop with Tommy—he'd keep hounding her until she became his perfect Jesus-loving wife. Connie pictured his whole cult, plus a few people from Suborney on the verge of joining it like Pete was, huddled together beneath the bedroom window of her new top-floor apartment. All night and day they'd kneel and pray, until she jumped out that window to her death or crawled out to them shouting, "I believe!"

It turned out to be nine minutes to the office, but once Connie got there, she decided she needed another job so she wouldn't have to explain so many things. At noon she drove to the Citadel Mall to look for clothes, starting with JC Penney but not staying long because it reminded her of her mother's store in Sidney. Plus, she wanted better outfits—nothing more from chains or bargain bins. She was young and beautiful and would have money to spend letting people know it soon because she wouldn't have a teenage son eating up her paycheck.

Connie tried on skirts and pantsuits and laughed at herself, not sure if she looked like a woman coming unhinged or a woman finally adding up to more than the sum of her parts. Someday Tommy would understand why she'd lied all those years, and then he'd beg her to forgive him for torturing her. Maybe in another year or two, after he knocked up his own horny teenage girlfriend and learned what responsibility meant. Because Richie sure couldn't tell him. Richie, who'd been in prison for every cut and scrape and piss-soaked pair of pants.

She found a peasant skirt she loved, creamy yellow with green and blue embroidered leaves, but didn't buy it. She couldn't try on new personalities yet because the one she wore in Suborney wasn't finished with its job. Connie took Hancock Road going southeast and spotted a nice neighborhood just twenty minutes from work. It was that long to Suborney, too, in case Tommy got sick of his shiny new dad and moved back to Mangum Street. She'd get together with him there for supper once a week, more often when Tommy gave up his ridiculous saxophone and went to Pikes Peak Community College to learn something useful.

In the parking lot of a Kmart, where she stopped to look for bargains out of habit, Connie passed an army guy in camouflage fatigues siphoning gas from his truck into the tank of a woman with two toddlers. He sucked on the tube and pulled it out expertly once the gas got flowing.

"Did you hear, ma'am?" he said as Connie walked by, and she

flinched at the *ma'am*. "The Shah just died. No reason left not to get our hostages out and bomb the shit out of that damn country."

"I see!" Connie said. The soldier spat, and for a few footsteps she smelled nothing but gasoline. She reminded herself to get one of those siphoning tubes at Kmart—maybe the kind with a pumper ball on it so she wouldn't have to taste gas. Might come in handy if her tank went empty on the road. Actually, it was something she absolutely had to have. Her life depended on it.

＊ ＊ ＊

All day long the circle around Connie's house changed shape and composition. Twenty-seven citizens of Suborney came out, though some didn't even last an hour. At first people put a lot of space between themselves, like they might at a concert in a park. But the prayers were too diffuse, out of sync, like a band that hadn't practiced, so the Sons and Daughters placed themselves strategically to pull the circle tighter—just as Connie had predicted.

"I pray for Connie Sandor," one of them would say every minute or so, to keep the crowd on task and improve the way they sang *Amen*. Tommy roved around the circle, holding people's hands and making sure they knew he was praying the hardest.

"I pray for Connie Sandor," called Wally Ogrean, who had always been too quick to call the woman a whore behind closed doors and to call her son a bastard. "That she finds peace in herself and doesn't shut out the people around her."

"I pray for Connie Sandor," added Pete Sowell. "So she and every mother in the world can get back to loving their sons."

Brother Worrell lit candles on Connie's front and back steps. Some people thought about their own mothers, some about their children, some about the battles that Connie had won and lost with Tommy. Some about the battles they'd won and lost with themselves, as they'd tried to keep their own children growing up right.

"I pray for Connie Sandor," said Julie Parness, "that she'll know what fights are worth fighting and keep her son close while she can."

"I pray for Connie Sandor," said Mother Meg, "that someday she'll embrace her child's father the way she's been embraced by the people of this town."

"I pray for Connie Sandor," called Thorpe, "that she can stand in peace beside her son and be grateful for what she's given to the world."

"I pray for Connie Sandor," said Tommy, "that speaking the truth will help her love God like she's meant to."

After that came a string of long *Amen*s, one rolling into the next. Brother Benjy and Mother Meg brought the bread and wine so that everybody could have some before the sun got too strong. A few people got their minds messed up from the heat and kept stumbling around for more bread, more wine.

"If you pass out," Mother Meg told everybody, "we'll have to stop praying for Connie and start praying for you. Go home and drink some water every once in a while."

The Sons and Daughters let the people from town have the shady spots, and that helped the circle last longer. Brother Zypanski brought Tessy over, but she stiffened up once she got close to Connie's house.

"What do you say we go inside?" Zypanski suggested. "Heal the place up a bit?"

Tessy, hidden beneath a white sheet, scratched his arm in protest. When Melanie looked under the sheet, Tessy thunked her chest three times—her sign for wanting to go home. Then she let out a brutal, hacking cough that dragged on for a minute and a half.

"It's all right, girl," Melanie told her. "Just keep on loving till you can't anymore."

❄ ❄ ❄

After suppertime prayers at the Jesus and Mary house, and long after the circle at Connie's house had broken up for good, Tessy woke with a nightmare. Nothing could calm her down, not even swinging back and forth in Zypanski's long arms. She sang up a storm—long, convoluted, jazzy lines that made Tommy grab his sax and play along softly from a corner of her room. When Zypanski left, Tessy motioned Tommy over until his bell was a foot from her chest. He breathed out a soft middle B♭, and Tessy grunted, so Tommy eased down the keys until she nodded at his F. Then she sang him a scale—

F G♭ A♭ A B D♭ E♭ F

—and Tommy made it jump and lurch and twist around itself. He spun it and threw it in the air so it came back down in pieces that he shuffled like a deck of cards until it fell back into the scale again, in its original order, pure and strong like Tessy started it. When Tommy's sax fell silent, she sang him another scale, this one starting with E. He followed it gently, negotiating its too-many flats, then picked it up and strutted with it. Tessy kept the scales coming, giving Tommy seven of them to keep, one for every day of the week. Then she hacked again, with snot clogging up her tiny nostrils, and her head slumped over.

"You're leaving us, aren't you?" he asked. Tessy clasped her good hand over Tommy's and closed her eyes, and he kissed her forehead. He stepped out of her room to find everybody kneeling by the doorway. Zypanski took one look at him and started bawling on Benjy's shoulder. Thorpe started blubbering, too, but there wasn't a shoulder close enough for him to rest his head on. *She's the child I'm about to lose*, his eyes said to Tommy as they stared at each other, *and you're the child I already lost once.*

Tommy broke their look and went to the living room to put away his sax, then rummaged through the kitchen for a pen and paper so he could write down the scales and give them names. *See My Broken Body Weeping. Reach Inside Yourself to See It. What Must Love Mean Now, My Brother?* He spilled himself onto the kitchen floor, and his empty hands moved through each of them, memorizing their notes in his flesh until his fingers cramped up. Down the hallway, Tessy's bedroom door opened and closed.

"She wants you," Zypanski whispered. Tommy couldn't tell who went in, but he knew that everyone would get the call. Maybe even himself again, before she was gone.

Nobody in the house could sleep that night. They all lay in the living room on their unzipped sleeping bags, clutching each other's hands for comfort as Tessy coughed. Zypanski sat in her room crying, then came out and announced that she wanted to die in the house— with all of them around her—instead of going to a hospital. Tommy freaked out at the prospect of a second child he knew dying in that room and started hyperventilating.

"The cops'll come for us if we let her die," he said, his voice high and shaky. "They just arrested some people in Pueblo who wouldn't take their son to the hospital."

"It's what she wants," Sister Melanie said. "Please, Tommy, don't make this hard."

"How can you tell what she wants when she can't even *talk*?"

But nobody would listen to him, and Thorpe eventually took him out to the arroyo to give everybody else some peace. Tommy sobbed over Tessy and hummed out her seven songs, and Thorpe held him— comforting his son, finally, the way he'd dreamed of for so long.

"It can't be two kids dying in that room," Tommy said. "Wesley died in that room."

"That's probably why she picked it. Tessy knows things. She can tell who loves God and who doesn't. Your friend Wesley did."

"What does she know about me?"

"Enough to give you her music. It was everything to her."

Those words broke down the last of Tommy's defenses. Tough guy Tommy. Linebacker Tommy. Gonna-Be-A-Marine Tommy. And there, with Richard Thorpe's arms around him, all the times he'd ever wished to cry on his father's shoulder met at once. He cried with his father like he'd never cried with his mother. He cried for Tessy like he'd never let himself cry for Wesley. Father and son clutched each other like two wrestlers who've decided once and for all to give up the battle, only to find that the battle never ends.

24

Late Sunday night at the Big Chief Motel, Connie winnowed her three trash bags of belongings down to one. The innumerably sided weapon inside her had cracked open, and its venom permeated her bloodstream evenly so that every single part of her was ready to use it. No inch of her would hesitate when she did what she had to do— win back her son, or make Richie Thorpe lose him.

"Will I ever see Tommy again?" she wanted to ask the Magic 8-Ball sitting in a box of junk back home, though she knew it would say, REPLY HAZY TRY AGAIN or OUTLOOK NOT SO GOOD. Connie finished watching a show on PBS about galaxies being born and dying, then went out to her truck and set the trash bag full of stuff she planned to keep on her passenger seat. She left another one, over-stuffed with junk, for scavengers in the alley behind the motel. The third bag already sat, full of gasoline-soaked rags, in her truck bed.

Maybe the gasoline was a bad idea. Unnecessary. Cops and firemen always knew if a blaze started with gasoline—hadn't that been the first thing they'd looked for at the showroom in Nebraska City and had never been able to find because Richie didn't need it? Connie wouldn't either, she decided. But what if she wasn't as strong as Richie and needed the boost gasoline would give her?

Connie showered at the Big Chief, caressing her taut musculature in the lavish way that Richie used to, and traced her fingers over her entire skin to check for spots where the venom might have coagulated. She found one on the inside of her left thigh and one above her right knee, like knots of misplaced gristle, and crunched them with her knuckles until they broke. She flopped onto the bed naked when the hot water ran out and felt the last remnants of those knots floating just beneath her skin. Almost close enough to reach, to grab onto and pull.

She didn't care that the polyester bedspread beneath her felt filthy. This skin wouldn't last long. This name wouldn't either. There were hundreds of women she might be next—Linda Coventry, Anna Dormatti, Stephanie Nicolet. Hundreds of pleasingly shaped, gleamingly skinned buckets for men to drop their needs into. Empty wells for them to shout into, wanting to hear back nothing more than their own names uttered with desire. She would never let herself expect anything more from a man again.

At one o'clock on Monday morning, Connie parked her truck on a forlorn shoulder ten minutes east of Suborney by foot. She walked through Suborney Creek so she couldn't be traced and carried the bag of gas-soaked rags. She stopped a quarter-mile or so from the church, a lot closer than Richie had been to her father's store that night in Nebraska City. Connie stepped out to the rock in the middle of the creek where she used to read and watch Tommy play, then took off her sandals and stuck her feet in the water to wash them even though they were already wet.

Jesus got his feet washed by a sinful woman, she heard Tommy's voice say. *Don't see why a sinful woman can't wash her own.*

But hadn't Justin Stannard said on the radio that she *wasn't* a sinful woman? No, he'd said she wasn't a *wicked* woman. Connie pondered the difference between those two words as she washed her feet tenderly, slowly, but she didn't know if she was washing them to spite her son or to acknowledge his rightness and power. And there was power in the boy—he'd learn all about it now that Richie had gotten hold of him. What would the two of them do to punish her?

Blow her house off the ground and hurl it down on her, probably. Like the Wicked Witch of the East in *The Wizard of Oz*, but with her head sticking out instead of her shoes so she could utter a few last melodramatic words.

What would those last words be, and would she say them to Richie or to Tommy? *Bubble. Crouton. Mammoth. Albacore.* Words that added up to nothing. She would never need to say those words, though, because once the church burned down, both of them would know who gave out the punishment in her world. Connie decided against using the rags because it would be a confession of weakness that might prevent the fire from starting at all. She knew she could make fire with blood and sound and will because she'd felt that power growing in her guts—the hook, the meteorite, the snake, the venom. Now the time had come to give them full birth. The time had come to be Richie's equal, to fight against him and Tommy and that deformed little girl who stole her breath.

Connie faced the church, pulling out the gray utility knife in her jeans pocket and setting it on the rock without a sound. She pictured Richie by the chain link fence in the moment when he first licked his own blood and tried to breathe like him, move like him. How would he feel if he knew that he'd taught her, in that very moment, exactly how to destroy what he loved? And who would die in this fire she set? Someone had to pay the price for her father's strangulation by smoke, for the parching of his lungs. An eye for an eye, a life for a life—it was the most ancient human way. Richie? He knew fire too well to ever let that happen. It could be Tommy, running into the church to save everybody's precious *stuff* and never coming back out again.

But the Sons and Daughters kept all their churches empty, didn't they? Nobody would run in trying to save anything and be involuntarily slaughtered when the one in Suborney burned to ash. Connie saw a hint of silent lightning through a gap in the trees as she tried to conjure fire within her. Good—it meant she had some cover. The lightning was too far away to strike the church, but an obsessive weather watcher like Ron Ulin would surely be able to tell the fire department exactly when he saw it. *Yes, there was lighting*, she could hear him say. *It woke me up. It didn't seem close enough, but . . . but . . .* Then his words would fail him, and he'd look away from whatever fireman he was talking to and out over the smoldering remains of Suborney.

"For public safety reasons the church on Tumbleback Road will be demolished tomorrow." That's what the Suborney newspaper would say, if the town had deserved a newspaper. Exactly what the Nebraska City paper said about her father's store. After that church was gone, she could burn all of Richie's other churches to ash too. The one in Sidney could be next, with Eldon Thorpe asleep in it. Maybe *he'd* be her eye for an eye, a dead father traded for a dead father. Once she did that, who could say what else she might do? Who could say what her limits were?

Don't get drunk on the power, Connie reminded herself. *Not before you even prove it.* She focused her mind and her hate and resurrected that moment with Richie by the fence in every detail—the cadence of his breathing, the nutmeg and barbecue smell that rose off his skin. She took hard breaths that bobbed her head and shoulders like an upside-down pendulum, leaning her so far forward that her face nearly touched the water, then so far backward that she hovered at the edge of her balance. As Connie sank into her movements, a sound crawled up from the back of her throat, not words or music but a guttural chant, a voice from beyond the grave and before the womb. Like the sound her father must have made when he choked to death on smoke, losing his breath as he searched the burning building for his precious stuff.

His stuff, his stuff, his stuff. Phrases like that helped Connie chant, and they drove her deeper into her rocking and breathing. *My son. No good. To war. To hell.* After she'd rocked for so long that she couldn't break her rhythm, she finally heard a tune embedded in her growl— four slow, even notes, rising like lazy versions of the piano arpeggios she'd learned in grade school. She and the sound became one: every-thing that had happened to this mortal once called Connie Sandor, this mortal once called Jeannette Holmquist, had whittled itself down to the rocking and the breathing and the phantom notes that forged themselves in her throat, in her lungs, in the cavern of her mouth.

It was time. Connie grabbed the utility knife and slid the button forward to expose its blade. As she rocked, she sliced her fingertips open—first the five right ones, then the five left—so quickly that she barely felt it until the knife clattered to the rock and her fingers spasmed in pain. Connie held them over the water and squeezed the blood out of them as fast as she could.

"You think you're the only one who can do this?" she growled to Richie Thorpe, wherever he was. Connie sucked her fingertips, which bled so profusely that she couldn't swallow all the bracing, salty liquid. The words inside her disappeared, and the growl at the back of her throat took over. She gave up thinking that she could suck the pain out of her fingers and plunged them into the creek instead, giving out one last grunt as she smelled something in the air.

Smoke? But the smoke didn't come, so she doubted herself. Maybe she didn't have enough of the metallic poison in her bloodstream to light a fire from afar. It had brought her to this point but couldn't take her any farther. Connie hunted inside herself for the parts of her that used to need Richie Thorpe in the first place, the small incomplete-nesses that she couldn't name, then or now. In her darkest corners she found the mouthless forms that crawled along the bottom of the sea before language, before people, before mammals, before vertebrates. She called them to her center and felt them swarming inward, then settling between her navel and her pubic bone.

She felt the same irreducible, ineradicable hunger that drove Jean-nette Holmquist in 1962 and still drove Connie Sandor in 1980. Her hunger and her hate came together as she focused on the church, on the picture of herself as Mary on its wall. That's where the burning would start because she was nobody's virgin and had brought forth her child in nothing but sin. She pictured the flesh-colored paint of Mary's face curling up from the heat that she planted inside it and eventually giving off tiny, weak flames. They danced from her face to her arm, then down her arm to the hand that so gently held her son's. Then they climbed up Tommy's arm and from there onto Tommy's face, where they burst alive and couldn't be stopped.

"There, Richie," Connie said, finally smelling smoke from the church. "If I can't have him, you can't either." She'd made fire from nothing, but it was too soon to congratulate herself. The fire had to stick, had to burn the whole building to nothing. She tasted her own blood again, sucking on those cut fingers that might never heal, that would change her fingerprints and make her impossible to identify. Then nobody could pin the names Jeannette Holmquist or Connie Sandor on her body, which was still beautiful and could still carry the seed of another man, even if no other man could give her a seed like Richie had.

"My son, my son, my son," she chanted, knowing she might never see him again. Connie feasted on her own blood until she saw smoke rising into the sky above the church. Then she calmly stepped off the rock and tiptoed through Suborney Creek with her bag of gasoline-soaked clothes, which she'd burn somewhere later. A hundred miles away, a thousand miles away. She carried it twenty-five paces in her right hand, stopped to lick her bloody fingers, and carried it the next twenty-five paces in her left. Shouts of "Fire!" filled the air as she slipped quietly through the water, past the inquisitive, open door of Sam Kurtep's house, past Pete Sowell's gas station, past the junkyard, and toward her waiting truck.

Then, as she ran full tilt, Connie Sandor and Jeannette Holmquist both disappeared from time, disappeared entirely from the human record. These women—these lies, these false entities, these creatures so drowned in deceit that they seemed to have been born from it—had once lived on earth in the flesh but were no more.

✻ ✻ ✻

The Sons and Daughters—minus the semi-exiled Thorpe and Tommy, who were out in the arroyo—still couldn't sleep because of Tessy and instead sat in the darkness of the living room talking. Tessy's breathing sounded awful, despite the wet sheets that hung around her like a tent, and they wondered if she would last the night. If it started sounding like the end, Melanie was ready to run out and fetch Thorpe and Tommy.

"What are we going to do about those two?" asked Zypanski. "Are we moving on with 'em or moving on without 'em?"

"We can't think about moving on yet," said Worrell. "There's nobody to take care of the church."

"I mean when it's time. Aren't we always saying we'll all know when it's time?"

"Right now we need to *give* it time," piped in Melanie. "Let Brother T and Tom-Tom figure out who they want to be."

They all looked at Mother Meg, waiting for her to weigh in. Tessy inhaled sharply, but the breath didn't come out right away, and everybody in the room held their own breaths with her. Beto crossed himself with his stump. Then a cough finally came from Tessy's room, and they let themselves exhale.

"It's not our decision to make," Mother Meg finally said. "When we're ready to go, they'll come with us or they won't."

"They won't," Benjy piped in. "Not right away. Too much to work out."

"You know I've defended him a million times," said Worrell, his shoulders slumping as his mind relented. "But yeah, I think we move on and give 'em time. They'll catch up if they need to."

As they prayed for Thorpe and Tommy to do what was best, the smoke from the church reached them, and Tessy's lungs shrieked like a stuck door hinge. They stepped outside and saw the flames, then Zypanski wetted down Tessy's tent while the others packed up their essentials—a practiced ritual that took all of three minutes. Mother Meg squared away their supplies on the sled and tied the rope around her waist. The men nestled Tessy on her traveling blanket and stood ready to walk out of Suborney with her on their shoulders, just like they'd walked into it. But the flame-engulfed church—and the wind that pushed the fire straight for the houses of Suborney—told them that some lives were more in danger than their own.

"I'll wait with Tessy," Mother Meg said. "Get everybody out of their houses. There's forty-three people—count 'em off."

"Shouldn't we get Brother T?" asked Benjy.

"He's coming soon enough." She knelt beside Tessy with a hand on the girl's chest. Everyone else ran straight for the houses, shouting "Fire!" and "Everybody out!" They knocked on every door, honked the horns of every car they could get inside of to wake people up.

Out in the arroyo Tommy and Thorpe didn't smell the fire right away because they were burning their hate and comparing it. Thorpe's looked like bright orange pearls, and they joked about Tommy's hate changing color someday like his hair probably would. Then Tommy heard the din of car horns from Suborney and stood up and smelled smoke.

"Did you start that?" he asked Thorpe.

"Start what?"

Thorpe stood up and smelled the smoke, too, and they raced up the bank of the arroyo to Tumbleback Road. They could see the church surrounded by a red-orange halo, and Thorpe dropped to his knees. Tommy tried pulling him up until he saw his father's hands clenching and unclenching to bring the rain.

"Go to the creek," Thorpe said. "Pull the water up, get it around the houses."

"Who the hell would—?"

"Doesn't matter. You raise the creek—I'll bring the rain."

Tommy ran to the Jesus and Mary house, where he found Mother Meg sitting on the lawn next to Tessy. "She alive?" he asked, and then he crouched down to check for himself. Tessy's mouth hung open to breathe, and her eyes looked like they couldn't even see him from a foot away.

"For now," said Mother Meg. Then Thorpe ran up, looking like he'd been hollowed out and filled with sawdust.

"This is my fault," he told her.

"Yep," she said. "You're the one who let it happen, so get that rain down now. Tommy, show the water what you can do."

He ran straight for Suborney Creek, wondering exactly what Thorpe had *let happen*, but stopped in his tracks in the middle of Road X when he realized that he didn't know where his sax was. In the church, at the Jesus and Mary house, at his mom's? No idea. The last he remembered was playing it with Tessy. He saw truck headlights coming his way and flagged down the driver.

"The church got hit!" Ed Dolman yelled, not quite stopping. "Is Tessy still alive?"

Tommy nodded and watched Dolman peel out toward the Jesus and Mary house, then said a quick prayer for Tessy as he ran toward the creek. He tried to get his marrow moving, thinking about Tessy and all those old people who might die tonight if he couldn't raise the water. But Suborney Creek didn't move. He had to be *in* the water, and he had to be still—a complete blank inside—to bring up the creek with all that fire around him. He reached the spot where he used to swim while his mom sat on the rock and read her mystery novels, the spot where he and his newfound father had sat on the rock and cooled their tired feet.

This was the place. Tommy stepped into the creek up to his ankles and held his hands up by his shoulders, begging God to let him have the water, but something looked wrong with the rock. There was a bump on it in a place where it had always been smooth, and Tommy stepped closer to see. It was his mom's gray utility knife—the one she used to cut open cardboard boxes, the one he used himself to score drywall before snapping it into pieces.

There was blood too. His mother's blood, it had to be, pooled in one of the rock's indentations. Looking at it, he knew his mother set the fire with the same kind of black magic Richard Thorpe had, that her own son had. She did it not just to get back at the father but to ruin the son too. It was personal, a message, a warning. Her way of letting him know *Your father brings rain, but I bring fire.*

"You're the one who let it happen," Tommy said, repeating Mother Meg's words to Thorpe, and he understood. If Thorpe only had the balls to walk into town and say the truth, then Connie would never have had the chance to burn down the church. If he hadn't taunted her, smeared her lies in her face, then the hate inside her would never have grown this needy or this strong.

Tommy pictured his mother on the rock, shedding her own blood to bring fire. What parts of herself did she cut? How deep? Did she beg God to start the fire, like he begged God to raise the water? He laughed aloud at the thought, and his marrow decided to bring the creek up and sweep away the knife and the blood. His marrow didn't even ask him—it just made Suborney Creek surge and washed the evidence away with it. The blood that might have been identified in a lab as Connie Sandor's. The knife with fingerprints on it that could have been identified as hers by any rookie cop with half a brain.

Not that anyone would have known it was evidence, except him and his mother. And he'd gotten rid of it for her without even having to be asked. She started the fire so he'd know her power, and she left the knife to find out if he was on her side or not. Now that the test was done, Tommy wanted to punish his mother for making him pass it. He wanted to twist her arms behind her back and launch her at the cops. Wanted to laugh while they shoved her to the dry Suborney dirt and cuffed her wrists.

But no. She was his mother, and he loved her in ways he couldn't name. His marrow swelled and lifted the creek to his waist, sending the knife and blood far downstream. The water rose to Tommy's ribs, and as soon as he felt his strength coming back—the moment he believed he could flood Suborney and save it—the creek receded without any reason. He was weak, and he hated himself for it, and the weakness and hate spun into a whirlpool that sucked Suborney Creek down into the earth. It sucked all his will down with it too. In the face of his mother's power, Tommy couldn't keep a grip on his own. The water fell six inches with every breath he took, and it kept on falling even when he refused to breathe at all. He wondered if he really wanted the same thing as his mom—hadn't he fantasized more than once about burning Suborney to a crisp? Lighting an American flag on fire to protest the coming desert war he'd die in, then watching that fire turn Suborney into a desert itself?

"Up, you fucker!" Tommy yelled, but the water kept retreating into the earth as if it agreed with the Sandors and didn't think Suborney deserved to live. He kept one eye on the water and one eye on the church, which glowed like a jack-o'-lantern. The fire had burned through the brush around it and was ready to burn through its roof, which meant it would soon catch the tall trees and start coming after the rest of town from above.

Up, up, up, he told the creek, but its water did nothing. It spited him, laughed at him. He felt little drops of rain falling down and knew they came from Thorpe, but why couldn't the man bring more? Did his father know who started the fire, and did that truth paralyze him as much as it paralyzed his son? Suborney gave off a collective cry of panic as everyone who could walk packed their most precious belongings into whatever cars they could still drive. The Sons and Daughters, ready to be the last ones out or not escape at all, helped whoever couldn't help themselves. Tommy left the creek and jumped right in with them, racing for Mrs. Culp's house because she wasn't strong enough to even crawl out. Then he saw her on Brother Z's shoulder, about to get loaded into Sam Kurtep's truck.

"Get Ginny Caslow!" Sam yelled to Tommy. "She's next, then Maggie Gander, and that should be everybody."

"What about Jim and Marcine?" Tommy asked.

"Already done," Zypanski told him, closing the truck door on Mrs. Culp.

Tommy stepped closer to him. "My moth—"

"Doesn't matter how it started," said Zypanski, cutting him off with a hard glare. He climbed into Sam's truck bed and slapped the side to get Tommy's attention. "Caslow house, go!"

Tommy ran the shortcut while Sam drove the long way around. Beto had Ginny Caslow in his arms at the front door but couldn't get the tricky screen door open with his stump, so Tommy turned the handle and flung it open for him. Inside he grabbed her cat from its hiding place under the kitchen sink, figuring Jesus and Mary wouldn't want his mom to kill a cat any more than they wanted her to kill a person. When he came out, Benjy shouted at him from Maggie Gander's house across the street.

"Got an old lady who won't let me touch her!" he shouted, and Tommy ran over and pulled her out of her bed in her bathrobe. What kind of person would rather burn to death than let a black man save her? But Jesus and Mary wanted her saved because she might turn around someday. Just like he'd turned around, Tommy figured. Though he couldn't find Jesus or Mary anywhere, not with all the smoke and shouting. Definitely not inside himself, where his mother's blood and his mother's utility knife had crowded out everything else that was there only moments before. All the love he hadn't let bloom yet, all the petty hates he let live too long because he didn't know how to kill them. His mother's single, titanic NO—shouted against him, against Richard Thorpe and the Sons and Daughters, against the whole town of Suborney—drowned out everything else.

"Where's your mom?" asked Sam, once Tommy got Maggie into his truck. The Sons and Daughters, except for Thorpe and Mother Meg, all sat in the bed, their faces dripping with sooty sweat.

"Somewhere!" Tommy called back. "I'll go check."

He couldn't look the Sons and Daughters in the eye because he was scared that they already knew his mother started the fire, just like they'd known all along whose son he was. He took one last glance at the bunch of them—people he loved, people who'd shaped him, people he might never see again—then ran to his mom's house. He might never see her again either, and if he did, she'd have a different name. She'd be an old woman by the time he tracked her down in seventeen years. Or thirty-four, or fifty-one. Maybe on her deathbed, ready to unfurl every secret.

Tommy went in the back door and saw the kitchen gutted, saw WHO IS MY FATHER? in blue ink on the bare counter and laughed like he was ready to lock himself inside the house and burn. His mother was long gone. In the living room all their old pictures had been cast to the floor, and he half-expected to see every pair of eyes crossed out. Had she done this before or after she started the fire? Or had she done it silently the day before, while the town circled the house and prayed?

Tommy went outside and felt raindrops but nothing that could put out the fire. He even saw a heavy cloud above the burning church, but it yielded nothing even when his marrow called to it. Even when he dropped to his knees and prayed and held his hands up by his shoulders. Then he felt the wind coming for him and him alone once more, coming not with water but with fire this time, and he ran for the deepest part of Suborney Creek to escape from it. Usually the water reached his chest, but now it barely came up to his ankles. He heard the first fire truck pulling into town, ready to save what property it could now that all the people were out. *Nobody's going to die*, Tommy reassured himself as he lay flat in the shallow water, plunging his face in and hoping that would help him raise it. *Nobody's calling me a murderer. Nobody's calling my mom a murderer. Or my dad.*

The water still wouldn't rise more than an inch—as if it would do any good now—so Tommy crossed the creek and hopped over the barbed wire onto Carl Mangetti's land. He barreled through neck-high hay toward the little shack where he always used to hide whenever he needed to run away from his mother. Back when his voice first started cracking, when he told her that if she didn't say who his father was, he'd turn into a monster who killed and killed.

He got to the shack and locked himself inside, deluding himself into believing that he was safe on Carl's side of the creek. He moved a spool of barbed wire and a moldy bale of hay to look through his old peephole at Suborney, which glowed orange as more and more of it caught fire. *Coward*, he called himself. *Chickenshit.* Tommy knew he wasn't safe in the shack because a fire could jump that creek, especially since he'd sucked it almost dry. It happened in '74 and '77—hell, it probably happened once every three years since before they built Suborney, since before the Indians. A bit of lightning and a little push of wind, and the fire went wherever it wanted to.

Thorpe was the only one who could do anything, and it looked like he was as powerless as Tommy. Jesus wouldn't even help them because they'd both failed him at the moment he needed them most. Jesus felt so far away from him now that he seemed like only a name Tommy gave to what he didn't understand. *He healed me*, Tommy told himself. *He put his hands on me, and now he's gone, swept away.* Then he heard Thorpe's voice—no footsteps, no rattle, no knock— and he wondered how long his father had known about his hideout. Wondered what spy had tracked him there and why that spy hadn't worked harder to send him a message from his father.

"Everybody knows you'd come here, Tommy," Thorpe said. "Don't wait for 'em to find you dead and say you deserved it."

"You want to let my mom get away with this?" It was more an accusation than a question. "Did you know she could make fire?"

"She's gone. You want to be the one to track her down this time?"

"Sure in hell do."

"Well, good luck." Thorpe thunked something against the shack door. "Open up."

"Answer me! Did you know she could do it?"

"I'm the one she got it from. I'm the one to blame."

"You said that once already."

"And I'll say it again." The thunk came once more, harder. "Open the door—I got something of yours."

"I don't want anything from you! It was wrong, your little trap. If you just came out and told me straight up, none of this shit would've happened."

"Open the damn door!" Thorpe barked, but there was panic in his voice too. The air around them got hotter, more volatile. Another blast of wind moved the fire closer—maybe into the trees above the creek, Tommy thought. He opened the shack door to see Thorpe holding the sax case and looking like he'd walked through fire to get it. It had been in the church all along, Tommy remembered. Right in the middle, where he was going to play Tessy's songs in the morning. When Thorpe set the case on the ground, its vinyl skin completely charred, Tommy saw burns on his hands.

"Tessy'd want you to have this," Thorpe said.

"Don't bullshit me about Tessy." Tommy yanked the case, its handle half-melted and still hot to the touch, into the shack. "You wanted to walk into a fire for somebody's stuff just like my grandpa, but come out alive. To prove you love me, prove you're the better man."

"Save it for later," Thorpe growled, looking over his shoulder at the flames. "We've both got staying alive to think about."

"Why the hell should I bother?" Tommy's face looked rejected, orphaned. He kicked the sax case. "I should play this thing until it melts in my hands."

"I failed you, Tom-Tom."

"Don't call me that."

"I failed you. But that doesn't mean you should sit here and burn to death by yourself. Come look for Jesus with me."

"Jesus isn't walking with you. Nowhere *near* you. It's black magic, the shit you do."

Tommy clasped and unclasped his hand, sneering. As his father deflated, the only thing Tommy knew with certainty was that following Richard Thorpe and following Jesus weren't the same thing, even though he'd believed they were for a few short, perfect moments of his life. Moments he thought he could seal up, like a scene in a glass snow globe, and carry forever. But that globe rolled out of his hand and shattered. The wind kicked up again, and he watched the fire start to devour the trees above the creek.

"Tommy," Thorpe said, fear creeping deeper into his voice. "It's getting closer."

"Let it." The man Tommy had felt himself turning into ever since his true father came to town blew away from his skin like a dry corn husk. Blew straight for the flames. "Why did she do it? Does she even care who lives and dies?"

"Ask her yourself. She'll go west, that's all I know." Thorpe grabbed his son's shoulder. "If we don't *run* now, it'll get us. Come with me, Tom-Tom."

"I can't walk with you." Tommy shook his head more than he needed to.

"Then walk wherever you want. We'll meet up somewhere." Thorpe grabbed him and hugged him. "Nebraska City."

"Sure," Tommy said with a dead, unbelieving voice. He didn't return the hug but didn't slip out of it either. "Or Lincoln. Your first prison cell."

"My first prison cell," Thorpe repeated, stepping back to let Tommy see his father broken—his whole face as beaten as his bad cheek, all the things he never got to tell his son plastered onto his blubbering lips. Tommy saw the truth of this man whose absence he'd built his entire life around. Whose arrival had burned down all the lies inside him and left behind only the hollow spaces that those lies had once filled.

Thorpe mumbled something incomprehensible even to himself as he stared down at his boots. Then those boots helped him do what he did best: walk through the night. Tommy watched until Thorpe disappeared into the hay, heading east, then looked up at the burning sky and said a prayer for Tessy. A thank-you for the music she'd given him. The music he had to give the world now because she couldn't anymore. Or wouldn't soon.

Tommy picked up his sax case and pointed himself in the opposite direction as his father. He headed off alone, not sure where he was going, because he was Brother Thomas Sandor, a son of Jesus and a son of Mary. Everything he'd learned from the Sons and Daughters was weeping out through his skin, and the only way to get it back was to put one foot in front of the other. Because God made him for walking, whether he knew where he was walking to or not. Whether the world cared who he was or not. Whether the wind tumbled him east or tumbled him west or pinned him down right where he was forever.

"One more step," Tommy told himself and his burning world. "One more step." He walked deliberately and sincerely because every single touch of his feet against the earth was its own mystery, its own finality, its own wonder. No matter what ghosts his steps would uncover, or what ghosts the steps of others would uncover in him.

ACKNOWLEDGMENTS

I'd like to thank the many people whose time, attention, and patience went into this book:

Those who read it in its early incarnations and helped me to shape and refine it, particularly Elizabeth Kostova, Bret Lott, Mary Clearman Blew, Neil Connelly, Rolf Yngve, Andrew Krivak, Emily Besh, Connie Connally, Jeremiah Chamberlin, and Maya Sloan.

The entire team at the University of Nebraska Press, particularly Ron Hansen and Alicia Christiansen for believing in this novel, Elizabeth Gratch for her fine work with its text, and Anna Weir for telling the world about it.

The Kimmel Harding Nelson Center in Nebraska City, which gave me time and space to work on the sections of the book set there, as well as the Nebraska City Public Library, which helped me explore the area's history.

The mentors and literary professionals who have been in my corner as I wrote this novel, particularly Robert Olen Butler, Margot Livesey, Steve Katz, Ben Fountain, Suzanne Gluck, and Arsen Kashkashian.

My literary communities in Colorado, especially Robert Garner McBrearty, Laura Pritchett, David J. Rothman, and David Mason; and South Dakota, especially Christine Stewart, Patrick Hicks, and Adam Luebke; as well as literary friends around the country and the world—who are too many to name—without whom life would be much less bright.

My wife, Jennifer, and sons, Lucas and Landon, who have been with me every step of the way on this book's journey.

Karol and Agnes, now more than ever.

To order or obtain more information on these or other University
of Nebraska Press titles, visit nebraskapress.unl.edu.